Champion of the Rose

Andrea K Höst

All characters in this publication
are fictitious and any resemblance
to real persons, living or dead,
is purely coincidental.

Champion of the Rose
© 2010 Andrea K Höst. All rights reserved.
V.22-06-2011
www.andreakhost.com
ISBN: 978-0-9808789-4-3
EBook ISBN: 978-0-9808789-5-0
Cover art by: Julie Dillon

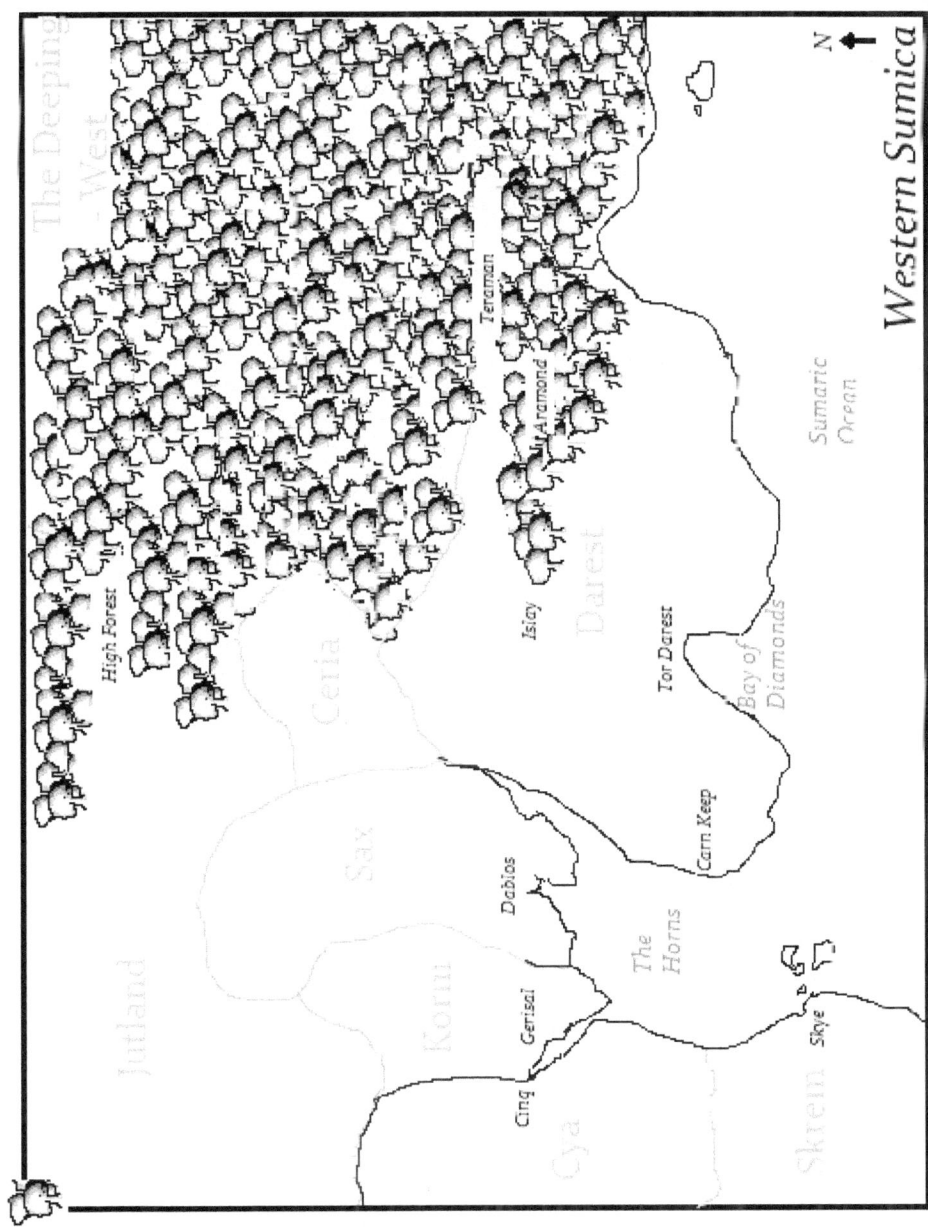

Western Sumica

One

After a morning spent sorting through the previous Champion's library, both Soren Armitage and the aide lent her by the Chancellor were so dust-laden that they were beginning to blend into their surroundings. *Grey hair to match grey eyes,* Soren thought, tucking usually black strands behind her ears. *A grey life.*

Without warning, the door crashed open, and the nearest pile of books lost its tenuous grasp on balance and slid into a heap. Three other piles slumped after it, puffing out dust redolent of old paper and slowly decaying binding. Soren sat back with a grimace, while her assistant for the day, Halcean, lived up to her red-headed nature by colouring hotly.

Oblivious, Aspen Choraide whisked into the room and stopped in the centre of the resulting tumble: a handsome blonde set off well by white and icy-blue linen. In all the poisoned throng of the Court, this was Soren's closest excuse for a friend, an apprentice mage not even willing to risk his position with open partisanship while he tried to coax his way into the new-minted Champion's bed. Soren was by turns infuriated and tempted by his trifling. At least he managed to laugh with as well as at her.

Today he was overflowing with excitement, well above his ordinary benign enthusiasm for life. Almost vibrating. "There's a rose!" he said, barely able to get the words out for the sheer delight of them. "A rose!"

"What of it?" Halcean asked, a decided snap to her voice as she rose out of the dust cloud he'd set off. She glanced pointedly about the room, which was festooned with carvings of roses.

"The Rathen Rose!" Aspen shouted. "There's a rose!"

He waited for their reaction, but Soren could only stare.

"That's impossible," Halcean said.

Making an exasperated noise, Aspen grabbed Soren's arm and pulled her to her feet, knocking the few remaining piles left and right. Soren, who tried to set certain limits to her treatment, attempted to free herself, but Aspen only tightened his grip and so she quickened her pace rather than be dragged across Fleeting Hall. The doors to the throne room were thankfully closed, but there were plenty of passers-by to witness their progress.

It was a brief trip, for the Garden of the Rose was only a short distance left of the Champion's rooms – directly opposite the Hall of the Crown. But Fleeting Hall was a palace hub, always busy, and by the time they'd reached the sunlit paving of the Garden a dozen or more people trailed them, scenting drama.

"There!" Aspen tugged her beneath an arch into the sunlight and flung a hand in theatrical accusation. "What did I tell you? Impossible? It's impossible to miss!"

It was indeed. Wound around the grey stone pillars and creeping across the exposed arches of the Garden of the Rose was the Rathen Rose. The leaves were small, black-green, and hid countless thorns. Today, for the first time in two centuries, it bore a flower.

"Sun's Mercy," Halcean managed, staring but making no attempt to approach. She would know the reputation of the Rose. Even Aspen in his excitement did no more than stand at the very edge of the garden.

Soren, her heart knocking against her throat, walked slowly forward and the double handful of people who had crowded to see stepped back to give her room. It was almost respectful. At that moment, she knew that everything was going to change.

For all she'd tried to make the best of being the most important nonentity at Court, uselessness irritated Soren, and she'd been looking about for change. But for there to suddenly be a Rathen? To be Champion in more than name?

The bloom depended from a cane wound around one of the narrow arches of stone overhead: a half-open cluster of petals so dark a red they were almost black, with a hint of richer colour at their heart. The very tip of each petal was rimmed with silver, like the lining of a storm-cloud, and as she lifted her hand it moved in response, dipping to the accompaniment of a dozen indrawn breaths.

The knowledge that it would be wiser not to do this before such an audience made no difference to her hand. Try as she might, Soren couldn't stop her arm from lifting, her fingers from brushing the soft, velvety petals. It was very like her annunciation as Champion, when a pressure behind her eyes had robbed her of all will and dawn had found her in Tor Darest, a week's journey walked in a single night.

"Teraman," her throat said, and a little thrill of power ran down her arm and buried itself somewhere inside her. It felt good. The rose moved away, out of reach.

"Teraman?" repeated Aspen. "What does that mean? Is it the heir's name?"

Soren shook her head and moved further into the small, stark courtyard. Aspen held out a hand, but didn't try to follow. He valued his fine features far too much to risk scratches. Instead, as Soren seated herself on a neglected stone bench, he turned to join the babble of excited conversation, speculating on an event no-one could have anticipated.

The Rose had been planted by Domina Rathen, the first mage-queen of Darest. It had been the core of the royal succession: a flower would bloom for every child of her line, enduring for the span of their life. All the Rathen Kings and Queens had been confirmed before the Rathen Rose. When the Rathen bloodline still existed.

"Champion!" Jansette Denmore, an engaging ninny who had recently become a favourite of the Regent, squeezed her way through the crowd and blithely brushed aside trailing, thorn-heavy canes to reach Soren. "Champion, who is it? Who is the new Rathen? How can this have happened?"

"I suppose that's what I must find out," Soren said. She was beginning to recover from the shock of seeing the rose, to think of what would come next. How wasn't really important, but who would be everything. Somewhere, a child of Rathen blood had been born, and Soren, as Champion, would have to find that child and protect it. She'd never felt more dismayed.

A sudden hush brought Soren's attention sharply back to her surroundings, and she looked up to see everyone sinking into obeisance. The depth of the courtesies told her who it was even before enough people had moved aside to reveal a medium-sized man clad in a snugly cut demi-robe of pristine white. He was far paler than Aspen, white-blond hair brushed sleekly back from a delicate brow, and it was a current fad of the Court to compare his skin to alabaster. His eyes were sapphire rimmed with dark, made brilliant by a crystalline blue-white radiating from the pupils, and they missed nothing.

Aristide Couerveur, the Regent's son. She'd never met a man more suited to his position in life. He already wielded as much power as his mother, and when he took the throne he would rule without wavering. Soren wondered who had run to bring him the news that this was no longer true, that the Rathen Rose proclaimed an heir to keep him from rule. There were not many who would have the nerve.

She'd only suffered a single interview with Lord Aristide, the day she'd arrived in Tor Darest. He'd asked her about her background and seemed amused by her answers. Afterwards he'd left her alone, setting a precedent for Soren to be ignored by the power players of the Court just as the previous Champion had been. Duly dismissed.

Whatever the reason, Soren had been eternally grateful for her failure to attract his interest. Darest might adore its Diamond Couerveur, but beneath the open worship was a strong thread of caution. His manners might be mild and exact, his face and figure attractive, but the sweet smile which accompanied his commands did nothing to diminish the consequences for those who crossed him. He might be considered even-handed, primarily interested in the fortunes of the kingdom, but he was also a powerful mage who did not tolerate enemies. And he was never at a loss.

The intense self-possession which characterised the Regent's son had not failed him. The glance he gave the dark rose was only brief and his gaze dropped immediately to Soren and fixed there. There was no sign of displeasure. He even retained a hint of a smile, though he was accounted to want the throne more than life. Then he turned his head a fraction, eyes keeping hold of Soren's as he addressed those who stood behind him.

"You may leave us."

The words were soft-spoken, and had immediate effect. Aching to stay, but not daring to risk provoking even the mildest displeasure in Lord Aristide, the onlookers shuffled back, all but Jansette. Secure in the Regent's favour, or oblivious to the Court's undercurrents, she remained standing at Soren's shoulder.

"You have something to say to me, Lady Denmore?" Lord Aristide asked.

"Not just at this moment, M'Lord," Jansette said, in her unaffected way. "I wish, rather, to ask the Champion about the new heir."

"I see why it is my mother admires you, Lady Denmore." Lord Aristide made some minor adjustment of his demi-robe, so that it fell in perfect folds over his white linen breeches. The steady sapphire gaze shifted from Soren, to her private relief, and took minute catalogue of Jansette. From the tip of the pink embroidered slippers peeping beneath a sheer full robe of figured azure and rose, to the girdle of silver links and modestly high bodice of a demi-robe beneath the near-transparent full robe, Jansette was exquisite, and had a face to match her finery. Physically, she was just the sort of woman Soren found most compelling, but every time she opened her mouth, attraction went out the window.

Lord Aristide showed no sign of being at all undone by artful confection. "Leave us, Lady Denmore," he said, apparently deciding a direct repellent was necessary. "You may question the Champion another time."

"I hope so," Jansette said, turning the corners of her mouth down in a pretty display of confounded will. "You are unaccommodating, M'Lord." She dropped into an elegant courtesy, bobbed politely to Soren, then turned and trailed away. Lord Aristide waited until she had passed through one set of the wrought iron gates which separated the garden from Fleeting Hall, then turned back to Soren, who had risen cautiously to her feet.

"Sorting the former Champion's collection must be a formidable task," he commented, nothing in his voice or manner revealing his feelings about the rose suspended a short way above his head.

"It is indeed, Lord Aristide," Soren replied, having no particular desire to discuss anything with him. There was something inhuman about this man, and she felt a need to show neither pleasure nor fear in his company, no matter how nervous he made her. "Anestan's additions to the Champion's library ranged far outside the traditional lore of her role," she said, the words sounding false and unreal to her. The library? What about the Rose? "I'm trying to winnow it back to the original purpose of the collection."

"Which can be accommodated without the need to stack the shelves three deep and bury the furniture." He inspected Soren as he had Jansette, reminding her of the dust and grime she had accumulated over a morning of sorting. She was wearing leggings and shirt in the dark grey she'd practically been forced to wear by those who oversaw Court regalia, but had left off her surcoat. Countrified and underdressed, she supposed, but there was no point being embarrassed about how she looked. It was what she did which would matter.

"Such a task is beneath your dignity, Champion," she was informed. "I am sure there are others within the Court whose time would be better spent. I will see to it that the collection is returned to its core content during your absence."

"Thank you," Soren said, resisting any impulse to echo "in my absence?", as only a fool would. "It will be useful to be able to find the books it seems I must read."

"Not must, surely? The example of the past might give guidance, but the Champion-Rathen coupling appears to have reinvented itself each time. Absolute loyalty works in many ways."

Impossible to guess what he meant by that, he who had the most to lose by a new-born Rathen heir. Nor was it easy to produce an appropriate response. "A number of the treatises and histories are very dry," she extemporised, still trying to accept the prospect of behaving like a true Rathen Champion.

He made some slight movement, which Soren was hard-put not to react to by stepping back. Then she froze, for a tendril of the Rathen Rose had descended with languorous speed to wrap itself around the slim, white column of his throat. Aristide lifted his chin, but did not seem even surprised by the circumstance. True, the

Rose was known to react to attacks, but she had never before seen it execute what appeared to be a quelling threat.

"It will be more than interesting to see the defences of Tor Darest active," Lord Aristide said, still unperturbed. If anything, he seemed perversely entertained by the situation, his eyes glittering. "Much of the palace is bound in magic, enchantments which have lain dormant since the death of King Torluce. Quite impossible to use or modify without the participation of a Rathen."

"Do you want to modify them?" Soren asked, annoyed and dismayed by this contribution from the Rose. How could she bring the conversation to an end with Lord Aristide in a noose? The Rose was not helping in the slightest by reacting to entirely unspoken threats.

To Soren's surprise, the tendril obligingly decamped, unwinding from Lord Aristide's neck and lifting back into the canopy. A thorn had left a scratch, very red against his pale skin, but not deep enough to produce more than a tiny, thread-like droplet.

"Thank you," he said, with a slight inclination of his head, and Soren could not think of a way to convincingly deny any involvement. "Your predecessor showed no sign of being able to effect the palace enchantments," he went on, delicately blotting his throat with the back of one hand. "But perhaps the existence of an heir makes all the difference. Did the Rose react to your will before today?"

"I don't know that it's reacting to me now, Lord Aristide," Soren said. She did not even begin to sound convincing.

"Do you not?" He treated her to the purely sweet, almost rueful smile which made the Court's blood run cold. As if he was chiding some clumsy stratagem which neither impressed nor disturbed him. "When you return with the heir, you should experiment."

"I – perhaps." Soren was starting to feel sick, totally out of her depth. She was far too blunt a person to make embroidery of words. "My apologies, Lord Aristide. It seems I have a great deal to do, and should start immediately." She bowed, employing what skill she had learned since arriving in Tor Darest.

"Of course." He returned her courtesy and stepped aside.

Soren didn't allow herself any unseemly haste as she headed to the gate, though she wanted to hurry, the back of her neck itching. She would have to see the Regent as well, and Arista Couerveur was as unnerving as her son. Then–?

"Champion."

"M'Lord?" She stopped and turned, but found it difficult to meet the bright, amused gaze.

"Teraman is a small township in the north-east," he said, with the air of one doing a favour. "Deep in the forest bowers. You will probably find it mentioned in the histories, for several Rathens died near there."

"Thank you, M'Lord." Soren bowed again, feeling none of the gratitude such help should inspire. Lord Aristide knew the birthplace of the child who threatened to displace him. She would have to get there before another Rathen died in Teraman.

Two

There was something to be said for the conflicted anger tightening Soren's stomach. At least it was familiar. Soren didn't consider herself weak, but she knew her failings. All her life she'd dragged her feet and stumbled through the opportunities her mothers had sent her way because they inspired no spark of certainty, did not draw or repel her, made nothing inside leap up. Nothing fit.

The irony of having the choice made for her by the Rathen Rose had dismayed but not overset her, at least when the future it laid on her involved nothing in particular. Being made Rathen Champion had been a shock, but she'd never questioned her ability to be a living anachronism, for all she resented the worthlessness of the role.

Now a life belonged to her. There was a baby out there she was supposed to protect and support and guide. And Darest. Hardly something she could abandon halfway through because it "didn't feel right". But of all the things she'd thought to be, a true Rathen Champion fit worst. Even starting on the task seemed ludicrous.

Concentrate on the moment. No possible way to put off going to formally notify the Regent. And then–? Go to Teraman. Be Champion. Rise to the occasion. She shook her head at the absurdity of it, then made a brief visit to her rooms to clean off the dust and don one of her surcoats – black with a restrained border of climbing roses in silver and gold thread. It was as close as she could come to girding her loins.

Emerging from her rooms into uproar, Soren took a deep breath and strode toward the towering arch which separated Fleeting Hall from the Hall of the Crown. By fixing her gaze on the briar-rose carvings which wound up either side of the arch she was able to avoid anyone catching her eye, but it was not so easy to escape a hand closing firmly on her elbow.

A woman in the livery of one of the Barons. "What is it?" she asked, trying to tread a thin line between polite and brusque.

"Don't you know?" There was an edge of derision, but it was as quickly reined back, replaced with a sudden, cautious courtesy. "Why Champion, I come with–"

"Interruptions," said another voice. "Do you propose keeping the Regent waiting?"

"M'Lady Rothwell," Soren murmured, turning with concealed relief to face a woman of statuesque frame. Another of the power-brokers of the Court, Francesca Rothwell had shown Soren a few moments' kindness when she'd first arrived in Tor Darest, and did her a second favour now, turning Soren back toward the Hall of the Crown.

"Come to me after you've seen the Regent," Lady Rothwell urged, her voice deep and richly persuasive. "There is something I have for you."

"I–" Soren hesitated, then nodded and smiled her thanks. "I will, Lady Rothwell."

"Good girl. Now go."

Soren did as ordered. Others were moving forward, determined or hopeful, but she twisted past them as best she could, and even the most eager did not follow into the Hall of the Crown.

Nothing had changed since the first and last time Soren had ventured into the Rathen throne room. It still felt like a dead place, abandoned and gutted. The dust was so thick on the floor that only faint streaks of pink and gold suggested colourful secrets. Most of the doors were hidden by murky tapestries, the rooms beyond unused since the death of the last Rathen King. Only a faint trickle of natural light crept through the grime miring the windows around the upper gallery, and shadows lurked in all corners, particularly on the twin stairs reaching up and back toward Fleeting Hall. But the blackest reaches were at the far end of the Hall, where the Rathen Throne must stand. All Soren could make out was a vague outline.

When she'd first seen this place, Soren had been perplexed by the neglect. It was true that the enchantments of the palace would prevent any but a Rathen monarch from using the Throne and royal apartments, but why the dust and cobwebs and complete lack of light? Understanding had only come after a few uneasy dreams where she had crossed that darkened hall over and over, hurrying toward the open door to her left where a warm golden glow promised a place without shadows or fear. The effect transported her again, as she stepped over the threshold into the Regent's Court, blinking and inhaling fresh air from open windows, and the scent of flowers and more expensive perfumes.

According to Aspen, what was now the Regent's Court had once been a retiring room for those waiting to be granted an audience, and so was free of Rathen-specific enchantments. It opened onto a private garden and the Regent's apartments, which had similarly once been the preserve of exalted guests. The Coueveurs had created the Regent's Court soon after the death of King Torluce, but Soren gathered that it was Arista Couerveur who had chosen to bring petitioners through dark abandon into a room of light and colour, full of bright tapestries and flowers cut daily.

Adopting as correct a posture as possible, Soren fixed her eyes on the figure sitting upright among a nest of cushions and downy furs on a coppery throne. An audience with the Regent was a chancy thing, for Arista Couerveur had reigned long over ill-luck and decline. In distant Carn Keep, Soren had heard tales of her series of favourites, of her brilliance, her failures, and her inevitable, impending overthrow to her son's ambitions. A month at Court had taught her that the Regent was not mad, nor necessarily inconstant, and that in Darest her will was still law.

She was a small woman, as pale and poised as her son, and looked little more than a decade his senior. Magery. Unlike Aristide, the Regent always dressed in the most sumptuous of robes, all brocade and silk in vivid, glowing colours. Today she wore sunlight on water: white-gold dapples sparkling on myriad shades of blue and green, oversewn with a glitter of her signature emeralds.

"Champion." The Regent spoke before Soren reached the throne, her voice brisk and matter-of-fact. "An animal will be made available for your journey. Do you wish an escort of the Guard?"

Taken aback, Soren instinctively shook her head, then searched for a justification for her reaction. Stupid decision, when she had no combat training whatsoever, but how could she say no and then yes? And, truly, she didn't want an escort.

"Thank you, Lady Regent," she said, abandoning any attempt at a reason. "That won't be necessary."

"As you will." Arista Couerveur's lips curved, and Soren realised that the Regent was not in the slightest way upset by news of the rose. She seemed almost...smug. Pleased by the prospect of an heir to the throne she held in custodianship?

"This is a Writ of Passage," the Regent said, holding out folded parchment bound with red ribbon. "Use it to command any assistance you require."

"Thank you, Lady Regent." The Writ felt stiff and crisp in Soren's hands, and smelled of fresh ink. Soren fidgeted with the ribbon as she found herself being surveyed with more attention than Arista Couerveur had ever before directed her way. It was a little like the sun coming out on a cloudy day, that bright, piercing gaze washing over Soren from head to foot. A judgmental god, weighing and measuring this untried Champion.

"Go make ready," the Regent ordered, not revealing whatever conclusion she'd reached about Soren's capabilities. Soren just bowed, eager to retreat.

"Bring the child back safely, Champion," Arista Couerveur added, as Soren reached the door. There was steel in this command, and Soren was left in little doubt that the Regent wanted the new Rathen heir intact.

Of course, unlike Lord Aristide, the Regent was not truly threatened by a new Rathen. At least another twenty years before the child could take the throne, and that might well encompass the rest of Lady Arista's life. Immortality was not granted to mages, just a lingering youth. It was Aristide Couerveur who had the greatest stake, who would surely do anything and everything he could to prevent the day a Rathen returned light to the Hall of the Crown.

Lady Rothwell's chambers were in the New Palace, built after King Torluce's death and lacking the sense of swooping grandeur provided by high ceilings and arches. Soren had initially thought that residence in the New Palace was a mark of disfavour, that the Regent kept her friends close and accommodated those less pleasing in the compact, utilitarian New Palace. But it was more complicated than that. Arista Couerveur kept her enemies as close as her allies. Lady Rothwell's New Palace apartments were a sign that she was not pivotal to the Court's machinations, despite her family's power and wealth. Neutral.

A white pitch of anticipation followed Soren through the palace, and she was reminded of her first few days in Tor Darest. But then she had only been a curiosity. Now faces turned toward her with avid fascination, and there were even a few following to see where she went.

The attention made her shoulder blades itch, and in her gold-embroidered black it was impossible to avoid notice. With a thousand courtly schemes crumbling in the shadow of a dark flower, few dared show even displeasure when she strode past their attempts to catch her eye. Pleasant as the prospect was of no longer being treated as a joke, Soren's imagination simply ran up against a wall when it came to contemplating her sudden shift of status, the end to her quiet skulking about the political fringe. The Champion had once been a force to be reckoned with. The first Champion, Kittredge, had been Domina Rathen's most trusted guardswoman. Kittredge had stood by the mage-queen's side as she established her realm, and had been woven into Darest's defences. At Darest's height, to become Champion was the wish of every Darien child, for it brought power and acclaim and honour in equal measure, to balance a world of responsibilities. All Rathens were mages, but the Champion could be friend, adviser, teacher, lover, sibling. Whatever that Rathen needed most, whatever would make that Rathen stronger. The Champion was the realm's protector, second in consequence only to the one who sat the throne.

Domina Rathen had created a process which did not allow for variation. For every Rathen ruler, a Champion would be found: proclaimed by magic, some even said shaped by magic. For the last two hundred years, there had been no Rathens, but the enchantments continued to find Champions. The four who had been proclaimed since the death of King Torluce were nothing but reminders of Darest's former glories.

And now a single rose threatened to change all that.

So was she to have some kind of mentor role to Darest's next ruler? Parenting mightn't be that bad, with the help of the child's mother, but Soren knew little of state-craft. And she had no taste to match swords with Aristide Couerveur, to be shoved to the centre of Court intrigue.

With this daunting prospect in mind, she was ushered into a receiving room where Francesca Rothwell waited alone, a long, linen-wrapped bundle on a table before her.

"Champion." Lady Rothwell smiled her welcome and indicated a seat for Soren. "I will not take a great deal of your time."

"I'm curious to know what it is you have for me," Soren said, though she had not till that moment thought about it. Trying to work out how a Rathen child could be born without a Rathen parent had proven more engrossing.

"This." Lady Rothwell indicated the bundle which lay between them. "It's been in my family's possession for a long time now." She gestured for Soren to unwrap it.

Already uncertain, Soren almost snatched her hands back when her fingers grazed something which sent a wave of pins and needles through her skin. Her hands recognised this, whatever it was. It was like encountering a lost limb, all unexpected.

Despite wanting to feel such surety for half her life, Soren was slow to continue. It pulled you off-balance, something like that, and her head hadn't stopped spinning since Aspen had made his triumphal revelation. But she couldn't sit here quailing before Lady Rothwell. Gingerly, she picked the last of the wrappings away.

The sheath was dull with age and care, the hilt softened by braided leather strips which had seen the touch of many hands.

Soren did not draw it, did not even want to pick it up, not when it insisted on telling her she'd been missing it all her life. She had not.

"I'm not a swordswoman, Lady Rothwell." And had no desire to be, whatever protection a blade might offer.

"Indeed, not all the Champions were. Its power is as much as a symbol as a weapon. This was Kittredge's sword."

The first Champion. It was an ancient thing, then, and probably bound up in all the magic which surrounded Soren's position. Probably. No probably at all. This thing was trumpeting its presence at her.

"How did it come to your family, M'Lady?" she asked, trying to control an urge to clasp the sword close. That was far more unnerving than Lord Aristide and the Regent put together.

"King Torluce's Champion survived him for several years and he was of the Rothwell line. When the first Rathenless Champion was proclaimed, the sword was in the hands of the family, and they did not consider it necessary – did not want, to be truthful – to give it up." Lady Rothwell leaned forward to brush her fingers against the binding. "So much history. A symbol of the way things were."

The way things were during the reign of the Rathen mages was a popular subject no-one discussed. Not publicly, at least. The Couerveurs had not been incompetent regents, but some vital balance had been upset with King Torluce's death. Encroached upon by The Deeping to the east and aggressive trade from the west, Darest was unlucky, cursed, at the very least no longer the power it had once been. Too much had been bound into a single bloodline, too many treaties, too many enchantments. A wealth of tradition and trust and inspiration. Without the Rathens, Darest had begun to fail, had now been altered almost beyond recognition. Few spoke about the decline, let alone put forward any ideas on how to arrest it. They muttered of Fae curses and did nothing.

How did a new-born Rathen come into this setting? And how in the world was Soren supposed to be any of the things a Champion was meant to be, when she was neither mage nor armswoman nor courtier? Just Soren.

Why had the Rose chosen her to be Champion? She'd never had a calling, never shown a particular talent for anything. Unlike brother Romadin, she'd been an indifferent student, capable of following their two mothers along the musty path of scholarship but not of devoting herself to it. Nor had she felt the urge to join her sister Rain and their father plying the sea-routes. Soren had never excelled, never loved anything enough to want to do it her whole life. She had a level of learning, after so many conscientious lessons, and knew her way around boats and trade-logs, but they were not her vocation, any more than the herding or the herb-craft or the fishing which she had tried as her blood-mother sought a pigeonhole to fit her in. Competent at many things, master of none, she'd been Carn Keep's maid-of-all-work, neither satisfied nor disconsolate with her lot. She knew how to bind a book and cast a line, and had no interest whatsoever in politics.

And would get nowhere trying to *out-fish* Aristide Couerveur.

Soren picked up the sword, her eyes half-closing at the unexpected and quite physical pleasure which flowed through her grip on the hilt. Her entire body tingled. The thing was most definitely hers; now what was she going to do with it?

Whether she was the stuff of Champions, or capable of wielding a sword, Soren had no option but to at least attempt to save the Rathen child. Despite the machinations of the Court, she would have to mark her own course. And believe it wouldn't end in disaster.

Three

H er name's Vixen, Champion."

Soren looked the mare over dubiously. A far cry from the sturdy former plough-horse she'd been permitted to ride back at Carn Keep. Not so many hands high, but Cob had been an imperturbable mound of a horse who would never think of shying or bolting. This showy bay pranced about the stable yard, tossing her head and apparently attempting to master the latest dance step. Being thrown was not how Soren wished to start her attempt to fulfil the role of Champion. Just starting was bad enough.

"She don't buck," put in the stableboy, apparently delighted to witness the Rathen Champion setting out. "She'll see you halfway to the Tongue before you know it."

And save the kingdom before afternoon tea? Perhaps, if she'd just stop still long enough for a horse-clumsy Champion to get on board.

To Soren's surprise, the boy proved right. Though peculiarly sensitive to anything which rattled, Vixen was well-trained, with an even gait kind to riders long out of practice. Her worst fault was an inclination to try and work open saddlebags left too handily in reach.

The first thing Soren did, once through the palace gates, was thrust her surcoat to the very bottom of those bags. She had no intention of riding about the countryside in clothing which announced her identity to every passer-by. The charcoal-grey shirt and leggings would serve her well enough, and she could purchase other clothing along the way.

After that, Soren tried to deal with the sword, but it refused point-blank to stay settled on anything but Soren, falling loose or poking stubbornly from every other place she tried to fasten it. She eventually gave in and used the harness Lady Rothwell had provided to strap it across her back, feeling boastful. It was heavy, but at the end of the first day she found herself reluctant to take it off, despite how little she liked its continued insistence that it was hers and that she was terribly glad to have it.

Planning for the future became a matter of working out everything she should do and then drawing a line through the things which she'd be stupid to attempt. The first item she'd eliminated was returning to Tor Darest. Soren was tolerably certain she wouldn't be able to protect herself in the capital, let alone a child with a claim to the throne. Even if she credited Aristide Couerveur with every virtue in the world, he was not the only interest at Court with a stake in a Rathen child's sudden death. The few allies she thought she could count on – Lady Rothwell and possibly Aspen – would not be enough to ensure the child saw its first birthday, let alone twenty and the Crown.

Which meant the best thing Soren could do was find this new Rathen heir and then somewhere to hide. For a very long time.

Going home was out of the question: she would not bring Court intrigue to a scholar's retreat, and Carn Keep was the first place anyone would look. For a moment she amused herself with the thought of descending on Tscharen, babe in arms. But Tscharen had a son of her own now, and would hardly welcome an old lover with a kingdom's worth of enemies in tow. It would have to be some anonymous place where a young woman and a child could lose themselves, in a crowd or a wilderness. A crowd would probably be better. She would have to leave Darest.

The prospect was both exciting and appalling. So many places she'd never seen, so many things which could go wrong.

There was a great deal of choice to the West. Sax and Ceria, Darest's nearest neighbours and probably too close. Jutland, beyond the northwest mountains, was out of the question. Raising the next ruler of Darest as a nomadic plainsman was surely not a good idea. Korm was too clannish, Skrem too violent. Perhaps Cya? But Cya and Sax were pushing hard against each other and Darest. She'd be mad to take Darest's heir into their territory.

South across the ocean would be too risky during the next few months, when every port would be watched. To the north and east, Darest was bounded by The Deeping, where few humans were permitted to live. Even if she could gain permission, there would be little safety to be found in the sprawling realm of the Old Race, called the Fair or the Fae or elves or a half-dozen other things. They had their own games of politics, and enchantments which made the Rathen Rose seem tame. And for all their rules and laws, she'd heard too much about Fae curses and their wish to reclaim their gift-kingdom to trust them with its heir.

But beyond The Deeping were human lands. Kingdoms which shared no borders with Darest, and had no great interest in Rathen children. It would be a journey of many weeks to reach them, but she could surely find a hiding place there, if anywhere.

She decided this over a week of sun-lit and unmolested riding, north along busy roads to Islay at the tip of the Tongue. Then she turned down the failing trade road east, travelling into a place of trees, tall and close to either side of a near-swallowed road. As she passed through the small, lonely townlets which scratched a brave existence in the north-east, Soren's thoughts shifted to the more immediate future. What, for instance, was she going to do once she reached Teraman? Ask to inspect every babe born in the last few weeks? Hope one happened to have a convenient birthmark of a crown or some such? And then try and spirit it away, whatever the wishes of the parents? She still hadn't thought of a reasonable explanation for a Rathen without Rathen parents, and she was at a loss over how to go about identifying the right baby and assuming Championship of it.

"Champion?"

Soren started, jerking Vixen's reins. She'd stopped at a stream, still an afternoon's ride out from Teraman, and there'd been no-one visible when she'd slid out of the saddle. Vixen lifted her head and snorted, put her ears back, then returned to thirsty drinking. Water first, in this early Autumn warmth.

"Don't look at me," said the voice, so naturally Soren did, searching for the source. A young girl was crouched beneath the small bridge crossing the stream. She was about twelve, berry-brown, and more than a little damp. Pulling a frantic face, she waved a hand, urging Soren to look away. "Pretend I'm not here!"

"All right." Soren studiously turned her attention to the trees – a mix of walnut and tall, black-barked loram. Hoping to make Teraman before dark, she'd been feeling increasingly ambiguous about what was to come. The girl was the first person she'd seen since Thissen, the last village.

Struck anew by the sheer unreality of everything happening, Soren could only try to be practical. "Who are you?" she asked.

"Nina, Champion. Lucia's my heart-sister. You are the Champion, aren't you?"

Soren admitted that she was. "Are you hiding under the bridge for a reason?"

"They're looking for us, Champion. Mama and Mama-la sent me to tell you what to do, when you get to Teraman. Don't look!"

"Who are 'they'?" Soren asked as she stared obediently at the small round leaves of the lorams and suppressed a faint urge to laugh. The situation appealed to her sense of the bizarre, if nothing else.

"Everybody," Nina said, sounding more than a little overwhelmed. "Strangers started arriving a week ago, but mostly they kept to themselves. Then the news came – about the Rose, and that you were coming to make Helena Queen. After that, everything changed. No-one'd believed Lucia before, when she said that the lost prince had come to her. Not even Mama-la, I think."

This was getting convoluted. "What happened?"

"Well, soon as Mama-la heard the news, she had us grab what we could carry. Then we went down the back. We were still on the stair when they rode in, and we had to keep quiet, between the walls, while they searched the inn. Jutlanders. From the trade caravan. Garrison men came and ran them off, but they haven't gone far, Mama-la says."

"Jutlanders?" That certainly wasn't who Soren had expected to be taking an interest in the Rathen heir. New factors, spinning her tentative plans all awry. "What was that about a lost prince?"

"Don't you know, Champion?" Nina asked, suspicious and uncertain.

"I only know that the heir is – or was – in Teraman, two weeks ago."

"Oh." The little pause spoke volumes. Champions were supposed to do better than that.

Then, in a flurry of words: "The lost prince was one of the Rathen princes that got killed in The Deeping centuries and centuries ago. Our inn's named after him. He haunts the woods just a ways north of Teraman, and people who cross his hidden grave are doomed to die before a week's gone by, and to see him's a bad omen, but sometimes he comes to girls out walking alone and lays with them if they please him. And he came to Lucia, and she had Helena. Mama and Mama-la weren't a bit pleased."

"I can well imagine," Soren said, weakly. It was some sort of explanation, at least, for how a Rathen child could suddenly come into being. It sounded like the Teraman situation was already a hopeless muddle. "Where is your family now?"

"We've a hidey-hole in one of the safe places in the Tongue. Mama-la said to say that the Jutlanders, or even the garrison men, are sure to have spies out to see if we try and contact you. That the garrison men sent someone to Thissen to follow you along, sure enough. She says to say that you can trust Mesdie Cantlever or Rimana, but none of the rest, no-how. They'll be watching, in hopes you'll be leading them to us."

"I understand," Soren said, tightening her grip on Vixen's reins as the mare decided to wander into the shallow stream Vixen turned her head and looked back at Soren speculatively as she moved further into the water. "The grass is just as green on this side, wretched beast," Soren said, to hide her dismay. Maybe anyone watching would assume everything she said was addressed to the horse.

Nina, after a short hesitation, continued. "It's all fixed that Rimana'll put you in the right room tonight, and you can go through the wardrobe and down the back stair. Go real late, after the moon's passed over the Temple gates, and I'll be on the stair waiting. If'n I'm not there, go back the next night, same time."

"I'll do that, Nina," Soren promised, still watching Vixen, feeling solemn and absurd and hopelessly overwhelmed. "And if – if I don't come after two nights, tell your mothers they should leave Darest, will you? Until the child is grown."

There was no reply, so Soren risked a glance. Nina was biting her lip, holding back tears. But she didn't say anything else, and Soren thought it best to move on, if there really was someone watching her.

Back in Vixen's saddle, she gazed about, but saw no sign of spies. Soren was a child of the seashore, used to sand, rocks, and grassy hills dotted with grazing sheep. Woodcraft wasn't something she'd had occasion to learn. She could be completely surrounded, and would never know. Champion Stumble-blind.

The girl had been clever to hide at the stream. Anyone travelling from Thissen would be sure to stop, exactly where Nina could pass on her message unnoticed. Far less suspicious than drawing Soren to the side of the road at a place where there were only trees, which would be exactly what a shadow would be watching for. A lead to a girl called Helena.

It sounded like the heir's grandmothers had dealt with the situation as effectively as possible. And the babe and her family were taking refuge in a 'safe' place in the Tongue? Soren hadn't known there were any.

More than eight centuries ago, Domina Rathen had performed some signal service for the Queen of the Old Race and been rewarded with the vast tract of land which became Darest. The histories theorised that the place was a disputed territory among the Old Race, and the Fae Queen had abruptly ended an age-old feud by handing it over to a human. Despite the valuable orchards, and rich land waiting to be cleared, Domina Rathen had initially found it difficult to convince settlers that Darest was no longer part of the Deeping, that all the dangers of the Faerie realm had been withdrawn. Time had proven Domina Rathen right. Darest was safe.

But that guarantee had held true only while Rathens still lived. The Rathen bloodline had been whittled down to its last King over two hundred years ago. When Torluce had died, the forest had come back, licking across the border. It wasn't as if it had sprung up overnight, or if farmers hadn't been able to chop the trees down. But they'd grown in such numbers that people became convinced The Deeping was trying to take back its own. Families gave up the fight and moved on to less chancy ground, leaving their farms to fall into neglect. A spate of disease, of bad luck, the discovery of gold just over the western border; it had all added up until there was a great swathe of forest cutting off the north-east. An entire town, Aramond, had been abandoned, slowly swallowed. Every year the Tongue stretched a little further west, grew a little thicker in the middle. The past catching up with Darest.

It was not long after the Tongue had taken shape that it began to be whispered that 'things live there', that the Fae had cursed Darest, were even living in the Tongue. Some of the enchantments of the Old Race had certainly returned, and it had grown almost as dangerous to venture into the Tongue as it was to wander unescorted from the trade road through The Deeping.

A half-dozen villages such as Teraman lived uneasily along the road which ran between The Deeping's northern border and the Tongue. Soren had seen evidence of continued maintenance in recently uprooted saplings and lopped branches, but she still found that the trees pressed too close. She hoped that, wherever Nina's mothers had taken their family, it truly was safe.

Four

The first and best thing Soren noticed about Teraman was the space. The people of this village had managed to maintain their fields, and the only trees within its bounds were small and confined to even rows, heavy with nearly ripe apples, pears and peaches. Late afternoon shadows stretched from the wall of trees behind Soren, but had not yet reached the centre of the massive clearing, where warm sunlight glowed on thatch and shingle, promising comfort and safety. A loose sprawl of perhaps thirty homes made up the heart of the village, with a handful of farmhouses scattered among the fields. A steady tang, tung, tang announced a blacksmith hard at work. Closer by, two young voices spiralled into shrieks of laughter, and a handful of toffee-cream cows moved toward a milking shed, bells around their necks clanking in time with their unhurried gait.

And soldiers. They were waiting by the fence of one of the farms, two women in the uniforms of Darien swear-swords. They'd already seen her, were stepping forward with a kind of attentive respect Soren suspected she should find complimentary. Since turning tail and running had long since become impossible, Soren nudged Vixen to a faster walk, and soon reached them. They both saluted crisply, with no suggestion of irony.

"Welcome to Teraman, Champion Armitage," said the older and darker of the pair. "Captain Sharwell, of Elder Garrison, presents his compliments, and asks that he might speak to you at your earliest convenience."

Trying to work her mind around her new status, Soren simply smiled and gestured for them to lead the way. They saluted again, then formed a miniature honour guard at either side of Vixen's neck, who inspected them until certain they weren't carrying the appropriate treats to reward the long day's journey. The younger of the two, round-cheeked and pink, kept stealing glances up Soren. It was hard to guess if she was impressed by what she saw: a tallish woman with enough looks to make her pretty, and a stupidly long sword strapped across her back. She wasn't even wearing the surcoat.

It looked like she wouldn't need the Regent's Writ of Passage to gain the Garrison's help. The fact that everyone seemed able to recognise her without her full uniform didn't make Soren any more enthused about wearing it. No doubt it was the sword giving her away now. But it hadn't been possible to leave it behind.

Soren shifted uneasily in her saddle, attention straying from the buildings ahead. Why hadn't it been possible? She'd managed to get away without fanfare, and it wasn't as if Lady Rothwell would have held it against her if she'd chosen not to take a valuable heirloom along for the ride. She certainly wasn't capable of wielding the thing: she'd unsheathed it in the Champion's apartments, just to see how it fitted her hand, and nearly gouged the ceiling trying an overhead swing. Simply possessing the sword hadn't given Soren the ability to defend herself, only confused her with the tingling pleasure she experienced when handling it.

Leaving it behind truly had been out of the question, much the same as staying in Carn Keep had been impossible. Because she was Champion, and the Champion's place was with the Rathen ruler or, failing that, with the Rathen Rose. And the Champion's sword, now that she'd touched it, had become part of her. That last night in Tor Darest, she'd been unable to rest until she'd fetched the sword into the same room, though she'd managed to refrain from actually sleeping with it. Just thinking about not keeping it with her made her uncomfortable.

It would, Soren suspected, be equally impossible for her to do anything to harm the babe, Helena. She was bound by magic to do everything in her power to help the future queen of Darest.

There was no element of choice at all.

Annoyed by the thought of control, Soren rode into Teraman. The blacksmith, a woman with shoulders to put an ox to shame, stopped her work and came to stare critically. A boy made some comment and pointed, only to be shushed by his father. Curtains fluttered and doors opened – wide or just a crack depending on the courage of the occupants. Soren chose to appear oblivious as the two guardswomen led her to a large, solidly constructed building.

A painted forest decorated the board swinging beside the inn's metal-bound doors. It was only after intent study that Soren made out a small, smudged shape among the towering trunks, a flash of white face looking back over one shoulder. The Lost Prince.

As Soren drew back on Vixen's reins, the door opened and two people came out. The man's bearing and air of command would have told Soren this was Captain Sharwell, even without the insignia on his arm. He looked up at her and saluted. The woman, stout and neat behind a creamy apron, spared Soren a single judicial glance, then withdrew.

"Welcome to Teraman, Champion." Captain Sharwell was a small man, with grey specked through brown hair. "I'll try not to tell you too often how very glad I am to see you," he added as she slid from the saddle.

"Thank you. I'd be glad to know what's been happening here." Soren regretted that she had to start by lying to the man. She doubted Captain Sharwell would be supportive of her plans to decamp with Darest's heir, even if she could trust him not to have an agenda driven by Aristide Couerveur's ambition.

"That makes two of us," Sharwell replied, stepping back and gesturing toward the inn's door. "I'd call the last week a shambles, but that might cast too positive a light. Come in, and I'll give you a full report, made slightly more palatable by some excellent cooking."

Leaving Vixen to her escort, Soren followed. The inside of the inn was cool, dark after the sunlight, and smelled of ale and stewing apples. Blinking, she saw stairs straight ahead and a public room to the right, unexpectedly crowded. Everyone had twisted around in their seats to watch her come in. No-one spoke.

The Captain turned left, toward the open door of a private dining room. Discomfited, Soren hurried after him, then stopped. Someone was looking at her, a very specific presence dwarfing the avid curiosity of the crowd. Standing just inside the second doorway, she looked over her shoulder and saw, alone at a table in the very far corner, a lean and saturnine man who wished her gone.

Blinking again, Soren tried to understand what she was feeling. All she saw was a man dressed in dark clothing, leaning back in his chair, watching her. Black hair, thin but definite brows, and strong features set in cynical lines. Attractive. And lit with blazing anger, for all his easy pose.

It was the Rose. The power which had become part of her was alerting her to the man's presence, revealing what lay beneath the surface. There was not an actual sense of threat, just that strong impression of tight fury.

"Champion?"

Now was not the moment to pursue the warning. Soren stepped further into the next room, allowing Captain Sharwell to close the door and shut away the interested spectators and the man the Rose was telling her was important.

"We reached Teraman the morning after receiving the Regent's message," Captain Sharwell said. He poured Soren a glass of water, then sat down opposite her. "With orders to keep an eye on the child and await your arrival."

Of course the Regent wouldn't have left recovery of the heir to Soren alone. She should feel relieved, not annoyed. "You know who the heir is?" she asked, reminding herself to behave like someone who hadn't had a conversation with a girl hiding beneath a bridge.

Sharwell grimaced. "Have you heard the tale behind this inn's name, Champion?"

"I know that Crown Princess Sethane led a hunting party from Teraman into The Deeping, about two hundred and fifty years ago," Soren replied. It had taken her too long to find even that. There was certain to be more than a paragraph devoted to the loss of an heir of Darest in the histories, somewhere in the tumble of books covering her floor. "None of them were ever seen again."

"Not alive. Searchers found a few limbs."

"They offended The Deeping?" She'd heard plenty of stories about the dangers of The Deeping, but something must have gone seriously wrong to end the life of a Crown Princess. A Rathen mage.

"The hunt had the approval of The Deeping," Sharwell said. "There'd been deaths in the area, a farm had been attacked. So they went out, they never came back. She must have succeeded – the Princess – even if it did cost her life. Whatever it was, it left Teraman alone after that."

"And where does this lost prince fit in?"

"The Crown Princess had a couple of cousins in her party," Sharwell replied, shrugging. "One's been sighted in the area on and off ever since – your standard infrequent haunt. Fading now, judging from the number of reports. But a tradition grew up – unmarried girls would claim that the lost prince had come to them. I always thought it was an excuse. With the garrison so close, Teraman girls have a tendency to find themselves starting a family without the security of a life partner." He shrugged, and rubbed his chin.

"So we come to the heir?"

"Ye-es. Lucia Meddescalf, the eldest daughter of the owners of this inn, claimed that the lost prince had come to her. Child arrived in due course, a girl she called Helena. Then we get the message from the Regent." He grimaced. "If we'd been the only ones getting messages, matters would have gone more smoothly, but it seemed like every second traveller had heard about the new Rathen and how Teraman came into the picture. Busiest the place has been for a century. When too many were inclined to stay, and a handful of distinctly unsavoury types drifted in, Mistress Meddescalf and her wife allowed me to station a couple of men as guests, though they declined my suggestion that they remove to the safety of the garrison. Seems like they didn't really believe the child could be Rathen." Captain Sharwell sighed, and put his hands flat on the table, giving Soren a straight look. "I'm not attempting to shuffle the blame, Champion. I made the decision not to act."

"What happened?" Soren asked, voice muted. She was glad to have met Nina. If it wasn't for the girl's message, she'd be spun sideways by this news. As it was, she felt more sympathy for Captain Sharwell than she would like. But if she planned to leave Darest, she couldn't take him into her confidence.

"Jutlanders."

Soren aped surprise, and felt she'd overdone it.

"Riding escort with a merchanter train, until they stopped in Teraman. Only a half dozen, but more than enough to take out the two men stationed at the inn. Young and glory hungry. They tell me ransoming the Crown Princess of Darest is 'name-worthy'."

"You caught them, then?" Nina's description had left Soren picturing an entire clan descending on Teraman.

"Oh, yes. A couple made a break for the road, but we rounded them up quickly enough. No-one's too eager to stray into the woods around here." He smiled thinly, then shook his head. "But they stormed the inn, left both my men and a number of others injured, and sent the entire Meddescalf clan out of the window."

He was looking very grim and stiff-backed, and Soren felt a pang of guilt. "So they escaped?" she said, disliking her pose of innocent ignorance more and more. She hated playing games with truth.

"They did indeed. So thoroughly that we haven't been able to find them since."

Soren didn't say anything, finding herself incapable of putting on a further show of horror or astonishment, let alone haranguing the man for this turn of events. Her face felt stiff. Sharwell shifted uncomfortably, and colour darkened the tanned skin of his cheeks. Then he turned one of his hands over, a device to dismiss the moment.

"We've scoured the road, of course, but it seems they must have headed into the Tongue or The Deeping."

"Why would they do that? Instead of making for the garrison?"

"Possibly Mistress Meddescalf felt the wiser course was to remain out of sight until you arrived, Champion. There are places within the Tongue which are said to be safe, and we've been attempting to search these, with the help of some of the locals. Slow going, since there's too much risk spreading the search among a number of small bands, and we've only a minor mage assigned to the garrison. My hope is that your arrival will draw them out."

His hope, and that of anyone else taking an interest in the heir. "Could they have made for Tor Darest?" she asked.

"Unlikely. Some doubt even the existence of the safe places; actually crossing the Tongue would be courting death. And they certainly haven't travelled along the trade road." He gave her an assessing glance. "Is there any chance, Champion, that you—?"

Soren shook her head, then lifted a shoulder equivocally. She was very aware of the weight of the sword, of the harness currently pulling to the left because she'd pushed the sheathe to the side so she could comfortably sit down. "I don't sense the heir's presence, if that's what you mean," she said. "The Champions have had only their title, since the death of King Torluce. I will try what I can, but I'm afraid that's very little."

"Even a little might be enough," Sharwell said, though he was obviously disappointed. "Would you care to refresh yourself, before eating? I've had a room kept for you."

A blank-faced man wearing a lieutenant's badge was summoned and escorted Soren upstairs. She paused to look out over the public room again, busier than before. Dozens of faces lifted to follow her progress, but the man in the corner was gone. She felt uneasy, not knowing where he was. He could be waiting upstairs with a knife and a grudge. He could be heading for Lucia and Helena, or just away. But she was careful not to pause to search for him, obediently following the Lieutenant to a door well away from the stair.

The room, which was presumably the one with a wardrobe you could walk through, was not large and was dominated by a cushiony bed. Her saddlebags were already empty and hooked neatly on the wall next to the small window. Checked curtains puffed inwards, allowing her a glimpse of a twilight town walled in black forest. No assassins, this time.

A lone bird called: two warbling notes. The moon was directly above, slowly drifting toward the far side of the sky, and Soren was being watched.

She'd dined excellently with Captain Sharwell, glad when he'd chosen to focus the conversation on Teraman and its environs and hadn't objected to her retiring early. After an intensive investigation of the back of her closet she'd napped until midnight. Now, looking out over Teraman from a dark room, she found herself listening to three people breathing.

One in the lane directly beneath her window, quick and light. Another across the road which joined the lane, with only a sidelong view of her window. There was a faint, moist gurgle to that one's breaths, as if on the verge of a cold. The third was on the rooftops, sitting in the shadow of a chimney near the building she thought was Teraman's temple. Slow, deep inhalations, almost as if the person was asleep.

Of all those in Teraman, these were the only people whose breathing she could hear. The ones who watched. The ones the Rose chose to point out. She wasn't a mage, didn't have the senses to detect the power within, but could hardly deny that the Rose was working through her. Out in the night, the man across the road swallowed a cough. It felt like he was in the room with her.

Why, so far from its garden in Tor Darest, was the Rose's power becoming tangible? Because she was closer to an actual Rathen than she'd ever been before? Because now, unlike in Tor Darest, danger truly threatened? She'd told Sharwell she couldn't sense the heir's presence. Now she closed her eyes and tried to reach for the child whose life was to be her centre, her focus. Somewhere, out in this same night, was the future Queen of Darest.

Or nothing but three people, watching. Experimentally, Soren moved forward, twitching the curtain against the wind. The one below caught back a breath, and across the road she heard a sigh. The one on the roof snorted.

Staring at the shadow of the chimney, Soren decided that this was the man from the inn's public room. A huge assumption, but she didn't doubt it. One of the others would surely be stationed there by Captain Sharwell, and the third an unknown. All waiting to see if she'd make contact with the family of the missing heir.

Knowing where the lurkers were hidden was a boon. Soren left the curtain to the wind and lay down on the bed. Their breathing kept her from dozing and, when she decided at last that the moon would surely have passed beyond whatever temple gate Nina had been talking about, it was a useful guide to their failure to detect her as she fastened her sword to her back and eased her way into the wardrobe. Her prior search had revealed a catch which released a false back. With only moonlight in the room, the stair beyond was a black well which could harbour any and everything.

The detachment she'd felt while waiting faded. Immediately, her strange sense shifted its attention away from those outside to the quick, nervous breathing of the one who waited at the bottom of the stair. Nina.

Soren had prepared for this moment, and when her heart caught up to her head she carefully lifted her re-packed saddlebags to her shoulder. She didn't know if she'd be coming back. The leather creaked, dragging her off-centre, and she moved with excruciating care onto the steep, narrow stair. Both doors had to be closed behind her.

Insensibly cheered at having successfully shut away three spies, Soren inched down, hugging the rough wall and feeling for each step. She'd lost track of Nina and found that when she tried to locate the girl, her own heartbeat and nervously ragged breath deafened her.

What was she doing? Creeping down a hidden stair in the middle of the night, off to smuggle a princess to safety. Rain would love this. Her sister was the most adventurous of the three Armitage siblings, and after Soren's annunciation she'd had a few pithy things to say about just who should be the Champion of the family. Romadin would have brought Captain Sharwell with him, always confident that right and wrong were clearly separate. Soren had the dubious pleasure of feeling that she was doing wrong, while unable to see another clear course. She felt sick, more than a little frightened, and, beneath it all, excited. After two weeks' of travel, she was eager to finally see the Rathen child.

"Nina?" she murmured, when she thought she was almost at the bottom of the stair.

A puff of wind touched her face, then the girl's whisper: "Take my hand, Champion. We've got to go quiet here. It's narrow an' it runs along the back of the common room, out to the icehouse."

Soren didn't reply, simply squeezing the small fingers which found hers. Trying to move silently while carrying saddlebags and strapped to an oversized sword proved more difficult than she'd expected, but the few scrapes and single tap would surely be put down to mice. She hoped.

Five

T hey travelled for at least half an hour, splashing along the course of a stream choked with overhanging bushes. It was an uncomfortable, itchy journey accompanied by far too much mysterious rustling in the underbrush, but no attack came. Nor did that strange awareness of observation return, though this was no guarantee they weren't being followed. Half Teraman could be trailing them, for all Soren would be able to tell. She was truly out of her seaside element.

Strange to feel so alive.

"We have to go on hands and knees here, Champion," Nina said, her hand warm and sweaty in Soren's. "It's not far now."

A fortunate thing, given the weight of her remaining saddlebag. She'd packed them both with care, trying to anticipate all eventualities, and left the more disposable concealed in the short passage between The Lost Prince's cellar and its icehouse. The single bag had still become an aching burden, and she would be entirely glad to stop.

"Why is it safe for us to travel this way?" she asked, shifting the bag to her opposite shoulder.

"Running water, Champion." Nina's tone indicated she found the Rathen Champion sadly ignorant. "We got to leave it now, but nothing'll come close here. The bushes are spiny, so keep low. There's boards either side."

There wasn't enough light for Soren to see what Nina was leading her into, but with the child's guidance she found wide, rough boards which seemed to have been shoved beneath a stand of extremely thorny bushes. They formed a low, uninviting passage away from the streambed. Nina was already scuttling ahead, but Soren hesitated. She wasn't particularly afraid of the dark, and so long as she went slowly the bushes weren't a major issue. Yet for the first time it had occurred to her to wonder if Nina was who she'd claimed to be. Trapped in a thorny tube, she would be at the mercy of someone who wished the Rathen Champion ill.

A bit late for cold feet. Besides, the use of the secret stair in their escape wasn't likely if Nina was only pretending to be the innkeepers' child. Feeling a little scared was natural, but it was no good letting nerves overcome common sense.

A few jabs to the spine later, Soren found herself facing a tall, dark figure who patted Nina's shoulder before saying: "Welcome, Champion. I'm Riese Meddescalf."

"Soren Armitage," Soren replied. "Thank you for sending for me."

"Didn't see what else I could do," Riese Meddescalf replied, bluntly. "I don't relish spending the rest of my life skulking about an abandoned temple."

"Is that what this place is?" Soren could only make out the shape of a wall ahead, and the faintest crack of light.

"One of the Selunic retreats as was." The innkeeper moved back toward that line of light. "Best crowd close, Champion. Don't want to keep the door open long."

As Soren moved forward, the woman tapped on the door. Immediately, the light within dimmed to nearly nothing, and then they were moving forward into a single, dilapidated room. A guttering lantern revealed a woman who was Nina's image, and a girl perhaps five years Nina's elder – younger than Soren had expected. She was darker than her heart-sister, more like her blood-mother, who proved to be tall and statuesque, with near-black hair and hazel eyes.

Soren lowered her bag to the floor and immediately looked around for the heir.

"I suppose introductions are the first order of the day," Riese Meddescalf said. "You know Nina, of course, and this is Lucia, my eldest."

"Champion." The girl, Lucia, bobbed briefly, then busied herself turning the lantern back up.

"My wife, Jesmy," said Riese. Jesmy nodded, reserved and unforthcoming, and Soren tried to smile at her, but almost all her attention was taken up by the bundle the woman was lifting from a nest of blankets. Her stomach was a tight knot. At last.

"About time you were feeding her anyway, Lucia," Jesmy Meddescalf said prosaically. She surveyed the baby cradled in her arms, then stepped forward so that Soren could view the new Queen of Darest.

Sleepily, the child blinked. She had dark blue eyes and long lashes, but only a thin fuzz of black hair. Pink lips parted in a minute yawn and she shifted in her grandmother's arms. Her skin was the flawless cream of the very young. Beautiful.

And not Rathen. Not remotely. Soren knew it as she knew the sun would rise in the morning. There was no response within her, nothing like the force which had brought her to Tor Darest for her annunciation, or had spoken the name 'Teraman' at the touch of a rose. There wasn't even the same intense awareness which had made her look at the man at the inn. This was just a pretty baby.

Idiot. Thousand times fool. She'd gone looking for a child purely on assumption. Why should a Rathen appearing out of nowhere be newborn, after all? A fully-fledged Rathen made just as much sense as a baby fathered by a ghost. And what had she met with, when she'd arrived at Teraman? What had the Rose told her?

"How old is Helena?" she asked, her tone not quite hiding suddenly discovered doubts.

"Three weeks tomorrow," said Lucia, then looked down and away, betraying awareness of the why behind the question. The girl knew perfectly well that there was nothing Rathen about her child.

As her daughter became the picture of guilt, Riese Meddescalf made a noise full of understanding, anger, and disbelief. "It was that smooth-talking lieutenant, wasn't it?" she said, sounding rather more relieved than anything else. "Sun, Moon and Sky, Lucia, do you have any idea what you've done?!"

"*I've* done?!" the girl retorted, with sudden fire. "What have I done except what dozens have done before me? Forgotten the herbs or the moon's quarter and found no-one to stand by me except a story about a ghost? I didn't suddenly announce that the Rathens had come back. I didn't bring Jutlanders and Cyans and half the garrison to camp at the inn!"

"You could have told us, you silly chit!" Jesmy said. "Why insist on the excuse after all this?"

"You never–!"

Disturbed by the raised voices, Helena coughed, then started to wail. Argument forgotten, there was a rush to soothe her. A babe's cry in the forest would be a beacon to any who searched.

Soren looked around the makeshift home the Meddescalfs had made out of this retreat of Selune's worshippers. Solid but neglected, with only a few sticks of furniture and nothing resembling comforts. The shutters were plastered with mud and leaves to stop light escaping, and a curtain, currently hooked to one side, had been tacked above the doorway. There was no arlune, no icons of Selune visible, but perhaps the retreat's dedication to the Moon afforded it some protection. The thornbushes outside certainly did.

Safe, in other words. But not forever. Eventually the garrison, or someone else, would find them.

"Mama-la?" Nina walked slowly forward. "Mama-la, does this mean we can go home?"

Riese Meddescalf looked at her heart-daughter with a mix of pain and regret, while Jesmy briefly stared at the ceiling, then turned back to Soren. "Champion?"

As if she might know the answer, could do anything to fix this mess. Soren wished she could reassure them, say that it would be all right. "There's few who'd believe the truth," she said instead. "Not when there is an heir, and that heir is in Teraman. If I went back there now and announced that Helena was no Rathen, they'd only search the harder."

Nina's face crumpled, and she would have headed for the door if her blood-mother hadn't caught at her shoulder.

"That's it then?" Riese Meddescalf asked. "There's no way back?" Her face was stark and sombre, facing down the prospect of abandoning her home and livelihood to escape those who would kidnap her granddaughter. Simply because Lucia had sought the refuge of a lie everyone had taken for granted until the blooming of the Rathen Rose. Soren immediately decided she couldn't let that happen.

All she had to do was think of some way to stop it.

Breathing in the dark.

Soren froze halfway along the fence between forest edge and icehouse. One of her hands protectively touched the babe-sling suspended against her midriff, and she almost laughed at the sheer futility of the gesture.

Over in the pitch-black shadows cast by the icehouse, the person who waited let out his breath – a soft, disparaging tuh! which Soren shouldn't be able to hear – in response to a movement the lurker shouldn't be able to see. The man from the inn. No need to see his face. The prickle down her spine was enough, the curling twitch of power saying here, yes, look. Look at this, your future, your central concern, your problem. Your King.

It was no use blaming herself for not understanding; the important thing was that she'd found her Rathen. With Teraman full of people who seemed determined to interfere, the best thing to do was get him far away as quickly as possible. Of course, unlike Helena, he was liable to offer an opinion about what happened next.

Glad she'd left Nina at the forest's edge, Soren started slowly forward, her stomach clenching tighter with every step. The subtle alteration in his breathing when she moved told her that he truly could see her, despite the moon-cast shadows. He must have watched her leave, and known that all she'd be able to do was come back.

"Your Highness?" she whispered experimentally, stopping bare feet from the person whose breathing she could hear so perfectly. Her eyes gave her only a suggestion of a shape, a black form leaning against the small building's wall. Her pulse was falling over itself, her chest all mashed with nerves, excitement and a peculiar kind of dread. If she reached out, she would be able to touch him. Rathen.

"So you're not completely oblivious," said the man who was to be King. The words were terse, exasperated, with an underlying note of the anger she'd been shown when she first saw him. "What possessed you to fetch back that nursling?"

Soren touched the sling again, tracing the curve of the head and the soft, cushiony body. Since she was certain he could see her, she simply grasped the doll around the neck and drew it from the sling.

"A straightforward sort of diversion," she told him, glad her voice didn't betray the knocking in her chest. This wasn't the moment to analyse why being close to this Rathen stranger made her so apprehensive. "If someone spots me riding toward The Deeping with a babe in a sling, they won't keep scouring the Tongue for the Meddescalfs. And they'll have no reason to watch the road between here and Tor Darest."

He paused before replying, and his tone was a touch less scornful when he did. "Riding? The stables are guarded."

"It's difficult," Soren agreed, rather hoping he'd produce a better plan. The horse was one of the many holes in her own. "But so would escaping on foot be, after being spotted."

"True." The admission was grudging, as if he wanted to be angry, to find fault with her. "Wait here," he added, and thrust a heavy leather object into her hands. Her other saddlebag. Before Soren could object, he strode away toward the inn, not bothering to keep out of the light cast by the crescent of moon.

Biting her lip, Soren silently cursed the man to whom she was supposed to devote her life. There was nothing she could do but sit and hope that he didn't get himself captured. This Rathen, whoever he was and however he had suddenly appeared in Teraman, did not seem a tractable sort. Shepherding a baby definitely would have been easier.

Thoughtfully, she replaced the doll in its sling. The unease which had gripped her lessened with his departure, leaving her another thing to worry about. Why this impression of not-quite-threat? For all he was a mage, she hadn't expected to feel scared of the Rathen she was supposed to protect. Or whatever it was she was feeling. Imminence.

Her intense awareness of his breathing had dropped away, so she closed her eyes, trying to recapture it, trying to focus. The wind played on her skin, and skirled noisily through the trees. A distant something rattled, and she heard a woman's voice speaking soft and low. But nothing out of the ordinary.

Then, muffled but unmistakable, the sound of a horse. Disbelieving, Soren stood up as her Rathen rounded the corner of the icehouse, Vixen in tow. He'd even saddled her. And in no more time than if he'd been collecting his own horse, without any difficulties about guards at all.

Rathens were mages. It was a point she'd do well to remember.

"Give me time to get to the eastern edge of the clearing, then ride out. I'll wait in the forest on the right side of the road." Without another word, he dropped the reins and walked off.

Soren decided not to be exasperated. The man was going to be King, after all. An efficient sort of King, if this was any example. Obnoxious arrogance was something she'd just have to learn to ignore.

Sighing, she turned her attention to Vixen, who reached forward a questing nose. "Hello to you, too," she said, catching up the dangling reins. "Miss me?"

Vixen snorted wetly onto Soren's neck, then abandoned her investigation to sample a grassy tussock.

Duly dismissed, Soren loosed the saddle so she could strap the saddlebags in their rightful place, then played with Vixen's mane until her Rathen could have walked twice as far as he'd specified. She still didn't have the least idea who he was, or how he came to be alive so long after the death of the last Rathen. At least he seemed to have quickly grasped the importance of this diversion. An infant Rathen could have one day denied Aristide Couerveur the Regency. A fully grown Rathen need only have his Champion proclaim him beneath the Rathen Rose to take the throne.

Soren doubted Arista Couerveur would be pleased.

Six

As she turned onto the road to the eastern edge of the clearing, an astonished shout told Soren she'd been spotted. Urging Vixen into a canter, she searched among the sharp-edged shadows for the source of the cry and found a pair of swear-swords directly ahead. Two men, who stared at the pale sling made so visible by the moonlight. Despite knowing she carried only a doll, Soren still felt an urge to shield her midriff protectively. And to apologise for her deception.

Surprise gave the advantage. As she passed, one man made a half-hearted snatch at Vixen's bridle but missed by inches. She caught a glimpse of his expression, full of confusion and shock, and felt like the worst of villains.

Resolutely, Soren focused on the looming forest, which could not look more black and unwelcoming. As soon as she was in the shadow of the trees she slowed Vixen but didn't stop, in case the men she'd just passed noted the abrupt cessation of hoof beats. She trotted a short distance down the road before reining in and sliding from the saddle, her pulse only a trifle frantic. Vixen snorted and bumped against her in the dark, no doubt wondering what all this start-stopping was about.

Wasting no time, Soren headed into the trees on the right side of the road. The ground was very uneven, and she stumbled in a muddy hole, then had her ankle scored by a fallen branch as it cracked beneath Vixen's hooves. A horse wasn't exactly a subtle animal and as soon as she was ten trees in, Soren stopped. Vixen nosed her, and tugged back toward the road.

"Just a little while," Soren murmured, though she wanted to shriek and then sit down and gasp. It was the first time she'd ever done anything like this – the sort of thing that would make enemies, which would effect people's lives, which wasn't...right?

She scratched the mare's soft neck to take her mind off the consequences to Captain Sharwell's career, and was thankful when Vixen stayed still while a trio of riders raced past. They'd been quick off the mark, and more were sure to come.

Continuing to reassure Vixen, Soren edged past a few more trees, wincing at every twig which snapped and cracked. The light of the waxing moon turned the forest to pitch and diamond, highly disorienting. Travelling along Nina's stream had been a great deal easier.

A fallen tree at the edge of a narrow band of moonlight presented a tempting seat, but, wary of snakes, Soren gauged Vixen's opinion before approaching. When the mare paced to the full length of her reins and dropped her head to crop at grass beside the exposed root bole, Soren was encouraged enough to seat herself on the rough trunk, then close her eyes and listen.

The three riders were still at full gallop, hoof-beats distant and receding. Insects chirred and scuttled, with Vixen and the wind-busy trees a distracting accompaniment. A dog barked, but she couldn't hear anything else from Teraman.

She could hear breathing.

He was some distance west of her, moving steadily in almost the right direction, and without any of the hesitation which should accompany a stealthy search in the dark. Fascinated, Soren followed his progress as he moved to roughly the spot where she'd entered the forest, then began methodically casting inwards. She knew the very instant he saw them, because he stopped halfway through taking a breath, then exhaled and began walking straight toward her. Soren stayed where she was until he was just on the far side of the strip of moonlight.

"Do you want to wait till dawn before going on, Highness?" she asked. It came out all stifled, because she'd again been squashed by an impression of a hammer waiting to fall. It wasn't a very pleasant sensation, and filled her with doubt about just what sort of man was to be Darest's next King, and how in the world she was supposed to live up to being his Champion.

"Not likely." His tone was abrupt, impatient. "Sharwell's not nearly as incompetent as I'd like him. There's no—"

He stopped as Vixen lifted her head, and a single horse came galloping back down the road between Teraman and the garrison. Returning to report their failure to immediately catch up.

"Time to get well away from here."

The forest seemed less threatening now that she was travelling through it. With Summer shifting to Autumn, the coin-shaped leaves of the lorams were beginning to pale to yellow, and the choked remnants of Darest's orchards were heavy with fruit. Birds gossiped cheerfully as they plundered the trees' bounty, and occasionally a rabbit or some other small animal would scuttle to safety. As the sky grew brighter, the wind dropped, and now that Soren could see enough to not be falling over every second branch, the walk was surprisingly pleasant. The Tongue's reputation for danger had so far gone unfulfilled.

Much of Soren's attention was, of course, devoted to surreptitiously watching her Rathen. He walked on the far side of Vixen, and just a little ahead, moving with a controlled, easy stride. She had so far observed that both his hair and eyes were black with a hint of blue. The hair was fine but thick and looked like it might have a soft curl if it was not clipped so severely, while the eyes were peculiarly long. His jaw was firm, neatly defined rather than heavy, and his nose had a suggestion of a hook. These were features which corresponded to the portraits which hung in the Old Palace, back in Tor Darest.

For all his ease in the forest, it did not look as if he'd spent his life outdoors. The tan was too light. Vertical lines were just barely etched on either side of his mouth, and there was a developing crease between his brows. Late twenties, Soren guessed, but with mages it was always hard to be sure. His clothing was sturdy quality, black from boots to collar, and he was carrying no weapons, no pack, and no clue to just who he was and how he'd come to be in Teraman.

The main thing which had stopped Soren from asking a thousand questions was his expression. He so plainly did not want to be in this place, dealing with pursuing guards and Rathen Champions, that she held her tongue as the sky turned colours, then faded and brightened to a cheerful blue. Tramping steadily in his wake, Soren alternated between regretting the substitution of this sour-tempered man for Helena, and growing increasingly concerned about why she felt so strange in his presence.

It was possible that the racing pulse, the mashed feeling in her chest, was because of the Rose. She hadn't felt its presence so strongly since her annunciation, when she'd been pushed to the back of her mind while her body walked to Tor Darest. There was a certain similarity to the sensation she was experiencing now. But then she'd been in some kind of trance, so overwhelmed by the force of Rathen power that she'd been a watcher in her own body, and hadn't felt anything at all until she was in the Garden of the Rose.

Perhaps, after so long without a Rathen, the Rose was anticipating the moment when this one was proclaimed King. If it was going to do this all the way to Tor Darest, Soren thought it likely she would go completely insane. And she didn't understand why she'd have such a sense of foreboding, if she were merely suffering from too much Rathen power.

Unless the Rose knew of some problem with this Rathen, and was having doubts. If it was capable of such complexity. The histories never made the Rose's abilities clear, but they'd been explicit about the workings of the succession. The eldest child of the direct line ruled, with no room for variation. They would be proclaimed even if they were a babbling idiot, or a depraved murderer. Could she really go ahead and crown, then protect, a killer? What if the Rose gave her no choice but to Champion him?

The question made Soren smile. He was a bad-tempered mystery to be certain, but there was no cause to denounce him as a monster just yet. She did need to stop pussyfooting around, and find out just who and what she was dealing with.

Fortunately for Soren's patience, the cloud lifted from her Rathen's face before mid-morning, and he began to look less like an argument waiting to happen. "What name should I call you?" she asked, as soon as she judged it wise.

He glanced at her and for a moment that inexplicable anger flashed in his eyes. Then he shrugged, subsiding into irritability. "Strake will do."

That told her precisely nothing. "Are there any precautions we should take? For travelling through the Tongue?"

He glanced around, as if forest dangers hadn't occurred to him. "I suppose there's a possibility that we'll fall across something not already running to get out of our way. Do you have any hope of wielding the sword?"

"No training," Soren replied, wondering why he thought it necessary to be so scornful.

"Are you mage?" He grimaced when she shook her head, looked as if he was about to say something scathing, but changed his mind. Instead, he gestured ahead. "In Darest, at least theoretically, you're only slightly less immune to Deeping roamers than the current King. The Covenant is bound through the Champion and if there's one thing the Fair will do, it's keep to the letter of a bargain. So every stray Deeping beast, enchantment or meal-worm should bend over backward to avoid so much as inconveniencing either of us. But unless The Deeping's changed beyond recognition, Faerie magic will also twist everything in its favour, and the Covenant covers a Rathen ruler, not a Rathen heir." He made a face like he'd tasted something nasty. "Treat it like The Deeping. Avoid circles, pools, the oldest trees, all the animals and anything resembling a nest or cave. There's a lot you should be able to do with the sword in the way of protections, even without a decent arcane grounding. I'll see to that later."

He picked up his pace, and for a few moments all Soren could do was stare. How could this man Strake know so much, speak so authoritatively about the terms of the Rathen Covenant?

"Who *are* you?" she asked, when she found her tongue. "Other than Rathen?" She ignored the impatient look he threw back at her. "It's something I'll need to know if I'm to proclaim you, after all."

"True enough." It was a grudging admission, and he paused as if he didn't want to go on, then sighed. "Aluster Veristace Rathen."

When Soren showed no sign of recognition, his mouth turned down, then took on a wry twist. "Son of Chenath Rathen, sister to Queen Tiarmed."

Soren was relieved to hear a name she at least recognised. Queen Tiarmed's reign had ended about two hundred and forty years ago, during the decline of the Rathens. She'd been King Torluce's great-aunt, or some such. And mother of the Crown Princess Sethane who'd died at Teraman.

From there it was an easy path to follow. A Rathen, a contemporary of Princess Sethane, suddenly appearing in Teraman. She'd even found him in the Inn of the Lost Prince.

"So one of the hunting party survived."

Instantly, a shutter slammed down. "After a fashion." And he walked away.

"Oh, for pity's sake," Soren muttered, as he strode off through a stand of loram. How did this help? If he really was a Rathen prince, why was he so hostile toward the Rathen Champion? What had she done except obediently turn up to collect him? Why did he sometimes look at her as if she were the proverbial red rag before the bull?

He was going to be King. Her role was to protect and advise him, but she supposed that didn't give her the right to demand answers to questions. If he wanted to stalk about scowling at her and acting like she was some terrible imposition, then that was his prerogative. No-one said a King had to be polite, and objecting might only make him surlier.

Soren suspected that the Rathen Champion was not permitted to smack the future King across the back of the head, either.

Around midday, he started asking questions.

"Tell me about the Regent," he said, after they'd forded one of the myriad shallow streams which criss-crossed the Tongue. He sat down on the bank and pulled off his boots, emptying a trickle of water out of each. Soren, who had avoided getting her feet wet through the simple expedient of riding Vixen across, dismounted and looped Vixen's reins around a branch within reach of the water. She was still wearing the sling and the doll Nina had contributed, and took the opportunity to pack them in her saddlebags before making a proper inventory of the bags' contents. This was as good a time as any for lunch.

"What do you know already?" she asked, wishing she'd thought to stock proper trail rations instead of relying on the towns along the trade road.

"That there's a Regent."

Soren glanced at him, but he was busy rinsing and wringing out his socks. The tone hadn't been sarcastic.

"Arista Couerveur," she said, glancing between him and her meagre stock of food. There was only a couple of days' worth of dried meat and flat bread, and a compacted mash which had once been honey biscuits. Vixen swung her head about when this was unwrapped, questing with her mobile upper lip, and Soren couldn't resist feeding her a fragment.

Naturally her Rathen was now watching with that barely-tolerating-fools expression. Soren refused to be flustered, and concentrated on explaining Lady Arista. "She's past seventy. One son. She's very clever, and very...strict. A quick but cold temper. Early in her rule she did much to strengthen textile production, to increase value from the hemp and flax crops. Lately, she's...focused more on the Court." Played with her favourites and sparred with her son, but how to put that in words that didn't sound petty?

"Who was Regent before her?"

"Lady Arista's father. The Couerveurs have been Darest's Regents since King Torluce's death."

"So, Queen in all but name."

"Yes."

"And this son is heir apparent. Teraman was full of Lord Aristide, and how he'd see the innkeeper's whelp dead before Harvest Festival."

"Lord Aristide has a reputation for–" Soren hesitated, trying to decide just how Aristide Couerveur's reputation portrayed him. "–efficiency."

"Oh, very circumspect." Strake flipped a fragment of bark into the stream, mouth twisting. "Disposing of rivals is a habit, is it?"

Soren didn't answer immediately, sitting at what she hoped was a safe distance and spreading out a cloth for their sparse selection. For the moment at least, she wasn't suffering that fear-flight reaction to his presence.

"Lord Aristide doesn't, I think, seek conflict, but he's not merciful to his enemies," she said, selecting her words with care. "I suppose the best known example is the Basquets. Vereck Basquet was a spice merchant who supplied out of Atlarus. Cinnamon and pepper, mainly, and wanting to expand into cloves."

"With The Deeping across the border?"

"Mm. It's almost cheaper from Atlarus. Lady Rothwell has had a monopoly ever since the embargo." She paused, because the embargo had been only forty years ago, and she was beginning to realise the scope of what she'd have to explain. He'd known a different Darest, a vigorous prosperous kingdom where his extensive family had ruled. In context, his ill-humour was more than understandable.

"Forty years ago, The Deeping cut off all trade with Darest," she continued. "Lord Elling, Lady Arista's father, had been offering inducements to Shapers to try and reproduce some of the Fair's most valuable exports. Not just cloves, but the medicine alums and perfume trees."

"Any succeed?" Strake asked, absently. He seemed more interested in the attempts of a tiny spotted fish to swim upstream.

"Not well. Not with viable seed-stock, anyway." Deeping mages were unparalleled Shapers, modifying plants and animals to match their needs. While Darest had been able to produce a variety of enchanted clove which would flower locally, true Shaping was judged in the seeds, in the ability to produce more plants without any magic at all.

"The Deeping reacted as usual?"

"There's been no Deeping ambassador in Tor Darest for half a century. The Regent shares Lord Elling's views on The Deeping – that the Fair are attempting to slowly steal Darest back – and her rule has not been without similar incidents. If the Rothwells didn't own half Darest's ships and have Deeping links, I expect we'd still be using the Western Kingdoms as middlemen." Soren lifted one shoulder. "Sax profited well during those years, and Cya prefers Darest to be waning, not least because they're land-hungry. They also draw a great deal on the mines on the Sax-Darest border, and they're not on good terms with Sax. Vereck Basquet had Cyan connections."

"I'm sure Aristide will surface somewhere in this morass."

Soren swallowed a mouthful of honey biscuit, and decided to censor any gossip delving into Lord Aristide's keenly guarded privacy. The malicious rumours Aspen delighted in repeating changed with every telling. "Lord Aristide courts The Deeping," she said bluntly. "That's the core of many of his conflicts with the Regent."

"And presumably Vereck Basquet's downfall." Face intent, Strake was still watching the fish struggle against the current. He was really very attractive when not scowling. There was something about those long eyes, dark and cynical, which was making Soren feel short of breath. And he was the temperamental man she had to deal with for the rest of her life. She hoped he'd stop interrogating and start talking to her, sooner rather than later.

"Basquet didn't enjoy the outright success he'd hoped for." Soren said, trying to suppress wayward thoughts. "The Rothwells could match his undercutting. But as the year wore on, Basquet began to win out on quality and quantity. Then one of Basquet's ships foundered and an accusation was laid against Francesca Rothwell."

"And then it was proved to really be the work of the Basquets?" Strake asked, sounding bored.

"Not quite," Soren replied, shifting uncomfortably. "Lady Rothwell freely admitted that she'd obtained a stone which would scupper a ship unless a counterspell was regularly cast. And then had it concealed among one of her own shipments. Basquet had been buying low-quality cloves and switching them with the Rothwell shipments."

"We still haven't sighted this Aristide," Strake pointed out.

Soren nodded slowly. She was feeling dizzy now, as if the world was moving in two directions at once. As if someone was standing above her, about to put down their foot. What was it about this Rathen? "The Regent's judgment was that Basquet pay recompense," she said slowly. "Enough that he would be years recovering. Lord Aristide suggested that the fine be lessened if Basquet could retrieve Lady Rothwell's property."

Strake snorted, then looked appreciative. Soren could only be glad he didn't glance in her direction, to see her struggling for composure. "A challenge, of sorts," she said, hurrying to the end. "Basquet hired a half-dozen mostly foreign mages, and lost two ships trying to retrieve the cargo and stone. Then he was required to pay the full fine. It ruined him."

The dizziness was growing worse, as if her mind was being crushed in a fist. Was it Strake, or were they being attacked? She stood up, looking around, and immediately felt better. Relieved and dismayed, she stepped away from the stream, and the oppression vanished altogether.

She looked back at her Rathen.

Strake was watching her, but didn't seem to understand her abrupt removal. "And did Lady Rothwell ever mention where she obtained a stone so cleverly enchanted that a half-dozen could not counter it?" he asked. "Do I even need to ask whether Aristide has a singular reputation as a mage?"

"He does and she did not. But there are none who doubt its origin."

"Is he popular?"

That was hard. "Yes and no. He's—" She faltered. "I wouldn't say Dariens...love him, but they want him. Imitate him, court him, worship him in a way. He is very powerful and formidably competent. There's a great deal of anticipation for his rule."

"Indeed." The tone was flat.

Soren stomach twisted, and she moved closer to Vixen, feeling quavery. The mare turned an ear toward her, then permitted Soren to stroke her nose. Why was this happening? She was almost certain it was the Rose making her feel so strange, but she had no idea why it pulled her in two directions.

She was sure she didn't want to find out.

Seven

S outh-west of Teraman, roughly in the centre of the Tongue, small grassy hills rose above the trees. Burnished by ample sunlight and specked with flowery clover, they were a bright, airy break from the forest canopy. The trees were widely spaced, so a horse could canter unimpeded, but Soren didn't suggest that they ride. She didn't want Strake sitting up behind her.

Fidgeting with the reins, she watched the swallows which had come with the afternoon breezes to make precise sorties about their legs. Although that intense oppression had not recurred, there had been moments in the last two days when she'd felt its shadow. Always when she came too close to this Aluster Rathen, to whom she was to devote her life, and who she now carefully avoided touching. She hoped he hadn't noticed.

It was an irksome, unhappy situation, and all the speculation in the world wasn't going to provide her with a solution. If Strake would be a little more forthcoming about his recent past, she'd feel better able to broach the matter with him. But he brushed aside any probing and treated her as a necessary evil, not a confidant. Nor did he entirely hide that he thought her an inadequate excuse for a Champion, whom he had no intention of trusting. All she'd been able to gather was that he'd only been in Teraman a few days, certainly not two weeks ago, and he wore everything he owned.

A knowledge of recent history had so far proven to be Soren's most useful contribution as Rathen Champion. As soon as she'd given him a bare outline of Darest's Court, Strake had wanted to know about the formation of the Tongue, then the decline of the Rathen rulers and everything which had happened in Darest since. Between those questions he'd required a run-down on all the neighbouring countries, and even pressed her for detail about Atlarus, far across the ocean to the south and magnificently stable. It felt like she'd been talking non-stop and getting no answers at all.

Studying Strake had told Soren only a little more. He seemed impatient to get to Tor Darest, but not eager to be there. His reaction to her recital of the accidents, petty feuds and sicknesses which had decimated the ranks of the Rathens had been tightly bound anger tinged with incredulity. So many Rathens had died in the short decades after his hunting trip – a family of fifty or more whittled away until only Torluce remained. But he'd kept what grief he felt well hidden.

At the moment, he was absorbed with the swallows as they turned about his feet, coming daringly close to snatch up insects startled out of hiding. There was something mesmerising about them, arrow-swift iridescence, purple-black. They skimmed in circles just above the grass, making abrupt, effortless turns so that their pale breasts and flaring underwings, tinted a delicate mouse-brown, were momentarily exposed. Strake had watched them for hours.

Nor were swallows the only thing to capture his attention. Yesterday he'd stopped to enjoy a stand of loram well into its amber-gold stage, and then lagged behind when he caught sight of a passing stag. That morning, she'd woken to find him watching the sky change shade through the branches overhead. Soren found these intent studies reassuring. An apparent appreciation of natural beauty surely made him not...wrong.

Wishing she could believe that, Soren gazed down the slope into the forest to their right and spotted what must be the remains of the old trade road which had once run from Tor Darest to Elder Garrison. It was interrupted in places by vigorous stands of loram, and most of the remaining stones, wide and flat, were cracked and disrupted by encroaching roots. But as a whole the structure was far more enduring than the rutted east-west road she had travelled to reach Teraman. Soren studied its gentle curving course along the base of the hills and saw in the trees ahead the remains of a roof, then a tumble-down spire.

"That must be Aramond," she said, and was rewarded with a moment's abstract attention. "I'm not sure just how long ago it went. Eighty years, I think, and half-empty before that. They weren't able to keep the north-east road clear, and traders began taking the long way 'round."

"Strangled to death," Strake said, his voice muted. Then he scowled. "What an idiotic waste."

"Do you expect resistance from The Deeping to your return?" she asked, while he scanned the distance for more of the ruin. She had found he would occasionally answer direct questions when distracted.

"Not once I'm crowned." He glanced at her. "But I'm sure North and East would be less than sorry to hear that I'd met an unhappy accident on the way. And unlike the obliging Captain Sharwell, they won't have believed for a moment that baby was Rathen."

'North and East' were the two Deeping lords who had long ago disputed the land which was now Darest. 'When North and East meet' was an old way of saying 'near enough to never'. When the Tongue had reached Aramond, never must have stopped seeming so far away.

It was unlikely the original Fair were still alive. There'd even been a change of Queen in The Deeping since Domina Rathen had been granted a kingdom, but the little gossip which leaked over the borders suggested that the two families maintained the old animus and were behind the influx of trees. Only the Fair could take centuries to invade. Or to exploit a loophole in a contract.

"I may as well look it over, see what can be salvaged," Strake was saying. "Tomorrow morning. We won't reach it today. Can I hope that Islay hasn't been abandoned?"

"Not yet. It's up against the trees, and lost a lot of trade with the close of the north-east road, but the orchards there are flourishing, and the hives."

"With any luck, they'll have a spare horse."

They followed the road to the end of the line of hills and set up camp, a process somewhat hampered by Strake's interest in the chorus of birds paying homage to the setting sun. But at least he was not above fetching firewood or searching for ripe fruit.

"So we've covered a few of the people who'd like to kill me," he said, after whispering for a moment to a carefully constructed pile of dry twigs, which hastily whuffed into flame. "What about allies? Any outside the borders?"

"Skrem, perhaps," Soren said, doubtfully. "Sax. Neither are in the position to take Darest themself. Neither would like to see Cya do so. No-one would."

Strake nudged a twig further into the fire with his boot as she piled an armful of wood within reach. "And is Cya poised and ready?"

"Not this year or next." She shrugged. "Maybe not this decade, if Queen Rithana continues to distract herself with Atlaran affairs."

He nodded, gazing west at the hazy apricot sky. She watched his hands clench and relax and wondered what he was thinking. Nothing about Cyans, she was certain.

Feeling dizzy again, Soren stood, wanting to get away. Then, entirely without meaning to, she reached up and slid her hand around the back of his neck.

At the moment of the previous Champion's death, Soren had been sorting through old bottles in the stillroom. She distinctly remembered pulling the cork from a squat bottle of clouded red glass and up-ending it so that a few grains of powder fell out. Then there'd been an overwhelming rush of something which had pushed her to the very back of herself. She'd been no more than witness as she put down the bottle and walked through a dark uncertain place. Until she found herself in the Garden of the Rose, she'd felt nothing at all.

Like now.

She could see the muscles in her forearm shift, but had only the faintest sensation of effort. She watched, completely detached, as Strake's first flash of surprise was replaced by anger. He had gone very still, and she could feel rather than see his struggle, just as she'd been aware of his initial displeasure at her arrival in Teraman. He was straining with every ounce of will to not bend his head. And the anger had become fear.

Then his face went blank. The implacable force crushing Soren had surged forward and simply quashed all resistance. There was no emotion in what followed. Strake and Soren weren't participating, and if the thing which joined their bodies felt anything of passion or triumph, the tiny fragment of awareness which was Soren could not sense it. She watched, listened to the evening chorus and the tossing of leaves, but there wasn't enough of her left free to react.

Then, of a sudden, the stifling wealth of power departed. Sensation, feeling of every sort, returned.

Strake's weight was pressing the scabbard and harness of the Champion's sword painfully into her back. For a brief moment he lay like any lover, lips pressed to one side of her throat, shuddering from the aftermath of exertion. Then an elbow pinned her upper arm, and in a flurry of movement he was off her. Gaining his knees, he paused momentarily, trembling with furious horror as he clutched at the ground. Struggling to sit up, Soren gasped as the man she was supposed to protect threw a rock and a handful of leaf litter at her, flinching as he did so, as if she were a snake or a water-mad dog. Then he was gone, scrambling to his feet and stumbling into the trees.

Blankly, Soren lifted a hand to wipe at her mouth, and found blood where the rock had struck her. For a moment all she could do was sit there, all grit and bruises, with her leggings around her ankles and her shirt wrenched open. She looked down at the sword's harness, cutting directly into the skin beneath her breasts, and began to shake.

This was impossibly wrong. The Champion was supposed to protect. Protect and guide and uphold and– The Champion was the person the King could trust above all other. The purpose of the Rose and Champion was to support the Rathen ruler. That was what they were for.

Soren stared down at her hands, at the delicate sketch of veins at her wrists. It did this. It was inside her, wound around her bones, and she was nothing more than its tool. It had reached out and done that to Strake and used her to do it, violated them both, and she didn't know why and she didn't know how to stop it if it chose to do it again and–

A blur of white and red made her blink, and she jerked. She'd been clawing at her wrists, trying to tear the Rose out. It stung, a couple of the scratches deep enough for blood to be trickling freely.

It was suddenly important to stand up, to snatch her clothes into some semblance of order. A noise kept trying to escape her throat and she choked when she tried to swallow it back. Reaching over her shoulder, she grabbed the hilt of the Champion's Sword. She still hadn't mastered the trick of freeing the weapon in one easy draw, and jerked at it savagely when it caught.

A cry, an angry shriek, burst from her throat as she threw the sword after Strake. It spun in an arc toward the trees, briefly reflecting apricot sky before it fell out of sight. Soren staggered, and fetched up against Vixen, who snorted, but didn't object when Soren flung arms about her neck.

"A puppet," Soren breathed into the short, soft hair of Vixen's neck. "I'm a puppet!"

Puppet, monster, anything but a true Champion. She could hear Strake breathing. He was running, very quickly, and was already at least a quarter mile away. He ran and ran, and then he stopped, and made a choking noise and coughed. She thought perhaps that he was being sick. He coughed again, and this time it came out as a sob. Then he began to weep.

Grimly, Soren tried to shut him away, pushing blindly at a sense she didn't know how to control. The sound of tearing breath faded and she gulped, hugging Vixen tighter. The mare was a marvellously solid thing. Warm and alive and as dependable as Soren was meant to be.

She wasn't altogether sure how long she stayed there, hanging around Vixen's neck, feeling false and wrong and soiled. The sky paled, and tiny insects rose to whine and bite. The rush of wind through leaves replaced the evening chorus, only occasionally punctuated by the rising call of a star-chaser. Vixen grew restless.

Then Soren heard breathing, slow, soft and even, just within the trees to the north-west.

It wasn't Strake.

Eight

Every hair on the back of Soren's neck rose as she slid her arms free and turned, staring. The moon had not yet risen, and the black blobs of trees could well hide an army. Wobbling, she took a step, trying to focus the Rose-given sense. Whatever was out there was little more than fifty feet away, moving at a slow walking pace, toward her.

Immediately, she was overwhelmed by a sense of peril, nerves all over her body coming alive. If the Rose had screamed aloud, it couldn't have made its warning clearer.

Jolted into action, Soren ran – directly toward whatever was approaching. She was desperately trying to remember the course of an arc into the trees, with a flash of apricot at its peak. Strake had shown her a basic way of creating a protection, simply by inscribing a circle into the ground. She couldn't do it without the sword.

Guided unerringly by the connection which had existed ever since she'd gone to Lady Rothwell's rooms, Soren plunged down the slope into the trees. Only fifteen feet separated her from the unseen presence as she reached, spine crawling, for a lump of metal she barely knew how to use. She was panting in tiny rapid gasps, convinced that at any moment a nightmare would leap out at her: red, slavering tongue, claws like sickles, and teeth whiter than stars. It was so close.

Soren's fingers found the worn hilt and she tried to snatch herself out of range of a monster's leap even as it abruptly stopped moving. She stumbled backward up the slope towards Vixen, racing on jelly-knees, the heavy sword wavering in her grip. The mare was standing quietly, and merely flicked her tail as Soren approached. If the gusting wind carried scents other than apple and grass, they were not the kind to panic a horse.

But the Rose's cry of danger was unrelenting. Skin flinching from an attack which hadn't come, Soren traced a circle around

Vixen, trying to make at least an indentation in the grass. The sword's hilt grew warm in her hand, which was the only sign Soren was able to detect that she was doing more than griming the tip. The circle would, Strake had told her, keep out basic attacks.

And it was not necessary. Without even coming close enough for her to see it, the thing in the dark began to move away.

Toward Strake.

"Oh, Lady Moon. Grace of Night. Help me." Soren's breath was still coming in spurts, the futile prayers juddering between gasps. He was a mage and infinitely more capable of defending himself, but he was out there alone without even a knife. Without even his self-command, after what had been done to him.

Vixen still didn't seem to think anything was wrong, except that Soren was thrusting the bit into her mouth at the end of the day, completely against routine. Soren had never saddled a horse faster. She dared not try riding bareback. Not in the dark through a forest with that thing roaming around.

She could hear them both now. Strake hadn't moved, was no doubt wishing he'd left her stumbling around after Helena. The soft, steady breathing had been moving directly toward him, but now began circling to the right. Already halfway between her and him.

It knows where he is as surely as I do, Soren thought, fitting one foot into a stirrup which would not stay still. It knew the moment I touched that sword. That makes it no ordinary animal. Something out to kill him. Fae magic, Fae—

Soren fell, flat on her back in the grass.

Startled, she tried to stand back up, but her legs wouldn't work. She grabbed at the stirrup swaying above her head, but trying to lever herself up only sent her sliding under Vixen's belly. The mare, far more perturbed by Soren's strange behaviour than anything lurking out in the forest, almost trampled the Rathen Champion in her haste to get out of range.

"Sorry," Soren said, too shocked at that moment to do more than make inane apologies. She tried to stand again, and this time managed to gain her feet. The world spun, the dizziness worse than before, and she felt crushed, pulled in two directions at once by the tumult behind her eyes.

Landing back on her knees, she groaned, lifting a hand to her head even as the conflict died away. Vixen was watching from just outside the circle, ears pricked forward and reins trailing about her hooves. Stars glittered above and the wind rushed peacefully over the hills. Out in the night an unseen thing stalked the Rathen heir. And the Rose wouldn't let her go try and stop it.

Fear and confusion fell away to anger, and Soren struggled to her knees. "Let me up, you wretched shrub," she demanded, pushing back when the Rose tried to box her behind her spine. Whatever else, she would not be this. She would not allow herself to be made a puppet, would not bend to an enchantment meant to serve and protect, and she certainly would not sit in a protective circle while something tried to kill her Rathen.

To Soren's surprise, the tight feeling in her chest went away. But the dizziness was worse than ever, her head reverberating like a struck gong. This time she fell hard enough to hurt.

Staring up at stars which were squiggling in little circles, Soren realised that the feeling of struggle was not her own. The Rose was fighting itself.

Why? Why attack Strake and then try to leave him unprotected? Why the internal battle? It seemed something had gone seriously wrong with the enchantment overseeing the Rathen succession. Unless there had been some sort of sabotage. Could Lord Aristide have tampered with the Rose back in Tor Darest, perverting it to his ambition?

Whatever the case, Soren had to try and take advantage of this wobbling conflict. Climbing to her feet, she set her jaw and pushed at the pressure within. An implacable edict. She would not be stopped. Strake was the Rathen heir and she would protect him. That, after all, was what everyone said she was here for.

Dizzy struggle evaporated. Even the sense of impending doom, of panic and danger had gone. But half a mile away the thing which stalked the future King drifted closer, and she was running out of time.

Riding at night was chancy even without factors like abandoned roads and unseen monsters. Despite the moon edging above the trees, Soren dared not attempt more than a fast trot, and found herself occupied with ducking branches instead of evading dagger-sharp claws. Vixen had picked up on her mood and was skittery and uncooperative, but still did not show any awareness of the presence which so excited the Rose. It was just ahead now, about twenty feet to the right of the road. She'd have to ride past it, within easy reach of a sudden rush.

Too frightened to hesitate, Soren drove Vixen to surge forward, closing her eyes to slits as she tried to stare through the dark. There was no catch, no change in the even pace of the thing's breathing. She was sure it turned its head to watch her fly past, bent low over Vixen's withers, but it did not so much as pause in its steady course toward Strake.

Strake.

Her Rathen had found the crumbling ruin of Aramond, and was standing at the mouth of a street suffused with silver. He was facing away from her, staring up at the half moon rising above the blockish shadows of crumbling buildings. Although he didn't move as Soren broke into the open, she'd heard the sudden intake, then his deep, shaky breaths as Vixen gained speed along the road. Steeling himself to deal with her.

Her stomach turned over, but there wasn't time to cringe. She reined Vixen to a halt bare feet from him and blurted: "We have to get out of here."

For a moment there was no response. Then his head lowered, his back utterly straight, unbending.

"We?"

Total rejection. It shrivelled her.

"Do you imagine I have any intention of travelling with you? Trusting you?" Scorn competed with furious loathing.

His anger reignited Soren's own. "I imagine that whatever it is chasing you about means you no good," she snapped. "I think you know something about why the Rose wants you dead. Why it did...that to us. Why it tried to stop me warning you." She couldn't hold back an exasperated, frantic noise, swallowing a volcano of doubt and antagonism as the shadow drew ever closer. "I think we need to get out of here. You can yell later."

Strake turned to study the forest at her back. "I don't see anything," he said, flatly. But he searched the black and silver trees again.

The Rose chose that moment to start pummelling Soren with a lifetime's fear and urgency. Vixen, her reins jerked about, danced in a little circle as Soren tried to control the urge to run as far and fast as she could. The pushing sensation had returned, along with the dizzy argument behind her mind, and she lost vital moments thrusting it away. It at least seemed easier, now that she knew that she could.

"Why is it doing this?" she cried, then shook her head. The stalker had stopped, a stone's throw away. "There isn't time." She held a hand out to her Rathen, who was watching her with the wary stare of someone who has discovered a madwoman. "Believe me, we have to go. Now."

He hesitated, eyes fixed on her hand. Not wanting to touch her. But something of her urgency must have communicated itself, because he grasped the back of the saddle and, avoiding contact with Soren as much as possible, swung himself up behind.

The thing in the dark let out its breath in a puff. As Soren turned Vixen, it rushed forward, crashing through bushes in a finally audible charge. The shouting tumult of the Rose reached a crescendo of panic, and then the sky went away.

Vixen screamed.

There wasn't time to even glance at the empty blackness around them as the mare began leaping in all directions at once. Strake, niceness forgotten, clutched at Soren's waist as Vixen spun in a circle, bounced forward, tried to rear beneath their combined weight, then leapt back the way she had come. Soren, her knees wedged into Vixen's sides, hauled desperately at the reins. She felt like she was swimming through treacle, and it was either this sensation or the flat nothing surrounding them which had sent Vixen into an ears-back paroxysm.

"Hold her!" Strake ordered, his voice strangely blurred. He slid left, nearly pulling them both from the saddle, then with a curse pushed Soren forward so he could grasp the reins, adding his strength, but Vixen had the bit in her teeth and continued to rocket back and forth like a bird beating itself against the windows of a small room. "Look for a path!" he shouted. "A door, a—"

"—light?" There was a patch less black than the rest, a depression rather than a guiding beacon.

Strake followed her direction, and immediately wrenched Vixen's head around, the bit grating horribly. They bounced toward the depression, and this time the treacle-drag was barely noticeable. Vixen squealed again, then bolted.

"She'll ruin herself!" Soren gasped, clutching at the pommel. Strake had somehow taken possession of one of the stirrups, and was perilously close to evicting her from the saddle, pushing her forward onto Vixen's withers.

"Better to let her run it out than stop," he replied, the voice at her ear sounding abruptly more collected. "Stopping wouldn't be healthy."

"You know where we are?" Soren stared dizzily about at black nothing. How could emptiness feel so crowded, so stifling? And why couldn't she hear Vixen's hoof-beats?

"A Walk. A path between, a gate. A quick way to get from one place to the next. In this case, an escape route."

He pulled her to a safer position in such a punctiliously matter-of-fact way that she was forcibly reminded of what had so recently passed between them. She could feel the rigid tension in his arms, now bracketing hers. She was still sticky from him, for Sun's Sake! Neither of them were ready to be pressed up so close, all rushed and jolted by Vixen's frantic pace.

"I think I came here when I was annunciated," she managed to say, talking from some vague notion of keeping both their minds away from the angry horror of that memory. "Th-the—" She pretended Vixen's jouncing gait had caused that quaver, refusing to make everything worse by sounding so mortified. "The Rose was riding me then, though," she said quickly and flatly. "So I didn't really take it in. I can only assume we're heading to the palace now. Why is it a bad idea to stop?" Inane, stupid words. He'd been raped, they both had, by the very thing meant to protect him.

"A Walk is compressed. Nothing is quite solid, or truly insubstantial, and time doesn't work the same way. I've never managed to cast one, not many can solo, but I know that stopping or turning from course has caused disappearances. The travellers never come back."

An unusually garrulous speech for Strake, especially now they were bent low over Vixen's neck, their breath half knocked out by the mare's pace. Soren tightened her grip on the pommel, bracing herself, far too aware of the way their bodies surged together, of how he must be hating her.

Still, she forced herself to ask: "Why did it do that to us? Why does it want you dead?"

He didn't answer.

"I have to know," Soren continued, with as much asperity as she could muster, trying not to sound so pathetically lost. "Don't you understand that? I don't know if I'm actually capable of protecting you, but I can at least try to stop the Rose from leaving you to the clutches of whatever that thing was. And I have a far better chance of doing that if I know why all this is happening."

"You'd know more about that than me." Strake was regaining the caustic edge to his voice.

"You know what happened to you at least!" she cried, exasperated. "Why you're still alive, what it is that's hunting you."

"No," he said, with immense reluctance. "I don't."

Nine

S o far as Soren could tell in the stifling absence of the Walk, they had been travelling for less than an hour when the dark went abruptly away. Fortunately Vixen had slowed to a tired walk and simply stopped as the world returned, lifting her head. The Garden of the Rose, already outlined by the nebulous light of early dawn.

Nothing moved. No coil of thorn and jagged leaf whipped down, and not a hint of pressure touched Soren's mind. It could very well just be a plant. Overgrown, neglected, mute.

Strake immediately slid from Vixen's rump, eager to get as far from Soren as possible. After admitting ignorance, he'd fobbed her questions off with such a sudden return to anger that Soren had given up the argument. It was impossible to debate with a man who was pressed up against your back, saying curt, furious things directly into your ear.

With mixed feelings, Soren dismounted as well and patted Vixen's sweat-damp neck. The mare would be thirsty, but Soren was reluctant to let her near the small rectangular pond which lay toward the back of the Rose's Garden. The birds never drank from it. Birds didn't enter the Garden at all.

Turning, Soren forgot all about her horse. Strake was standing arrested, staring up at the dark, velvety blossom which represented his life. The colour was leaching from his face as she watched, leaving him a peculiar waxy tan.

"What wrong?"

"It's black." He spoke like a man returned from a visit to a neighbour to discover his house burned to the ground: the dismay was almost drowned by astonishment. He could not quite believe what he saw.

"That means something?" Soren spared a nervous glance toward Fleeting Hall. There were always guards posted at the doors to the

Hall of the Crown. She could see the warm glow of their lanterns, but they were surely too far away to hear. Other palace staff passing through were far more of a risk, one which would increase as the sky grew brighter.

Her moment's inattention had given Strake the chance to regain his composure. He never seemed to lose it for long, and had reverted to impatient and unfriendly. "It doesn't matter." He glanced back at the flower as if he would rather it wasn't there. "You have a duty to fulfil, Champion," he continued, giving her the title with angry sarcasm. "Perhaps you should stop wasting time and do so."

He meant that she should pronounce him King. The ideal moment, when they were before the Rose, and no-one knew that the heir was anywhere near Tor Darest. She wondered how she was supposed to go about it.

And if she should.

"First tell me what it means, that the rose is black."

The anger was immediate. He seemed to grow taller, bridling up so that it was suddenly impossible to deny that this was a Rathen, royal blood, heir. Even Vixen felt it, tossing her head and stepping back. Her hooves struck the paving like a summons.

"You think this a matter of choice?" The words were calm, but he looked as if he were about to hit her.

"Not at all," Soren replied, also standing as upright as she could, clutching Vixen's reins until the leather was sure to be imprinted into her skin. The muscles of her shoulders tightened in anticipation of a blow, but she forced an entirely false calm into her voice.

"You're heir and I'm supposed to proclaim you," she continued. "But this seems to be one thing that the Rose isn't rushing to force me to do, and I want to know why. Stop acting as if I have anything to do with what's happened to you, for you know – you must know – that it's the Rose which will make you King and the Rose which did that to both of us. Both of us, mark you. You can stand there and glower at me all you want, but that will only make it more likely we'll be spotted. And then...I guess you'll have to gamble on other people's loyalties."

"Trying to blackmail me will get you nowhere," Strake retorted. He was flint, perfectly inclined to wait and see how the palace would react to him.

"Oh, will you get down off your high horse?! Do you think that instead of stamping about making the worst of everything you could attempt to work with instead of against me? You've the temperament of a fest-hall cook, but you're to be King. I have just as little choice about that as you. But if I'm to spend my entire life running around trying to keep you safe, I need to know what's going on. You mightn't know for certain why you're alive, or what's chasing you, but I'd wager you've a better idea than I do. You know what happened to you before you all of a sudden turned up in Teraman. You certainly know what it means that your rose is so dark. Stop sulking and give me an explanation."

"Sulking?" He said the word with infinite affront, but spoiled it with a wry twist of his mouth. Shaking his head, he looked down.

"I–" The full weight of what she'd been saying crashed down on Soren. Arguing with a Rathen mage, with the future King. This wasn't what being Champion was about. But apologies weren't going to solve the problem, and he had at least stopped fuming. "I'm not your enemy, Strake," she added simply.

"Maybe not." A short stride took him directly beneath the rose, and he inspected the fragile silver rims of the petals intently. "It means I'm about to die."

Soren hadn't been prepared for this, and stepped back as if she could escape the implications of his words. Vixen, standing just behind her, nudged her in the ribs, but Soren couldn't spare any attention. "Die?"

"I've only once seen a rose go black, when my uncle lay half-alive for three days before finally giving in. More usually, the flowers only get blown with age – more open. At the moment of death, all the petals fall. A black rose...they happen very rarely. Cases of poisoning, sickness beyond the ability of any to cure, broken skulls."

"You haven't a broken skull."

"Not yet." He gave her one of his sour looks. "It seems I soon will. Is that enough explanation for now, or shall we wait for an audience?"

Soren stared up at the black rose. "What of the thing chasing you? And how you came to Teraman?"

Strake was looking toward Fleeting Hall. "Later," he said. "You have my word, if you need it."

There were footsteps approaching, steady but not hurried, and very near. Soren, the implications of Strake's impending death unravelling in her mind, looped Vixen's reins over her neck and moved to stand next to him. The black rose dipped to meet her and she paused, because she did not know what to say.

It was at this precise perfect moment that Aristide Couerveur walked into the Garden of the Rose. He was wearing a light, silky dressing gown over loose trousers, but was otherwise as impeccably presented as the last time Soren had seen him. He didn't even seem surprised.

There was no time to freeze or panic. Soren lifted her hand to brush the very tips of the fragile petals and looked straight into the eyes of the man she was about to disinherit. "Aluster Veristace Rathen," she said, then added with exacting simplicity: "King."

Several things happened at once. The rim of silver on Strake's rose flashed bright enough to hurt, the light shifting gold before it vanished. Strake made a small noise, a grunt of pain or effort. And a thousand bells rang.

Metal tongues in metal throats, falling over themselves in eager triumph. High as birdsong, deep as night, cascading everywhere and through everything. A clamour of acclamation so powerful that Soren's chest vibrated in sympathy, and only Aristide Couerveur's interested gaze kept her from covering her ears.

It wasn't easy to think in the midst of joyous cacophony. Soren's thoughts kept being bounced from their course as she tried to divide her attention between Strake's expression and the possibility that Lord Aristide would be rash enough to attack them in the Garden of the Rose. And a strange sense that she'd suddenly acquired a dozen extra eyes.

Since it was impossible to be heard in the riot of noise, and Strake and Lord Aristide were just standing surveying each other, Soren concentrated on herself first. An unlooked-for section of her mind seemed to have suddenly opened up, or been invaded, by...locks. Locks which were home to spiders, locks which were frozen with rust. Locks which were in part tiny killers; cold and patient. Shining locks, recently oiled, warm with use. A dozen hundred locks. And their doors. In every direction, doors. And musty stairs and cobwebbed windows and tiled roofs enduringly whole beneath their burden of leaves and dirt. Gardens, bright and blooming, and one parched, desiccated from neglect. Rooms empty and still, others warm with life. People. Walls and corridors and floors of stone and wood and marble, held together by a coiling all-pervasive force. All around them, everywhere. Infesting, upholding every part of the palace. The Rose.

And bells. She'd never known there were so many in the palace, indeed that there were any outside the Chapel of the Sun. But there were two at each corner of Fleeting Hall, warm and mellow. A cluster of twenty at the very entrance of the palace, turning and rocking above the great golden doors. And one massive cup of metal, just beyond the throne room, exulting the new King in a voice of silver thunder.

Soren nudged at a tendril thought, a fragment of will furnished with dark, serrated leaves and copper-green thorns. And the bells stopped.

"Thank you," Strake said, tone edging back into impatience. Soren opened her eyes to discover herself still a woman standing in a garden. With a palace twining through her mind.

She wasn't certain how long she'd been staring at things she couldn't really see, but it seemed to have been enough time for Fleeting Hall to collect the beginnings of a confused crowd. Some like Aristide still in sleeping clothes, and most staring up at the ceiling. Others were watching Lord Aristide, with the usual interest anything he did inspired, but they didn't seem to understand that the pair of people he faced were the heart of the morning's excitement. That the bells were for the King, for a new chapter in Darest's history. Bells for the end of the Regency.

They couldn't see her, Soren realised. Just her legs beneath Vixen's belly. A very strange thing, for a horse to be in the Garden of the Rose, but not nearly so curious as the sudden clamour of bells.

Then Aristide Couerveur went to one knee.

Thirty years at the heart of Court intrigue. It had certainly provided Lord Aristide with a performer's feel for the moment. Soren could not do more than guess at his feelings, but he did not spare any inch of depth as he inclined his head to the new King of Darest. He still looked like he was enjoying himself.

"Your Majesty," he said, star sapphire eyes meeting blue-black ink. "How may I serve?"

"You can get up, for a start," Strake replied waspishly, but it was too late. Disbelief ran through the Court: the Diamond Couerveur – kneeling! Then comprehension slowly dawned, and those nearest began dropping to their knees. A different kind of excitement spread across Fleeting Hall, a mix of fear and joy. Strake merely looked impatient. "If you would be so kind," he added.

Lord Aristide immediately rose to his feet. And smiled, that peculiarly sweet smile he was reputed to have given Vereck Basquet before he beggared him. "Would Your Majesty like to be conducted to the...former Regent?" he asked.

"In due course." Strake looked out over the twenty or thirty people kneeling before him to startled newcomers just entering Fleeting Hall. "One of you fetch the Chancellor," he said. "And the Seneschal. Presuming the palace still has one."

Soren only recognised a handful of the people who were gazing at Strake so avidly. Guards and servants mostly, for few people had apartments close to the Hall. She saw Aspen, and the Chancellor's pretty young husband, who looked particularly wide-eyed as he surged to his feet, bobbed like a cork, then hurried away toward the still-open door to the Chancellor's apartments. No-one needed to fetch the Seneschal, who had already appeared at the west entrance and stopped to stare.

"King Aluster," Soren said, as much to the crowd as to Strake. "This is Lord Aristide Couerveur, the Regent's son. Lord Aristide, this is Aluster Veristace Rathen, son of Chenath Rathen, who was sister to Queen Tiarmed."

"King," Lord Aristide added, and folded into another exquisitely judged bow. Again, there was no hint of hesitation or doubt in the observance. "Perhaps Your Majesty would care for breakfast?"

"Shortly."

Gratified to discover that curt and touchy was Strake's method of dealing with everyone, Soren gestured to a porter. "Take Vixen to the stables," she said, catching hold of the mare's bridle as she sidled toward the pool at the back of the Garden. "See that she's well looked after."

"At once, Champion!" With a startling puff of self-importance, the man jumped to take the reins. Soren stroked Vixen's neck one more time, trying not to feel that she was sending away her only support. She wished she could concentrate.

It did not seem possible to shut off the ebb and flow of information through her mind, though it did tend to recede to the background when she focused on what was happening immediately around her. But even as she turned back to Strake, she was discovering that she knew that there were exactly eighty-three people in Fleeting Hall, that dozens more were running toward it and seven away, that the Chancellor and his husband were a few moments short of their apartment's door, and one of the cooks had just upset a pot of water over the kitchen's main hotstone, sending up a cloud of steam. That the whole palace was a pageant silently playing out in her head.

With a wrench, Soren brought her attention back to Fleeting Hall as the Chancellor emerged, his husband in tow. Though he was properly dressed, with the thick silver chain of office around his neck, the Chancellor's dark hair was standing in uncombed clumps. He ignored the Seneschal as she wove her way toward them, blinked twice at the sight of Strake, Soren and Lord Aristide, then bowed briskly.

"Chancellor Dominic Gestry," Soren said helpfully. Gestry was an olive-skinned man with a handsome-ugly face, all his features seeming too large, but somehow coming together into an attractive whole. He'd been the Regent's favourite some years ago, his position his reward when her interest waned. He'd managed to retain it by proving circumspect and just ambitious enough.

"What are Your Majesty's orders?" he asked now, acting like he'd been serving Strake for decades, and not at all dishevelled or short of breath.

Strake was frowning at the inner corners of the Garden of the Rose, where the scourers never dared venture to collect fallen leaves and scrub away dirt and mould. He turned to look the Chancellor up and down, then said: "Inform Darest of my return, and despatch the appropriate messages to our neighbours. I will expect to meet with the Regent after lunch, then address the Court. The afternoon will be divided between an initial briefing from the Court Shaper, Councillor of Mages, Marshall of the Army, and Apexes of the Sun and Moon. Then I will meet with those of the Barons who are currently at Court."

Before the Chancellor could even nod, let alone compose some sort of response, Strake turned to the Seneschal, who had reached the edge of the garden and was curtseying deeply, her Keys of Office clattering.

"Seneschal Mara Sedurian," Soren murmured. Thin, prim and highly political, the Seneschal's most public battle was with the Chamberlain, sparring with him constantly about the division of their duties. Her expression suggested rapid thought, but like everyone else she did not seem prepared to simply reject the new King. Aristide Couerveur, after all, had not.

As Strake gave the Seneschal the same quick survey that he'd awarded everyone else, the crowd finally broke its silence, those furthest away beginning to murmur explanations to newcomers. Only a few were still on their knees. In other circumstances, Soren might find their stunned confusion entertaining, but too many were stealing quick glances at the man two steps to her right for her to forget possible consequences. Lord Aristide gave no sign of being perturbed by the fact that Strake had not spared him a further glance. She couldn't imagine what he was feeling.

"I'm told that part of the palace was sealed after Torluce's death," Strake said, brusquely, as the Seneschal opened her mouth to speak. "Get it cleaned. Start with the throne room, then my apartments. The Champion will see to your people's safety. But first find me somewhere to bathe and breakfast."

"I–" The Seneschal struggled briefly, then bowed her head. "Of course, Your Majesty. If Your Majesty would follow me?"

Strake held up a hand to put the Seneschal off and turned to Soren. "I'll see you for lunch," he said. "Will you be able to shepherd the cleaning crews?"

"Yes," Soren said simply, because it was hardly the moment the launch a discussion on her sudden dual existence as person and palace. And she was, besides, quite sure that she could. When she'd had more time to think, perhaps it would be clear why.

Turning away, Strake paused to look Lord Aristide over again. "Perhaps you would like to inform your parent of my arrival," he said.

"Very much indeed, Your Majesty," Lord Aristide said, with a wonderful sincerity. "Thank you."

Strake barely lingered for the answer, was striding across Fleeting Hall, the Seneschal only just managing to keep ahead of him.

"You appear to have crowned a whirlwind, Champion," Lord Aristide said, too soft for any but Soren's ear. Soren, whose attention had flicked away to the Regent, rising grandly from Jansette's bed, glanced jerkily at the man at her elbow and found his smile quite impossible to gauge.

The prospect of Lord Aristide as enemy frightened her, and she looked back at the full, dark flower which represented their new King. His explanation of the colour briefly drowned out the palace

"It means I'm about to die."

 Ten

There was nothing Soren wanted more than a quiet place to hide, if only for a year or two. Instead she had a crowd of servants, all lye, linseed and unconcealed excitement as they turned out the fabled living quarters of the Rathen rulers. Soren was too shakily weary to even appreciate it, her head full of cotton regret.

"My Lady Champion, you must advise me!"

Avoiding a scourer laden with disintegrating bed-linen, Soren turned to the Master of Apparel. He was one of those small, dapper men who seem to live on a diet of nerves and ill-considered romance. "What is it?" she asked, as her newfound inner eye flicked across a dozen rooms to find Strake in her own apartment, moodily leafing through the books she hadn't had time to study. She'd been carefully not looking at him ever since he'd climbed into his bath.

"It is the King," the Master of Apparel replied, with a nice rising note of alarm. "He will not allow me to dress him!"

Strake was certainly not prowling about her rooms naked. Nor was he still in his trail-worn clothes, though his current outfit was something very similar. "How so?"

"Everything I have shown him, Champion, he has rejected out of hand. He has turned his nose up at any thought of a demi-robe, and even the simplest of stockards prompted him to accuse me of trying to dress him like an Atlaran. His opinion of shirts suitable for wearing without outer robes does not bear repeating."

"But you have dressed him all the same?" Soren asked, her sense of the absurd slowly stirring to life.

"Much against my better judgment. I have been obliged to outfit His Majesty in a manner best suited for stable-work, or some coin-scraped huntsman. It is not suitable, Champion. It is not suitable at all!"

Not fashionable, at any rate. Following Lady Arista's sumptuous tastes and Lord Aristide's shining precision, Strake's penchant for undecorated black was going to look sadly out of place. It was interesting that the Master of Apparel had decided to appeal to Soren. He was the first but not, she suspected, the last.

"He is King," she said now, with as much gravity as she could muster.

"Champion, you must–"

"He is King," Soren repeated. The Master of Apparel opened his mouth, closed it, took another breath to speak, stopped, then reluctantly nodded.

"Thank you, Champion," he said, unhappily, and turned away. Soren watched him go, thinking over the power of that simple statement. If Strake took it into his head to wear a transparent lime-green nightgown who could gainsay him? The Master of Apparel should be grateful for unrelieved black.

"Are you ready to open further rooms, Champion?" the Seneschal asked, having crept over while the Chamberlain was busy displaying his vigilance over a cabinet full of outrageously valuable statuettes.

Soren was starting to realise that one of her major difficulties as Champion would not be playing politics, but staying away from it. The origin of the feud between Seneschal and Chamberlain was murky: something about a woman they'd both wanted. The result was constant struggle. Soren suspected they were as eager to impress the new King with the other's incompetence as their own efficiency. In Strake's absence, they had resorted to proving themselves before Soren.

The loathsome prospect of adjudicating courtier's games was finally too much. Awake since the previous morning, Soren did not really care about the replacement of hundred year-old mattresses, or whether statuettes of emerald and topaz should remain where they were or be conducted at once to the Treasury, let alone which court official should be doing what. The Seneschal had barely given her a chance to bathe and snatch breakfast before chivvying her off to oversee the unlocking of doors. And, because she'd wanted to give the impression that the Champion's much-vaunted powers over the palace protections required her physical presence, Soren had allowed it. But standing about watching people dust was ridiculous.

"So long as you use the keys, Seneschal," she said, decisively, "you will not be troubled by the palace defences. I will be with the King in my receiving room, and will expect lunch at noon. Advise the Chamberlain to leave valuables where they are found."

Without another word, Soren walked away. She'd discovered that there was a door linking the royal apartments to the Champion's rooms, but headed in the opposite direction. She wanted another look at the Hall of the Crown.

Scarcely possible to believe this triumph of art had been lost to neglect. In permanent gloom beneath layers of grime it had been huge and threatening, with only a hint of splendour in the half-seen sweep of the banisters and the glimpse of carving on the doors. Ignoring the curious glances of stray scourers, Soren stopped just beyond the door to the royal apartments and drank it all in.

Vaulted beams of burnt honey curved molten over a generous two stories. The same wood formed a single sinuous line of banister, up the curving flights of stair, and all the length of the galleries to merge with the wall behind the throne, holding the Hall in an embrace minutely etched with roses. The room's five doors, a darker shade of honey, were also festooned with intricate carvings. Petals and leaves, thorns and vine.

The floor was glory. Sunset marble, awash with the most delicate of reds, gold, pinks and yellows. It drew in every ounce of light and gave it back as depth, revealing more and more of its kaleidoscope mysteries until it became a thousand layers of colour in an ever-receding horizon.

Soren found it entirely mesmerising, not least because her strange, new-found sight made it feel like she was staring at the inside of her own skull. But if she hesitated too long, someone else would find the nerve, or gall, to question her about Strake. And though those who had approached her so far had reluctantly accepted her statement that the King would address the Court later that day, there was sure to eventually be one who would not. Besides, Soren had answers of her own to discover.

During her journey to Teranan, the Champion's apartments had been transformed from over-stocked library to muted luxury. She even had an actual view into the Three Fountain Garden, now that the wall she'd thought contained only shelves had proven to possess a wide windowsill. A few dozen books remained, and she found her King sitting in a chair reading a particularly old and decrepit specimen. A selection of others were piled on the floor beside his feet.

Strake read with the same expression he wore when watching sunsets. Engrossed, introspective, those long, blue-black eyes still markedly cynical, but the hostile irritability absent. He held himself with a loose-limbed poise, and was attractive in a way which was signally his own. Amazing the mix of sick dismay and pain the sight of him could conjure.

But despite the Rose's efforts, despite her own heart-felt wish not to, she still felt a curl of desire when she looked at him. Even without being King, he'd soon have half the Court after him. She did not think that she would enjoy watching the inevitable attempts, any more than she was going to find any pleasure in talking to him now. Because he was her Rathen, just as the sword was her sword. She kept recognising him in some fundamental way that she thoroughly distrusted. Not dealing with him didn't seem to be an option, no matter how much he went out of his way to make her not want to. No matter how thoroughly she'd failed him.

Memory of that violation was a gaping chasm between them, which no words could possibly mend. If she could undo the last day, if she could have lived up to the role forced upon her— She wished she understood why she was Champion, when she was patently a less than adequate protector, and nothing like a courtier, able to smooth over such a savage rift. But with little choice but to stumble on.

"Does that, by any chance, detail the supposed abilities of the Rathen Champions?"

He looked up, and for a moment barely seemed to recognise Soren in her embroidered black surcoat. But the now familiar anger was quick to follow, a shutter slamming furiously in her face.

Then he sighed and looked resigned. Sitting back, he snapped the book shut and gestured at the chair which faced his. "It's a journal of the last of the true Champions," he said, as she sat down. "Most of them kept some kind of record. This one covers the arrangements made after Torluce's death, but it's circumspect, to say the least. An occupational hazard. I doubt you'll find anything conveniently written down."

Last of the true Champions? She couldn't deny it.

"What did the Champion of your time do?" Soren asked, making herself be glad to be dealing with a person rather than an ill-natured storm. Being alone with him was desperately uncomfortable, but this had to be faced. "What was publicly known?"

Strake shook his head, but then said: "The Champion concerned himself mainly with directing the Captain of the Guard. When my aunt travelled, he would create the ward I showed you, and it's well known that the Rose detects poison. No-one was obliging enough to directly assault my aunt while I was around." He paused, as if entertained by the idea. "Still, he also enforced her rule of peace within the family, which was a challenge given our tendency to offend each other. Lockren would always know when matters had reached the point of daggers-drawn, and find his way to us before we'd managed a fatality. It was impossible to lock him out."

This image of constantly warring Rathens went some way toward explaining how the family had died out, dozens perishing in a few short decades. Soren tried to picture it: mages with blue-black eyes filling every corner of the palace, vying and clashing, kept in order by the Champion. If they'd all had Strake's temperament, it would have been more than a challenge.

"How did he stop you?" she asked, wonderingly.

"His mere presence was usually enough to damp matters down. But he was also a painfully expert swordsman and on occasion we saw the flat of his blade." Strake half-smiled at the memory, then frowned at her. "You're not wearing Kittredge's sword."

"My back is bruised," Soren replied, unwilling but unflinching. It was a question she'd anticipated and he reacted just as she'd predicted. The shutter slammed down, locking them in mortified silence.

The red lines on Soren's wrists throbbed, refusing to let her forget her own anger, the helpless fury at being made a puppet by the Rose, the shame and violation she would have to face. But that assault did not change the political forces shifting to accommodate a sudden King, did not spare her time to recover and reconcile. "What about outside the palace?" she asked, hoping in her blundering way to distract him back on course.

Strake had turned his head so he was no longer looking directly at her. She watched the muscles shift in his face, but could only wait, and curse the Rose. Images of the palace began to infiltrate her thoughts: the scourers hard at work, Aspen sorting through a pile of old books, Fleeting Hall unusually busy, children fighting a battle with fallen leaves in the east garden. Lord Aristide, alone and unsmiling–

She could push the images away and they would become background, a flicker at the far corner of her attention, but it did not seem possible to banish them.

"We had better luck prosecuting our little feuds outside the palace," he said, sooner than she expected. He was still not looking at her, and the air of quiet ease was gone altogether, but he was talking. "Even then Lockren would too often interfere. He was not a mage, and occasionally we attempted to disguise our activities, but with negligible success. We never attempted to strike at him directly. The reputation of the Rathen Champion was formidable enough."

"But the stories are so unspecific," Soren said, looking at him steadily, refusing to give in to squirming discomfort. "I'm constantly told that the Champion controls the protections of the palace, but the only visible weapon is in the Garden of the Rose itself – the canes strike at anyone who tries to interfere with it. While there are endless murky tales of thieves who have tried to loot the sealed apartments since Toluce's death, never to be seen again, I can't actually see any evidence of...I don't know. Traps doors or spikes, aside from a couple of locks which actually are snares. If there's enchantments set for the Champion to use to eviscerate stray assassins, I don't seem to be able to touch them."

"You said you could keep the cleaners safe," Strake pointed out, at last looking back at her. But the constraint hadn't gone, wasn't ever likely to.

"I think I can," Soren said, struggling with guilt and an overwhelming sense of incompetence. "I'm not altogether sure I could attack them, though." She frowned into the distance, but didn't make the attempt, scared of accidentally killing someone. "Hardly the thing to experiment with."

"I'll try to oblige you with an attack." Dark eyes flickered, and he took a breath before going on. "My aunt's Champion was uncannily omniscient, but since he was so thick with the Captain of the Guard, we could never be certain if that was thanks to informants or the Rose. It seems that you telling me what the Champion can do would be more productive than the other way around."

Soren nodded. "I can see everyone," she replied, watching Lord Aristide cross Fleeting Hall, beautifully indifferent to the ever-increasing crowd. "I can see all of the palace, and even just outside it. Anything within sight of the walls, I suppose." She tried looking out over the city and the bay from the palace roof and shook her head. "No distance. I can see about five feet from the wall, not even to the stables or the New Palace."

"New palace?" Strake repeated, evidently more surprised at this last than anything which had preceded it.

"Built just after Torluce's death," Soren explained. "I suppose because so much of the Old Palace had been sealed off."

"Where?" he asked, looking unexpectedly worried.

Soren gestured generally east. "Past the stables. It's more an extension than anything else, for it's mainly residences and connected to the Old Palace by Dathan's Walk. It has its own kitchens and laundries." She looked in subdued astonishment at the tight, closed expression of pain on his face. "What was there before?"

"Gardens. A small wood, for riding." It was apparent that Strake could scarcely believe they were gone. "Is there anything else I should know?" he asked, with an angry, disgusted bite to the words. "Have they turned the Temple of the Moon into an out-house, perhaps? Planted turnips over the floral clock?"

"Floral clock?" Soren repeated carefully, and his eyes flashed angry-bright before he slumped, and waved a hand in negation.

"I see I shall need to tour the premises sooner rather than later. And the city. What condition are the royal apartments in?"

"Dusty," Soren replied, watching him lock obvious hurt away until he merely looked a little more cynical than usual. "Mould and spider-webs and dirt. I couldn't see signs of mice, though it was obvious moths in plenty had made it their home. Anything of cloth, and much of the furnishings are in a bad way, but the structure itself just needs cleaning."

"It takes something to damage. So, you can see everything within the walls? What's the Regent occupying herself with?"

"Talking with the Lord Marshall," Soren replied. "She's set her servants to cleaning out the room which has served as an alternate throne room." She narrowed her eyes, watching the packing. "It rather looks like she's planning to move to a different part of the palace altogether."

"Saves encouraging her to go. Can you see the Treasury? Or the 'old Treasury' as I've no doubt it's known? Is there anything left in it?"

After surveying the shut-away rooms, which constituted practically a third of the palace, Soren decided the one just south of the Hall of the Crown was the old Treasury. It certainly had a formidable door. "Chests," she said, after a moment. "I don't know what's in them. Tables with things on them, weapons in racks on the walls, some rusting, some not. Why would they leave all these things there?"

"The throne isn't the only thing which is Rathen-specific," Strake replied, the edge back. "What else can you do?"

"Open and close locks, doors, windows," Soren said, moving the hall door by way of demonstration. Muscles supplied by the Rose. She could easily have sprung every lock in the palace while lying in the bath. "I think I could turn on those lights in the Hall of the Crown, and the plumbing in the rooms which have it. I stopped the bells. I don't seem to be able to shift anything which isn't meant to be moved."

"What are the Regent and the Lord Marshall talking about?"

Soren shook her head. "I can't hear what people say at all. It's not even like I'm really seeing the inhabitants of the palace. Painted dolls, performing behind a wall of glass. A puppet show." Full of embarrassing detail. She had managed not to watch Strake bathe, refused to even think about the privies, and had enough hard detail on who was sleeping with whom to keep Aspen busy for a year.

And, like any drama with several hundred players, there was far too much going on at once. If her mind was on Aspen, busy admiring himself in a mirror, she did not see what Aristide did until her attention flicked to him and found him talking to one of the Barons – Peveric. A hasty alliance? Aristide was looking as amused as ever, and Peveric solidly commanding. He made some gesture with his hand, and turned away. If they had sealed some bargain, Soren could not decipher it.

"No sound at all," she repeated, then added cautiously: "But I can hear you breathing."

As she'd expected, the shutter slammed up. "Breathing?"

"It's how I knew where you were in the forest," she said, keeping her voice as matter-of-fact as possible. "Wherever you are, I seem to be able to hear you breathe, know where you are. I still can't hear what you say, though," she reassured him. "Sometimes I can hear the breath of other people–" She paused, and tried to locate Jansette Denmore by her breathing, but that did not work. "When you were watching my window, I could hear the other people watching me, and I could hear the thing hunting you–"

"You could?" He sat up straight, as if this was the last thing he was expecting. "Are you certain?"

"Very," Soren replied, not knowing what to make of this latest development. "The Rose was having hysterics. The thing came and looked at me first – it wasn't more than a dozen feet away – and then it went straight after you."

"You're sure?" He seemed only half conscious of her presence, too caught up in rapid thought. "Could you see it?"

"No." Soren was silent, eyes on his. Her expression would say it all. You know more than I do. You need to explain.

She waited.

"We were visiting Aramond," Strake said finally, staring at a point well to Soren's left. Voice, expression, posture: all were eloquent of his reluctance, of the effort it took him to speak. "My cousin, Sethane, was courting the Baron of The Oaks. We'd been there some weeks when a report came of an attack out of The Deeping. A farmer cut to pieces, not two feet from where her husband was preparing dinner.

"A message from Tor Darest came close behind. There had been deaths within The Deeping. The Tzel Aviar had tracked the killer across the border and requested permission to pursue into Darest. A joint hunt was arranged, and we headed for Teraman."

He shifted in the chair, turning the book he held over, smoothing its discoloured cover. The Tzel Aviar, or 'Warden of the Borders', was an official of the Fair who dealt with problems caused by Deeping magic straying into neighbouring territories. Soren only knew that the current Tzel Aviar was a man reputed to loathe humans, and certainly hadn't done anything about the incursion of trees.

"We couldn't track it by magic," Strake said, a small vertical line appearing between his brows. "Even the Tzel Aviar could do no more than hunt the faint physical traces it left, and follow its kills. We could not tell if it was man or beast. Not a troll, as the Tzel Aviar first believed. Its victims were ripped by claws, but it did not feast. No troll would behave so.

"After treating a bullock and a child the same as the farmer, it turned back to The Deeping. And we followed. A frustrating journey – we seemed to constantly blunder past it no matter our precautions, and by the time we would find its track again it would be hours ahead. Eularin, the Tzel Aviar, suspected that it was heading for the citadel of Seldeering, some five days on. She suggested an ambush."

Another pause. He was gripping the book tightly now, its boards cutting into his fingers. "There was one logical point, a trail up an escarpment. We set wards and laid a web of spells which would hold fast anything larger than a rabbit. And waited.

"Two days later, the escarpment exploded. No warning at all, just a loud noise as rock flew in all directions. I was one of the few not injured. The Tzel Aviar was killed outright, some of the horses, two retainers." Those long dark eyes were bleak, but he continued the story in the same forced, flat tone. "We found traces of blood where we'd laid our trap, but no corpse. No blood-trail. No way to tell whether the hunt had achieved its aim. We had too many injured to continue. We set out for Teraman.

"Four days from the border, we woke to find the Baron of The Oaks spread in pieces around the camp. No sign at all of the guardsman set to watch. Or our horses." He looked at her then, for the first time since he'd started speaking. Just a quick glance, to check her expression perhaps. Soren was sure she was pale, her face as set as his. She had no idea what to do or say.

"The blood was still wet," Strake went on. "Still warm. Sethane summoned keleyards. You know what those are?"

Soren had heard of them. "A weapon of spirit," she faltered. "Will and magic."

He nodded. "They look a little like hawks. Or blades. Or sunlight. They circled out from the camp, ready to strike anything which moved. Vanished among the trees." He paused, lips forming a word, then he lifted one hand, fingers splayed, spoke soft words. An image spun into existence, a woman standing among golden trees. Her face was bruised, and tears streaked her cheeks, but her eyes, long and blue-black, were full of cold, furious determination. A hunter's resolve.

Then her eyes widened and she threw up one hand. And fell, crumpling into a heap, her image melting into a glimmer of light on the rug.

"We could not revive her," Strake said, and his voice shook with an effort he could not hide. He was sweating, sitting as if he endured some torture, an ordeal far greater than words.

"She was cold, as if she had been dead for hours. While we covered her body the last two retainers broke and ran. There was a sound, a branch breaking, a scream cut short. I stood with Vahse, another cousin. Back to back, swords at ready. There were no trees close, no way for anything to approach unseen. We heard another scream, far distant, then...birdsong."

"Birdsong?" Soren repeated, unable to help herself. She had to fight down the need to tell him to stop, to apologise for asking, to reach out.

Long eyes closed, opened. For a moment she thought he wouldn't go on, then, in a thread of a voice: "The forest did not care what was happening, did not seem to notice. Birds called. There was a lark. Not close, but very clear. We stood there, waiting for something to find and kill us, listening. There is an almost frantic elation to the song of a lark. I could feel the press of Vahse's shoulders, warm against mine. The trees were in Autumn dress, the wind only light as it rattled the leaves. Vahse made the smallest sound, as if he had choked, and jerked against me. His elbow hit my ribs."

He hung there, on that memory, staring into the past as if it were about to fall on him. Then he hurried to the end, plainly bent on getting the tale over with. "I could smell the blood even as I spun. I cast as I turned, pushing everything behind me away, panicking. I caught a glimpse of Vahse's body, split and tumbling among whirling leaves. Golden. Red specks, liquid shining. I did not see what killed him. Not at all." The words choked to a stop.

"What happened then?" Soren asked, when it seemed he would not go on.

"I don't know." Strake was white. He reached down to place the book on the top of the pile, and she could see marks on his palms from where he had been gripping it. Then he straightened, as if that simple action had put everything at a distance, and his voice was stronger after.

"Everything around me kept changing, dark and light. Trees of every sort. I don't remember walking, but I always seemed to be in a different place. There were people, a dozen or so, just glimpses. It lasted a handful of moments, no more. Then–" He shrugged. "I'd lost the sword, had a scattering of coin in one pocket. No blood, no bodies, no creature. I wandered several days, then found the road to Teraman. Found myself a Champion."

The words were incalculably bitter. He gazed across at her, a muscle jumping in his jaw. "Are you carrying my child?"

Soren couldn't quite manage not to flinch. This was a leap to the heart of things.

"I don't know."

"But."

"But." She found her hands had closed into fists and forced them to relax before she met his eyes again. "I can't think of any other explanation for the Rose doing that to us. If it thought you were about to die."

"Champion brood mare." The words were cruel, but his anger had already drained away. "I don't know the reason for the black rose. I thought it must be the hunter, that it had somehow found its way to now, as I had. But we couldn't track it with magic, and I don't see why you'd be able to, any more than I understand why the Rose is so willing to abandon me in favour of a...hastily-produced successor. If the thing we encountered in the Tongue is the same that the Tzel Aviar hunted, then it has formidable magical defences. But is that reason enough for the Rose's behaviour? Whatever the case, I don't intend to be shuffled aside. I don't intend to leave anything of Darest to the Rose's devisings."

"What do you mean?"

"The Rose is bound into the Covenant and the succession. The palace, the Rathens and Darest itself, all intertwined into one. A way of strengthening, making what is formidable almost insurmountable. All very well, when there are Rathens, but it hasn't been good for Darest these last two centuries. Whatever else Domina Rathen planned, she certainly did not intend for Darest to be held in limbo by its own protective enchantments. And never beneath a thousand Suns would she expect a Rathen to tolerate being treated as—" He stopped, face a mask of anger. Took a breath, as if he needed it to control his voice. "That is not something I will tolerate. Tomorrow – no, the day after – I intend to study the foundation of the Rose's enchantments. With a view to unmaking it."

"Do you expect me to object?" Soren asked, for he was staring at her with evident hostility. What Strake was proposing would significantly weaken the Rathen possession of Darest, but Soren could not be anything but supportive of removing the Rose's ability to make her a puppet.

"I suppose not." Strake glanced away, controlling himself, and the hard lines of his face eased. He took a deep breath and looked back up at her. Almost human; resigned and weary and rather worried. "What's your name?" he asked. "Your first name, I mean.

They were full of 'Champion Armitage' at Teraman, but nothing else."

"Soren." It had never occurred to her that he would not know it.

"I need you to understand something, Soren," he said then, so grimly that Soren straightened. "What the Rose did to control me– You are not a mage, so you wouldn't have experienced it the same way. You would have had no way to resist it, would have...drowned in a moment. But I fought. It was holding my head under water, and I was struggling with every scrap of strength to lift my head, to break free. Fighting death of self itself." He looked sick. "The Rose is too strong for any individual mage. I drowned, and then I – we – were used as we were. I'll try to remember that you were as unwilling, but you must understand that as I struggled to lift my head, to take 'breath', it was your face I saw. And I can't simply erase that."

He stood up, prowled around to stand behind his chair as if he wanted it between them. "Intellectually, I can't blame you. On some level, I even recognise the Rose's motives, if that's what they were. But that makes no difference to what I feel when I see you." He looked down at his hands, resting on the high padded back of the chair. "I am hardly the most temperate of men. I've had my enemies, taken my revenges. I have never so wanted to punish another human being as I do you."

He smiled, thin-lipped and sour, at the expression on her face. His own was still pale.

"You're fortunate I'm not so petty as I am quick-tempered. I tell you this only because you need to remember that whenever I see you, for a moment I am drowning. Hating." He shook his head. "I would never have believed I could so want to hurt someone, to humiliate, to make them suffer."

Soren didn't, couldn't, say anything. After a prolonged pause he went on, staring at the far wall.

"Even without the possibility of a child, I don't suppose it would be politically wise to send you somewhere out of the way. Especially if the Rose's doom is unavoidable. So I will master this, teach myself not to react as I have been. Just remember that I have a temper. And that I don't want to be the first Rathen King to beat his Champion to death."

It was at this faultless juncture that the Seneschal arrived with their midday meal. Awkward silence reigned, Soren thickly miserable and Strake brooding over his wine. They did not say another word to each until they went together to the newly pristine throne room, where Soren watched Strake sit for the first time upon his throne.

Then the Regent came to deliver a brief and gracious speech of welcome, before announcing that she was quitting Tor Darest.

Eleven

A palace never truly sleeps.

Night is the realm of cats and mice, owls, spiders, moths, roaches. Even a nest of furry grey torlindars hidden among the kitchen stores. Their perilous Court scuttled and squalled, hunted, mated, battled and died while those who ruled the day lay snoring.

The borders between the two dominions were constantly crossed. Countless visits to chamber pot or privy, bed-hopping of every description, fractious babes tended by weary nurses, and a handful who read or talked or watched Selune gazing back at them. And there are always guards, exchanging desultory comments, playing cards, making rounds of empty corridors.

Lack of light didn't impede Soren's view, confirming her belief that she wasn't really seeing at all. Nor did it matter whether she had her eyes open, or was even conscious. Exhaustion had finally shown her sleep despite the constant distraction, and even then the palace trooped through her head, a silent pageant slipping between vision, memory and dream so fluidly it became a tangled whole.

The fourth time Soren opened her eyes it was a little before dawn and she was weary to the bone of her dozing observation over the palace, and the tangle which made waking such torture. Three times during the night she'd woken a beat behind the strangled cry and bolt-upright jerk of her King. She'd watched him gasp and shudder, pace about the newly refurbished royal bedchamber, just two rooms away, then finally settle back to sleep. He hadn't done this in the Tongue, and Soren suspected she knew too well what haunted him now.

What do you do when your King has nightmares about *you?*

Haunted by an overwhelming sense of failure, and unwilling to lie in bed any longer, Soren rose and dressed, though she left her so-distinctive tabard off. The door to the Hall of the Crown was still guarded, not by the tall Jutlanders who protected the Regent, but a man and a woman wearing the same black touched with gold as Soren's uniform. The Master of Apparel had turned his energies to outfitting the King's Inner House.

Ignoring their salutes, Soren strode east through the dimly-lit palace, fingering the mageglow she'd slipped into her pocket. The double door to Dathan's Walk and the stable yard was also guarded, by a less distinctive pair. They saluted just as smartly though, and opened the doors as she approached. Newfound respect.

Soren walked into sweet relief: the chill, dark nothing of outside, where she saw only what was in front of her.

She'd discovered this the previous afternoon, after Strake's marvellously pithy address to the Court. After the briefest of explanations he'd dismissed the curious crowd and headed out to inspect the changes to the palace grounds. The moment Soren had stepped outside she'd found herself almost human again.

"Not surprising," Strake had told her over dinner. "There has to be limits. It obviously has range outside the palace, especially where you're concerned, but the constant flow of information of this 'palace-sight' would be ruinously expensive outside the area of the enchantment."

Beyond its limits, Soren couldn't summon up the palace at all, but she walked into the stables listening to Strake's breathing. Sleeping deeply, and she would know when he woke. That would surely be enough to allow her a small freedom.

It was pitchy dark inside the first of the long stables. Soren stood a moment listening to tiny noises made by unseen animals, and was careful to set the mageglow she'd liberated from the Champion's apartments to a soft glimmer before taking it from her pocket. Sparing the eyes of the horses was as much a consideration as not waking whatever hands or minor officials infested the stables.

She was not three stalls along before she found what she was looking for.

"Hello Vixen."

Stupid to go hugging horses, but spending the day standing at the side of a man who was trying not to hate her had left Soren needy. The bewildering mix of dismay, concern and desire she felt around her Rathen was not helped by the fascination of the Court or the weight of the palace. Among so many, she found herself very alone, and it was with considerable regret that she'd found time to write her mothers a most circumspect composition which could be translated as "stay away for now, until I'm sure it's safe". It was a sensible move, but not a comforting one.

One thing Strake had said to her cut deeper than anything else. She'd yet to puzzle out a reason for the Rose to choose her above all others as Strake's Champion, but he'd brought a horrid possibility to light when he'd called her Champion Brood Mare. Little as she wanted to be Champion, Soren loathed the idea of having nothing more to contribute than any woman capable of bearing. But, she told herself, the idea didn't make sense – the urgency of attack had brought on the Rose's attempt to breed a Rathen, if that was what it had been. She didn't know if she was pregnant, didn't know the why behind that coupling, and mustn't fall into the trap of making herself less than what she was.

Indifferent to ride-ly woes, Vixen tried to eat the apple Soren had wedged into her other pocket.

"Put me in my place," Soren laughed, and pressed her cheek briefly against the soft hair of the mare's neck. Then she fed her the apple, and looked about for a saddle.

On the maps, the Kingdom of Darest looked like a shakily-drawn square leaning east. It was a large, mostly flat country, its few mountains trailing along the border with Sax and Ceria to the west. The northern and eastern borders were consumed by trees, slowly being absorbed back into The Deeping, while south was entirely coastline, deeply notched by the Bay of Diamonds. Tor Darest spread across the low hills at the apex of the Bay, where the Eldavar ran into sea.

Established by the wealth of Domina Rathen and blossoming in the security of Rathen rule, it was airy, had wide streets, flowing lines and few scars. But, like the north-east borders, the edges of Tor Darest were fraying. As the Tongue slowly licked across Aramond, that region's occupants had trickled south and west. To Islay, to Tor Darest, or all the way to another kingdom.

The city had changed to accommodate those displaced from the north, especially in the flat valley close to the wharves east of the Eldavar. These crowded boxes made stark contrast to the wide orderly streets with their sewers, ornamental streetlights and large picturesque houses.

'Tor Darest is like a splendid Queen with mud on her face.' Soren couldn't remember who had said that to her. Aspen's tutor Fors Cabtly, perhaps. It was a not inaccurate description. Even in the domain of the wealthy 'on the hills', fading whitewash and weeds creeping out of pavement cracks spoke the same message. Darest was in decline.

West of the river's mouth was the royal preserve, with the palace on Seduna Hill and only the wealthiest private residences to the north. Soren rode south, to a hill which sloped down to the beach and formed a kind of parkland open to all.

People claimed that if you stood on Vostal Hill on a clear morning, it was possible see Atlarus reflected in the sky above the Sumaric Ocean. Cities of towers and fountains, populated by firebirds, dragons and the coal-skinned mages who rivalled the Fair for their complex nobility. All Soren saw were gulls, swirling up in a column as they followed the fishing fleet out to sea.

Turning back, she looked up at the palace, wondering why it faced away from the beauty of the south. Toward the forest. Her domain, the world which filled her head. When she was inside, it was hard to believe there was anything beyond the bounds of the Rose, and the ocean could very well be a world away.

Her King still slept, and the beach stretched empty and tempting along the western shore of the Bay of Diamonds. Shafts of sunlight were just breaking over the far hills and soon the choppy water would begin to sparkle and earn its name. Vixen shifted eagerly, ears pricked as she contemplated the possibilities of the surf.

"Let's go," Soren murmured, allowing the nebulous beauty of the moment to wash away roses and Rathens. Weeks with Vixen had taught her that there was more to horses than a slow plod, and she rode down to the beach and raced the waves along the damp, tight-packed sand. A throat-swallowing gallop through the thin sheets of foam, with the cry of gulls and the shush of surf her only accompaniment.

And breathing.

The bubble of exhilaration burst. Abruptly exposed, Soren slowed Vixen and looked around. Up ahead, where Vostal and Seduna met in a tumble of dark, angular rocks, two somethings were breathing.

They reacted to her searching stare. Soft gasps, something she thought must be hurried whispers, though it was difficult to be sure without the words. Then, sheepishly, two ten-year children emerged from behind one of the larger rocks. They carried a bucket and a rake, and bowed clumsily. Collecting mussels.

She inclined her head, smiling to show she was not annoyed by their presence, then rode on, wondering why she had been able to hear two children who plainly posed no threat. Experimentally, she attempted to call up the breathing of Lord Aristide, whose activities she had watched carefully all the time she'd stood beside her King.

Nothing.

By the time Soren reached the stables, she had decided that the Rose allowed her to locate anyone – and anything? – which watched her or Strake from hiding. It was an explanation which matched her previous experiences, though it did not quite account for the way she had followed the progress of Strake's pursuer through the forest. Still, a theory to start with.

During her absence, the stables had been overrun by thin, scruffy boys and girls in their early teens, busily removing the night's deposits. Without compunction, Soren handed the salt-spattered Vixen over to the first one who looked her way.

"Have tack ready in her stall at all times," she said, trying to sound assured without being as curt and dismissive as Strake. Then she went back into the palace.

It came over her in a wave. The kitchens were a hive of activity, the Seneschal had already rallied and was lecturing her forces, fresh guards were in the process of relieving those who had stood through the night. Energetic children demanded attention or played quietly, the most enthusiastic lovers discovered each other anew among tumbled blankets, and every second person made more work for the night-soil attendants. Less than an hour past first light and hundreds were awake.

Soren had been braced for it, but still her step faltered just within the east door. She picked up her pace, gazing for a moment on Strake's continued slumber, finding Lady Arista coldly surveying the progress which had been made packing her belongings, and then checking on Lord Aristide. The Regent's son was still in his bed. He lay relaxed and quiet, blinking occasionally as he stared up at the ceiling. Just looking at him made her deeply uneasy.

Aristide Couerveur had attended Strake's address to the Court, standing to the back of the crowd. Now only a Baron's heir, he had not been included on the list of people Strake wished to speak with. Abruptly relegated from the Court's centre to the margins, he had made no attempt to approach his new King since their first encounter. Soren wondered how many people who had firmly been in the heir's camp the previous morning would abandon the pale precision he preferred to follow Strake's tastes? The Court would look as if it were beset by crows.

True to form, the Diamond showed every sign of finding twisting circumstance a source of immense entertainment. Contemplating him prompted Soren to abruptly alter her course as she crossed Fleeting Hall, and head for the door of the Royal Mage's apartments, which lay between her apartments and the Garden of the Rose. She glanced toward the garden as she did so, but had no wish to look upon the black petals which blotted Strake's future.

There were a few spectators to watch with interest as she turned the door's handle, but none were close enough to hear the double-click as she released the lock at the same time. Inside was an apartment very similar to her own, and almost as over-stacked with books as hers had been before the advent of the rose. The Court Mage, Fors Cabtly, was still in his bed, cuddling close to the equally plump figure of his wife. But that only suited Soren's purposes the more.

Aspen's room was as fastidiously neat as the man himself. He even slept in the exact centre of his bed. Soren studied the remarkable symmetry of the room, then sat down beside Aspen and touched his arm.

His first response was a long, deep inhalation, then his eyes cracked open. He breathed in again, and smiled, still mazed with sleep. "Sea-foam, sweat and sand. I can smell the beach on you, nixie."

Soren sat back. "Are you always this poetic first thing in the morning?"

"Only when someone lovely comes to seduce me," he replied beatifically, then rubbed his eyes.

"I wanted to ask you some questions."

"I thought you would." A little more awake, Aspen gave her a cat-with-cream smile. "On the desk."

Surprised, Soren moved across to the neat stack of books positioned in the exact centre of the spotless desk. Places were marked with strips of blue ribbon. Histories. "I see you've been busy."

"Currying your favour, my sweet. Though, really, why I should be at all helpful when you've gone and let that fribble Fisk worm his way into the King's good graces, I don't know."

"You didn't happen to be there at the precise moment he decided he needed a secretary," Soren replied, absently. For a time Strake had asked Soren questions before interviewing each of his officials, but had soon tired of her ignorance of Court minutiae and appointed a random footman to be his personal secretary. The man was barely out of his teens, and still looked stunned by his sudden change of circumstance, but he had proven to be a rival for Aspen's crown of gossip.

She opened the topmost book and found a record of Strake's birth. Aluster Veristace Rathen. Nearly two hundred and eighty years ago.

"There's not a great deal on him," Aspen put in, watching her speculatively from the bed. "A very obscure Rathen you've found for us. But, Sunshine!, he's a stunner isn't he? No portrait could do justice to those eyes."

Aspen waxed lyrical about Strake's looks while Soren opened book after book, discovering only mentions of a long-ago prince, child of the Queen's sister. He'd had a brother called Domari, a sister named Kassandia, seemed uninvolved in the politics of the time and was not famed for skill in sword or sorcery. Barely a blip in history.

The last two books covered the time after the disastrous hunt: the annunciation of Kassandia as Crown Princess, the investigations which had followed and led nowhere. It did not sound as if The Deeping had been helpful. Soren was held captive not by speculation and accusation, but rather a list of just who had been part of the hunt. Princess Sethane and the Baron of the Oaks. Prince Aluster, and Prince Aluster's betrothed, Vahse.

"Another cousin," Strake had called him. He had been subdued and factual and kept completely to himself the importance of the man who had stood pressed against his back, and died.

"They're made for each other, of course," Aspen was saying.

"What?" She felt blank and numb, struggling to fit this news into the situation. Strake had lost the man he loved, and then himself. And when he'd won free from whatever enchantment had thrust him out of the past, he'd discovered he'd lost everyone else. It was Vahse, the deepest hurt, he'd kept to himself.

"King Aluster and Lord Aristide," Aspect said, drinking in her distraction. "The entire Court's seen the possibilities of it. Both born for the throne. Both mages. Both absolutely reeking with looks, not to mention the kind of drive it will take to get Darest back on its feet. Formidable men make the best matches, don't you think?"

"For the entertainment value perhaps," Soren replied, quietly appalled. Lord Aristide and Strake? But it did make a kind of horrible, inexorable sense. "It was Lord Aristide I wanted to ask you about, actually," she continued, trying not to picture her Rathen in the arms of the gleaming, silky-sharp Diamond.

"How so?" Courtier to the core, Aspen lit up at the prospect of a chance to demonstrate his knowledge, and no doubt to chalk up a debt.

"I..." Soren shook off panicked, pointless jealousy. Strake was asleep and Lord Aristide still lay in his bed, staring up at the ceiling. "Yesterday, almost everyone the King spoke to – Fors, the Chancellor, the Chamberlain, the Marshall, two of the Barons, even one of the Apexes – went straight from the Hall of the Crown to Lord Aristide."

Aspen laughed. "You have had your spies out! Even the Chamberlain? He doesn't care for the Delectable Diamond at all. But of course they all went to him. Can't you guess why?"

"I can guess a lot of things. I want to know."

"I'm gratified." That she thought he could answer, she supposed. Aspen tucked his knees beneath his chin, for once looking almost serious. "You do realise what our late-come King asked them to do, don't you?"

"Report on the state of the kingdom."

"Well, yes. Some of them are competent enough to answer, I suppose. Poor old Fors is in the worst state – he doesn't know whether he's coming or going. He's a jobbing word-mage: he fixes things, performs entertainments and carries out whatever little tasks the Regent cares to throw his way. He's competent enough for that, but he's never poked his nose into anything like what King Aluster wants. Tell him how many mages live in Tor Darest? The entire country? Rival kingdoms? How many are born with true-mage potential? Brief him with their capabilities, their loyalties? Whether there's been any instances of blood-magic? A summary of the efforts made to get rid of the Tongue? The state of the Shaping projects Lady Arista abandoned? I tell you, Fors reeled out of the throne room. And when he could walk straight, the Diamond was the first and only port of call."

"What about the others?"

"Oh, I dare say the Lord Marshall knows how to run his toy soldiers well enough, but since Peveric made a point of calling on the Diamond, the Marshall would only consider it wise to find some excuse to do the same. I'd bet the Chancellor went to him because he's the only one who actually understands to the letter The Deeping's ban on our trade He may have had to wage a running war with his mother to do it, but the Diamond's the one who's kept this kingdom staggering along these past five years or more."

"I had no idea it was that bad."

Aspen shrugged. "Occasionally something does spark Lady Arista's interest, true. Especially if it runs counter to the Diamond's wishes. But—" He tipped one hand sideways. "Darest defeated her long ago. Fors tells me she was really something when she was young. Brilliant, resolute. Full of ideas and thorough at implementing them. If she'd been Rathen, if this country didn't seem so set against success, well – who knows how she'd be remembered? But what can you do when your every scheme goes sour? We should be glad all she did was withdraw her attention from everything except the latest pretty piece of flesh. And, of course, frustrating her son at every turn."

Lady Arista was standing alone in the centre of her throne room, now stripped to the walls. She had been gracious to Strake, but very formal and determined. There were responsibilities in the Couerveur Barony which were long neglected. She thought it best to demonstrate a clean break to the populace. Naturally the King could call upon her for anything, but after so many years of service, it was time for her to leave Tor Darest.

Straightforward acquiescence was as hard to believe as the Diamond's mild acceptance of Strake as King. "So they go to Lord Aristide simply for answers?"

"Some." Aspen was watching her closely. "If they're fomenting rebellion, they're keeping very quiet about it, naturally enough. But—" He paused. "Our new King isn't being terribly tactful by simply ignoring the Diamond's existence. Love him or loathe him, there's few who won't admit that Aristide has put everything into Darest. That all the Couerveurs have. A lot of these visits will be nothing more than a statement of support. I mean, the Rathens are the rightful rulers and I don't think anyone's seriously contemplating throwing our new Rathen straight back out into the cold. But Aristide is *Aristide*. People owe him favours, debts. A lot are truly loyal, bought and paid for long ago. They aren't pairing him with the new King just because they'd look so good together."

A reward. Soren didn't know what to think.

"Of course," Aspen continued, with an euphoric smile, "playing match-maker is not nearly so fine a thing as getting the alluring Aluster naked and slippery. What do you think, oh Champion? Do I stand a chance?"

"I haven't the slightest idea," Soren said, then looked away as Strake woke up. For a moment, he and Lord Aristide were in the same position, lying blinking at the ceiling. Then, with typical energy, Strake was out of bed. A whirlwind crowned, not leaving a moment spare for empty loss.

Time to go stand at his side through another day full of questions. She would tell him this possible explanation for the meetings with Lord Aristide, but certainly not that they would look good together.

Her Rathen. Just what was she supposed to protect him from?

Twelve

"Champion?"

The tall, brunette's voice was familiar, though Soren couldn't immediately place her face. A sheen of red in the hair, pale skin, a scatter of freckles, but it was the not quite veiled assessment in dark blue eyes which finally jogged Soren's memory. The Chancellor's junior-most aide and assistant book wrangler, Halcean Veth.

Soren waited as the woman joined her. Strake had spent the morning inspecting the city, the afternoon disposing of diplomatic audiences, and was at the moment studying political maps with the Lord Marshall. He'd not given himself a moment's rest all day, and besides trailing him about, Soren found herself with a list of people eager to 'consult' with her. Who wanted to carry tales and gossip about the King, or try to convince her to coax him to support some scheme of theirs, redress some ill.

She wasn't altogether sure who it was she was supposed to be talking to now, let alone what kind of answers she could give them. She murmured some greeting and hoped Halcean wasn't going to be another who thought she'd help her climb into the King's bed.

"Are you finding it easier to find your way through your apartment now?" Halcean asked.

"Was it you who was lumbered with cleaning out the rest of my library?"

"I was that unfortunate," the aide replied. "It was dusty and dull," she added with bland forthrightness, "but it seemed a pity not to finish what I'd started, and it's stood me in good stead in the claws-out battle for the prime appointment of the day." She executed a short, graceful bow. "I present myself, a gesture of goodwill from Chancellor Gestry. Should you want an aide?"

Startled, Soren blinked, then said: "And should I want an aide?"

Halcean's mouth curled up at the corners. "They're this season's prize accessory." But her eyes remained assessing, searching Soren's face. "I won't pretend I don't want you to want one," she continued, still with that deliberate honesty. "It would be a real step up for me. And there's a lot I can do for you – keep track of your appointments, organise your apartments, make sure you hear all the gossip you should."

"I already hear that."

"Thanks to Mageling Choraide? But who'll tell you the gossip about *him*?"

"He does that, too." But it was a fair point. Soren knew every second courtier had their networks of spies and sources. And hateful as she found the idea of participating in games of petty intrigue, she needed to know what was being said if she were to even keep her head above water.

More importantly: "I could do with someone to stand buffer between me and everyone suddenly wanting a meeting. Sort out the merely curious from those who genuinely need to see me."

"And those out to curry favour." Halcean's smile had become conspiratorial, underlaid by relieved pleasure. A plum position, landed more easily than she'd perhaps anticipated.

Amused at the stupid sense of power accepting Halcean had given her, Soren started forward once again. "Feel free to take over any of the empty bedrooms in my apartment," she said. "Having gone to the effort of cleaning them out–"

She broke off, spotting Aspen's tutor, Fors Cabtly, lurking outside her door. He was rumpled, and his usual rose-cheeked self had been replaced by a sweaty pallor. Fors' second interview with Strake had not gone well. Since no-one at Court held the title of Court Shaper or Councillor of Mages, Strake had quizzed Fors on the duties performed by both during his aunt's reign. Fors had attempted to answer every question, which, Soren thought, had rather made it worse. Since Fors had always treated her with an absentminded courtesy, Soren summoned a smile as she reached him.

"Champion. Soren." Fors touched her arm, moth light, then his hand fluttered away as if he feared to give offence. "I would, I wanted to ask... Has the King said anything? Will he–?"

"I don't know, Fors," Soren said, quietly.

"Was he angry?"

Disbelieving would be a more accurate description. "I think he understands that the role of Court Mage is not the same as these...former offices."

Tact did nothing for Fors. "I have lived here half my life, Champion," he said. "Nearly thirty years. I don't know–" He stopped and shook his head. "The ground has shifted, Champion. I don't know – I don't know if I can rise to the occasion."

Sorry for the man, embarrassed by his evident need, Soren fumbled out a few words of sympathy. Fors hardly seemed to hear her. "All for the best, of course," he said. "I would have liked to have helped, but–" His mouth squashed down. "I am not a politician, Champion, and I don't think I would like to be. But I have served long and faithfully. And I am good at what I do. Tell him that, will you? As a favour?"

She promised, and Fors turned to walk slowly back to his rooms. He looked old and crumpled. And frightened.

"Not a politician," Halcean repeated softly.

Soren started, having quite forgotten the aide's presence. She gave her a searching glance, prompting the woman to shrug. "Court Mage wasn't the most prestigious position. Councillor of Mages now – even if he thought himself equal to it, do you think Magister Cabtly would be allowed the role?"

"Allowed?"

"As Councillor of Mages Lord Aristide would remain central to the Court. As it is, he has no formal role – the King hasn't even sent to speak to him – and whatever else, the Diamond isn't going to accept the role of just another Baron's heir."

It suddenly felt less than circumspect, to be having this conversation out in the open. "Is there anyone more suitable?" Soren asked neutrally, pulling the door to her apartment safely closed behind them.

"Probably not." Halcean bit her lip. "I'm talking out of turn. My apologies, Champion."

"It was a valid point."

Palace sight had revealed Halcean's muffled consternation, followed by swift calculation. A sudden sense of loss touched Soren. Halcean wasn't disguising the gain she hoped to make – one of many cultivating the Rather Champion, now that the title meant something. It was another level of isolation.

"Call me Soren," she said, abruptly, and turned to smile at her new acquisition. For the moment motives didn't matter: she would be happy to have anyone to stand between her and the importuning hordes. If Halcean could keep the worst of them away, she would happily help her advance.

But Halcean was sleeping safely in her new bed the next morning when Soren returned from another stolen dawn with Vixen and spotted Aristide Couerveur standing by the entrance to the Garden of the Rose. It was too much to hope he was not waiting for her.

Palace-sight allowed her to watch him unknowing: curiously expressionless, his star sapphire eyes hooded. Then, as she reached a point where she could not escape seeing him, that faint, infamous smile curved his mouth. It was quite impossible to imagine him scrabbling to retain power when he did not act like he'd lost any.

"Can I help you, Lord Aristide?"

Lord Aristide simply held a hand out toward the Garden. More than a word, then. Why was it she was always sweaty and dishevelled when she encountered this over-pristine man?

Unwilling but resigned, Soren walked through the nearest arch and looked about at the dark-leaved canes and single flower. She supposed that in this place, where she could shred a man just by wanting it, she should be at her most confident. But all she could think of were the fading scratches on her wrists.

Lord Aristide walked beneath jagged leaves with perfect equanimity. "I will not keep you long, Champion."

"What is it you wish to say to me?" she asked, in as politely neutral a tone as she could manage. But it was hard to banish the thought of Strake in a quicksilver embrace. She wished Aspen had never suggested it to her.

Above Lord Aristide's head, several of the canes shifted, a sinuous curling patently not caused by any breeze. The Regent's son looked up, exposing his white throat, but Soren clamped down on unruly thought before there could be a repeat of the briar noose episode. She refused to make an enemy of the man until he made an enemy of himself.

The subtle line of Lord Aristide's lips had altered, but she thought the resulting expression was more appreciative than anything. "I wished to pass on an observation, Champion," he said. Shifting position, he held one hand toward Strake's rose, as if measuring its size. "Black."

"Yes?" Soren managed to sound uncomprehending, but Lord Aristide's lips only curved to full glittering enjoyment.

"I am not the only one who might seek meaning in the colour," he continued, with the gentle tone used to explain a harsh world to a disappointed child. "Inevitably, tomorrow, the day, week, month after, a whisper will become rumour and then fact proclaimed in every alehouse and sitting room. A black rose. Inevitable death."

"Everyone dies," Soren said, though she was shaken. These past two days, watching Strake firmly take up Darest's reins while the palace whirled through her head, it had almost been possible to forget the expression on his face when he'd seen the rose. He had kept so unremittingly to the task at hand, maintained such unwavering energy, that Soren had found it difficult to credit the idea of his doom. He was not injured, showed no sign of failing. Whatever they had encountered in the Tongue had certainly not followed them through the Walk to Tor Darest, and any local hazards had to overcome walls and guards and Soren.

But the rose was still black. No wonder Lord Aristide had seemed so completely unperturbed by Strake's return.

He was watching with an air of patience. Then, to her surprise, he said: "Whatever else, I do not relish the uncertainty which the black rose will bring. You need to plan for the reaction."

"Won't it advantage you?" she asked, stupidly. He rewarded such heavy-handedness with a weary expression.

"It wouldn't benefit Darest. I shall leave it to you to judge whether that is of concern to me." He glanced at the rose. "Since the threat to the King has evidently existed since his sojourn in The Deeping, I would suggest that he seek answers from the Fair."

She couldn't quite credit the idea of Lord Aristide giving her advice to pass on to Strake and some measure of that response must have shown on her face because his expression changed subtly, and when he spoke again his voice was silk cut with razors.

"I also felt I should congratulate you, Champion." Taking two steps, he moved to stand just behind her. A low tendril hung before his face and he gazed at the small cluster of red-green leaves at its tip. "Such commendable promptness," he added, as Soren stared at the heart of the cluster, at the burgundy sepals of a mote-sized bud.

Lord Aristide must certainly have enjoyed her reaction, which was to flinch, then send the bud shooting up above the stone arches, tucking it completely out of sight. "My felicitations," he said. Glittering, glass-cut courtesy.

Soren stared at him. She had resigned herself to a nervous wait for her next woman's blood, and this was probably the last way she would have wanted to learn that she really was pregnant. Rather than make any kind of response, she leaped to an abrupt tangent. "How was it you were there, that morning?" she asked. "How did you know to come before the bells rang?"

Star sapphire eyes glinted with renewed amusement. "I am a mage, Champion. I knew that the Garden was the first place you'd go, if you succeeded in returning with the heir. Ordinarily, I would not risk establishing a casting so near the Rose. But I wanted to be there."

"Why?" It had not been to attack. He had made no move to do so.

Lord Aristide looked down the length of Fleeting Hall to guards wearing black and gold before the door of the throne room. His face was blank and closed and Soren thought that 'Diamond' was not the right name to give to so opaque a man.

"Because I promised myself a long time ago that I'd see my mother's reign to an end," he said, with cold honesty. "And now I have. I thank you for that, Champion."

With a dry, eloquent bow, he turned and walked away.

Seeking solace in the luxury of a bath, Soren clutched at her knees and tried not to exist. It did not seem possible to take in the reality of her pregnancy. There was no joy, not even any room to think. She felt crowded, cut by Lord Aristide's barbs and overwhelmingly crushed beneath the constant tide of the palace.

It wore on her even more than she had anticipated: all the bed and bathroom visits, the strange things people did when they thought themselves unobserved, the constant motion demanding her attention. People's lives, made petty by distance and silence, sheer numbers and unrelenting observation.

Lying in water up to her chin, she watched Strake wake up and make his way to the privy. Twenty-seven other people and a handful of animals were doing the same thing. At least half the palace still slept. The Chamberlain's husband was in a borrowed room, working up a frantic sweat with a gangling young woman who resembled the Baroness of Runath. An elderly woman had fallen down the stairs of the west residences and a small cluster of scourers, all wide eyes and flapping mouths, stood about her. Dolls, waving their arms.

Every single Champion had watched the Court as she did. No matter how they felt, however wretched or sick or tired or dismayed to be pregnant – they had no way to hide from the intimacies of hundreds. It was a wonder Rathen Champions did not have a reputation for going mad.

Yet the idea of returning to Carn Keep, of not living in this place, of ignoring whatever responsibility she might have to King and Kingdom and escaping a life for which she wasn't suited, seemed to be beyond her. She constantly thought about it, had ever since she'd first come to Tor Darest, but could not go beyond the thought. Her head just did not want to work that way.

The Rose again. It had to be. Taking away choice, just as it had taken away the control of her body, back in the Tongue. It had even stripped her of privacy along with freedom, had displayed her pregnancy for anyone to see. For Aristide Couerveur to throw in her face.

Puppet Champion. How could all the stories have been so wrong? Life-long servitude, where she couldn't even call her dreams her own.

What if Strake couldn't destroy the Rose? She had to accept that it might not be possible, that she would spend the rest of her life in the palace crucible, battered by the constant sight of everything. With people like the Diamond cutting her to pieces. Not to mention her King.

Enough.

Soren squashed all her helpless hurt into a ball and pushed it away. Then she breathed deep and slow until the useless self-pity receded. This life had become hers, and she could at least choose to be more than a cipher while she wore the uniform of the Champion.

She could start with palace-sight. Horrible as it could be, it was a tool she most certainly could use. Time to get out of the bath and try and do her job.

Strake was talking to Fisk now, issuing a long series of orders. One of them would be for his breakfast, so Soren dressed in anticipation of an invitation. He was looking withdrawn this morning, gazing out the windows of his receiving room at the neglected garden which lay at the heart of the King's residence. Elsewhere, the Captain of the Guard and Lord Aristide matched swords, a regular practice bout. Jansette Denmore arrived in the palace, walking purposefully toward the western halls. The old lady who had fallen down the stairs was finally carried off to the ministrations of a physician. A cook was screaming at a scourer who stood among shattered dishes.

Lady Arista had left for Ritmar yesterday, as quietly as the movement of a Baroness' entire household could manage. Jansette Denmore had remained behind, but Soren had not seen any sign of argument between the former Regent and her lover and was duly suspicious. Jansette was a person who seemed to go everywhere and talk to everyone. A veritable mine of connections, who, frustratingly, had found rooms in the New Palace, where Soren could not keep a close eye on her.

All the Barons were naturally next-most interesting. They'd been primarily concerned over how the new King would deal with the ever-difficult question of taxes and the army portion, and had invariably brought it up in the audience he had granted each. In return Strake had been uncommunicative, curt and demanding. The King was fully aware of his station.

Not that anyone had objected. So early on, and with the Couerveurs at least publicly compliant, they were all waiting to see what would happen. Waiting to see if this sudden gift of a Rathen could turn the kingdom's fortunes, waiting for Strake to give them a reason to think themselves better off without him. Making contingency plans.

Lip-reading was definitely a skill she would have to acquire.

Combing her hair, Soren divided her attention between Jansette Denmore and the table attendant who was laying two places in Strake's receiving room. Both of them were beauties, and had dressed to display a sweetly enticing curve of breast. Jansette was far more exquisite, her skin so fine Soren could not help wondering what it was like to touch, but it seemed this morning the Denmore talents were to be wasted on coquetting the Chamberlain, while the table attendant worked at captivating the King.

Fretfully, Soren watched this first attempt to win Strake's favour. She knew she was going to witness many, many more, but this morning her situation seemed particularly invidious. She wished she could stop thinking of him as her Rathen. She wished not to be carrying his child.

It took Strake some time to notice the attendant's display, but he finally glanced at her and looked amused, then lazily appreciative. The woman immediately bent to adjust the fall of the tablecloth so that her breasts bulged into handfuls just waiting to be cupped.

The King of Darest's response was to stand and walk out into the parched garden, where he stood staring at the brittle yellow weeds. His back was rigid, jaw set, brows drawn together. All the muscles of his face and throat stood stark and clear. Anguish. It was the first time Soren had really seen him act like a man who had lost everything. Scarcely three weeks ago in his memory.

The attendant, horrified, said something and hurried away, obviously convinced she'd angered him. Soren rather thought that she'd momentarily roused him, and now his anger was directed inward. After the loss of his betrothed, and then what the Rose had done to them–

Watching his grief hurt. Soren sighed and wished she knew whether she even liked her mercurial King, and whether she could mend the fences between them. He had resented her from the first, and what little accord they might have built had been shattered by the Rose. The last thing he would want was her sympathy.

A short time later Halcean opened the door to Fisk, then came to relay an invitation to join the King at breakfast. By the time Soren reached his receiving room, any hint of loss was banished, and Strake was back to gazing moodily out at the ravaged garden.

"Why has it been left in this condition?" he asked as she came in. "It looks disgraceful."

"It looked worse yesterday," Soren replied, making an effort to be equable and detached and not nearly so battered and unhappy. "They carted out a forest of dead vine."

That simmering, baulked expression darkened his face when he looked at her, but she was prepared and far less ready to quail. What had happened to them in the forest may have made it nearly impossible for them to deal easily with each other, but she wasn't going to spend the rest of her life creeping and cowering.

"I expect they'll finish clearing out today," she continued, carefully ignoring his irritation. "If that isn't soon enough for you, I suppose I could pitch in. What was it like before? It smells like a stillroom."

"An ornamental herb garden. There was a reflective pool with a mosaic. Brilliant blue and green stone."

Soren tilted her head, feeling the boundaries of the garden. "The pool's full of dirt. But it seems intact."

Strake was duly surprised and, to Soren's satisfaction, no longer a thundercloud at the breakfast table. Not reacting to his irritation seemed the best way of handling it. A pity she would soon have to ruin the mood.

"That's not sight," he was saying. "How do you know?"

"It's part of the palace." She shrugged and sat down at the table, surveying steaming pancakes and fruit compote. "It's like knowing I still have toenails."

He snorted. "Very poetic. Tell me, then, what rooms are beneath the palace? The structure of the Rathen enchantments is supposedly down there, and I'll need to reach it if I'm to take it apart. But if there's a way to access it, it was kept very dark. I don't particularly want to take up the throne room floor getting rid of the Rose."

This proved more complicated than the garden, for, apart from the wine-cellars and a couple of simple storage chambers used by the kitchens, there didn't seemed to be anything beneath the palace. Aware of Strake's critical gaze, Soren surveyed the sprawling building room by room.

"I can't see below," she said, eventually. "But there's a sealed chamber behind the treasury, with a stair which goes down. Beneath the big bell."

"Behind the throne?" He stopped spreading preserves, teeth bared in a satirical grin. "Old Domina had a sense of humour. Can we get to it without a battering ram?"

"There's a door of sorts in the treasury," Soren said, doubtfully feeling her way around the walls. "Very concealed."

Strake finished off a pancake in three neat bites and selected a peach from the tray. "We'll take a look after breakfast." He checked off a few points on their schedule that day, then ate in silence, shifting his chair so he could continue to gaze out at the garden. Soren watched him without looking at him, just as she divided a fraction of her attention between different members of the Court. Jansette was now engaged in a teasing conversation with a young man who went bright red at every second thing she said. Lord Aristide had returned to his rooms and begun the ritual of either meditation or incantation he had undertaken every morning of Soren's observation. Fors Cabtly and Aspen were having a solemn discussion. Lady Rothwell, whom Soren had not had a chance to speak to since her return, was crossing Fleeting Hall with her daughter. She knocked on Soren's door and spoke briefly to Halcean, but Soren didn't move, deciding to find the time to meet later.

"Fors Cabtly asked me to make representations to you on his behalf," she said, since Strake was spending more time staring at the garden than eating. "And it is true that he has performed the duties given him by the Regent perfectly well."

"You'd best not encourage people to treat you as a conduit to my ear," Strake said, voice flat, but added: "Though there's little you could do to stop them."

Soren just shrugged, and watched him frown at an unoffending salt cellar.

"Cabtly occupies the rooms of the Councillor of Mages," he continued, his tone suggesting that this was somehow Soren's fault. "I've no objection to his maintenance role – Sun knows the palace needs jobbing mages, and it seems like Darest's stock of them has been whittled away to nothing – but he is not even a shadow of a Councillor of Mages. That posturing sprat apprenticed to him has more base ability, coupled with an impressive lack of drive. I'm looking about for a better choice."

Soren made no comment to this. He surveyed her lack of expression then grimaced. "Other than the obvious. The one the every second person has tried to shove down my throat."

Precisely why he hadn't done it, Soren realised. Why no audience had been arranged with the man who had been ruling Darest in all but name. Her Rathen did hate to be pushed. "I suspect it would be more...comfortable to work with Lord Aristide than against him."

"I've seen enough of that one to know how 'comfortable' I'd be if I strayed from whatever plans he's fomenting." He looked, of a sudden, sourly amused. "Especially if Fisk is correct in telling me he hopes to marry his way to control of the throne."

"That could be said of most of the Court," Soren observed neutrally. She hadn't realised Strake's new secretary was passing on this variety of gossip.

"The man has every reason to wish me dead. Should I clutch a viper close to my chest?"

Soren wasn't altogether sure if Strake wasn't arguing just to be contrary, or if he'd been completely set against the Regent's son. "I met Lord Aristide earlier this morning," she said, deciding that there would never be a safely predictable opportunity to tell Strake he was going to be a father. Now that the Rose had made delaying the news nearly impossible.

"Earlier? A dawn rendezvous? Did he ask you to make representations as well?"

"No. He knew the meaning of the black rose and said the knowledge would inevitably spread through Darest."

"Causing uncertainty and all manner of calumny no doubt. Did he offer to show me a way to avoid it?"

"Just made the observation."

"No solution?"

"He suggested calling on the Fair."

"You said he courted them, didn't you? Very eager to have the Fair back, and passing messages through you won't get him anywhere."

"I'm not sure why he chose to. But I suppose he could just have been leading up to – he did point out something on the Rose I didn't know was there. A bud."

For a moment Strake looked blank, then he lifted his eyebrows. "Didn't know? What happened to it being like knowing you still have toenails?"

"I need to direct my attention to pick up details like that," Soren said, feeling lost. His lack of reaction was more disconcerting than any towering rage. "Turn to the page of the book, open that particular window in my mind – whatever analogy you care to use. I haven't been looking at the Rose." She fidgeted with her knife, then began segmenting a peach as if lives depended on the result.

It was not until her eyes were turned away that Strake revealed the blow. Soren struggled not to react to the piercing hurt suddenly evident on his face, the loss and pain rapidly overtaken by anger. One of his hands closed on the table's edge; strong, finely-made fingers gripping cloth and wood as he stared at Soren, so assiduously bent over the task of dissecting breakfast. On the verge of throwing the table at her.

Then he sighed and passed his hand across his eyes, slumping back. Controlling his anger, as he had promised. Soren waited a moment more before looking up, feeling sick. It was so hard to know how to deal with this man who was her King. Making him not hate her seemed quite as important as ensuring he didn't die.

"I don't think it likely anyone but Lord Aristide would have seen it," she said, because she guessed that Strake would only withdraw if she pushed. "Few go into the Garden. And I've hidden it now."

"They'll see you soon enough," Strake replied, dourly. But the anger was a dull simmer, no longer directed at her. "I suppose I should look on this positively. An heir would be just the thing to soothe the nervous once news of my imminent death gets out. It is something I would have had to see to in due course."

But at his own speed and choosing. He didn't have to say it.

"Your death hasn't been very imminent," Soren said.

"No."

"Perhaps the flower is black because of the period when you weren't alive, even if you weren't really dead. It mightn't be a future event at all."

"Very optimistic." Looking particularly saturnine, Strake pushed back his chair. "We're wasting time."

Without another word, Strake left the royal apartments, Soren trailing in his wake. His personal guard and the carrot-topped Fisk attached themselves, but Fisk was quickly dismissed and the guards left to stand outside the Treasury. Firmly locking the doors, Strake turned to Soren with grim expectation, and she suddenly realised that if he succeeded in destroying the Rose she would lose more than the Champion's burden of sight.

Strake would not be her Rathen.

Thirteen

"So where is this door?"

Soren, sliding a bar across the inside of the Treasury doors, gestured toward the far wall. The Treasury was freshly cleaned, the shelves and benches gleaming and laden with ornate chests and odd-shaped lumps veiled by dust-cloths. It all looked highly intriguing, and Strake's order not to open anything must have been particularly frustrating for the Chamberlain during the turning-out.

Ignoring the mysteries of the chests, Strake crossed to the centre of the wall opposite the door, where it was unobstructed by benches. The stony surface was blank and smooth, with no sign of join or crack. He looked back at her, ever impatient.

Soren touched the wall, aware of an absence, then nodded when Strake pressed his hand to the smooth stone. "It's waiting for you."

Strake grunted and drew his hand back as Soren felt the lock change. A thin line of light climbed from floor to ceiling, expanded and was gone, taking the wall with it. It left a doorway into a yellow-gold room where dust-motes tumbled in sunbeams above a grimy stair.

"Not sealed," Strake said, surprised. He gazed up into the throat of a massive bell, suspended high above their heads. It was just possible to glimpse blue sky beyond its circumference, though the dazzle of light made Soren's eyes smart.

"The sun's only just over the horizon," she protested. The light couldn't be natural.

"Redirected." Strake had already started down the stair. "Could be a power source, maybe even for protection."

That sounded like a reason to not charge blindly forward, but it was a little late for caution. If there was any trap, it was not something Soren could feel and at any rate hadn't blasted her Rathen for trespassing.

As Strake summoned a magelight, Soren followed less precipitately. The clear, steady glow picked out every detail of stairs long neglected, filthy with dust and grime. She'd had at the back of her mind an image of a long corridor stretching all the way to the Garden of the Rose, where literal roots were twisted into some form of spell, but as she descended she saw only a short passage ending in a room with no sign of plant life.

Halfway down the stair, the palace went away.

The simple relief of nothing made Soren pause. Wonderful, how taking one step forward could make her feel human. But then she hurried to catch up. Strake would more likely be protecting her from any attack, but she would observe the forms of being his Champion. She supposed she should start wearing the sword again, though she had grown more wary of the compulsive need to keep it close.

"Stone-deep 'chanting,'" Strake commented, more to himself than Soren. He was standing in the centre of the chamber, looking around at walls of glossy black stone covered from ceiling to floor in precisely drawn runes.

"What does that mean?" Soren asked, glancing up to confirm that the runes were on all four walls, even above the entrance. The ceiling and floor were bare. There was nothing else in the room.

She touched the stone, and found it cold and slick, almost like glass. The runes, white streaked subtly with pink, were not on the surface, for all they looked painted on. Rather, like the coloured streaks in marble, they were part of the stone itself.

Strake had not answered her question. She wasn't certain he'd even heard it. Brows drawn into a straight line, he moved to the wall left of the entrance and commenced reading.

Runes were one way to bind magic to will. You didn't need to have an inner source of power to use them, just as you didn't really need fingers to paint. Born mages had an affinity which could not be reproduced, not to mention magic on tap, but of all the different breeds of enchantment, runes were the most accessible. All you had to do was learn to read them.

Wryly, Soren left Strake to it. With a kerchief and sufficient application, she was able to clean herself a seat on the stair, just below the point where she was 'out' of the palace. Then she sat in the sun among lazy spirals of dust, taking advantage of the unexpected gift of quiet to think about babies.

The last time Soren had been planning a child she'd been eighteen and convinced she and Tcharen Esten would be together for the rest of their lives. They were going to live happily ever after: the typical girl's dream of an ideal marriage, with only a third to choose to get them with child. Then Tcharen had discovered Vetris Rilmonney and wanted him to be not a third, but an equal partner in a tribond.

If she was entirely honest, Soren would have to admit that Vetris was not evil incarnate. Or ugly, or corrupt, or something other than a sharp-witted merchant Soren's love happened to want as well. But Soren hadn't been attracted to him, certainly hadn't wanted to share Tcharen with him, and it had all been downhill from there.

Four years was a long time. Soren had trysted with a handful of men and women since, but not contemplated marriage or babies. Twice shy, she supposed, or just hadn't stumbled across someone she wanted to set up housekeeping with, let alone a nursery.

Like Strake, it was not a decision she appreciated having made for her.

So early on, she simply didn't feel pregnant. But that bud meant a Rathen heir, and she was fairly certain Strake would have mentioned getting anyone else with child. Wouldn't he?

The image of her King seeding the countryside with Rathens pulled at Soren's spirits. She knew she should not feel so intensely possessive about a man she had known for less than a week, one who had made her no promises and was free to bed anyone he pleased. A tiresomely rude man with a too-quick temper and very evident antipathy. She needed to rid herself of this conviction that he was hers.

Besides, if he wanted to ensure the family never died out, multiple consorts might be a bad tactic. A whole slew of rivals for the throne would create more problems than it solved.

Dismissing suspicion, Soren thought over the formalities she would have to put off until she was prepared for the whole world to know. An offering for the child's health in the Temple of the Moon would be tantamount to a public announcement, and it was unlikely she could write to her mother with news of a grandchild without the contents of the letter being inspected. Lord Aristide already knew, it was true, but there were too many others whose congratulations might be accompanied by more than a knife-edged smile. At least the usual embarrassment about having a child without a partner's bonded support wouldn't count for much – polite social rules didn't count for kings, and the rich never had as much pressure to provide the security of marriage. The Rose handily took care of any possible squabble about paternity.

The most she could do was think of names, and even that presented complications. She'd long intended to call her first child Shaol. The name had been in her family for generations and would do for a girl or boy, but she wasn't sure she liked it with 'King' or 'Queen' attached. And Aluster Veristace was sure to have an opinion. About too many things.

If he succeeded in destroying the Rose, Strake might choose to take the child and send Soren some place where she could not serve as a reminder of his ordeal. An easier route than struggling with fury every time he saw her.

Soren found that her hands had closed into fists, and forced them to relax. He had not proved a pointlessly cruel man, at least so far. But a flicker of unease still ran through her, something she recognised as being outside herself. The Rose. She hadn't felt it this way since they'd left the Tongue.

Worriedly, she looked down the stair and discovered the room dark, magelight gone. But before she could leap to her feet, her eyes adjusted to the gloom enough for her to make out Strake, watching her from the shadows.

"Can you unmake it?" she asked, when he didn't move.

With the Rose a subdued coil at the back of her head his dim, shaded figure became a threatening unknown. Why did he just stand there? But then he stepped forward into the sunlight, and though the Rose's unease didn't go away, Soren was reassured by the way he spared a moment to gaze up the shaft of the bell-tower at the dance of light and dust. Her imagination had served her images of a mind-blasted zombie, of her Rathen suddenly run mad or again possessed by the Rose. Whatever he had learned, he was still Strake.

"It's possible."

Without pause for explanation he walked up the stair, swiping at the grit on his boots before re-entering the Treasury. Soren followed, thinking she'd never seen her Rathen so subdued.

The palace came back, and she slowed, distracted by a stand-up fight between two guardswomen in the garrison. Lord Aristide alone in the East Garden, the Seneschal staring at herself in a mirror, Aspen lost as usual in a whirl of gossip. Strake watching her with a shuttered frown as she walked into the Treasury. He ran his hand along the side of the entrance and the wall obligingly returned.

"Possible at what price?" Soren asked, and he looked at her sharply. Not out of anger or fear, but something less easily read.

"It's an atrociously complicated spell," he said. "Different from what I expected. The Rose itself is a construct rather than an entity. A set of instructions." He began lifting dust-cloths from odd, obviously arcane objects and testing the locks on the chests, opening what he could. Prowling about, as if he didn't want to explain.

"Are you saying it's not sentient?" Remembering the struggle of wills at the back of her mind, Soren doubted this very much.

Picking a string of tarnished bells out of one of the caskets, Strake poked at the wadding which prevented them from chiming before setting them on the bench beside a dome of silver and crystal.

"It's not any one thing," he said. "The plant provides a living shell, but it has no 'being'. I understand now why it created Champions even when there were no Rathens. In a way it can't not create Champions – half its functions seem to rely on interaction with one. Certainly the divinations covering the palace require a mind the Rose doesn't own. So it needs Champions just as much as it needs Rathens. And Rathens... Did you see the colour of the runes?" He waited until she nodded. "Domina Rathen's blood, mixed with I don't know what. She must have bled herself half-dry to finish that room. It not only provides a means of identifying her descendants, it's where the Rose gets its power. It draws it from Rathens."

"Not just the King?"

"Just the King at the moment." Bitterness flashed in his eyes and he continued turning out the chest of bells without really looking at them. "It can store power, so it was still able to create Champions these past two centuries, but even with my return – perhaps thanks to my return, given that Walk – it would be the weakest it has been since it was first created."

"Making it easier to destroy?"

"Very much so." He glanced at her again. "I'd have to look into it further, but pulling it down might be as simple as destroying that room – and dealing with the power left unbound by the structure of the runes."

The Rose was no longer jittering at the back of her mind, but Soren was less than reassured. Strake was not behaving like a man who had discovered his enemy was weak. She wanted him to declare that the Rose would be gone within the day, wanted to have her head her own and her Rathen provided the vengeance he needed to stop hating her. And she saw no sign in his face that she would be given these things.

"Do you think it will try and stop you?" she asked, and her voice came out small.

"It might not recognise the threat." He made an impatient gesture at her incomprehension. "It's not a person. It's a list of orders. Defend Rathens, the palace, the borders themselves in a way. Divine the proper heir, a suitable Champion. It would stop anyone but King and Champion from entering that room, but preventing the Rathen Ruler from dispelling it isn't its function."

"But I could feel it. Fighting against itself."

"Two rules conflicting. And the stronger – protect the bloodline – won out against the weaker."

"Protect the King."

That goaded look was back. It gave Soren barely a moment's warning before he suddenly swept bells, casket, packing, and the rest of the contents of the bench to the floor. Crystal shattered, muffled bells clunked, and a black sphere rolled slowly away. Outside, Strake's guard glanced toward the door, plainly uncertain what if anything they'd heard.

Soren had taken a step back, her stomach a roil of anger without focus. Sun send her a better-tempered Rathen, or at least some way of dealing with this one without being constantly pitched into storms. Or some way to touch him he would accept.

He was standing frozen now, face blank, watching the sphere as it disappeared under a bench. Outside, the younger of the pair of guards pressed her ear to the door. Soren watched Strake's hands, already closed into fists, contract even tighter.

Then he bowed his head. With an exasperated grimace, he righted the fallen casket and knelt on the near side of the crystal shards, picking up the largest fragment.

When Soren bent to help, he spared her a fraction of a glance, and said: "Leave it." The tone was curt and he looked down before continuing. "An exercise of my mother's. I clean up whatever mess my temper causes."

But you're King now, Soren thought, staring at the blue-black crown of his head. His expression was intent as he worked, attention given entirely to bells and slivers of crystal. If possible, she felt more shut out from his thoughts than ever before. What was going on?

Holding her tongue, she stood discreetly back as he filled the casket, then swept up the smaller shards with one of the dust cloths. Outside, the two guardswomen had stopped trying to listen at the door, and were now talking earnestly. It did not seem they would risk bursting in.

"Where is Aristide Couerveur?" Strake asked then, fetching the black sphere from beneath another bench.

"In the East Garden." Soren spared a moment to watch Jansette curtseying before a seated Lord Aristide. Pale and golden, their hair shone in the late morning sun. Lord Aristide was looking particularly amused.

Depositing the sphere in the top of the casket, Strake unbarred and opened the door, walking between two guards who had leapt frantically into position a moment earlier. He strode off purposefully, with the air of a man going to perform an unpleasant task. There was little Soren could do but close the Treasury door and follow, pretending not to notice the looks exchanged by the guards falling in behind her. He was heading directly toward the East Garden.

Was he actually going to discuss the Rose with Lord Aristide? Talk about what it had done to them? Soren sorted her options, for her one resolve since she'd learned she was pregnant had been that her child would never know how it was conceived. She would rather be thought ambitious, or a tool in some pragmatic plan on Strake's part to ensure the Rathen succession. To have anyone else know the details of that last night in the Tongue was doubly distressing, for it would only increase the chance of the truth making its way to her child.

He had said that he could unmake the Rose, that it was possible, but quite obviously there had been some snag in the detail. Some unanticipated complication more difficult to accept than the loss of the Rose's protections. What had he discovered?

Fourteen

The quadrangle known as the East Garden was a lonely place. With the palace's water drawn by enchantments, the well in the centre was a neglected decoration, and the until-recently sealed doors to the southern buildings had long meant there was no through-traffic. The carpet of grass was bisected by a path and circle of stone around the well, lined with white standard roses. Sparsely-stocked beds ran along all four walls, subdued in Autumn but still sprinkled with spots of red and yellow. One wall was cut by tall spears of cypress, drawing the eye toward roof and sky, and there were rows of windows in every direction, behind which a small audience was already pausing to watch the King come to visit. But still there was a sense of isolation. Emptiness.

Shortly before midday, the sun was directly overhead, but the day was not warm and occasional clouds even dared to dim the garden's sole occupants. Lord Aristide was seated on the furthest of a cluster of garden benches nestled in the south-east corner, and Jansette stood before him, wearing a prettily earnest expression as she spoke. When Strake strode in, Lord Aristide turned his head a fraction, but Jansette did not seem to notice until the Regent's son rose and swept into a bow. Turning, she made an appealing picture of confusion, suddenly confronted by the King.

As ever, Jansette inspired in Soren a mix of desire and dismay. Such beauty wasted on such an idiot. It was different to see her in person rather than palace-sight, to experience the full effect of her perfume and that peach-milk skin. Soren was not the least bit surprised when Strake stopped to survey her as he would a sunset or swallows.

Today she contrived to look astonishingly young in white and pale yellow, with high neck and long sleeves. She curtsied less gracefully than usual, peeking up at Strake's closed expression, and then past him to Soren as if appealing for help.   Exquisite, delectable.

It was Lord Aristide who stepped forward, while Soren tried to dislodge the memory of Jansette and the Regent's last night together, along with a few past fancies of her own.   She refused the inevitable image of Jansette and Strake.

"Your Majesty," Lord Aristide said, "may I present Lady Jansette Denmore?   One of the lights of the Court."   He looked truly appreciative, as if introducing Jansette to his King was something he only wished he'd thought of sooner.   They were themselves a pair, Soren realised – both displaced from power by Strake's return, both seeking new roles.   Perhaps even the same one?

Strake, however, was not in the mood for flirtation, no matter how beautiful the woman.   "Denmore?" he repeated.   "A relation of Baron Lucas?"   He was already looking impatient.

"Only distantly, Your Majesty," Jansette replied, and proffered up a charming, tentative smile.   "I should, I mean I wish to, would like to say welcome home.   Your Majesty."   She sank immediately into another curtsey, this time with weightless ease, then hurriedly extracted herself from the encounter, whisking past the guards now stationed at the garden's entrance.

Soren watched Jansette's face as she paused to glance back, then moved so she could watch the encounter through one of the many windows.   Pleased with herself.   But Lord Aristide had already switched to a more formal stance, and Strake was gesturing for him to sit back down, so Soren could not spare the attention to try and analyse a past favourite's false fit of nerves.

"What can I do for you, Your Majesty?" Lord Aristide asked, as Strake planted himself in the middle of the bench opposite.   Soren, who had no mind to be eternally standing in a corner during Strake's conversations, chose a third bench and smoothed her surcoat over her knees.   This all felt too calm, after her expectation of epic confrontation.   The morning had been set aside for vanquishing the Rose, not sitting in a garden opening manoeuvres with Aristide Couerveur.   It conjured an entirely different sense of peril.   Why wouldn't Strake tell her what he'd discovered?   Why was he suddenly here, apparently planning to take the most difficult hurdle of his short reign?

For an overlong moment both men indulged in intent, critical survey, to which Lord Aristide added splendid insouciance. His ease suggested a gathering of friends indulging in some particular pleasure. Since Strake's return he'd had time to consider his situation, speak to his allies, judge whether it would be possible to take the throne. Strake had not so much as offered him a conversation, which many had read as Lord Aristide not being in the new King's favour. Now, turn-about – the King had come to the Diamond Couerveur. Darest's future would ride on this encounter.

"I suppose," Strake said finally, "the question is not should I appoint you Councillor of Mages, but whether you would accept the position."

Fascinating to watch the subtleties of reaction. Lord Aristide's ever-glittering smile turned almost wry, star sapphire eyes searched blue-black, and he sat slightly back. It was re-evaluation.

"Would I be insulted, you mean?" Quite without any hint of silk.

Strake nodded, once.

"So you are willing to suggest I might have reason to consider Darest mine. But anyone would tell you that. The true question is whether I am willing to kill you for it."

Bald indeed. Lord Aristide direct was rather worse than honey-coated calculation. But Strake simply said: "Can you answer it?"

"Not yet."

Not yet? Could he actually contemplate admitting a desire to kill Strake – to Strake's face? It was a move that spoke of extreme confidence, and of a sudden Soren was reminded that she did not know how to use the palace defences. They were not in the Garden of the Rose, instead were in the part of the palace where Lord Aristide had his apartments. She had no idea of the loyalties of the guards who had escorted them here, but among those who watched from the windows were the Diamond's personal servants. Not to mention Fisk and Halcean, both looking anxious, and Aspen, hurrying to catch this much-anticipated meeting. Word had spread like lightning through the palace, and they would soon be standing shoulder-to-shoulder at the windows. There came one of the Barons, the Captain of the Guard, an ambassador. Strake had made this spectacularly public.

Lord Aristide did not betray his awareness of the audience by so much as an eye-flicker. "As to insults: do I understand that you would expect me to interest myself in infractions against the laws governing mages? And have duties similar to the Tzel Aviar?"

"That is the primary role of the Councillor of Mages. I am not fool enough to limit you to it." Strake's tone was desert dry. "Why waste a resource? The Councillor is also an adviser. Advise."

"While you make the decisions?" The smile, the courtier's manner, revived into sudden, dagger-sharp vividness, and Soren held her breath. Challenge and challenge.

"Bar one. Tell me when you've made it."

Strake did not get up and stalk away. He was not after all throwing down a gauntlet to an enemy. An impatient man, he wanted to get down to business, which meant having Aristide Couerveur decide whether or not he was going to kill him. Now.

It was the antithesis of courtier's games, the dance of debt and consequence and double-spent loyalties which had been Tor Darest for years. Lord Aristide shook his head, eyeing his King's set face as if he could not quite believe him to be real. Then, seeing Strake was truly waiting, he fell to introspection with effortless self-composure.

Impossible to negotiate what he truly wanted. Strake could not, would not give Lord Aristide Darest's rule and he'd made it absolutely clear how firmly he planned to grasp the reins. At best the Diamond could hope to be allowed a position of influence, perhaps eventually trusted, possibly forever held in suspicion. He could never have the free hand he'd long worked towards, which his mother's twisted hate had denied him. Although Strake's energy would be a breath of fresh air after Lady Arista's interminable blocks, to Lord Aristide the Whirlwind King must bring with him the taste of ash, of bitter, permanent defeat.

Unless he chose to murder for the throne.

There was only one answer right now, of course. Strake had given Lord Aristide no warning. Even if the Regent's son had managed to suborn Strake's bodyguard, he had no way of knowing

Soren couldn't use the palace defences. Let alone what measure of mage his King might be. So he would say yes, take on the role of Councillor of Mages, and be free to choose his time.

Strake was playing the role of the man too practical not to use a good blade, for all he could be positioning a knife at his throat. What had changed his mind? He waited, mouth flat, as Lord Aristide stopped gazing into the middle distance and shifted those brilliant blue and crystal eyes to Strake's face. Then with easy grace Aristide stood, looking down at the man who had taken the throne he considered his own. Strake did not move. Somewhere above Soren's throat, the Rose coiled, shifted, and slid into nothing.

"My family has long known that Darest prefers a Rathen," Lord Aristide said, murmur-soft.

He added a word in a language she did not know, but would always recognise. A word of power. Then another, a distinct object in itself, before raising one hand. Streamers of brilliant light trailed into existence, and he continued to speak: low-voiced, sibilant.

All around them faces echoed the reaction Soren's would surely have been if she had not the advantage of seeing Strake's. Dozens of mouths gaped to black circles – shock, anger, and in more than one case anticipation – but her Rathen, though he looked faintly surprised, showed no unease. If this was an attack, Strake was meeting it with the sanguinity of a god.

The two bodyguards had not been suborned. They made it halfway across the stretch of green before Soren signalled them to keep their distance. Swords shimmering in the light from Aristide's casting, the two women stuttered to a halt and gaped at the coiled lace of power forming between the two men. Soren had no more idea what was going on than they did, could only take her cue from her Rathen and keep her composure.

Mages of the Diamond's calibre rarely resorted to verbal crafting, which meant this spell had a level of complexity or permanence requiring more than will and gesture. Like yarn wound into a ball, the light was contracting into a solid sphere, a moon where shadows which could be fern leaves or sea monsters roiled beneath the surface. Lord Aristide stopped speaking, but a susurrus of fugitive syllables whispered on, faded to the edge of hearing, and were gone.

What remained was a perfect orb, twice the size of a man's head, trapping the world in silence. Even the wind had died away.

"I would not have asked so much of you." Strake's words were tenuous and distant, as if they could barely escape the pull of the orb.

The glitter came back, this time leavened with a self-mocking edge. "Having found myself without the stomach to pull Darest apart for the pleasure of calling it mine alone, I have no mind to waste my energy continually proving that decision."

Strake simply nodded, matter-of-fact to the end, and rose to press a hand firmly against the white surface. Twining dragon shadows fled before ripples. "I'll leave the wording to you."

More ripples, as Lord Aristide matched Strake's position, touching his right hand to the opposite side of the orb. Soren held her breath. This was obviously to be some sort of oath, a very binding one, but it would take mental gymnastics of a high order to start viewing the Regent's son as a trusted ally. Would he really go through with it? Or was it a trick?

"On my name, then," said Lord Aristide, voice suddenly clarion clear. "I will not seek to harm you or your heirs. I will not attempt to gain the throne of Darest at your expense. I...will protect and support you."

"On your life," Strake responded, with calm finality.

A tidal-wave of ripples swept the orb and it began to contract. Lord Aristide's arm jerked, and his eyes went wide with pain. Soren looked hastily from his face to Strake's, but her Rathen remained quietly intent. Both men kept their hand to the swirling surface, or perhaps could not draw away, but Lord Aristide was the only one in obvious difficulty. He stood it well, setting his teeth and not flinching again as it shrank. Soren became convinced she could smell burning flesh.

When they were both standing arms outstretched, with barely an apple's worth of orb separating their palms, the light suddenly flared from white to gold to a deep bruised red, and funnelled into Lord Aristide's palm. Their fingers brushed.

Strake dropped his hand away. There was a hint of admiration in his eyes when he said: "More than I would have done."

"Perhaps." Lord Aristide's focus was on his palm, touching the result of the spell like paint not yet dry.

Keeping to her seat with arduous restraint, Soren could only make out the details with palace-sight. A complex pattern of light lurked beneath the skin: almost filling a palm which showed no sign of burns, it was not a rose as she'd first thought, but a knot of lines woven into attractive symmetry. White shot through with threads of colour: silver, blue, gold. And it moved. The sliding hints of fin or claw or vine had transferred from the orb.

Half-remembered bedtime tales finally gave her an explanation. The thing had to be a *saecstra*, an enchantment of the Fair which featured in many of their great tragedies. More than an oath, it was judgment wound in promise. Lord Aristide would wear the mark for the rest of his life. And if he broke the vow just made, it would kill him.

Soren had to remind herself to breathe around her disbelief as Lord Aristide arranged himself neatly back onto his bench. He had just bound himself almost as thoroughly as she was herself. *Why?* She did not doubt for one moment that he considered Darest his, that he wanted its rule. How could she possibly be expected to believe that he would bind himself away from any chance of gaining his fondest wish?

Then she remembered – it had only been a few hours ago. Lord Aristide knew the meaning of the black rose. He'd just put himself in a perfect position to take control of Darest when the Rose's mysterious doom caught up with this inconvenient Rathen King and left behind a politically incompetent Champion ripe with child. All he had to do was wait.

"What would you like me to advise you on first?"

The glitter-smile was back, along with that air of private enjoyment. Whatever the truth of this profound, flamboyant gesture, he was still all sweet acid and darts.

Strake was again looking particularly saturnine as he returned to his own seat, but like Lord Aristide he moved beyond spectacular life-oaths as if they were everyday happenstance. "What should I expect from your parent?"

The now-dozens who watched were far from as calm, mouths flapping in excited speculation. The King had aligned with the Diamond. Without palace-sight Soren would only see the three of them, alone in the courtyard, with the two guardswomen retreating to the shelter of the nearest entrance. The Court were just shadows behind sky reflected in fine glass while King and Councillor conducted their day's business and the ripple of Lord Aristide's gesture, of this new-formed alliance, spread through the palace. The sheer unreality of it all made her head ache.

The delicate bow of Lord Aristide's lips had curled into pure delight. "That would depend on what circumstances offer her," he replied. "She will see little value in a direct move. Darest declined too greatly under Couerveur rule, and your appearance has provoked widespread anticipation of a return to heady days of wine and roses. You need not fear open insurrection. Not enough Dariens would support it."

"Outside interests might."

"True." For a moment star sapphire eyes again found the middle distance. "Quite possible that someone might make her an offer, despite long coldness to our neighbours. But – no. That would mean ruling under the auspices of another. An intolerable thing. No, from my lady mother you will receive surface support. By appointing me, you lose any slim chance you may have had of more."

"And beneath the surface?"

"A mule in the traces." He seemed to find the image particularly agreeable. "Whatever your endeavour, she will attempt to lead it into disaster, for she is well-versed in presiding over plans come to naught. That has been Darest for too long." Absently, Lord Aristide massaged his newly marked hand.

"If she should try and kill you, it would most certainly be an incident which would either finish me as well, or have me up for the deed. She could not risk my gaining ascendancy in the aftermath."

"I'll keep that in mind," Strake said: blunt acceptance of future treachery. "Do you have a recommendation for Court Shaper?"

"Do you need one?" Lord Aristide dismissed his own question with a unhurried turn of the hand. "There are two major Shaper steadings. Goldenrod is in the north-west, close to the Cerian border. A word-mage and true-mage at the heart of it. Married, powerful, competent, their focus entirely flora. A trifle obsessed, as Shapers tend to be. I've had little to do with them, but they report hopes of a strain of coloured flax. If that's true, I'd suggest leaving them to it. Fletcher's Marsh Farm, the other steading, works with both flora and fauna but recently fell into crisis. The classic story – someone, the stead holder in this case, produced creatures too smart for their own good. Many adventures were had."

Lord Aristide curled his lips in apparent disgust. A Shaper operated on a deeper level than an enchanter and the results were far more enduring. It was one thing to shape-change a man so he could live beneath the water, another to make it possible for him to father children with the same ability. And you could not return those children to 'normal' like you could disenchant a cat spelled to understand speech. Even the Fair rarely Shaped intelligent creatures, simply because too many things went wrong working magic 'beyond the blood'. Blame it on trial and error, or the Moon being jealous of her realm of birth and death. The result of Shaping sentients was too often something you could not control.

Could Strake want a Shaper to help him with the Rose?

If this was the case, Strake was not admitting it to Lord Aristide. "The Court Shaper advises as an expert, and inspects steading projects," he said, terse as ever. "Subordinate to the Councillor. Appoint whoever you think most appropriate. It's not of immediate concern, but I prefer not to have Shaping unsupervised. Which leaves what is of immediate concern."

"Being?"

"Tell me."

Another drawn out moment of assessment. On these rare occasions when he forewent sugar crystal venom, Lord Aristide would go very still, and his mouth would relax from its habitual slight curl. It was, Soren realised, exactly how he looked when he lay in bed in the morning staring at the ceiling. She wondered what he thought about, between waking and rising.

"We aren't producing enough," he began now. "Lack of goods and high impost make us an unattractive port, which means the trade between the far east and the western kingdoms travels straight past the Bay of Diamonds. Few take the land route. Without funds or manpower, we cannot maintain sufficient garrisons, and anyone outside a large town believes themselves exposed. People flock to the cities and live hand-to-mouth rather than risk the supposedly blighted countryside, leaving large tracts undermanned or deserted. Which leads to even lower production, and we take another turn down the spiral."

He paused, gauging Strake's reaction, then sat back before continuing. "There are other factors. What we do produce is mainly raw resources, which we export at a poor profit. Some of our most valuable, like the silver mines, are failing. Taxation is badly distributed, and we spend our revenues unwisely. The Tongue grows ever wider. It's not a desperate case. We can feed ourselves and are not beyond luxuries. But it is a long time since Darest flourished."

"The mines are depleted?"

Dissatisfaction glinted in Lord Aristide's eyes, at the question or lack of silver. "They've near emptied out the vein, but there should be others. I sent a diviner, but she did not return and I have yet to establish whether it was accident, murder or something else."

"Its lack at least makes the border less attractive."

"The iron is draw enough. There are two major factors holding back invasion from the West. The first is the belief that an attempt to take Darest would only lead to The Deeping resuming the kingdom – if it is not already doing so. But perhaps the more powerful is the West itself. Sax would not see Cya in Darest, Cya would certainly not see Sax more than double its size. They block each other. Korm and Cera might even assist us, should they see the region's balance begin to shift."

Strake nodded, and went back to an earlier point. "Increasing production is a slow business. A Rathen presence might boost confidence, but it will not arrest this cycle."

"No. In the near future I want to focus on trade."

A shadow of a frown touched Strake's eyes, then cleared. "Establish ourselves as the market-place, let others supply the goods?"

"Exactly." A school-master with a quick pupil, Lord Aristide leaned forward, sketching his thoughts with one hand. "The Westerners sail all the way to the east to trade with places like Kaldeban, and eastern merchants pass Darest to sail up the Horns to Cya. At the moment the Bay of Diamonds represents a detour for them, and too often they do not make us a port of call, but cross from Sumaric Heads directly to Sapphire Point."

Strake wasn't looking precisely encouraging. "In the past the Cyans would arrive in Tor Darest with half a hold to trade and half to take east. They would stock the best Darest had to offer and travel on. Long journeys with high profits and higher risks. I imagine it should be possible to convince more than a few of the advantages of shorter trips, but again this is a slow business, with many whose interests are invested in the older patterns. What kind of inducements, other than dropping the port duties, do you propose offering?"

"Hold races," Soren said, and they both stopped, straightened, and turned to her. Not so much affronted as remembering she was there. "Or a tourney," she went on, refusing to feel rankled. "Or duelling illusionists, which are always popular. Whatever takes your fancy, so long as there's a large purse and plenty of things for people to bet on. Coordinate whatever it is we usually import from the east and the west, and order supplies timed to arrive in the week leading up to your races. Best to use several rival cartels, and let slip who will be there. They'll be fighting each other off to get here first."

They were still staring at her, disconcertingly blank, and she had to fight a tide of heat in her cheeks. As well a fish might sing, apparently. "It's what my heart-mother does, though of course on a smaller scale. Carn Keep lives off the proceeds of the Midsummer Festival for the rest of the year."

"I will have to appoint your mother another of my advisers," Strake said, but although his tone was dry, they took the suggestion very seriously. Deeming it too late for a harvest festival, they began tossing around the viability of Spring races.

Relocation to somewhere with paper to make notes became necessary as the discussion carried on into lunch, then the afternoon. They could well go for days without break, Soren thought, and were very likely to, given the amount of resources they intended to invest.

Soren contributed little to the planning, speaking up only when they touched upon something where she had particular knowledge, but she was learning an extraordinary amount. About Tor Darest, but primarily the two men who wished to rule it.

That they were both highly intelligent, decisive men she had already known. That restoring Darest was important to both of them was obvious. That they were very alike was becoming increasingly clear. More than just shades of blue eyes.

They had hardly become bosom-chums, though. Total capitulation did not fit with Lord Aristide's ruthless image, and the honey and acid quickly returned, just as Strake had almost immediately fallen back into his terse, demanding habit. With distinct, definite opinions about just how they should proceed, their discussion involved a good measure of feint and thrust, and ever-wary observation. Fortunately, they were both willing to concede a point in the face of compelling argument and in their own ways she thought they were enjoying the sheer magnitude of the task ahead, and a comrade-in-arms to tackle it with.

But Soren, watching them while she crossed Fleeting Hall, could not help but remember again that Lord Aristide had made this move knowing both the doom predicted for Strake and the existence of the child he had fathered. Were these all plans he would carry through alone?

And she could not help but wonder why her Rathen had not so much as mentioned the Rose.

Fifteen

S trake announced Aristide Couerveur his Councillor of Mages, and the Court approved. The stories of an impending marriage strengthened, and those who had wavered rushed to show their allegiance to King and Councillor. Fors Cabtly was the first to pay the price of change, losing position, apartments and even his apprentice, though Aspen admitted he had not so much transferred his tutor as received permission to temporarily keep his room. Fors' new apartment, as befitted a mere jobbing mage, did not stretch to housing more than his immediate family.

Strake made few other appointments, and held off further replacements while he strove to learn enough about the Darest of now to make more sweeping changes. He had not reached the point of simply accepting everything Aristide told him.

Ambassadors began to trickle in, along with outlying Barons, come to pay their respects. No-one made any open attempt to object to the Whirlwind King, and the Court settled into a kind of watchful anticipation.

Soren missed dreaming. Missed the rambling epics of day-to-day routine, the skewed tangles of past and future loves, the crystal sharp urgencies where worlds were saved and forgotten before dawn. She'd never been one to clearly remember her dreams, but she was used to waking out of all manner of night-born oddity. Now, she had only the palace.

Possibly what she saw while sleeping included conjurings of her own mind, but it remained obstinately focused on privies and gardens, lovers and loiterers. So many people. Far too much of Strake.

He slept badly, still had nightmares. Ten days now, and he continued to toss and turn through the night, sometimes bolting awake, sweating and shaking. And Soren would wake with him and watch as he paced or pissed or read. Once he had sat with a hand covering his eyes. Her Rathen.

On the morning of the eleventh day of his reign, Aluster, first King of that name, turned and sighed, burrowing beneath blankets. His mouth quirked and relaxed, the shadow of lashes shifted. No nightmares for once, not about the frozen moment of death at his back, or the Champion who had betrayed him.

Soren slid out of bed, impatient with this morning ritual of waking only to continue to watch Strake sleep. Scurrying over the chill floor to dress, she felt no drowsiness despite only half a night's rest. One of the compensations of the Rose, like being able to move about dark palace rooms without worrying about uncovering a mageglow.

She had watched Strake too much this last week, seeking signs that his anger was easing. Over and again palace sight had revealed him looking fixedly at her when she was turned away, had shown intent study slide to a frown he could not hold back, his eyes flashing resentment or pain, sometimes outright anger. And then the shutter would come up, with only a hint of constraint leaking through as he plunged back into plans and preparations.

It had been too much to hope Aristide wouldn't notice. He and Strake spent most of every day together, and though Strake watched her more when they were alone, it was inevitable that Aristide's bright gaze would catch first the constraint, then what lay beneath it.

He kept any speculation to himself. In fact, both men were being entirely circumspect. So far as Soren could tell, since Aristide's oath neither of them had said a word which did not involve things like merchant fleets, flax crops or the viability of transforming the problem of the Tongue into a shipbuilding industry.

Wisdom on Aristide's part, Soren thought, glancing at him curled in the centre of his bed. He always looked so young in sleep, vulnerable. It was those lips, soft-sweet and deceptive, more suited to an infant. The *saecstra* was a coil beneath half-closed fingers. She alone of the Court knew that when he slept it seemed to come awake, whirled and twisted like there were dragons chasing their tails beneath his skin, trying to break free.

Despite the certainty of the spell, and her speculated explanation, she still couldn't trust his sudden capitulation. But careful observation had revealed nothing she could mark as preparation for betrayal. To all outward appearance, Aristide was willing to simply cement his position, playing the long game. Strake had even started to greet him with something akin to relief, thanks in part to the man's exclusive focus on business. For the rest of the Court was in full pursuit.

He had lost all patience with the onslaught. Fisk still hadn't recovered from whatever Strake had said to him when the secretary had tried his luck, and now crept about like gallows-bait. The only person who'd had any hint of success was Jansette, and that mainly because she'd twice more met Strake briefly, showed open admiration, then hastily left. That had roused his curiosity, if nothing else. Soren was sick of the entire business, of her head's insistence that he was her Rathen despite her heart's ambivalence. And especially of the palace. She lived for her dawn escapes.

The guards at Dathan's Walk saluted as she approached, and drew open the double doors. They were a weary, depressed pair who obviously found the Champion's morning departure the most interesting thing on their watch. Or a harbinger of their release, since they were never there when she came back. Soren smiled at the older of the two men, feeling sorry for him and pleased when he nodded his head. And then she smiled in earnest, for she was outside, with a cool breeze nipping at her face and the palace merely a building at her back.

This is the only time of the day I'm actually me, she thought, tugging a red-streaked apple from one pocket and a mageglow from the other. *There isn't room for me inside the palace. If I'm lucky, Strake will decide he does want to look over Islay before winter sets in, and then I'll have entire days of not being the palace. Perhaps I can convince him he really wants to look over Carn Keep, and I'll be able to visit Mother. Tell her about the baby without fear of telling the whole world. And talk to someone who sees Soren first, who lets me be someone other than Rathen Champion.*

I need to be held.

Soren paused to look up at the stars. More than a few had offered to do just that in the past week, for the Champion had most definitely become a person of consequence. Aspen had been graceful, but Lady Rothwell's daughter Varian evidently now thought Soren marriage material and had been persistent despite refusals. Regretfully, Lady Rothwell was mother enough to see the advantages of her daughter's pursuit of the Champion, and liked Soren enough to want her part of the family. That was a door Soren would rather not have had closed.

Halcean now obligingly screened out people wanting an audience with the Rathen Champion purely for romantic purposes. The number of propositions was sure to change when her pregnancy was known, though it was difficult to say whether they would increase or decrease. But that would surely be months off, and her surcoat would long hide a thickening waist.

No use continuing to hope it somehow wasn't true. The child she hadn't chosen would come. Some time soon it would become more than 'the baby', an abstract idea that did not seem to belong to her, no matter how many buds Aristide found on the Rose.

It was the smell which stopped her.

On a cold morning it was like a needle from sinus to brain. Rust and storm-dust and something else which brought Soren to a heart-pounding halt, apple in hand at the wide stable door. As her brain slowly processed the body's warning, horses whickered and shifted. The entire stable was awake.

Suddenly lack of palace-sight felt like an amputation. Soren squeezed the mageglow until it flared to its full brightness, setting long equine heads tossing at the glare. The stable was etched in sharp relief, stalls and rafters, bales of hay. And, winding through wisps of straw across the floor, a stream of black glinting red.

Third stall on the left. No glossy bay head poked over the gate, no dark mischievous eyes sized her up in hope of a treat. No soft nose or warm neck or any sign of Vixen except that shining swatch of blood.

Quite without thinking, Soren wrapped her arms protectively across her stomach. Shadows swallowed the stable as the mageglow was blocked, then fled as she caught herself. She turned, seeing nothing but anxious horses and the same walls and buildings she'd seen every morning. Less Vixen. Plus blood.

Nothing leapt out at her. Fingers falling slack, she dropped the apple. It bounced in the dust and rolled to one side, still gleaming from Soren's efforts to polish it. Nothing leapt out. A grey to her right blew noisily and thumped the wall of its stall. Nothing.

Unable to bring herself to go forward, Soren went back. Her chest kept fluttering. The Moon knew how her face looked, for when she tapped on the Palace doors, the guards who opened them took one glance and drew their swords.

"What is it, Champion?" the shorter of the pair asked. He had more crow's feet than face, but he moved like a young man to put himself between Soren and the dark. The other was only a step behind, suddenly exuding alert competence.

Their reaction spurred Soren to try and pull herself together. The Rose was silent. Because she wasn't in immediate danger, or because it had withdrawn its protection from her, as it had Strake? Or had it simply not known that someone or something had come in the night to butcher her horse?

"One of you fetch the Captain of the Guard," she said, and was proud her voice wobbled only a fraction.

The younger man immediately saluted, and left at double-pace. Soren turned and walked back to the stable, followed by the other guard. She'd dropped the mageglow as well. She couldn't remember when, but there it was, a harsh white star sitting in the dust a foot from her apple. The guardsman saw the blood and swore.

"Don't go too close," Soren said, forcing her throat to work. "There may be signs which can be used to track the killer."

He nodded, looked around, then hoisted himself up onto the nearest gate and leaned forward so he could peer into the stall. Soren made no move to follow. She would not allow that sight into her head.

As she watched, the guard turned his free hand palm to ceiling and, fingers splayed, lifted it in commendation to the Moon. Even the mask of laugh-lines couldn't hide grim shock as he climbed down.

"The blood's drying," he said, peering at every corner of the stable. "Not hours ago, but it didn't just happen."

Soren turned away. She supposed if the killer had still been here, she would not even have had the chance to see that Vixen was dead. Or perhaps the Rose would have stopped her, or it. Countless experiments had not provided her the trick of using the palace defences, but surely–

Cold metal pressed against her fingers. An unstoppered flask, thin and smooth. The guard's eyes were kind, fatherly. Soren made no more pretence of composure, tilting the flask to her lips and letting a draught run down her throat. Vicious cheap stuff, but it served its purpose, burning her back into some semblance of alive. Returning the flask with a nod of thanks, she checked Strake's breathing. Still asleep.

Had Vixen been killed by the same creature which Strake had hunted long ago? Was that what they had encountered in the Tongue? But how and why had it suddenly emerged here? Why Vixen? Why no warning from the Rose?

An explanation occurred as she bent to pick up her abandoned mageglow. She had spent the last week expecting some move from Lady Arista or one of the more disgruntled Barons, or any of the faceless thousands she suspected of wanting to do away with her Rathen. What better way to hide an assassination than to link it with a past killer? A few random deaths to match those recorded in the histories. Then Strake.

Grimly, Soren sorted through her tumble of palace dreamings, trying to isolate who had been on the move. But what she saw asleep was always an uncertain mess. And wasn't it wishful thinking, seeking a human killer rather than facing a seemingly invincible monster out of the past?

The guard began examining the ground at the stable entrance, but since this was one of the most trampled areas of the palace grounds, Soren doubted he'd have much luck. She turned her attention to the palace wall, and the well-lit gatehouse. The grounds were not strongly fortified, but the wall was still too high to simply scramble over, and the gatehouse and watchtowers were manned night and day.

If it was the thing from the Tongue, it had to have reached the stable somehow. Perhaps the wall posed little obstacle. Perhaps it had come through the gatehouse.

In answer to her thought, a swear-sword appeared to raise the portcullis, no doubt anticipating her morning departure. Not widespread slaughter, then. Just Vixen. Just Soren's horse.

No more morning rides, Soren thought as the Captain of the Guard, Helaine Vereck, arrived trailing a handful of guards she'd evidently collected en route. Vereck was a competent woman of few words, and she needed no direction to do her job. In short order the entire area blazed with light, there were patrols scouring the grounds, and a snub-nosed young woman was examining the floor of the stable as if the hollows and scuffs actually meant something to her. Stable hands sleeping in the loft above were woken by the noise and had to be restrained from swarming the scene.

The Guard had a few minor mages in its service, and Soren waited until a sleepy-eyed diviner pronounced himself perplexed, then left. Very likely Vereck breathed a sigh of relief not to have her erstwhile commander watching, grimly intent.

It would not be true to say that Soren felt overwhelmingly relieved to walk back into the security of palace-sight. But it did allow her to make absolutely certain nothing was anywhere near Strake. She flicked her attention across Aristide, various Barons in residence, the Chamberlain, the Marshall, and anyone else who had ever prompted her to the slightest suspicion. No-one obliged her by being blood-spattered, knife in hand. Most were still asleep, only the Marshall fumbling through morning routine.

Trying to look everywhere in the palace at once made it a little difficult to walk in a straight line, but Soren proceeded to do so, searching out anomalies, any hint or sign. Anything.

News was spreading with disobliging speed. The most unusual thing in the palace at that moment was the number of people rushing to wake others and talk excitedly. Though the sky was barely shading toward dawn, the palace was rapidly coming alive. If there was a vital clue to be found, it was lost in gossip.

On cue, Fisk turned into the corridor ahead. Soren intercepted him and said tersely: "Go wake the King and tell him what's happened." Fisk, already brimming with excitement, looked caught between dismay and pleasure at her command, but didn't argue.

That done, Soren returned to her apartment. Halcean was just emerging from her room, and stopped in faint confusion at the sight of her charge returning so early.

"Forget something?"

Shaking her head distractedly, Soren watched Strake's face as Fisk reached him. The shutter came down during the hesitant explanation, but Strake kept any shock or fear to himself.

"Champion?"

Soren forced herself to turn her attention back to her aide. Halcean had thrown herself wholeheartedly into her new role, obviously finding considerable entertainment in handling the importuning hordes, but there'd been little chance to get to know her. She was far too much a stranger for Soren to begin to explain.

"I won't be seeing anyone but the King this morning," she said instead. "Keep them away."

"Of course," Halcean said, now wholly startled. Her expression as Soren headed toward her bedroom was one of proprietary concern, and Soren realised that to Halcean she would be 'her Champion' in a grey imitation of the way Strake was Soren's Rathen. The thought didn't help.

Her Rathen was dressing, efficient but unhurried. Soren watched him leave for the stables, waiting until he had passed out of palace-sight before she allowed herself weep.

It was not as if Vixen had even really been her horse. Property of the Regent or the Darien Crown, and mainly interested in Soren as a source of treats. And someone to gallop away with, madcap along a beach. And she did love to be groomed, vain creature.

Half Soren's tears were surely for the fact that there could be no more morning rides, that she could not possibly risk venturing out alone, or even in the company of guards. Man or beast, the killer would effectively keep her prisoner, here where she could safely see anything coming, could not help but see them, any more than she could avoid witnessing the gossips' delight, the quiet attention with which Aristide received the news, or the lowering frown on her Rathen's face as he returned.

There would be no Vixen to ride, anyway. Swallowing one last hiccuping breath, Soren rolled heavily off her bed and went to wash her face.

Halcean was hovering in the receiving room, and started forward as Soren emerged, only to sheer off when Strake knocked at the door. Casting a worried glance over her shoulder at her Champion seating herself in one of the receiving room chairs, the aide opened the door to the King, then removed herself from the room.

Strake took one look and said: "Crying over a horse?"

"I've spent more time with that horse than with you."

Her voice was rusty-dry, and he grimaced, then said: "You've been riding out on your own each morning?"

She just nodded. That was not what she wanted to talk about. "Was it the same?"

"Unequivocally?" He sighed, then sat down opposite her, leaning forward with his eyes on his clasped hands. "It looked very much the same to me. But I've read the histories, and there's enough detail in them for someone to reproduce the creature's manner of killing. Slashes like claws, continuing after death, the body uneaten." His fingers whitened, betraying what his face and voice did not.

"The Rose gave me no warning," Soren said, quite steadily. She'd reached the stage of numbness.

"It may not have known." Those long, dark eyes flicked up for an instant. "The way it's constructed, there would be little within the palace hidden from the Rose, but most of its divinatory abilities outside are linked to the presence of Rathens, or the Champion." His mouth twisted. "Of course, if warning you of the attack on the horse would have resulted in you running straight outside to be cut up yourself, it may well have deliberately kept quiet. But I lean toward the former. It's certainly not omniscient, may not even be able to reason complexly."

It just acted like it. Far too contradictory. "If Vixen was killed by the same thing that hunted you in the forest, how could it be inside the palace grounds? Why would it trail you all the way from Teraman?"

He shrugged. "That's what we aim to find out. Is Aristide awake?"

"Oh, yes." Aristide had returned to his morning passion for staring at the ceiling. He at least did not smile as he lay thinking over the morning's news. "What do you plan to tell him?"

This distracted Strake enough that he stopped trying to strangle his hands. "Most of it. He's far more a mage than I'll ever be, and I want to see if he can track this thing, or at least discover why the Rose was able to. Which means, yes, he'll know more about the Rose than is comfortable. Including that it attempted to prevent you from coming to my aid. But not everything."

Strake was very deliberately staring out the window. Soren didn't say anything at all and after a pause he continued. "The *saecstra* was a brilliant move. He was right – I would never have trusted him else." He shrugged again. "Yes, I expect he will think it very convenient if this Deeping monster kills me. But he chose the wording of his oath, and it leaves him little room to manoeuvre."

He stopped, his fingers again laced and white, his unease having little to do with Aristide. Carefully, he loosed his grip and settled his hands on his knees, breathing deeply. "I think he likes the prospect of reviving Darest too much to risk losing Rathens altogether," he said, with determined focus. "If I do die, you may be certain he will protect our child."

"I have no intention of letting you die," Soren told him. And meant it. She had no idea how, but she refused absolutely to ever face finding a pool of blood belonging to Strake. Never.

Sixteen

No light but *Selune's shall ever shine in her temples.*

It was a difficult edict. During the day, the temples kept their windows shuttered and curtained, and the entry hall screened by successively heavier layers of velvet drapery. Candles, even ordinary mageglows could not be used, and many of the smaller temples simply could not manage it, were constantly seeking funds for specially enchanted orbs which stored the light of the moon. Otherwise, the temple remained dark until the sun set, permanently a place of uncertain shadow.

Most of the larger temples followed the structure of a long hall with walls of black and a pool-studded floor of white before a ceiling-scraping arlune. Soren had already seen the temple through palace-sight, had been fully aware that glows had been placed beneath the water consecrated to the goddess, that the arlune had been similarly enchanted so that the entire sweep of white shone like the shaft of moonlight it represented. When she struggled out of the mercifully dust-free curtains, the room still made her gasp. It danced.

Halcean remained outside, ready to fend off intrusion, and palace-sight showed Soren two acolytes lurking behind curtains to her left. She ignored them, her attention flicking to Aristide and Strake as they passed out of the east doors to the stables. She listened to her Rathen's breathing, then shut him away as fully as she was able. She had come to make an offering.

It was invariably cold in a Moon temple, thanks to all the water. In this case it flowed the length of the walls along specially constructed channels to form a semi-circular moat. A narrow bridge projected out into the centre of this moat, terminating just short of the arlune in a densely padded prayer cushion.

The arlune itself was marble, far removed from Carn Keep's carved sandstone painted white. It rippled like the water beneath, carving out of the bracketing walls and flowing upward, narrowing to a pristine shaft which touched the dark ceiling. Kneeling on the prayer cushion, Soren looked up.

"Moon for birth and death, Sun for all the rest." Soren had not often come to the Moon's temple. When her brother's daughter was born. The deaths of two of her grandparents, a childhood friend, pets. She'd never felt so conflicted.

Gripping the edge of the prayer cushion so that she could not be tempted to reach out and steady herself with her hands, Soren leaned forward and rested her forehead against the chilly marble. Immediately, a faint headache she had not realised she was carrying lifted, and the swirl of palace-sight retreated to something distant and negligible.

To the Moon she gave two slow, sinking realisations. One spread black across a stable floor, and the other solidifying out of the chaotic aftermath of the Rose's assault in the Tongue. Painstakingly she reconstructed her bewildered loss and slow-burning fury at sight of that pool of blood. To that she admitted a shrinking desire for safety. Then she tried to piece together the suspicion of pregnancy. A great deal of that was anger and dismay, but despite it all she had to acknowledge an edge of pleasure, that she was to have the child of this man she desired. Child of a King, child of her Rathen. An offering required honesty.

She felt it flow away from her, combined recollection of death and conception, not erased from her memory but shared with the one who meted out the world's souls, and gathered them home again. The Moon did not reach out to her supplicants – there was no chance of the sudden, burning transcendence brought on by the fleeting regard of fickle Sun. An offering to the Moon brought more a reminder of a presence always there but hardly noticed, as an oft-worn scent becomes edited out of conscious notice. A connection to something immensely distant, remembered in return for memory. Mother's skirts. Comfort.

It could not bring Vixen back, but it would do.

"Let me help."

"What?" Soren looked up at her aide. Not willing to offer any more of her grief up for the Court's consumption, she'd retreated to her apartments to leaf through the histories, searching out more references to the killer while she watched the palace.

"Let me help," Halcean repeated. "I'm your aide, good for more than answering doors."

Halcean's eyes were intent, full of frustrated energy, but Soren hesitated. It didn't matter whether the woman offered out of ambition or sympathy, Soren simply didn't want to talk, didn't want to prod at the mass of fear and frustration tangled around her.

"What can you do?" she asked equivocally.

"I can be properly outraged!" Halcean grimaced, and held up a hand to forestall response. "I – ever since I came to Tor Darest, I've been watching how everything works. Learning who wants what, and how badly. And how I could use it to get ahead. I knew just what strings to pull to get myself offered for this position, and it was fun to do it. There's–" She hesitated, then hurried forward in a rush. "You do what you can, to advance your family, and most of the time I enjoy playing Court. But I don't think I've ever seen anything so completely unnecessary as killing your horse. Whoever did that – well, I'd like to see them regret it."

"So would I." Soren looked down, then rubbed her fingers across a line of old text, a fair description of a centuries-old death. "Who then?" she asked. "There are others to work out how it was done, to try and prove it. Tell me who, who has reason enough to – to hate the return of the Rathens so much that they'd try and mimic this? Because if we aren't facing the real monster, someone has to be willing to go on killing, to make it look like the King's past has tracked him down. Who has so much at stake to do that?"

Halcean bit her lip, her certainty faltering. "It does seem excessive," she admitted. "I mean, if they're able to hide their tracks well enough for a single death, why not just make it the King's and be done? Of course, the King's under better security, but they'd have to breach that some time, and this kind of thing will only mean he keeps out of harm's way."

"It would have to be a mage," Soren said. "Even avoiding the divinations cast for Vixen requires that."

"Or someone wealthy enough to buy one. There's few enough local mages, but plenty for hire elsewhere."

"So name your candidates. Whether or not you could believe them contemplating a string of murders, who has the most to lose?"

"Well–" Sudden caution.

"Putting the name Couerveur at the top of the list won't startle me, Halcean."

The aide shrugged sheepishly. "There's no point denying they've lost the most. Though Lord Aristide has recovered a lot of ground. Really, except for not being heir presumptive, he's in a better position now than he was before the King returned. King Aluster has started making changes Lord Aristide has tried to push through for years, and at the same time the mere presence of a Rathen in Darest has increased the number of ships in port. And people are staying on, hoping to ride the tide of new fortune. Lady Arista – well, you don't need that situation spelled out."

"Aspen told me there's stories she's secretly living in Tor Darest, keeping a close eye on things."

"Ha." The corner of Halcean's mouth curled up. "I'm sure. But Lady Arista might be the key in another way. Before King Aluster, the Court had been shifting to Lord Aristide's banner, but there were a few too fully invested in Lady Arista to do that. People who hadn't been exactly supportive of Aristide, or who he had little use for. The stand-out candidate for that would be Chancellor Gestry. Lord Aristide's never been overly fond of his mother's discarded favourites, and he's already begun to move against Gestry."

"He has?"

"The Chancellor – well, he hasn't precisely been lining his pockets from the coffers, but he's certainly used his position to his advantage. Old gossip's been stirred up this last week: minor sins coming back to haunt him, making their way to the King. I doubt Gestry will be Chancellor for much longer."

Dominic Gestry was talking to his husband, arms folded protectively across his chest, eyes shuttered and unhappy. More than his political life was falling apart.

"He's not a mage, is he?"

"No."

"Who else?"

Halcean hesitated again, obviously viewing the next candidate as possibly sensitive. She started to speak, paused, then said: "The Rothwells."

That was hard to believe, and Soren's expression must have shown it. "Not Lady Francesca," Halcean added hastily. "Her children."

The Rothwells were breakfasting in the Baron of Mogath's apartments. This was hardly unusual, since Lady Rothwell's lands were in Mogath. Mogath was a stolid, taciturn man who rarely shifted from impassive reserve, but it did not seem his guests were happy ones.

A frown was carved between Lady Francesca's eyes, and Varian Rothwell was not hiding her frustration. Their attention was focused on the fourth at the table, Lady Rothwell's son Everett. A year his sister's junior, he was a refined male version of his mother's stately presence, and currently in the throes of passionate speech.

"Why the Rothwells?" Soren asked, fingering the pages of the book again to hide the way her attention was divided. Strake and Aristide had returned to the palace, were heading toward Fleeting Hall. "I thought Lady Francesca had some kind of unstated alliance with Lord Aristide."

"The Diamond's a chancy bedfellow. And neither he nor the King seems inclined to remain daggers-drawn with The Deeping."

"So – ah." Soren raised her eyes in comprehension. "Trade."

"A monopoly is a hard thing to give up, and while Lady Francesca is hampered by a stiff sense of honour, Varian and Everett are not."

Everett was trying to convince Lady Francesca of something. Varian wavered. The Baron watched. Finally Lady Francesca delivered a short, obviously discouraging speech and left. Brother turned to sister, sister turned on brother. Watching the argument develop, Soren was glad she'd never been drawn to Varian.

"Is Lady Francesca in danger?" she asked.

"I don't know," Halcean said, as if that question hadn't occurred to her. "I don't know how far Varian would go. I think–" She paused, a wicked grin lighting her face. "I think Varian would far prefer pursuing more attractive possibilities, like marrying you, than cross her mother. Everett...he wants everything, and he wants it quickly. A man usefully bereft of moral check, as my own mother would say."

Brother and sister slammed out of the breakfast room, Varian not quite able to fix a mask over her temper as she stalked toward a palace exit. Everett said something evidently vituperative to her back, then walked on. Before he turned the corner, he'd lost all sign of ill humour, was even smiling. Left to himself, the Baron continued his meal. But he did not seem dissatisfied.

Interesting, but not illuminating. "You had someone else in mind, I think," Soren said, looking back at Halcean. "Before you produced the Rothwells."

"I–" Halcean stopped, shook her head. "No. You said we were talking motive, and I don't know of one."

"Still–"

Fisk, despatched from Aristide's rooms, knocked at Soren's door, and Halcean rose with an air of relief to answer it.

It was time, according to the King, for breakfast.

Aristide's taste leaned to the spare and elegant, and Fors Cably's departure had been swiftly followed by the transformation of the cluttered apartments of the Councillor of Mages. The rooms were large through lack of furnishings, and the rugs quite distractingly beautiful beneath bare walls of warm-toned oak. The breakfast rooms afforded a different view on the same garden Soren's receiving room overlooked, a discomforting symbol of Aristide's new position in the King's court. The Champion's apartments were bracketed by King's and Councillor's. A cosy little arrangement.

"It can't be scried," Strake told her, immediately Soren seated herself at the table. "Divinations were useless, and the tracker can't sort out distinctive prints."

"What were the tracks of the original creature like?"

"I don't know." Strake grimaced. "What little we found suggested something humanoid. It was intelligent enough to keep away from soft earth."

"Yet you succeeded in following it," Aristide said.

Strake paused to look distractedly at the array of dishes, his selections prompting Soren to put a warm roll on her plate and butter it.

"We tried using dogs," Strake continued, gaze on her now. "Again with little success. At times they seemed to sense something, but their tracking always led nowhere, so we sent them back. We tracked it by the corpses." He watched Soren's hand waver, and shook his head. "Small animals, torn apart. Birds. At times the trees themselves were scored, as if it could not help but claw at whatever it encountered. We'd find something like that, and then Theremel – our tracker – would laboriously search out every bruised leaf and blade of grass and broken twig."

"Fast enough to take birds, but not outdrawing pursuit? Striking out wildly, but controlled enough to kill a man while his companions slept?" Aristide's eyes were narrow, glittering. "Did you track it, or did it lead you?"

"That's something I'd like answered." It did not seem to be the first time the question had occurred to Strake. "The Tzel Aviar said it did not conform to any Deeping creature she had previously encountered. The elusiveness outstripped a nixie, the clawing suggests a troll. The arcane protection was of a level usually expected of one of the dragon-kind. We discussed the possibility of one of the lesser elves using some sort of artefact, or even one of the Fair run mad. The creature seemed to kill solely for the sake of killing. Selecting its targets with all the logic-illogic of a Deeping monster travelling for days just to slaughter a horse."

"There have been no reports of sudden deaths between here and the Tongue," Aristide commented. "Certainly no trail of corpses. But if this was done by an opportunistic local, they have superlative protections – a high order of magery. Unlikely that there would be a multitude of untraceable killers. Yet you say this is not entirely the case?"

While Strake matter-of-factly outlined the Rose's ability to observe inside and outside the palace, Soren made intent work of pulling the roll into small pieces. Aristide listened to long-guarded Rathen secrets with an air of polite attention, but when told that Soren could see everything which occurred in the palace he was not quite able to restrain the curling corners of his mouth. She wondered if he'd stop lingering in his bath.

Strake concluded with a description of the encounter in the Tongue. "Whether it was the same creature is naturally the issue. There's as much evidence for as against. If it was, then despite our failures it's possible to track the thing."

"The Rose offered no warning this morning?"

"No." Soren didn't lift her eyes from her plate to answer.

"The Rose is a type of *setherin* construct." Strake was frowning at her bowed head. "Operating through the bloodline and the Champion. It has some unconnected divinations, no real prophetics, and may simply not have been capable of detecting this creature when it was at any distance from the Champion or myself." He paused, turned over his unused fork, then added: "After making clear our pursuer to Soren, the Rose attempted to prevent her from warning me."

Aristide, arrested in the act of drinking, blinked over the rim of his mug. For once in his life surprised, but quickly recovering composure. He frowned at Strake for a long breath, looked at Soren as if he expected to discover an explanation in her face, then said: "If I might be indelicate, was this before or after your child was conceived?"

"After," Soren told him, refusing to make it sound like an admission.

There was no suggestion of triumph in Aristide's manner. "So it becomes a matter of whether you are doomed because the Rose cannot, or will not, protect you. But a *setherin* construct—"

"— might have the potential to accrue some semblance of self, after centuries of existence." Strake's unquiet temper showed in those long, dark eyes, and he focused on filling his plate before continuing. "Or perhaps it was the long dormant period after the death of Torluce, when it lay neglected and festering...or starving. The runes are still clear, but it could have warped, or grown beyond them somehow. In either case it would still be constrained by the original bounds of the *setherin*."

"If it has awakened." Aristide was sceptical. "What gain in destroying the bloodline? What advantage in seeing you dead?"

"What cost in saving me?" Strake looked back at Soren, his expression better suited to the study of a canker which must be burnt out. "Suffice to say that we don't know whether the Rose was aware of this morning's attack before the Champion discovered it."

"But it was definitely aware of the thing chasing us about the Tongue." Soren pushed her plate aside. "And it did not feel at all like a set of conflicting instructions. I think it was terrified."

"Or trying to terrify you."

Soren considered that initial dizziness, the trepidation she'd felt whenever she came too close to Strake, and thought that was more likely a side-effect of these conflicting orders. The jangling panic when the creature approached, so much stronger and more obviously alien to Soren's mind, had been overwhelmingly intense. She felt strangely impatient with this conversation, with her own hatred of what the Rose had done, of the myriad problems of Strake's kingship. She wanted Vixen back.

"At any rate, I felt nothing at all from it this morning," she said tersely. "And can't remember anything unusual during the night. The Rose's motives, or lack of them, seem. less important than finding the thing that killed Vixen – man or monster – and stopping it from killing you."

"One might lead to the other," Aristide said. His eyes reflected the morning light. "However, my first summation of the black rose has not changed. If the threat is linked to The Deeping, then a solution should be sought there. Contact the Tzel Aviar."

Strake's mouth flattened. "The same Tzel Aviar who has done nothing to stem the incursion of trees over the border?"

Aristide smiled, that peculiarly appreciative expression this time. "Before relations with The Deeping soured, the previous Tzel Aviar was called on twice in regard to the Tongue. The trees themselves cannot be proven magical. No overarching enchantment was found to be active." He shrugged, fluid dismissal. "In my lifetime, we have never officially called on Tzel Damaris, although he has dealt with occasional cases which have strayed into Darien territory. Possibly he would deal with the Tongue as ineffectively as his predecessor. And, indeed, every single mage who has made the attempt, including most of the Couerveur line."

"I do not care to bring the Fair into this matter," Strake said, obstinately. "Tzel Eularin was not able to track the killer." He paused, and looked frustrated. "But I concede that despatching a Deeping creature without the Tzel Aviar's sanction is not a diplomatic start."

"It will be remembered, at least, no matter how inimical your stalker. There is considerable pressure within The Deeping to close their borders completely." Aristide had taken up his mug once again, and was regarding his own reflection in the steaming liquid. "Queen Desteret does not openly favour the insular factions, but she has long allowed policies keeping humans out of The Deeping to gain strength." He rose abruptly. "If you would excuse me one moment?"

Strake waited until Aristide had left the room, then turned to Soren. "What do you know of this current Tzel Aviar?"

Soren looked at him in surprise. "Lord Aristide visited The Deeping during his training. He knows vastly more about the Fair than I."

"And he considers it important for Darest to have The Deeping as an ally," Strake said irritably. "I don't want circumspect answers trying to point me in a particular direction."

Soren was surprised at the implied trust, and supposed she should be pleased Strake retained a reserve about Aristide. Then he added: "Besides, I was hoping for another gem of country wisdom from your mother."

Thinking of her dryly acerbic heart-mother, it was hard not to smile. "My mother says that the Fair are people like us," she said. "Just people who happen to live several hundred years among the kind of magic most of us encounter only in legend. She says avoiding them is the best thing you can do."

"Not unreasonable. But not entirely practical. What of this Tzel Aviar?"

"They call him the Indifference." Strake quirked an eyebrow, but Soren's attention was momentarily drawn by Aristide in his bedroom, leafing through a number of books. Many of the pages were covered in intricate patterns, others with neat writing. He'd taken them from a panel concealed within the head of his bed.

"Indifferent to his duties?" Strake prompted, ever impatient.

"Suitors. He's said to be out of the ordinary, even among the Fair." She shrugged. "Carn Keep isn't exactly on The Deeping border, so I've barely seen any Fair at all – but there's a great many rumours about the man. Said to be a superb mage. Said to despise humans. Said to have been made Tzel Aviar as a punishment."

"For?"

"Feel free to ask him." Soren shook her head, watching Aristide leaving his room, book in hand. "He's held the position for something like eighty years. Whatever happened, it was long ago."

The wrong thing to say. Strake's face closed, just in time for Aristide's return. Soren regretfully watched Aristide survey their expressions, then turned her attention back to shredding her breakfast. She couldn't worry herself to the bone every time she upset Strake. He was only her King.

"This is the Tzel Aviar's sigil," Aristide said, placing the book on the table. It was open to a page dominated by a complex knot of Deeping writing, with 'Tzel Damaris' beneath it in Aristide's compact hand. "The request would best come from you."

Strake seemed still inclined not to make the request at all, but picked the book up without protest and rose to stand by the window. Fingers resting on the symbol, he frowned down into the garden as he cast.

Difficult to guess how long this would take. Soren stared at her Rathen's intent face and tried to remember the peace the Moon had brought her.

"Is my table so displeasing, Champion?"

Startled, she turned back to Aristide. He tilted a glance in the direction of her plate of bread-crumbs.

"No insult meant, Lord Aristide," she responded shortly. "I have no appetite."

"Understandable. And the Court will greatly appreciate the drama of a fainting Champion."

Soren wondered if Aristide had some misplaced idea of a pregnant woman needing to eat constantly. Or if he was just entertaining himself, baiting her. To get him to turn that blandly solicitous expression somewhere else, she took a piece of fruit and began to dissect it, but that only brought a spark of unholy amusement to his eyes.

"Does Baron Mogath have cause enough for treason?" she asked then, but did not have the satisfaction of surprising the Diamond.

"Mogath is not likely to involve himself in something as risky as regicide," he replied promptly. "For all he stands to lose if The Deeping thaws to us." An eyebrow quirked. "Everett Rothwell is under observation."

He was bland again, but Soren thought she heard the condescension of a master not interested in fencing with beginners. What was she to Aristide, after all, but some coastal girl who'd been transplanted out of her element? She was nothing but a conduit for the Rose's power; a vessel. Champion Brood Mare.

On the other hand, she'd be underestimating Aristide in turn to think he'd discount her. More than likely he was looking to the long game again, beginning to prepare the ground for working with her after Strake's probable demise. Soren sighed inwardly, wishing herself well away from this place where everyone's motives had to be second-guessed.

Then Strake turned from the window, handed the book to Aristide, and said: "He is coming."

Seventeen

Even a Deeping mage could not travel to Tor Darest in moments. The Tzel Aviar had told Strake three days, which palace security hurried to fill with patrols, searches and impressive energy. So far the result was precisely nothing, but that nothing at least included no more corpses. Soren spent less time following Strake about and more watching him and the palace in her head, trying to settle on how the Rathen Champion could meet the threat of murder.

"Are you absolutely, positively certain you wouldn't like me to carry you off for an afternoon of lust and abandon?"

"Do you think you could lift me?" Soren was by no means small or delicate.

"With the right motivation I expect I could stagger all the way to the couch," Aspen said, and shook his head when she laughed. "You do my pride no good at all, nixie."

"You're beyond injury."

"Cruel, cruel."

Aspen was a welcome distraction, outrageously flirtatious as he attempted to turn her thoughts from death. When a faint clink of crockery heralded Halcean's arrival, he broke off, then adopted a sprawling and over-comfortable position in his chair. Eyes dancing with unconcealed glee, he held a hand out imperiously for a steaming, spice-scented mug. Taunting Soren's aide had become his latest fad.

"Join us, Halcean," Soren ordered, accepting her own mug. While Halcean went to fetch another, she pulled a face at Aspen and murmured: "Stop it."

"No need to take up cudgels, my delight. She's well able to fight her own battles." But he sat a little straighter in the wing-back chair, and made a demure play of devotion to his cider as Halcean returned.

"You move rooms tomorrow?"

"Sadly. Too much to hope the Diamond would allow me to lurk about the wainscoting much longer. His sterling Robar has tidied me off to some remote corner of nowhere, quite as far from anything interesting as it's possible to be. And all my dreams of a sudden midnight encounter came to naught. I'm fated never to know if half the things they whisper about the Diamond are true." He tossed up a hand in mock despair, then sobered. "No news on other fronts. Endless speculation, but no-one willing to accuse, let alone put their hand up to slaughter. Not even a popular candidate, beyond this Deeping hobgoblin.

"The only change—" He made a moue of distaste. "There's been a revelation among the more poetic that our divine Aluster's rose is a very black shade of red, which does not at all fit with the descriptions and pictures history's left us. There's no limit to the speculation around that. The wisest heads have concluded that it reflects the nature of our new ruler, and predict dire events and calamities."

That would teach Strake for his thunder-cloud humours.

"You knew that one already," Aspen said, watching her closely. "I see I'll have to scare up something truly original for you."

"Or concoct it," Halcean murmured, softly enough that Aspen could pretend he hadn't heard. The look he gave her suggested their game of rivalry was about to be taken up a notch.

"Aspen, can you tell if a person's a mage?"

The quiet, grim tone almost drew corresponding gravity. "Not casually. Not unless they're casting, when I'd be able to feel the current of worked power. You can test a person you suspect of being a mage, if you've the time and energy and they don't hit you for your insolence, but since magic is everywhere, in everything and everyone, even tests can be wrong. The simplest way to know a mage is to keep track of the children of mages, the students of mages, and everyone who's ever cast publicly."

"And if I wanted to keep an eye out for mages casting? Could I tell?"

"Not a true-mage. I presume you don't mean a word-mage or, Sun forbid, a blood-mage?"

"Would I always be able to tell if one of them were casting?"

"If you were in the room, surely. No-one can mistake the sound of spoken magic, and I'd hope you'd notice if someone started etching runes about the place or sacrificing some hapless creature for summon-price. They could use a trigger spell, but trigger spells are hard, and unless you're really good they tend to...swell. They want to finish themselves, you see, and they push at you and unless you've said every word just right and left absolutely no wriggle room, you can't keep them in order too long."

"But still, I need to be able to tell if someone's casting – whether they're a true-mage or a word-mage with a trigger spell or whatever. Could you teach me?"

"You–" Aspen was imperfectly hiding his sympathy. "I suppose – yes and no. It's within the bounds of possibility. Anyone with a tongue can learn to be a word-mage, after all, and a spell could give a word-mage something of the senses of a true-mage. I could look for one, could even try to write one. How long it would take you to learn to cast it... It's a truly bad idea to cast without comprehension. No-one ever really finds a scroll, reads it and has the spell work. You have to pronounce everything just right, and what you think you're saying has an immense effect on your result. For such an exact language, there's a lot of shades of meaning in *elachar*. I could cast and maintain the spell for you. But–" He stopped, let his breath out. "You serve a Rathen mage, Soren. The Diamond supports him. Half the mages in Darest are in the palace, ready to point a finger at any intruding mage. Don't you think the threat of magic's sufficiently covered?"

"Do you? Truly?"

He wrinkled his nose at her. "Don't ask me for honesty when I'm trying to be reassuring."

"Even if all the known mages in the palace were going to leap to the King's defence, you just said that anyone could be a mage. Anyone could be Vixen's killer. Or another killer. The King certainly has a better chance of spotting a spell-caster than I, but I'm not always with him. And I want to–" Contribute. She didn't say it, didn't want to know how well Aspen thought the title of Champion fit Soren Armitage.

"You may be certain I'll leap to the divine Aluster's defence, at any rate," Aspen said, draining his mug. "How could I pass up the chance to win his gratitude? Let alone yours?" He stood, and bowed elegantly enough to rival the Diamond. "I must off. Do send word if you reconsider." With a final pert flourish for Halcean's benefit, he left.

"Lord Aristide's factotum found him rooms overlooking the barracks practice yard," Halcean said, when they were safely alone. "Noisy, but with a view."

Soren grinned. Aspen was sure to wax poetic about the morning exercises. But the time for lightness was past. "And have you narrowed on any candidates?" she asked.

"No." Halcean met her eyes with characteristic directness. "But I still don't think it's this monster out of the past. One that creeps into palace grounds unseen, kills a horse, then leaves just as quietly? There's no reason at all to believe the thing survived into the future as King Aluster did. You're right to concentrate on mages."

Not keen to discuss night-time encounters, Soren sipped at her cooling cider, inhaling apple and spice. "I'm told there's few capable of turning divinations."

"In Darest." Halcean's tone was derisive, and she caught herself up, ducking her head. "You'd only need one, true enough."

"Have you heard the same as Aspen about the black rose?"

Her aide hesitated, then said: "Yes. More that it's a doom-sign. That he's to die, and soon."

Truth had a way of uncovering itself. Soren could only hope no-one came up with the bright idea of announcing her pregnancy to allay concern.

That speculative gaze had been turned on her again, hastily redirected as Soren looked back up. When Soren made a wry face, Halcean laughed, adding a shrug to admit her curiosity. "You don't like this at all, do you? No, not whatever murderous wretch butchered your horse – the palace, the Court."

"The Court isn't the nicest of places."

"Oh, it's not too bad. King Aluster – well, he's high-tempered I own, but I haven't seen any malice in him, which is an improvement on the Couerveurs. And even Lady Arista didn't over-stock the jailhouses with those who looked at her the wrong way, let alone line their heads along the docks. There's a lot of pointed conversation, and jostling for position, the occasional fortune staked on some political manoeuvre, but that's half the fun, isn't it?"

"If you say so."

"You come from a place where there's no gossip, no scuffles for precedence?"

"Well, no–"

"Everyone's kind and generous and well-intentioned?"

"Hardly."

"Then what's the problem?"

"The stakes are higher here. And–" Soren sat back, resting her mug on her knee, staring across the palace. The Rose's barbed contribution wasn't something she was willing to share with her aide, any more than her less-than-perfect relationship with her Rathen. "What I'm expected to do is different. I didn't have to involve myself in those kind of games, back home. Didn't like them, wasn't any good at them, nobody really cared if I didn't play."

"Power, prestige, position. A lovely apartment, free meals–"

"Delightful people to work with, and a horse to call my own. It's all part and parcel, Halcean."

"There's many who'd change places with you in a moment."

"I expect so." Soren smiled a little lopsidedly. "Until they knew what it was like." Then she laughed at the expression Halcean didn't try to hide, reminded of her sense of proportion. "That does sound pettish, doesn't it? Maybe I'm just homesick. Even with all your successes, don't you miss your family?"

"My family wants me here," Halcean replied matter-of-factly. "The useful youngest child, purpose-built for courtly machination. I've spent so long learning how to get every advantage out of Tor Darest that I doubt I'd know what to do with myself anywhere else. Nor," she added, with a conspiratorial grin, "is my family the kind you miss."

"I'm sorry."

As Halcean shook her head at misplaced sympathy, Soren's attention was pulled away by the sight of Aristide Couerveur, the Captain of the Guard and Lady Rothwell in the corner of one of the ballroom antechambers. Just what was going on? Aristide had been studying a transcription of the Rose's wall of runes, and was due to visit her to try and probe the Rose's secrets. Nothing had been said to Soren about Francesca Rothwell. And why were they just sitting silently in an empty room?

"You could always have your family come visit," Halcean pointed out, oblivious.

"I could. I will, I hope, before Winter closes in. My mothers won't be so busy, and perhaps things will have settled down."

Or Strake would be dead, and Soren would see how far the Diamond's avowed loyalty went.

"Are you all right?"

"Distracted," Soren replied, embarrassed by how obviously she must have been staring off into the distance.

"I'll leave you to it, then." Halcean smiled and gave her a courteous little bow. "It can be nasty at times," she added. "Even I don't like everything I do, all the time. But it's important to remember that it's all really just a game, that everyone's playing it. Don't worry too much."

"I'll try." But it was hard when Aristide and the Captain of the Guard were so obviously engaged in some manoeuvre they'd neglected to inform her about.

A few minutes later explanation came in the form of Everett Rothwell. He looked carefully around the room, eyes passing over his mother and her escort without so much as blinking. Lady Rothwell bowed her head, then lifted it, apparently struggling with an impulse to cry out some warning. Soren could see Captain Vereck tense then relax, the moment passing.

A woman came into the room, her face faintly familiar, her clothing that of a clerk. Everett's manner was peremptory, hiding relief. They spoke. A small, heavy purse was exchanged. They moved to depart.

Nothing changed to Soren's eyes, but suddenly Everett noticed the three seated in the corner: Captain Vereck grim, his mother with tears in her eyes but her chin held high and firm. Aristide, just the faintest curl touching his lips. Almost, Soren imagined she could hear another audience, reacting with approval to the dumb-show's denouement. Everett's reaction was certainly that of the villain undone: springing back, hand going to his belt knife.

So tidily managed. Guards appeared at the door even as the woman dressed as a clerk ran. Everett stood his ground, face bloodless. More words were exchanged. Aristide asked something of Lady Rothwell. She shook her head, said something which brought a touch of surprise, of disbelieving hope to her son's face. And then, with no flicker of triumph or compassion, Aristide moved one of his hands and Everett Rothwell was gone.

A small, brown thing fluttered on the floor. A sparrow, shaking and crashing its wings as if it had no concept of how to use them. Lady Rothwell quickly stooped and captured it, her face tightly closed against anger or relief. The players scattered, the Captain escorting guards and prisoner, Lady Rothwell carrying her transformed child: off to find a suitable cage.

Aristide came and knocked on the door of Soren's apartment.

Soren had to admire the ease with which Halcean left the Diamond Couerveur to kick his heels in the entry hall while she punctiliously went to consult the Champion on whether she was receiving visitors.

"Send him in," Soren ordered, feeling remarkably nervous after the scene she'd watched. "And you'd best go out yourself, I suppose. Come back in an hour."

Halcean nodded obediently, even managing to hide her no doubt avid curiosity as she bowed Aristide into the receiving room. Palace-sight let Soren see that practiced courtier's manner dissolve as he walked past her aide, leaving Halcean's face filled with speculation, and an emotion which looked very much like the one Soren now felt herself whenever she looked at Aristide Couerveur. It was a kind of frustrated fascination, wary and discomfited.

"Please sit down, Lord Aristide," Soren said, as Halcean closed the door, hesitated, then left the apartment. "Perhaps you'd care to tell me just what it was Everett Rothwell was trying to buy?"

"Death. Mine, interestingly enough." He sounded more bored than intrigued. "It seems I influence the King too much toward The Deeping."

Soren couldn't help but stare at him. He'd uncovered and countered a plot against his own life, had just turned someone into a bird for pity's sake! He was acting like he did that kind of thing every day.

But then, he probably did. Soren, who could see everything which went on in the palace, hadn't spotted whatever Everett had done to expose himself, nor even the preparation of the trap set for him. For all her expanse of vision, it was almost impossible to catch the important among all the everyday. She should thank Sun and Moon both that Aristide had chosen to ally himself with Strake, for Soren could do nothing to match him.

"You've come to experiment, I take it?" she asked, struggling not to let sudden desolation show in her voice.

"With your permission, Champion," He'd made no move toward any of the chairs, was considering her with analytical abstraction.

"Do I need to do anything?"

"Shield me from the Rose, should it seem necessary? No, Champion. You I will place into a trance, while I test this theory that a long set of instructions has developed a personality. It should be quite painless."

Though she was not at all worried he'd be anything but correct, Soren was less than easy at the thought of being unconscious in Aristide Couerveur's presence. And the mocking glitter in his eyes told her he knew that perfectly well. But she needed to know more about the enchantment driving her life.

"Don't let me keep–," she began, and found herself stopping mid-sentence. Her eyes had shut, and she couldn't open them, didn't at all seem able to move, though she did not quite feel as if she were asleep. Palace-sight showed Aristide just standing there, looking intent.

Mages. They were altogether dangerous creatures to have around. As Aspen had warned, she'd not been able to sense him casting at all, hadn't realised he'd started. Aristide could probably do that any time he wanted, without even visibly trying. What if he decided to turn her into a sparrow? Would the Rose stop him?

He sat down then, gaze still fixed on her. He was probably casting something else, but she couldn't even read satisfaction in his face. He was always peculiarly expressionless when he was alone.

Soren had been watching him too much. At first out of fear and suspicion, but that had been transmuted. She had to admit there was an edge of attraction, perhaps always had been, but misplaced desire was neither new nor remarkable. Rather to her horror, Soren had started to feel *sorry* for Aristide Couerveur.

It made her impatient. He showed every sign of thoroughly enjoying the cut and thrust of Court life, was certainly a past master of the political game. Everett Rothwell knew to his cost what it meant to cross him. Aristide had recovered brilliantly from the blow of Strake's return, was now operating without the direct interference of his mother, and had an excellent chance of becoming Regent in the all too near future.

But when he was alone, he never smiled.

At the very heart of the Court, his was a startlingly arid existence. Palace-sight had yet to provide proof of anything resembling a love-life, let alone tastes as baroquely perverted as rumour would have it. Aristide slept alone, woke to reports from his servants of the latest developments of the Court, worked from breakfast to late night, then slept again. The most social thing she'd seen him do was practice swordcraft with the Captain of the Guard.

Soren was at a loss to explain why it bothered her so much. He was no friend, was potentially her worst enemy. She never really had any idea what was going on inside his head, and was always made tongue-tied by his exquisitely polite unpleasantries. The magery he commanded frightened her, far more than Strake. And she wasn't going to find him any easier to deal with, lying here watching him watch her.

Turning her attention outward she checked on her Rathen, who was still embroiled in an overlong interview with the just-arrived Cyan ambassador. The palace had been growing ever-busier as outlying barons straggled in and representatives of Darest's neighbours arrived full of pomp and curiosity. Strake had been sleeping even less, and his jaw was set in a way which suggested he was struggling with his patience.

Restlessly, Soren moved on. Here was Baron Peveric talking with the Marshall of the Army. They were cousins of some variety, and the Marshall was popular among the troops he commanded. Darest's army was less than likely to hold up against an invasion, but it would be a pivot internally, should Strake die. The Marshall was no friend of the Diamond, and Peveric's careful façade of neutrality might not hold if it came to returning the Coeurveur regency.

But there she was again, thinking about what would come after Strake's death, as if it was a foregone conclusion, as if she hadn't made a promise to herself to keep him safe. She would not let the Rose dictate the future.

Her prime suspect for wanting to rid Darest of Rathers had just been neatly removed from play, but now she had the ambassadors to factor in. Sax had already had a representative in Tor Darest when Strake returned, and over the last week they'd been completing a collection for all the western lands. Cya's had arrived last night, with an entire retinue of hangers-on, any of whom could be a mage. They were all over the palace, and Soren found it impossible to keep track of every single person they spoke to, yet felt she surely must. Sax, Cya, Ceria, Korm, Skrem and even the Jutlanders – all the western kingdoms would be mulling the disadvantages of a revitalised Darest and every single one of them would surely have suitable mages at their disposal.

Jansette Denmore seemed to be stalking Halcean, following her as she wandered through the eastern corridors of the palace. Attention sharpening, Soren watched as Halcean, oblivious to her beautiful shadow, turned down a blind corridor and stopped to lean on a balcony looking over Vostal Hill.

Palace gossip was divided on whether Jansette had been cast off by Lady Arista, or was acting on her orders. The former favourite had gone from person to person in the palace, talking, flirting, bedding more than a few. Some had given her gifts, but she'd not been taken up by a new patron. Of course, like so many others, Jansette seemed determined to eventually win the notice of the King.

Why seek out Soren's aide? To Soren's interest, Jansette was considering Halcean in a thoughtful and completely un-vapid manner. Not the fool Soren had always thought her? Then all sign of intelligence was wiped away and she said something in that bright, artless manner, enough to catch Halcean's attention. Surprised, Soren's aide turned, responding with blank courtesy.

Jansette spoke again, blue eyes bright and wide, and Soren could well imagine the guileless tone which matched that expression. Whatever she said, Halcean shook her head in response, rejecting some question or proposal. Cocking her head to one side, Jansette said something else, bringing a sharp frown to Halcean's face. She shook her head again and made to walk away, but Jansette was quick to step between her and escape, speaking again.

Aspen had said that Halcean was able to look after herself, and Soren here saw that assessment confirmed. Hand going to belt knife, her aide produced an expression which suggested Jansette was the kind of creature normally found under rocks. Jansette reached and covered her hand, holding knife in place even as she said something conciliatory. Halcean stepped back angrily, spoke a definite rejection.

With a shrug, Jansette lifted her hands and retreated. Watching her depart, Soren tried to guess what the former favourite wanted. Most likely a way to get closer to the King, but for her own advancement, or on Lady Arista's order? So many possibilities.

The scene had demonstrated to Soren that she needed to think not only about protecting her Rathen and their coming child, but anyone closely linked to them. Personal servants like Fisk and Halcean, friends like Aspen. Halcean had weathered this encounter well enough, but how well would she do with someone less negligible? One of the Barons, or a foreign ambassador? And Soren would be a fool not to acknowledge the possibility that one of them might offer something Halcean found harder to reject.

Less than happy with this vision of a future of constant suspicion, Soren turned her attention back to Strake. The interview with the Cyan ambassador had drawn to a close, and a message from one of Aristide's servants sent her Rathen to Soren's apartments.

He stopped in the doorway of Soren's receiving room, surveying the curious scene of sleeping Champion and intent Councilor, then wordlessly took a seat. Leaning back, his frown first deepened, then eased as he waited until Aristide, some minutes later, blinked, then turned his head toward him.

"Anything?" Strake asked.

Surprised, Soren tried to move, but Aristide's sleep hadn't been lifted. Still, there was no reason she wouldn't be able to hear them speaking. She was in the same room.

"Not yet. No sign of a secondary mind, and no response to probes. What did Celaury have to say for himself?"

"Beyond offering Cya's raptures at the revival of my family? Underneath the froth, it seems Cya is willing to offer its aid and support in driving back these unwarranted incursions."

Aristide's eyes glittered. "Cya would not weep to see us at war with The Deeping," he said, sounding almost approving. "I trust Your Majesty was suitably grateful?"

"For the moment." The inflection said it all – you want me to court the Fair, but I am not so eager.

Of late, nothing seemed to delight Aristide more than to be reminded that Darest's future was in Strake's hands. His smile turned up to full glitter, and he inclined his head as if to mark a point scored. Then, suspiciously mild, he turned his attention back to Soren's still form.

Strake's mouth twitched, apparently entertained by this neat reminder of the black rose. He sat watching attentively as Aristide's gaze once again turned intent and abstract. On the surface, little had changed between the two. They were all business, with occasional verbal skirmishes as they settled differences of opinion. Strake had wasted no energy distrusting his Councillor, and had fallen into the habit of treating him as an old ally, even seeming to enjoy Aristide's Court manners. But Soren's fears of them tumbling straight into bed had proven unfounded. On occasion she thought she caught admiration in Strake's eyes, but he allowed no hint on the surface. And Aristide gave away nothing at all.

Roiling at the back of her spine. It was an extraordinarily unpleasant sensation and Soren squirmed, somehow moving despite Aristide's enchantment. Strake looked at her sharply and Aristide leaned forward. The roiling increased, accompanied by a deep unease. The Rose. Whatever it was Aristide was doing now, it didn't like it. Not at all.

It wasn't afraid, at least not so overwhelmingly as it had been in the Tongue. It felt very much like something which was being poked into waking: suddenly roused, startled.

Then – anger. For a moment Soren's skull buzzed, vibrating to some blow she couldn't feel. Aristide flinched and immediately she was awake, heart thudding hard, but with that tangible sense of the Rose fading even as she straightened in her chair.

"Something?" Strake was frowning impartially at Councillor and Champion both.

"Enough." Aristide rubbed his *saecstra*-marked palm absently, one of the few unconscious movements Soren had ever seen him make. He was paler than usual. "Not a mind, not a person, not in the sense that I was looking for. More an instinct. A sense of self-preservation which shouldn't be there, which isn't linked to the Champion outside the Champion being part of the enchantment. If it is self-awareness, it's not particularly developed, but it has access to a mind, to all the resources of the enchantment."

Sapphire eyes surveyed Soren. "I had little chance to judge, before it struck away my probe, but as instincts go, this seems the most basic – survival. If it felt itself threatened, it could well warp the function of the enchantment to the degree of protecting itself rather than any particular Rathen."

"Lovely." Strake's eyes were pitch.

"At the same time, its survival is entirely linked to the Rathen line. And – it is hardly conscious. It reacted to my probes only after I had made very definite incursions. A sleeping bear."

"Can it be unmade?" Soren's tone told Aristide far more than Strake had – that she had a horror of the Rose, that she wanted it gone, found it monstrous.

"The instinct alone? Not with any ease – it came very close to killing me, just then. A flea slapped away." His mouth curled up, but his eyes were thoughtful, curious. "The entire enchantment? Of course. Stone-deep chanting founders with the destruction of its runes. But that would take with it all the protections of the borders, the palace, the entire Rathen inheritance, and the localised power backlash—" He looked at Strake, who was white-lipped, intense. "— would be difficult to contain. I can try and isolate and destroy the instinct if you wish it, but—" That mocking smile reached his eyes then, lighting them with Aristide's acid brand of amusement. "But I value my life, and would sooner keep it."

"No." Strake's voice was heavy. "Leave it."

He stood, strode out of the room with the complete lack of social niceties which was the privilege of kings. Aristide watched him go, then stood and bowed to Soren, very pointed.

"Should I discover anything else, Champion, I will keep you informed."

"Of course." Her tone had an edge of its own, and his mouth curled up, but he left without a return dart.

She watched him, watched Strake in his apartment standing staring out at the herb garden. They weren't keeping her informed. Both of them knew something, both of them. Something they'd chosen not to share, a secret between them about the Rose.

It hurt.

Eighteen

Soren was studying Aristide's face, that deceptively vulnerable mouth hidden by the curl of his fingers. Patterns swirled in the palm of his hand, always more active when he slept. It had only been after he'd left that she'd taken in one thing he'd said: the Rose had come close to killing him. She'd thought him unaffected, but he'd spent a long time staring at the ceiling before he slept.

Something her Rathen hadn't yet managed: he was still up, reading one of the histories covering the last two hundred years. This had become routine – brandy, cheese and books to take him late into the night. It was, Soren suspected, part simple enjoyment and the rest a way of coping with the sheer loss those histories represented. Reading until he was exhausted, and less likely to be haunted with dreams. But a sleep-deprived king was a dangerously short-tempered one.

At least the amount of brandy, though generous, had not grown, and she kept a careful eye on the servants' preparations, just in case the Champion's much-vaunted ability to detect poison proved false. The day had left her tired, and she'd already covered the mageglows, leaving only the warm light of the braziers. But getting to sleep before Strake was always difficult, so she sat cross-legged on her bed, combing her hair.

A key turned in a lock. Mid-stroke, Soren blinked at a robed and hooded figure, crossing through the Regent's former throne room. In moments it was in the Hall of the Crown, heading toward a door opposite the royal apartments. Palace-sight made it easy for Soren to peer up at the face beneath the hood and discover Jansette Denmore, smiling and excited as she produced another key and unlocked rooms which were once and soon would again be the Chancellor's apartments.

Soren's initial thought was that this was to be an attempt on the Treasury, but Jansette worked her way around that guarded corridor and made a circuitous route to a doubly-locked door. One of the entrances to the royal apartments, rarely used, and unguarded because its lock was enchanted to respond only to the correct key.

Which Jansette held, it seemed. Suddenly the scene between Halcean and the former favourite was explained. Jansette had been busily finding a way to get to the King of Darest.

It quickly became apparent that another thing Jansette had collected was details of the security routines. She whisked along a route which neatly avoided encountering guards or servants and finally paused in one of the bedrooms once used by the royal heirs. Here she produced and kindled a tiny mageglow and set it and a ring of keys before a mirror taller than herself.

Faintly astonished, Soren watched Jansette shed the heavy cloak with a single, fluid shrug to stand in the chilly night air wearing a diaphanous wisp of nothing. She was, as Soren had noted on too many occasions, truly exquisite. Her skin glowed, fine curls tumbled past slender shoulders, the line of her neck and back was pure perfection. She smiled at herself in the mirror, then rearranged curls over her small, high breasts so they partially concealed what the transparent cloth did not.

Torn between outrage and intense appreciation, Soren sat unmoving as Jansette donned the cloak and again shrugged it dramatically to the floor. This time she adjusted the drape of gauze around her hips, then ran her hand upward from knee to inner thigh, apparently out of sheer gratification. She trailed fingers across the soft curve of stomach, stroked her throat. Voluptuous delight. And then, again the cloak, the shrug, another tiny adjustment.

Despite herself, Soren responded to the sight. But the performance wasn't for her benefit. Jansette had gone to the royal apartments, not the Champion's rooms, and all too soon she left the cloak on and turned to the door.

Not that it would open. It would be a peculiar kind of torture to watch Jansette turn this arsenal of delight on Strake, and all too easy to stop it. No door in the palace would open against Soren's will. Jansette could sit there until the servants cleaned her out.

Or perhaps, supremely confident in her charms, Jansette would make a fuss, call out for rescue. Strake would inevitably investigate and learn that Soren had intercepted such a peerless delight. Whether he had any inclination to accept Jansette's offer would be nothing beside his reaction to such a manoeuvre. He'd made it abundantly clear how much he despised manipulation.

Soren threw her comb across the room. Impossible man! He'd hated her from the start, for no reason at all, and there were times he'd had her on the verge of apologising for being forced to bear his child. He was keeping secrets from her! Why shouldn't she stop Jansette? Why should she have to second-guess every decision she made for fear of upsetting him? It was her duty to protect him, and that meant keeping a potential assassin out of his bedroom.

Albeit the only weapons Jansette could be carrying beneath that scrap of gauze were far from fatal, and the cloak had not fallen as if weighted. The main reason Soren wanted to stop her had little to do with Strake's physical safety.

With a groan, Soren relaxed her unseen grip on the door, just as Jansette reached it and slipped out into the corridor.

"Maybe I can go back to Carn Keep," Soren muttered to herself. "Get away from all the horse-killers, and leave Lord Ill-humour to be seduced by anyone who pleases." It wasn't as if her presence was making any difference to the conduct of the Court or to Strake's safety.

Sourly unhappy, Soren watched the little scene play out. Strake glanced up as his door opened and looked purely surprised as Jansette shut the door behind her and stood with her back to it. Then the well-rehearsed shrug, and he stared in earnest as she took one step forward out of the folds of the cloak.

Snapping shut the book held in one hand, he said something. Jansette's reply, delivered with that air of ingenuous gravity, surprised him to laughter. Whatever he said then was accompanied by an extremely sardonic expression, but still he put the book down and stood up, did not sneer or snarl or send her scurrying.

Nor was he precisely encouraging as Jansette crossed the room to stand before him, but surveyed her careful display with critical attention. The Lady Denmore was equal to the challenge, however, moving with unhurried aplomb and composing herself into a very pretty picture, hair falling away from that lovely throat as she gazed up at him, head tilted ever so slightly to one side.

Strake asked a question. Jansette's attitude was demurely inviting as she replied, though it was difficult to understand how it was possible for anyone to be demure in such a flimsy excuse for clothing. By comparison Strake looked overdressed, ready for sleep in loose hose and a grandly patterned bed-robe. The Master of Apparel was slowly succeeding in his attempts to inject a little colour into the royal wardrobe.

Kittenish, Jansette arched her back, then leaned forward until she was almost resting against his chest. The ecstatic enjoyment of her approach was obviously disarming. They spoke again, an exchange which brought a glint of appreciation to Strake's long eyes. He had not stepped away, did not move as a slender white hand touched his wrist, travelled up to trace his arm beneath the robe, then slid further still to twine around the back of his neck.

Soren only just anticipated it, knew a moment before Jansette tried to pull his mouth down how her Rathen would react. It was a fatal, inevitable error. Strake threw his head back like a shying horse, then gripped Jansette by the upper arm and spun her across the room. She bounced off the door, regaining her balance to stare back at her incandescently furious king. Soren had never seen Strake angrier, and wholeheartedly applauded Jansette's quick decision to gather up her cloak and leave the way she had come. In a few moments she was back in that empty bedroom, gathering up her keys, head cocked to one side as she listened for any outcry.

Strake hadn't moved, still gripped by the memory of the Rose's assault. He looked like he was grinding his teeth, quite capable of chasing after Jansette Denmore and beating her to a pulp And then he did follow her out into the corridor, but turned left instead of right and slammed open the door which connected the royal apartments to the Champion's rooms.

In her shock, Soren actually squeaked, then hastily leaped off her bed and retied her robe so she wasn't gaping out all over the place. On the far side of her apartments, Halcean sat bolt upright in her bed, jerked out of sleep by the bang.

Soren had barely fumbled tight the sash before her bedroom door was wrenched open and Strake was somehow right in front of her, tall as a mountain, eyes black as pitch.

"What do you think you're playing at?" He snarled the words, almost spitting in his fury.

Her mouth wouldn't work, and she must have gaped like a fool, but knew better than to pretend she didn't know what he was talking about. How could she have anticipated this?

"I – it – I wasn't sure whether I should make those decisions for you," she quavered, hating herself for the too-exposed fear. "She wasn't carrying a weapon."

"Don't you know an attempt to climb to the throne when you see it?" he snapped. "The last thing I need is another manufactured heir. Another trap." Sheer loathing dripped from his voice, and he lifted his hands, quivering, then paced around her as if he had to move or hit out. "The moment I set eyes on you, I knew I should have run as far and fast as possible."

This made Soren blink. But she had known it, remembered that surge of anger as she walked into The Lost Prince. Even before the Rose had assaulted them, he'd felt this way. "Why?" It came out as a gasp.

"Look at you!" He stopped pacing, made a violent gesture toward her face, then caught himself and turned away to stare at their images in her mirror. Two white faces: one frightened, the other furious. "As if I would obediently take the treat offered me. And then when I did not–!" He was vibrating with fury, shaking.

It was immensely difficult not to move away, for she very much wanted to put some distance between them. She was painfully aware of Halcean, now out of her bed and listening hard, obviously just able to hear Strake's voice and not at all sure what was going on.

"I don't understand." She forced herself to be soft and composed, to not provoke, to try and defuse.

The expression he turned on her then well recalled his words on their arrival in Tor Darest. That he had never so wanted to punish another human being. He lifted a hand, but this time it was only to summon illusion, sparkling into the air beside them, an eerie intruder to shift a confrontation's balance.

"We were looking for a third, Vahse and I." Strake's voice had lowered to a hiss. "Our tastes were shared and we made an image of our ideal and set out to find her. I never saw anyone even close, until that inn."

It *was* close. A tall, dark-haired woman with the same oval of face and exactly the same mouth. The build, the carriage, the eyes were all familiar. It reminded Soren horribly of her sister, Rain.

"Composite of my desires," he went on. "As if I would obediently perform at the first opportunity. And you ask me 'why'? The why I can't answer is why I haven't damned the consequences of destroying the Rose and gotten rid of you both."

"Both?" Soren echoed. She was still staring at the woman Strake and Vahse had been looking for. Not her face, but her. Very much her.

"Wonderfully arranged." Strake was pacing again, each step provoking a responding clench of Soren's shoulders, anticipation of a blow. "The Rose operates through the Champion, and the Champion carries my child. If I destroy the Rose, the power backlash releases through you, and thus makes me murderer of my own heir."

"And me." Her voice was breathy now, strangled by disbelief.

"Sometimes that doesn't bother me."

He was only getting angrier, working himself up with this flood of explanation, a litany of frustration and betrayed hope. On top of her fear, Soren added a flush of embarrassment, for Halcean had crossed into the receiving room, and was hesitating in its centre, concern written over her face. Soren doubted the woman could hear exactly what was being said, but the tone, the participants, would be clear.

"I'm sorry," she said, forcing the words past the tight lump of tears. "I wish there was some way I could fix this. That I could erase what happened, or make it less awful. I...I know you have nightmares. I know that it's the Rose you want to hurt. If there was anything I could do, you know I would. Anything at all. But I can't unmake it."

Strake stared at her, black fury riding his eyes. She could feel his need to hurt her beating down, growing stronger, boiling over.

Then he said: "Take off your clothes."

"What?"

"You heard me. Something you can do."

The look in his eyes was ugly, unlike any she'd seen there before. It didn't matter that this had been a thing she wanted, that he could have had her with a gesture, a glance. Lust wasn't what was driving him. This was for revenge, to kill the nightmares and the memory of being forced on her. An outlet for overwhelming anger. She wasn't sure he would let her leave. That would be even worse.

This was the moment Soren discovered how to operate the palace defences.

They coiled down out of the ceiling, vines of milk or moonlight; mist. Thorns longer than any plant's had a right to be, leaves serrated like saws. Glass snakes, flawlessly deadly. They glowed, leaving a vicious little trail of afterimages as they dropped to frame his face. He would only have to turn his head to see them, but he was frozen now, intent on her stricken eyes. Wholly gripped by old, cold, seething anger.

It would be ridiculously easy to tear him away from her, cut him, shred him as completely as Vixen had been. Keep him distant, impotently furious. Or kill him.

"Unless you'd like me to strip you?" he said, oblivious to threat.

She held her hand across the sash of her robe – a mindless defensive gesture as she frantically searched for some way out. If she attacked him, it would completely destroy whatever fragile relationship they might salvage after this. She wasn't even sure she could avoid killing him, if she let the Rose strike. But she couldn't let him rape her.

"It's only going to make everything worse," she said, brokenly.

He recoiled, something in the words striking him more surely than any thorn. A staggered step backward, as the glowing vines lifted like startled snakes, and then he whirled and slammed his fist into the panelled wall beside her bed, producing a sickening crack. Out in the receiving room, Halcean jumped, took two hasty steps forward and stopped again while Soren gasped with the effort of holding back the vines.

Strake slid into a heap beside her bed, Halcean bit her lip, torn, and Soren pushed the Rose away, refusing murder. And, without protest, it went.

Her Rathen was panting, as if he had run all the way back to Teraman. Palace-sight showed her a face filled with revulsion, self-loathing.

"Thank you," she said, softly. For not making me kill you.

He closed his eyes, looking drained. "It wasn't for your benefit," he told her, in a tone of bitter honesty. "Of all the things I never believed myself capable."

She sat warily on the far end of the bed, and focused on the defeated sag of his shoulders, willing Halcean to stay where she was. "Do you hate me so much?"

"Not you, the Rose. You were right in saying that. But still, your face—" He rubbed a hand across his eyes, as if he was trying to erase memory. His knuckles were bleeding. "Sun, there are times I can't bear to look at your face."

Composite of his desires. Welded with nightmare. She refused to apologise for her appearance.

"Would I really die, if you destroyed the Rose?"

He sat up at that, though he didn't quite seem able to look at her. "I can't see a way to avoid it. The Rose as good as dwells inside the Champion. It's taken root in you, uses the mind it does not quite possess to perform its functions. It's little wonder this instinct feels like a person to you. And that connection means if I simply pulled down the runes, all the power of the enchantment would release through you."

"There's no way?"

"I could attempt to channel the power – or have Aristide do it – but it would still have to run through you, all the power of the Rose. Shielding you from that – it would be like trying to sew with lightning."

As he looked up at her, his expression changed a little, and he stood, made a gesture of open remorse. "I can't apologise for this," he said. "It would be so wholly inadequate. Don't—" He shook his head. "I have never been able to guarantee my temper. If I – bar your door, call for the guards. Don't ever let me do this to you again."

She watched him leave, thankfully not even noticing Halcean transfixed in the middle of the receiving room. Reaching his bedroom he poured out a tumbler of brandy and swallowed it in one choking gulp.

"Are you all right?"

Halcean, a shadow in the doorway. Soren tried to think of something, anything, she could say to explain the dreadful scene away, but could only lift her hands. "I've been worse."

"Really?" Halcean's voice was equal parts doubt and sympathy. She looked as usual full of questions, but instead crossed quickly to the bed and matter-of-factly put an arm about Soren's shoulders, leaning her like a child into her side. "I won't ask. Just let it out."

Strake, face set, poured another tumbler of brandy and swallowed it. Soren, chokingly reluctant, tried not to weep. The *saecstra* shifted beneath Aristide's skin. Jansette, practically forgotten, slipped safely out of the royal apartments. The guards patrolled, the rats raided grain sacks, the sleepless yawned or shat or fucked. In the Garden of the Rose, a tiny bud grew minutely larger.

And that was the worst of it, far out-shadowing the King drinking himself into a stupor, the dreadful scene, the whole stupid mess of it all. The reason she was Champion. Not because she could save him from the Deeping monster, or for any words of advice she might think to give. Not even for being even-tempered or intelligent. Just because she was a leggy brunette with a nice mouth and the right sized breasts. Champion Brood Mare.

Nineteen

A poison morning: flat, bleak, spoilt. Soren wallowed in it. She hated Strake for hating her, for being more temper than king. She loathed herself for not yelling back at him, for giving a damn about him. Halcean she resented for suggesting being Champion was a possibility not a life sentence and for overhearing enough to see that wasn't completely true. The rest of the world she despised impartially.

Lack of sleep was no excuse. As ever she'd woken completely refreshed, but had only watched with sour malice as Fisk discovered his king in a reeking stupor. The secretary would be damned whatever he did. Strake woken on time and half-drunk, or late with a hangover, was not either way going to be a grateful master. Fisk had eventually tip-toed away and, from the looks of it, cancelled the morning appointments. If only Soren had taken the time to bully her aide into equal restraint.

"Drink it. It'll make you feel better."

Soren gazed at the steaming mug and felt queasy. "Halcean," she began, "I appreciate what you're trying to do—"

"No you don't." Halcean grinned, completely undaunted. "You'd appreciate me going away and leaving you alone. But, really, it will make a difference."

"Should I call you mother?"

"If you want." Halcean had left without protest the previous night, after Soren had recovered her composure a little and asked to be let alone. Now she sat down opposite. "I could sleep outside your door," she said, brightly. "Make a stab at faithful hound."

"What? Ah." Soren frowned at the woman. "It won't happen again, Halcean. Leave it."

"If you say so." Clearly doubting.

Well aware she was acting as irritable as Strake, Soren was not quite able to stop. Part of the problem was she wasn't sure just how much Halcean had overheard, and the possibilities made her squirm. Forcing herself to an even tone she added: "Jansette Denmore paid a visit to the King. It annoyed him."

"Oh!" Halcean looked disconcerted, then guilty and uneasy. "I should have said – Lady Denmore was pushing me to tell her whether it was true there was a way to the King's apartments through the Champion's chambers. And if I had a key."

"I'll have to set palace security on her." Jansette seemed a petty thing, one Soren couldn't rouse herself to care about. The woman's gambit had failed, and she certainly wouldn't try it again. Soren sniffed at her mug, a hot nutmeg and milk offering, then set it down abruptly and closed her eyes, swallowing hard.

Morning sickness. Bitter bile reminder of her contribution to the grand tradition of Rathen Champions, explanation for why a woman with no particular talent for court-play, sword or magery might be declared Champion. Chosen to quickly get a child from a doomed man.

Palace-sight wouldn't let her escape confusion turning to speculation on Halcean's face.

When Soren managed to open her eyes, Halcean didn't try to hide her comprehension. "You're–? I, well, congratulations, I guess."

The ambiguous tone almost managed to make Soren laugh. "Thank you."

"When are you going to announce it?"

"Not yet." 'Not ever' probably wasn't feasible. "Not at least till we know more of Vixen's killer. I'm too easy a target."

"True. Well–" Halcean sat back, having evidently adjusted to the idea of a pregnant Champion. "So, which do you want? Boy or girl?"

"I haven't really thought about it."

"But you must have!"

"Must I? What would you want, if you found you were pregnant?"

"A way to shield myself from my mother's wrath? A boy, I think. A girl would be too much like another me. Or maybe not. Who can tell? It's–" Halcean paused, looking at Soren thoughtfully. "It's a big change. But a good one?"

"It–" Soren felt choked by her resentment, but knew it was for the Rose, not her child or even its father. "Not a bad one. Darest needs its Rathens. Temperamental maybe, but they have a history of being good rulers, of bringing fortune. This one – Aluster is a good king." She said it with an air of surprise, but knew it to be true. Strake seemed to consider kingship not only his due, but a responsibility he had to live up to. "I think he will make a good father. And I think he will revive Darest."

"We can only hope." Again ambiguity shadowed Halcean's voice, reviving memories of violent argument to stain the early morning light. The aide stood and began tidying away the breakfast plates, keeping hands busy to deflect attention from her thoughts. "Is there anything you *would* like to eat? Fruit? Dry toast?"

"Water. Just water."

Soren had caught unusual movement through the corridors. A grim-faced guard, hurrying to Captain Vereck's office, where she delivered a message which produced a disgusted grimace. Captain and messenger both headed to Fleeting Hall and separated. Dreading what this meant, Soren waited silently as Halcean answered the door.

The Captain strode in, bringing a scent of oiled leather and steel, her salute as crisp as her uniform. "Another killing," she said, with a professional detachment Soren would never be able to emulate. "Over in the Vermissa – a cart-man found in the street. I'll take a team over, see if we can take a trail this time."

Soren had known what had to be coming, but she still could not quite keep back the surge of denial. For one person, some random unfortunate, their efforts had been far too inadequate. Should they have sent out a general warning? Urged people to stay inside at night, keep in groups, bar their doors, their windows?

They hadn't been sure. Had suspected a human killer, something unrelated. Still didn't know, for certain. It could be– But she wouldn't scrabble for excuses. Strake's Deeping killer had followed him home.

"I will inform the King," Soren said, and Vereck nodded, turning to depart. Reporting to the Champion was a formality, nothing more.

"The Tzel Aviar is due to arrive today," Soren added, checking the woman's departure. "He may want to see it. And Lady Denmore has – seems to have obtained keys to the royal apartments. Get them back, then find out who gave them to her and have them dealt with."

A flicker of curiosity crossed the professional mask, then another salute and the Captain was gone.

Halcean, hovering in the doorway, was wearing an expression of immense foreboding. She smoothed it away as Soren looked up, and kept her face very still indeed when Soren said: "Get the harness for my sword."

First shrugging her surcoat over her head, Soren buckled the harness on with quiet deliberation, then slid the long shaft of metal into place. The first time she'd worn it since returning to Darest.

Last night, Soren had faced an overwhelming desire to prove herself something more than a mindless baby-maker. For a time she'd imagined herself vanquishing all conspirators, hunting down the Deeping killer, perhaps even ridding Darest of the Tongue. Then she'd spent longer telling herself that being a parent, especially to a future monarch, was hardly a minor task, and that her child deserved more than her dissatisfaction. But the words 'Champion Brood Mare' had kept forcing their way into her thoughts.

Pathetic. While she'd been busy spiralling around her own self-worth, a man had been cut open, just as Vixen had been. Just like a long-past Crown Princess, her retinue, Vahse, and very almost nearly Strake.

The cold shock of knowing a man's life had been lost, a life she would surely have been able to save if only she'd been...more, had driven something out of Soren. She was neither mage nor swordswoman, but dwelling on her inadequacies made little difference to death. If there was no way to kill the Rose without killing herself, no way to stop being the Rathen Champion, then she would do what she had seen Aristide do: face the impossibilities, accept what she had lost, and make the best of it.

Difficult as she found it, her only strength was in the Rose, in the palace. Even if Aristide outpaced her at every turn, she would still serve wherever she could, and forget the question of how well suited she was to the task. She would go talk to Strake, would watch the palace, would do what she could, no matter how little it was.

But first... Taking up a heavy cloak, she set out through the palace to the residences, and a balcony which overlooked the river mouth. Her breath puffed mist. The Vermissa was almost directly across the water, cramped elegance set close to the docks and dominated by the Harbour Master's building and Baron's Court. Beneath a pale grey sky she could glimpse movement but nothing more. The Deeping killer could be anywhere.

So intent was she, Soren almost missed seeing the Tzel Aviar fly in. A faint speck above the bay became man-shaped, very upright and travelling rapidly. Soren had only occasionally seen mages fly, since most of them considered it a lot of effort best reserved for emergencies. A kind of magical sprinting, it was quick to exhaust them, and only the most powerful, like Aristide and evidently the Tzel Aviar, would use it to travel long distances. And even they could not easily manage a great deal of baggage, let alone passengers. Like running with an armful of rocks.

Tzel Damaris wore a backpack and carried two smaller bags slung about his shoulders. Covered up against the wind, with a scarf tied across his face, he was as peculiar as he was intriguing.

She thought he saw her. The muffled face seemed to turn as he sailed past, but he continued without hesitation around the curve of the palace wall, not crossing its boundary, and vanished from her sight. Gone to knock on the front gate.

It was not very long before he was escorted inside by a guard, a trailing porter now laden with the bags and coat. Soren was faintly disappointed to discover the much-vaunted Tzel Damaris to be not half so beautiful as his reputation suggested. He was handsome, certainly, as Fair usually were, but not extraordinarily so. Soft brown hair and creamy skin, fine bones and clear grey eyes. He was not even so tall as most of the Fair, was at least an inch or three shy of

Strake's measure. Still, it was not his face they needed. What if his magical talent also came up short? What if death followed death, every one leaving no trace or sign of the killer? How long before the vulnerable, the fearful – the sensible – left? Escaped this past-born threat? It would destroy Tor Darest, all Darest.

Aristide and Captain Vereck met the Tzel Aviar just inside the main entrance. Soren watched closely, but could detect no sign that the Deeping visitor was a particular ally of Aristide's, brought in as part of some deep manoeuvre. There was an exchange of greetings, and an air of formality about the brief explanations which followed. Then the porter and guard were despatched with the luggage, and Tzel Damaris was turning back the way he came, with Captain Vereck leading the way.

And for a moment, when only Soren could see his face, Aristide's expression changed, became a stiff, tense mask completely unlike his usual self. But before Soren had more than a bare chance to mark it, the look smoothed away, that courtier's mocking smile curled one corner of his fine lips, and he followed the others out of the palace.

Surprised, Soren waited until she could see the three, now trailed by another pair of guards as they rode toward Lustring Bridge. But there were no answers to be found gazing after them.

Soren went to her Rathen.

Strake didn't stir as she walked into his bedroom. He was slumped in the chair where he usually read, brandy tumbler lying on the floor. The decanter was empty.

She touched his cheek, her ungloved fingers cold enough to spark a reaction. He twitched, turned his face away, then opened bleary eyes to look at her. After a moment, dim memory and her expression combined to rouse him, to wince and put a hand to his head as he frowned at her.

"What is it?"

"Another death. A man in the Vermissa. Vereck's investigating."

The shutter came down. A deep breath followed to temper the blow.

"The Tzel Aviar has arrived. He and Lord Aristide have gone to inspect the – the body."

"Who was it?"

"A carter. I don't know any more."

He was slow to respond, shock combining with the aftermath of the night's excess. His eyes flicked over the sword strapped to her back, the set cast of her face. Then: "Wait in the breakfast room." Eyes more closed than open, he gained his feet and stumbled out.

She went to Fisk first, told him to bring a suitably light meal, then sat watching news of the carter's death spread. Excitement, fear, dismay far outstripping that awarded a slaughtered horse. But no-one obliged by pantomiming fiendish glee or committing to paper a confession of their plots and plans. The reaction of the various ambassadors confused her at first, until she realised that they found a violent death of little account compared to the arrival of The Deeping's Warden.

Her Rathen had gone to his bathroom, emerging wet, blue-lipped and shivering-sober. By the time he reached the breakfast room, only bloodshot, black-shadowed eyes and a certain corpse-pallor betrayed the night's trials.

That night lay between them: the anger, the hate and hurt and frustrated defeat. The desire Strake so obviously did not want to feel, twisted completely beyond bearing by the Rose's violation. And by silent mutual agreement they were not going to touch it. The Rose was a burden which would not be lifted without a price they couldn't pay, and neither of them wanted to poke that wound.

Strake faced breakfast with only marginally less enthusiasm than Soren, and she let him force down a few bites before beginning.

"Do you think there's any chance this creature, though it followed us here, isn't interested in killing you? It hasn't so much as tried to enter the palace proper."

He passed a hand in front of his face as if to push the question away, but didn't deny her assumption that it was the monster out of the past. "Speculation only takes us in circles. If this Tzel Damaris proves useless, we will have to bait the thing."

Soren stared at him, then poured a glass of water just to have time to recover. "I take it you're not proposing to stake out a goat."

"I've no intention of remaining a prisoner in the palace for the remainder of my life. Or cowering in safety while half Darest is slaughtered in my place."

The words hung in the air, waiting to be denied or refuted. Soren couldn't do it, didn't know if they were true or not. The thing in the Tongue had definitely been after Strake. Could it have come to Tor Darest for any other reason than to finish what it started? Kill the last living Rathen? Her Rathen?

Who was considering parading about hoping to draw the thing into the open.

"And what if having killed you it's quite prepared to go on killing?"

"Then you will have to give up morning rides," Strake said flatly.

Soren could not let that pass, had to inject acid into her voice to hide the hurt. "No doubt watching Lord Aristide battle it out with his mother will provide me with sufficient entertainment over the years."

"You don't think he'd emerge victorious?" The sardonic tone only just held back anger. "The more I know Aristide, the better I appreciate his oath."

"He is his mother's son." Soren watched the words sink in. "Lady Arista is still Baroness of one of Darest's wealthiest baronies, and she cannot stand to see her son ascendant. I don't think I exaggerate to say he hates her, and, admire him all you like, there are many he's crossed in the past, who are loyal to her. How much damage do you think they could do, between them?"

Strake made a discomforted movement, then sat back in his chair, accepting the argument. "I can reinforce Aristide's claims at least," he said, weary oppression in his voice. "A document in your care endorsing his regency should it become necessary. Would it be to the Baroness' advantage to kill our child?"

"That would depend on whether I'd any alliance with Aristide."

"Delightful." Strake stared across the table at her. When she met his gaze squarely he seemed to nod. "If I'm killed, you're left in the fire, I know. I'll try to avoid it. It's just – I want to face this thing." He looked embarrassed, as if revenge was a weakness. "It took everything from me. In a way it has already killed me. So I want, need it to be trapped and destroyed. I want to slice its heart out and grind it into the dirt." His voice quivered, then impatient irritation returned. A cover, she realised, for too-naked emotion. "I can't say I'm brimming with confidence that this current Tzel Aviar will come any closer than his predecessor. We tried everything within invention to track it last time, and did not have a city to protect. Tell me you have some plan which will bring it down, and I'll happily sit back while you stake out a goat."

"I'd like to draw it into the palace. See what it actually is. I think I've worked out how to operate the defences."

Even to her it sounded inadequate. His response was heavily tainted with the old derision. "Draw it how? You said yourself it hasn't so much as tried the door."

"I know." Soren wanted to yell the words, to try and force into his head some sense of how powerless being Champion made her feel. She threw out a hand, conceding the point with an angry lack of grace. "No use arguing over it until we've heard what Tzel Damaris has to say."

She bent over her glass of water, sipping it deliberately as her stomach churned. Palace-sight made her watch Strake watching her, his expression ambiguous at best. Then, when she was least expecting it, he stood and reached out, took the glass out of her hands and put it down before catching hold of her wrists, inspecting them. Faint lines were still visible beneath the cuffs.

"I'm trying not to fight you," he began, baldly exposed. "I'm not deaf to sense, but I – I'm used to being angry with people, but I've no experience with this kind of...festering grudge. Last – last night, everything before it, was no sudden outburst, forgotten once it's over – the sort of thing I do know how to deal with."

He sighed, fingers tightening. "I know perfectly well that being at odds with you is base stupidity. And that I have been indulging my anger. That will change."

An apology of sorts, for his ill-manner more than last night's rages. Soren slid her hands free, remembering his description of how it had felt when the Rose took him. Drowning.

It was past time they both started to swim.

"They're back."

Sitting on the floor among a circle of chests, Strake took a moment to register the words. Then he put down the latest in a series of coronets and rose to dust himself off. Trying to kill time and fear by sorting through the Treasury had proven a messy business, despite the scourers' labours.

Soren put her effort at an inventory on top of its badly decayed predecessor. It was an amazing array, giving a glimpse at the sheer wealth of the Rathen past. "Any chance we could use something from here as the prize for the Illusionists' Duel?"

"It can't all be 'chanted to work only for Rathens."

The words were casual, but then he picked up the sword he'd selected from numerous others and once again tested the edge of the tarnished blade. Soren didn't comment, merely following as he set out at his habitual brisk pace.

When the doors to the Hall of the Crown were opened and the Tzel Aviar announced, Strake was planted on his throne as if he'd been there all morning. His expression was closed, but he watched Damaris of the Wryve, bracketed by Aristide and the Captain of the Guard, as if he were a serpent sliding across the sunset floor.

Standing to one side of the throne, Soren was forced to adjust her opinions. Tzel Damaris, as she had previously observed, was a handsome man, moderately tall for a human but smaller than most of the Fair. Brown hair, grey eyes and a fine creamy skin were pleasant, but hardly extraordinary. Yet palace-sight had not begun to convey some quality of his composition, a way of holding himself, or simply a way of being which trapped all attention. It was, Soren felt, the difference between the floor Damaris walked upon, and a true sunset. One was beautiful, the other: fathomless.

Caught up herself, Soren missed Strake's reaction. By the time Tzel Damaris halted before the throne, her Rathen was austere and thin-lipped and his words of greeting sounded grudging. He wanted, Soren thought, to simply bark "Can you kill it?" and be done.

The Tzel Aviar's response was formal and measured, his light tenor carrying no hint of warmth as he passed on a decorous message of congratulation from The Deeping's Queen. Then, as if he also had no taste for further niceties, he moved directly on to business.

"The area of the death shown to me has been distorted by a powerful force, one which has the taste of the Moon about it. This meant I could not reconstruct the death by scrying the past, and no standard tracking method is effective. Possibly this is a natural defence."

"Can it be overcome?" Strake's question trembled on the edge of an explosion. It was clear at least to Soren that he wavered on the verge of holding the Fair responsible for past and present murders.

Tzel Damaris had the steadiest gaze. Unlike Captain Vereck, obviously suppressing all expression, and Aristide with a ghost of that glitter-smile, the Fae showed no sign of tension, of pleasure, even of concern. He was a pool without ripples.

"It is unlikely we will be able to follow it by magic," he replied. "There are possibilities I will pursue."

Watching Strake, Soren thought that his jaw had locked. That he wanted nothing more than to throw something or shake the Tzel Aviar until his teeth rattled and he promised miracles. Instead, he shifted his gaze, focusing on Captain Vereck. His lips were white, and the muscles of his throat stood out. Then he said in a reedy thread of voice: "Find it for me, Tzel Damaris. The resources of Darest are at your disposal."

It was a dismissal, abrupt after such a short-lived audience, and a profound relief. The Tzel Aviar bowed, Aristide and Vereck closed around him. A gesture sent Fisk and the rest of Strake's satellites into belated retreat, until only Soren remained to watch the King control his disappointment.

Wondering what she'd do about standing stalwartly at her Rathen's side when she was heavily pregnant, Soren shifted unobtrusively from foot to foot. Strake's face had become angular, full of planes, and he stared straight ahead at nothing, cold death in his eyes.

Eventually he turned to look at her, resplendent in black and silver. "In the histories there's a great deal made of the idea of a Deeping curse."

"One of the explanations for why everyone died," Soren acknowledged, resisting an impulse to stand up straighter. At least he had his own voice back. "A lot of things in Darest are blamed on Fae curses."

"The Fair don't talk of Darest's distant past, even if you ask them — why it was left empty so long, what happened to its inhabitants." He was staring straight at her stomach, hidden as it was by her uniform. As if she and everything around him were some strange nightmare, and he couldn't credit the evidence of his eyes. "Do you believe in this curse?"

Tricky. Soren waved a hand equivocally. "I think that Darest has had more than its share of ill luck since Torluce died. It's too soon to know whether your return will change the cast of its fortunes. But before — more than Rathens died in the plague that took the majority of your family. More than Darest suffered. Some of the other major deaths happened after Queen...your aunt died, and they were ascribed to a power play among the family itself. The accidents were not inexplicable, and seemed mainly due to a Rathen tendency to fling off after things with a lack of due caution. Do I think that someone assisted the decline? It's possible. How would we prove it? If you're asking me whether I think the Tzel Aviar will be more interested in concealing some truth, or ensuring your death, than tracking down this killer — I don't have an answer for you. I find myself giving no-one the benefit of the doubt any more."

He shifted that stare out over the Hall of the Crown. "What is he doing now?"

"Listening to Aristide." Who was evidently being his most exactly polite, with the malicious glitter restrained. Tzel Damaris gave him precisely the same amount of focus as he'd awarded Strake and, though Captain Vereck had left them in the empty guest apartments, there was still no sign of conspiracy between the pair.

As she watched, the Tzel Aviar slowly turned his head, looked across the room and then up, until he was facing the very angle Soren used to observe him. His face didn't change, became neither annoyed nor interested, and after a moment he returned his attention to Aristide.

Warden of the Borders. Even among the Fair it was a role few could aspire to. The Deeping was an empire: ancient, enduring and vast. Its people were singularly gifted with magic and that power was woven through forest and farmland, stone and river. The individual charged with resolving the disputes and troubles of such a land's borders could be nothing less than a consummate mage, steeped in centuries of lore. And, with the tiniest amount of effort, he'd just pointed out to her what that meant.

Disconcerted, Soren had drawn her focus away. Now she returned it. While he was in the palace, he would be part of the parade through her head, whether she willed it or not. She assured herself that it was hardly likely that the Tzel Aviar could observe her in return.

"What do you want to do with the rest of the day?" she asked Strake. She wanted to remind him that he'd that morning promised not to take out his anger on her, or perhaps just to hold him while he so obviously bled, but was half certain he'd throw her across the room. "Go through the rest of the Treasury?"

"No." Strake rose, but only to stand unmoving, still staring across the room. "Have Vereck give you more detail on the death. About the – this carter. Find out precisely why they could find nothing."

After a pause, Soren obediently headed for the garrison. But her attention stayed on her Rathen as he stood alone in his throne room. And she was not altogether surprised when he headed out through the palace and, for the first time since their return, visited the Temple of the Moon.

Twenty

W ell past midnight and Soren watched incredulously as a cloaked figure crossed Fleeting Hall, skirting the very edge of the Garden of the Rose to avoid the attention of the guards at the opposite end of the room. Jansette. Again.

This time, using every shadow available, she flitted past the Royal Mage's apartments and paused to fit a key to the Champion's door. Fuming, Soren slid out from the warmth of her blankets, and snatched up a mageglow on the way to her receiving room. With conspiracies and killers to worry about, bed-climbers were beyond tolerance. She would not be waiting till morning to speak to the Captain of the Guard.

When Jansette slipped into the receiving room, Soren was standing in its centre, arms folded and expression leagues from welcoming.

"Can I help you, Lady Denmore?"

After a frozen moment, Jansette surprised Soren by laughing, an appreciative chuckle. "Should I clutch at my chest and cry 'Undone!'?" she asked, lowering the hood of her cloak. Her hair glimmered in the light of the mageglow, but it did not seem Soren was to be treated to the shrug and tumble, or that there was only a tantalising wisp to reveal beneath the cloak.

Soren suddenly wished she'd brought her sword. The tone of voice, the words, the dry twist to the beautiful lips, the assessing gaze all belonged to a different person to the one she'd expected. And this time Halcean was safely sleeping, not ready to rush to the rescue.

"What can I do for you?" she managed.

"I know my response here – 'It's what I can do for you, Champion.' With a sultry purr, don't you think, and perhaps a hint of lowered eyelashes?" When Soren didn't respond, busy trying not to gape, Jansette's smile widened and she moved forward so they were standing chest to chest. Light perfume tickled senses. "I'm being shockingly unprofessional," Jansette added, and laughed again, soft and full of excitement. "Don't worry, you're quite safe – assassinations were never my taste."

"You're–" The conclusion was obvious. A professional, an agent. A spy. And a consummate actress, for Soren still could not quite credit that this was the same person. "What is it you want?"

"Well–" Jansette had somehow moved forward again, her presence quite overwhelming. "Now that I'm not in the bed of someone worth my wages, and failed so miserably last night, my posting's been recalled. And there's only one thing it'll really burn me to leave Darest without doing. I don't like regrets."

Amazed at how much not being a ninny improved the former favourite, Soren moved abruptly away. "Do you have other keys the Captain of the Guard missed?" she asked, trying to erase all hint of temptation from her voice.

"Not many." Jansette's smile was challenging, but she didn't immediately press her attack. "I'll offer you a trade, Champion. Some information I'm sure you'll be interested in."

"For?"

"Do you want me to be crude?" The toss of the head was a nice mix of invitation and teasing mockery. "Nothing this past month has suggested you'd regret paying."

"You won't get anywhere trying to blackmail me," Soren said, and immediately recognised an echo of Strake in her stiff tone.

"Oh, rot." Jansette's retort was derisive, her eyes still sparkling with obvious pleasure. She was thoroughly enjoying this. "Take the poker out, Champion. Soren. Ever since you arrived in Tor Darest you've been looking at me like I was the wettest of your dreams, fatally flawed. Believe me, if circumstances allowed I'd have been quick to oblige. That sober, statuesque dignity thing you've got going – I've been wanting to test that since I first saw you. Women like you shouldn't be allowed to put on uniforms."

Somehow, Jansette had neatly closed the distance between them, and backing away again only brought Soren to a wall. "Who do you work for?" Soren snapped, trying to delay. She wasn't the least surprised when the woman just shook her head.

"Don't you want to know what I saw?" Jansette asked, leaning in so the words were a thread of sound in Soren's ear, so that breast pressed breast and thigh slid against thigh. "I'll bargain low – a kiss, that's all. One kiss and I'll tell you just the thing you want."

And, for the moment at least, Soren didn't care about bargains or spies, but the discovery that Jansette's skin was just as soft as it looked and her hair spider-silk tangling fingers as Soren clasped the nape of her neck and did as she was asked. Jansette had no intention of just one kiss, though, and her hands were everywhere. But, for all the woman's beauty, for all that her exquisite form had been the subject of fantasy, Soren found she didn't want to go where this was taking them.

It wasn't a fear of consequences, or even the thought that Strake would be hurt if he knew. It was a realisation that a spy sleeping her way to secrets, calculating and intelligent, was rather worse than a pretty fool trading on her looks. And Soren liked that woman even less.

A shaky halt, but she held Jansette back, shook her head and said in quite a firm voice: "No."

"In love with your King?" Jansette, blue eyes displeased, possessed more acuity than Soren had ever dreamed. "Who's to know?"

"I will."

"Forget that," Jansette said, shortly. She pressed forward, but Soren would not respond.

"I'm happy to let him join in," Jansette added. "Sun, I'd ride that one raw any day."

"I don't think I'd enjoy that."

Jansette drew back, frowning at the tone. "I could wear you down if I had time," she said. "But that's the one thing I can't spare."

"Leaving on the dawn tide?" Soren asked, almost normally. Her skin was flushed, breath fast, but she was glad to have said no.

"Oh, well before, Champion. I've no taste for earning myself a cloak of feathers. I must say that for the Diamond: these salutary lessons are always so memorable there's none in the Court who don't think twice in their misdeeds. At least for a while." Jansette reassembled herself, then sat primly on a chair. Her bright, assessing gaze swept the room before settling back on Soren re-tying her robe. Jansette the ninny, bed-toy of the Regent. Naïve, ingenuous and blatantly ambitious and – nothing like.

Kicking her thoughts firmly away from half-fulfilled fantasy, Soren crossed her arms as a shield. "Tell me."

With a small nod, Jansette gestured toward the eastern portion of the palace. "Some nights ago I was returning from an assignation with a very talented little man." She paused, felt in her pocket, then dropped a key on the floor. "Married, sadly enough, and pretending to be faithful. But there's a useful window, and those blockish sills dotting the New Palace are wide enough for my purposes. I was working my way around over the stable yard when I heard–"

She paused, for dramatic effect or out of uncertainty, her fine brows drawing together. Soren, who had been expecting some secret of Lady Arista's, clenched her hands into fists, desire forgotten. Vixen. Jansette had been there when Vixen was killed.

"A nightingale, I think. Or a lark of some sort. One of those birds that sing, anyway. I don't waste my energy knowing animals. The moon was high and waning, not too long past full. A scatter of clouds kept blocking and unblocking the light. It made for uncertain shadows, and then sharp ones, and though I could see the yard clearly enough, the stable was in darkness.

"The song was coming from there. Just a bird I thought, but still I stopped and waited and stared. Because it – pierced. And it was moving, coming out into the yard. And there was – nothing." Jansette lifted one hand to wind a finger through one of her tendril-curls, twisting it tight and then pulling free. "It – I'm not telling this at all well, am I? But I was frightened, and I'm not very often. Hardly ever. And this was for so little reason; a bird, a sound. No threat at all. I told myself that it's easy to mistake where noise comes from, that a little bird would be easy to miss, down there in the night. And then–"

This time she tugged the curl, jerked it and stopped herself, smoothing it into place. "The light changed, the clouds moving across the moon, so everything became less sharp, less perfectly clear. And there he was – sunlight on dust."

"What?"

"You know – when sunlight at just the right angle picks out all the dust in the air? It's there all the time, but usually you don't see it? Well, he was there all the time, standing in the middle of the yard. Whistling. He moved away, and – it was very fragmentary, the image, as if he was walking between the moonbeams. I don't think I saw all of him, all at once, but I saw enough."

She fell silent again, then shook her head and stood up. "Dark hair and dark clothes, a pale face and little more to see from that height. But his hands, Champion. They glittered like they were sheathed in glass. Like they could cut."

"Was he Fair?" Soren asked as Jansette headed toward the door.

"Who can tell? He didn't have the height. But he looked young." She shook her curls back, and lifted the hood of her cloak so that only the curve of jaw and honey-stung lips remained. "That's all I saw. Are you going to call for the guards?"

It hadn't even occurred to Soren to do so. She should. Keep Jansette in Darest, question her about the Deeping killer until there was no possibility she was keeping anything back, and then start in on such interesting questions as who she was working for and what she had told them. But Jansette had volunteered the information about Vixen. There had been nothing to stop her leaving Darest secrets intact. Stolen kisses aside, she had exposed herself to pass on news of the killer. It was not something Soren could ignore, even to know who was taking such an interest in Darest.

"You wouldn't have come here if you'd thought there was a risk," she said.

Those lips curved. "There speaks one who doesn't know me at all. But I'll take the forbearance with thanks. I think I should dislike you for refusing me. What's the good of being so virtuous you won't even take the things you want, when they throw themselves in your face? But – instead, I think I'll give you something, just for free. The Diamond Couerveur–"

"Yes?" Soren's voice was tight.

"Ask him if he's missing a knife."

"Fisk, present my compliments to Lord Aristide and the Tzel Aviar and ask them to join the King to breakfast. Have Lord Aristide arrive a little earlier."

Strake's secretary might be growing used to organising the lives of important people, but he still looked a little daunted by this order. Strake had made it abundantly clear that he did not like business brought to his breakfast table, and his mood had been anything but mellow following yesterday's disappointments.

Aristide was the only one of the three awake, staring as usual at the ceiling. She watched him receive her message and rise, unhurriedly following his morning routine until he was the shining pattern of perfection which was awarded the name of Diamond. He hadn't varied his behaviour since learning of her palace-sight, but there was something very deliberate in his manner as he dressed, as if he could not quite forget the possibility of observation. Still, little difference. It made her wonder if yesterday was the first time she'd ever seen Aristide in an unguarded moment.

Watching someone dress became embarrassing if they knew for certain you were, so she pulled her attention away when Tzel Damaris was woken. There was little to be learned from watching him, anyway. Another one for habitual masks, or did he truly feel so little about whatever task he'd been set?

She joined Strake in his breakfast room, and found him frowning at a larger than usual table, set for four.

"Have they made some progress?"

"No. Well, not that they've said. This is something else." It was a cloudless morning, and she looked out into the garden thinking of Vixen, of the carter, and all those who came before. She wondered how far Jansette had travelled during the night. And where to.

Before Strake could work all the way up to being irritable, Aristide was ushered in, his glitter-sweet smile leavened by genuine curiosity. "Is there a problem, Champion?"

"Jansette Denmore called on me last night."

Strake's reaction told Soren she'd do well to avoid being propositioned in his presence. Dark brows snapping together, he looked briefly incredulous, then studied her face very closely indeed. Soren affected not to notice.

By contrast, Aristide simply smiled, on the edge of what could well be genuine amusement. "Lady Denmore has been very diligently searching for another...patron," he said blandly.

"Did you know she was a foreign spy?"

Just the faintest narrowing of Aristide's eyes told her the answer. "You have some proof of this?"

"Only her claim."

"Jansette Denmore told you she was a spy." Rather than being annoyed, Aristide looked appreciative. "Then I must compliment you both, for I certainly had no inkling. Spying, yes, but not for one of our neighbours."

"And how is this so important it warrants a morning summons?" Strake broke in, curtly. He was still studying her face, no doubt remembering just how Jansette had chosen to visit him.

"Because she told me two things. One was to ask Lord Aristide whether he was missing a knife."

This appeared to mean little to Aristide. He touched his belt knife, obviously present. "I am not a collector, Champion," he said. "I have no—" And then he was caught by 'could it be?' and stopped, those fine, pale brows drawing together. "I do not have a knife which could be stolen," he finished.

"Trump blade?" Strake asked.

"As I said, not a knife which could be stolen." But Aristide was frowning.

"Often a proving piece for a mage leaving his apprenticeship," Strake explained to Soren. "A knife not physically present, but always there to be called upon in times of desperate need. Not an easy casting, and one which takes days to reset." He looked at Aristide, then said: "Call it."

"It is not—" Aristide stopped again, plainly not able to set himself wholly at ease. "*I* would not be able to steal a trump blade," he said, and reached with one hand, a small movement toward nothing. Light flared, and Soren distinctly made out the shape of a weapon, no larger than a belt knife, with Aristide's fingers curving around where the haft should be. Then the light went away, and so did any hint of a blade.

Aristide's fingers closed in on themselves, hiding the swirl of the *saecstra*. He looked down at it, and the exquisite line of his mouth flattened.

"I shall look for it between my ribs, then," Strake said, with a philosophical note. "I take it the thing is very identifiable?"

"It was a gift. And it would...taste of me." The mouth was still flat, his entire demeanour one of a man taking stock of altered circumstances. Then the smile came back, curving up from one corner of his mouth and then the other. Aristide did tend to enjoy irony. "Depending on how it was handled, the thing would simply scream 'Aristide' to any mage who happened upon it, between your ribs or not." He met Strake's eyes and held them. Soren, watching in more ways than one, saw his fingers rub across the *saecstra* mark again.

"I'll leave a counter to your devising, then," Strake said, and looked back to Soren. Aristide's pale lashes lowered over those star sapphire eyes, then he, too, turned his attention to Soren, full glitter revived.

"And what other gem did Lady Denmore choose to share?"

Soren held up a belaying hand, and waited as Fisk knocked on the door and the Tzel Aviar came in. She saw them all seated before explaining, and they listened without interrupting. Further questions could only be countered with Jansette's claim of having nothing more and Soren was conscious of their dissatisfaction at not being able to interrogate the woman herself. But they did not push her on the point, and sat back to consider the development.

Aristide broke the silence. "Mage assassin?"

"Something less structured," the Tzel Aviar replied, in his unhurried manner. "This reinforces the impression of a natural defence. The Deeping births strange creatures at times."

"This one wears the form of a man," Strake said. He sat very upright, staring across the table at the Tzel Aviar. He hadn't expected this kind of killer. "The garb of a man. Can we rule out the motives of men?" Or Fae. He did not say it.

Tzel Damaris merely inclined his head, making no attempt to refute Strake's imputation. "We have gained no great advantage, knowing the killer is visible, or invisible, in moonlight. And any foe which falls within Selune's demesne will not be easily defeated."

It was true. None of the men had received Soren's news with relief. They could post the description, vague as it was, but where would that get them? A few slaughtered guardsmen, most likely. And the factor of moonlight was the worst. Birth and death were the Moon's, and Soren could not keep back an image of the killer as some soft-footed avatar of the goddess, intent on avenging an insult Darest, or its Rathens, had not even realised they had made. You could not hope to win, fighting a god.

"Will any of this assist you in tracking it by magic?" Strake asked, voice tight. The need to do something sat clear and square on him. Did it make it worse, to know that his family, his lover, had been killed by man and not beast?

"Little." The Tzel Aviar was not one to soften a harsh truth. "Experimentation on a subject which is not even present, to overcome such formidable protections, may be possible. Given weeks, months."

The Deeping man didn't press his point, didn't urge or warn or do anything but wait. And Strake said: "Very well."

Then they began to plan exactly what Soren did not want. Bait to trap a killer.

Twenty-One

"I still think this is woefully inadequate."

"So you've made clear." Putting himself at risk had improved Strake's temper immeasurably. He even gave her a glimmer of a smile between scanning the horizon for glass-clawed killers.

Soren shrugged under the weight of the Champion's Sword, and took a moment to try and believe that they could just march out to Vostal Hill with a handful of crack guards and bring down the Deeping killer. No casualties, no tears, and happily ever after.

There was a possibility it might work. The thing – the man – had shown himself capable of locating the hunting party even in the depths of the Tongue, and if Strake truly was his target would surely leap at the chance to catch him outside the palace defences. The difficulty, of course, was exposing Strake just enough and no more. Too many guards and the assassin would have to be mad to make the attempt. Too few and they would be...too few. But none of Soren's carefully reasoned objections had swayed Strake's determination, and neither Aristide nor Tzel Damaris had supported her. Why was it they had to rely on two men whose motives could only be suspect?

All three claimed she was to be their trump card. Aristide had said that with a particularly curling smile, to remind them all of missing knives and phantom plots. His point was that the Rose, unlike mages, seemed perfectly able to track the location of the assassin. Not only could Damaris and Aristide observe and attempt to discover why, but Soren could point out the killer's exact location and they would see if he was as immune to crossbow bolts as magic.

And so they were walking out on Vostal Hill, ostensibly to watch the sunset. A mere half-dozen crossbowmen flanked them and a less-than-pleased Captain of the Guard was bringing up the rear.

For Autumn the day had been quite pleasant, and Soren was busy being astonished at how many birds were lurking about a treeless hill, ready to explode into the air as they approached, and shriek or chirp or carol. But none of them sounded remotely like larks, and she'd stopped jumping whenever the latest flurry of feathers launched itself into the bleeding sky.

"Why let her go, Champion?"

Eyes made dark by the failing light, Aristide had trailed the question out like a hook for a fish.

"Because I chose to," Soren replied, shortly. She was not the one to be baited this evening. "What information she had gathered she already had ample opportunity to pass on. Her employer – well, could it be someone we didn't already think was taking an interest?"

"You can put the next spy to the question," Strake said, in mock consolation.

"I shall hope for one Lady Denmore's equal."

Strake smiled again; Aristide's darts never seemed to do more than entertain him. But then he was back to raking hill and shoreline for something which could not be seen. Aristide considered his profile a moment longer, then looked past King and Champion to the quietly composed figure walking at Soren's side.

Without palace-sight, she could not continue to study their faces without it being remarked upon. It made her feel like she was trying to tie a knot one-handed. When had that barrage of images become so much a part of her? What was the Rose making her into?

The Rose was, of course, the critical factor and one Soren thought Strake was wilfully ignoring. It had shown itself less than inclined to come to his aid in the Tongue, which made relying on a warning from it dubious strategy indeed. But Strake wouldn't accept her argument when she'd raised it out of Tzel Damaris and Aristide's presence. The Rose, he said, would be warning her, not him, and that would be sufficient.

Soren could only hope the Deeping assassin didn't come.

"Belsen Cove," Strake said, stopping on the crown of the hill to point across the bay. With the sun setting at their backs, the far shore became a raft of warmth: burnished gold and yellow-green above dark blue water. "It's a little further south than immediately convenient," Strake continued. "But if you're serious about those ships, that seems the ideal location."

"We need craftsmen more than a site, Your Majesty."

"And, of course, when that clutter in the dock area is cleared out, it would be natural for the city to expand south to meet your ship-builders."

Strake had made no bones about his opinion of the city's decay, and before Vixen's death the two men had been jousting over the feasibility of simply ripping out all the crowded, shoddily built houses which had been squeezed into the docks. Replacing them would be costly, but Strake did not seem able to stop worrying at the subject. His tone was always light, but barely covered tangible discomfort.

Although he had conceded that the port was a little impaired by the constricted access, Aristide was ever ready to sprinkle salt on any attempt to place the appearance of the docks above other priorities. He produced a particularly bland expression now and said, "If we do attract shipwrights, we could direct them to making cosmetic changes about the foreshore."

"You think the skills transfer?"

"It's all working with wood. Putting it up, tearing it down."

"Don't forget the masonry." Strake nodded north-east to the heart of Tor Darest, a patchwork of sun-kissed roofs and evening shadows on yellow stone. "Has ship design changed so much that sandstone is a major component?"

"Stone ships could be made possible."

They continued in the same vein, and Soren rolled her eyes, inadvertently catching the gaze of the Tzel Aviar. The Fae listened with the same stone-dropping-into-a-well imperturbability with which he met everything else. Faint concentration, no sense of emotion. It was highly unlikely that either Strake or Aristide had forgotten the Fae's presence, but the same quality of self-containment which captured the eye made it easy to accept him as a silent part of the background.

They had started down the southern slope of the hill, the same path she had followed with Vixen. Directly ahead and curving back to their left, the beach became an uncertain glimmer in the gloom of the hill. The lights of Tor Darest were hidden by Vostal's bulk and the shipping tower at Sapphire Point was the only gleaming mote to the south-west, where the coast travelled south from Eldavar River to form the western reaches of the Bay of Diamonds. The sun was now only a memory of colour and all around them was shadow beneath a darkling sky.

"This is the best time of day."

Strake, gazing up at the lucent heavens. A few faint stars wavered at the limit of visibility and the occasional gull floated in and out of view, heading across the bay to find a perch. It had grown markedly colder and the wind was picking up, bringing the tingle of salt. Above the shush of waves, Soren could hear perfectly well the breathing of the seven who accompanied them, but so far as the Rose was concerned, no-one and nothing else stood on Vostal Hill.

The sky, she thought, was exactly the colour of Strake's eyes. Blue and black at once. "When does the moon rise?"

"An hour or more." Aristide took a step forward as he spoke, then stopped and looked back at Strake for direction.

"We wait."

"I don't intend to do it all at once," Strake said, breaking a long silence. "But I mean to have Vostal Hill made into gardens."

This was directed at Aristide, who shifted on the rock he had chosen as a seat. "Why?"

"Because I'm not so profligate as to tear down that monstrosity called the New Palace and restore the garden which was there."

A pause. "There is a certain logic to that."

"No argument?" Strake didn't affect surprise, was simply asking.

"That would depend on your schedule." Aristide allowed sand to trickle from his palm. The moon, a crescent above the sea, did not cast nearly enough light to make this visible, but between them the three mages had enchanted the vision of the entire group, so that night became, if not day, a blue-stained dusk.

Dusting his hands together, Aristide stood. "We should return to the palace. A long delay in the chill will only make us sluggish. Another sortie later at night may bear more fruit."

Soren was surprised when Strake didn't argue, simply heading down the beach over the tide-smoothed sand. Perhaps the wait was preying on his nerves.

"Both the killings here seem to have occurred after midnight," Soren offered.

"Others did not."

She was not the only one who had learned the signs of temper which would creep into her Rathen's voice. Aristide turned his assessing gaze on the set of his King's shoulders, and the Captain of the Guard increased her pace. Now was not the moment for Strake to decide he had a better chance of drawing out the killer by sending his defenders away. He had the sword from the treasury strapped to his hip, and was gripping the hilt as if charging off into the dark with it drawn was the only thing which could alleviate his disappointment

"I hesitate to suggest further investigation of the Rose," Soren said, quite honestly. "But it may be the only way we're going to find this thing."

Aristide, keeping step with her, produced a gentle smile, as if he thought her far too obvious. But Strake's hatred of the Rose was enough to divert him.

"We know its abilities from the runes," he said, looking back with a predictably irritable frown. "Our energies are better spent trying to draw the assassin out. In the short term at least."

He hadn't liked his own qualification, and increased his pace. Worried he'd pull ahead of them, Soren felt a prickle of unease, then a pitch of dismay. The Rose. It had so rarely been tangible since their return, she'd almost forgotten that weird sense of conflict. Her step faltered and, on cue, breathing.

It was the Tzel Aviar who touched her arm, questioning her without words. Soren forced herself to walk on normally, then murmured: "On the crest of the hill. Can you see anyone?"

She didn't follow his glance up, already knowing the answer. The Rose was not shrieking its fear, but it was a definite warning.

And – the breathing sounded the same. Slow, unhurried inhalations. Not a monster, but a man.

"What is its location?" the Tzel Aviar asked. The words caught Aristide's attention, but there was no fear of exposure from that source. He merely moved a step closer to hear her answer.

"Almost directly above us. A little behind now and a couple of hundred feet away. Not moving."

"But likely to if we all turned and took aim. I wouldn't care to wager on the shot." They walked on in silence as Aristide surveyed the beach. Then, when Soren's nerves were screaming for the delay, he called: "Aluster."

Use of his given name, when Aristide had remained so determinedly formal with his King, was warning enough. Strake's long stride didn't check, but his head came alertly up and, staring ahead, he said: "Where?"

"Forty feet behind and well above. I've marked the general area with a scrape in the sand."

To their credit, only one of the guards so much as glanced, and he covered it well. Soren, her heart indulging in small cartwheels, took a much-needed breath and added: "It's still not moving."

"Too many of us here," Strake said, immediately. "I'll head back. Accompany me, if you will, Tzel Damaris."

With an unexpectedly accomplished turn for acting, Strake checked as if he had discovered some loss, looked down the beach, and then strode back along the line of their footprints in the sand. "Position for the best possible shot," he said to Aristide as he passed. "Soren, signal them when it reaches that stump-shaped rock."

Assuming that it came straight down the hill toward Aristide's barely visible mark, that it moved at all, that it would fall obligingly in with his plans. Soren struggled to put the Rose's unease at a distance as the Tzel Aviar wordlessly followed Strake down the beach, with the Captain of the Guard tagging stubbornly at their heels. The guards, proving their worth, drifted in a casual cluster in their wake, surreptitiously checking their weapons, none of them looking directly at the target rock.

"Just yell," Aristide advised. frowning in concentration. He was to try and break the assassin's invisibility while the Tzel Aviar performed divinations. "Is it moving?"

"It – yes." She could not decide whether to be pleased or dismayed as the presence shifted. A step, two, down the slope. Strake was drawing closer, his head bent attentively toward the Tzel Aviar, as if they argued some point. The guards were full of sidelong glances as they spread down the beach, and Aristide left Soren to follow them a short distance behind. It would be all too obvious if not for that protective cloak of invisibility, which surely made the assassin arrogantly careless. No way for him to know she could hear his every breath.

Strake glanced up once, eloquently casual. The man who had taken so much was less than fifty feet away, no sign of excitement or fear in his even breathing. It would surely seem the perfect chance. A quick dash down the hill, a single blow, and then the empty beach stretching south. How could they stop him, after all?

"*NOW!*"

Every crossbow came up, Aristide spoke softly, Strake's sword was in his hand, and–

Dawn. A flare of light so intense the seashore was bleached beyond Summer's height, though no heat touched them. It was like ten thousand mageglows had escaped their orbs, white knives stabbing into vulnerable eyes.

Soren's attention had been on Strake, not on the stump-shaped rock central to the burst. Even so she gasped in pain and clapped hands to her face, for the moment seeing only colours. But she could still hear. And concentrating around the tumult of a Rose suddenly beyond frantic, she found the quick breath of one no longer moving at a slow and steady pace, but running along the slope of the hill, angling down toward the beach. Toward her.

For the first time she drew the Champion's Sword without catch. It sang as it slid out of the scabbard and her breath sobbed in her throat as she whipped it over her head, the muscles in her forearm straining with the effort of not simply slamming it to the ground.

He moved so quickly! No human could run like that. She barely had time from realising where he was heading to grab hilt of sword and get it between them, blinking desperately to clear her vision. And then another breath, with a shameful measure of squeak, as she stared through streaming eyes at a beach where her partners in this mislaid trap stood or stumbled, clustering toward Strake because that's who they thought was at risk. And the thing, the sound of breathing, the assassin, moon-deadly, songless killer was right in front of her.

Only Aristide turned at the noise she made, to find her standing with Kittredge's sword outstretched, point at throat height confronting a nothingness which made footprints in the sand. The assassin didn't cut her down, didn't leave her slashed and bleeding to follow Vixen, Vahse, all the others into the Moon's embrace. Just stood there.

Another ragged breath. The blunt tip of the sword shook. A length of dull metal she was completely unable to use, except that somehow it held the killer at bay. She stared past that wobbling tip at Aristide, his hands sketching the beginning of some casting, face deadly serious. The Rose had gone as still as a rabbit before a snake. Another breath.

The light didn't change. There were no clouds to cast a shadow across the waning moon. And yet, between that moment and the next, he was there. Dark hair, a pale face, her own height. Dressed in black specked with dried rust. Vixen's blood. A carter's. Perhaps, she thought with slow dread, even Vahse's blood.

Jansette had said he was young. Beyond understatement, for this was a boy. Fourteen, fifteen at most. Fae blood to be certain, with a human adult's height and that child's face. Delicate bones contoured with shadows, eyes moon silver framed by improbable lashes. A smudge of dirt on one side of his mouth. No sign of claws.

Noise, voices, gathering reaction made no impact on her as she found the strength for another breath. Her arm ached, the sword an unsteady fingernail from the killer's chin. Monster, murderer. Child.

"*Tuath*," he said, though monsters surely should not speak, let alone with such a light voice, made husky with urgency. "*Tuatha, secra del.*"

As she struggled to make some sense of this, the Rose stirred abruptly back to life, not in reaction to the words but to bring her a breath, a presence suddenly falling into existence above her Despite herself she turned her head in reaction to the coil of unease shooting through her, looked up the hill and saw the outline of a figure, almost certainly Fae from the height, drawing back a bow.

Soren didn't see the shaft released, and the boy she held at sword-point had vanished before it struck home. But she heard its meaty penetration, and the tiny noise he made before he ran.

She turned, and watched the line of footprints appear until they reached the rock and grass of the hillside.   Then there were guardsmen everywhere, three galloping past her to chase the invisible, another pair scrambling up the hill toward an archer she felt she should tell them had already gone, vanished as mysteriously as it had arrived. But she needed to stay upright.

A hand on her back came as silent support. Aristide, his spell forgotten as he shifted his attention between the doubled pursuit. He was saying something, and she forced herself to concentrate on the calm reply of the Tzel Aviar as he and Strake came up the sand.

"Your casting was clean, Lord Aristide," the Fae was saying. "That at least provided an explanation for some of our difficulty. Another natural defence, for he would have had no chance to consciously turn that spell. Revelation warped became light. Anything cast on him, I think we will find, will turn and mutate."

He stopped, looking down. The tip of her sword had grounded in the middle of a booted footprint. Scuffed, jerking aside to suggest a near-fall. "The question of his immunity to conventional weapons has also been answered."

"And who provided that?" Strake was confounded energy embodied. He looked liable to take a limb off any who came near him, black gaze raking Soren's face before fixing on Tzel Damaris. "What explanation do you have for this?"

"None." Volcanic kings were nothing to the Tzel Aviar. "Evidently you are not alone in wishing this death."

"Tzel Damaris. What does '*tuath*' mean?" There was a note in Soren's voice which demanded no prevarication. "It's what he said. *Tuatha, secra del.*"

The Tzel Aviar was not quick to answer. For the first time a ripple in the pool. Surprise. And something she could not read. Then he answered.

"*Tuath* means 'please', Champion. *Tuatha secra del.* 'Please stop me'."

Twenty-Two

Darest was two steps short of severing all ties with The Deeping. The killer was Fair, and another Fae had attempted to kill him. When Tzel Damaris had produced no answers, refused to speculate, asked for time to confer, it had only been a sudden bout of self-recrimination from Aristide which prevented Strake from damning all Deeping aid and closing the borders himself. And since Strake did not believe Aristide's assumption of responsibility for more than two sentences, King had come very close to putting himself at war with his Councillor as well.

Vengeance had not only been snatched out of Strake's hands, it had been hopelessly muddied. An assassin for an assassin, and a child to hate. He would barely speak a word to Soren after, had been curt and cutting to everyone who had to deal with him. Pent up, he'd spent hours walking back and forth in his garden, aching with the need to fly into the worst sort of rage. That made it impossible for Soren to not lie watching him, and she was heartily relieved when he finally came in from the cold and found a particularly thick book to leaf through.

But even a furious king wasn't her true problem. A boy's face. Death standing right in front of her, and the sound of an arrow going home. The tiny choked gasp which had followed.

He had said 'stop me'. That was precisely what they had come to do, but if he'd meant kill, would he have run? He was a murderer, a dozen lives weighing the scales. Wide-eyed youth did not make him less of a monster. More, in truth. She should be cursing lost opportunity, or the archer for not aiming true. And for interfering before any sort of explanation could be got out of the boy.

What difference did it make that he was young? There was no wiping away the blood already spilt, no excuse to be manufactured for risking Strake or the rest of Tor Darest because a killer could say please. Tomorrow, Strake would demand answers from the Tzel Aviar, and the hunt would continue.

If she could only close her eyes without seeing a smudged, shadowy face.

Soren finally managed to sleep despite Strake's restlessness, grateful for once that palace-sight would steal her dreams. Guards trooped through the corridors in her head, and even the most enthused of gossips gave in to the day's toll. Her Rathen returned to his pillows, but lay for hours tossing and turning.

Then he was up again, all mute frustration. Out of his room and through the connecting door to her apartment, and her palace-wrought dream suddenly felt like a nightmare as she struggled to wake before he reached her bed.

Gasping, Soren grabbed a handful of nightrobe as she was plucked from her blankets. Dreaming his approach had made waking all the more disorienting, and her heart thundered with shock and fright. He didn't say anything, just turned and carried her back to his room, dropped her on the bed and climbed across her.

"Strake—"

"Shut up. Shut up, shut up, shut up!"

There was such a note of hysteria in his voice that she choked back protest as he pulled up blankets and wrapped his arms around her ribs, tight enough to hurt. Burying his face in the back of her neck, he squeezed his eyes shut and lay still, gulping a breath. Soren was reminded of nothing so much as a child denying monsters by refusing to look at them, and she with her heart tripping over itself, wanting to turn around and beat her fists against his chest.

It was beyond everything, to be hauled about in the middle of the night and then told to shut up. She preserved her silence only so she could calm herself enough to speak without shrieking, and marshal precisely what she wanted to say. And he fell asleep. Abruptly, completely.

Frozen and indignant, Soren lay in his arms. He had – what? Felt a sudden need for her, but couldn't bring himself to accept it? Thought nothing of jolting her awake, carting her about like some...some rag-doll and shouting her down when she so much as presumed to object?

She wasn't a temperamental person, but she had her limits. If he wanted her in his bed, he didn't get to shout at her. She had excused a lot of his behaviour because she could see it wasn't normal for him. It had only been a month since he'd stumbled out of the forest. The loss of Vahse was a still-bleeding wound, and the betrayal of the Rose a goad to fury. That evening he'd put himself at risk and seen the killer for the very first time, only to have all their plans come to naught. The Tzel Aviar's behaviour had added to the frustration.

Somewhere under the grief and anger there was a person she knew she liked, was drawn to in a way which wasn't simple physical reaction. She liked his cynical edge, and the way he would stop to look at beautiful things. But she wouldn't be able to cope with much more of him like this. Returning to her own bed would be the simplest option and she thought about that, and told herself it was stupid not to want to, until sleep crept up on her as well.

Fisk tapped on the door and came in, stared for a moment, then hastily backed away. This sequence woke Soren, and she blinked, watching the secretary try to hide a grin as he closed the door. To her surprise, he didn't immediately rush to share the news, though his air of keeping a delightful secret soon had the entire royal household whispering. Off in Soren's apartment, a concerned and speculative Halcean was making a related discovery, staring at an empty bed.

Soren shifted so she could look at her Rathen's face with her own eyes. Handsome, vital, and much improved for some rest. Everyone was going to think they were lovers. And she wanted them to be, was despite everything enjoying that he was lying beside her, warm and comfortable. No clear-cut resolution had come to her overnight, but she felt a curious stillness. If he'd asked her to his bed, she'd have gone perfectly willingly. Two nights ago he'd warned her to bar her door, but he hadn't hurt her last night, or even intended to. Just battered her with his anger. It was too much, this back and forth.

Not ready to talk to him, she followed the trail of gossip as Fisk made a great show of refusing to answer questions, then was unable to resist what was obviously a broad hint. From there it was all over the palace before he could take back the words, and she watched Aspen laugh, and Aristide offer no suggestion of interest; the scourers giggled while they waited for the Seneschal, and the debate in the kitchens grew heated. The Champion in the bed of the King. A few, quicker of mind than she, went immediately to the Garden of the Rose. She kept the bud well hidden, and resigned herself to another shift in status. A second letter to her parents would be in order, though it would come too late to beat rumour.

Strake slept late, catching up on too much lost rest. It was well into the morning before he shifted and stretched, brushed a hand along the warm figure beside him, then woke fully, grimacing. She sat up.

"Can I speak now?"

He had the grace to look embarrassed. "Of course."

Soren kept her voice completely even, flat and uncompromising. "Don't do this to me again, Strake. I don't want to start flinching when you come near me."

That made *him* flinch. "That wasn't my intention. I–" He broke off and sat up, his cheeks shaded a dull red. But he was forthright enough not to try and deny a fault, shaking his head. "I can't excuse it. I just – couldn't convince myself you were still alive. Couldn't sleep, because you weren't there. The only thing for it was to go and fetch you, keep you close so I could be sure you were safe. I spent hours with that thought, rejecting it, circling around it, completely unable to move past it. By the time I gave in, I was – less than polite."

He stopped when it filtered through to him that Soren's expression had shifted closer to dismay than anger. "What is it?"

"That's the Rose." She was sure she was right, and felt a twist of pure frustration. "It does it to me. Puts things in my head, odd certainties. I didn't realise it could do it to you."

"It puts things in your head." He said it slowly, scarcely able to bring himself to repeat the words.

"Like leaving Tor Darest, after first being proclaimed Champion. I wanted to go home, didn't see the least point in staying at Court to wear a uniform and do nothing. I decided to leave less than a week after arriving. And then I didn't, and whenever I tried to think about leaving, I'd list a great many reason to go and none to stay and – nothing. This blank space, where there should be choices, action. I don't think it's tried to make me do something, though – it's always been to not do something, to do nothing."

"Blank space." That held a note of numb recognition. His reaction so far had been horror rather than anger, and he stared into the middle distance, at a future of choices made for him. Then he shifted his gaze to Soren, whose life stood between him and ridding himself of the Rose.

"I'm sorry," she said.

Surprisingly, he laughed: a queer, bitter exclamation, but still founded on a genuine note of amusement. "I'm the one meant to be apologising to you, Soren," he said. "I'm usually better able to keep my manners."

"The circumstances are rather extreme." She felt out of place, sitting on the edge of the King's bed, pregnant to him, still very much a stranger. Fully clothed, sharing an air of weary loss, they would surely disappoint any gossip's imaginings.

"What was it that stopped you?" she asked. "That night?"

He knew what she meant: the night of Jansette's attempt. "'You'll only make things worse,'" he repeated, with obvious difficulty. "Something Vahse would say. He'd cut me down with a word if I tried to do anything in a rage. Laugh me out of my temper."

There was a pause, and Soren felt awkward, not knowing what to say. Strake just looked overwhelmed, then of a sudden wry. "I should first try to earn your friendship. It's what I've been pushing hardest against." The edge in his voice was directed at himself.

"I'd like that." Strake treating her as friend instead of servant would certainly make a huge difference. But they were both of them avoiding the most obvious of questions, talking about being friends. Had they gone beyond the point where they could separate desire from bitter defeat?

She shook her head. "The Rose is a bad matchmaker, isn't it? If I could see any reason for it, I'd think it deliberately set out to see us at odds."

"It–" He glanced away and then back at her. "What it did not complicate, I hardly...helped." His long eyes were intent, searching her face. "I've given you every reason to loathe me," he said. "But you don't, do you?"

"No."

"I'm luckier than I deserve, then." Almost expressionless, he held out a hand, the gesture reminiscent of Aristide's pointed courtesy. It seemed cold, passionless, but when she touched his fingers they closed tightly about hers. Still, he looked more upset than lover-like as he pulled her forward, bending his head.

Impossible not to think of the last time they'd done this, of the fear, fury and disgust which followed. Strake's back was rigidly tense, his grip over-tight, but his kiss was careful, delicate. Soren wanted to hurry him, pull at his clothes, and struggled to let him set the pace. She would not risk sending him into retreat.

Even as she thought this, his head came up. "There isn't any blank space in your mind for this, is there?" he asked, sounding thoroughly appalled.

"No. Gods, no."

"Good."

He'd lost a little restraint to the question, his mouth covering hers more urgently, searching for response. This time she met and matched him, had him on his back so she could watch his face while she pulled off her robe, and finally saw the desire she wanted. A few moments later he had their positions reversed, and they abandoned any measure of moderation.

Strake fell into thoughtful silence after, indulging in slow caresses. There was a sense of resistance gone, and it made a great deal of difference to how she felt being with him. But his expression was more sad than satisfied, and she knew he was thinking of Vahse. Only a month dead, and a new lover as much betrayal as release. A morning tumble was only a beginning to mending the fractures between them.

"Do you like being King?"

"What?" Startled laughter in the response.

"It's what I'd ask a friend." She had liked the idea of them trying to be friends.

He took a while to answer, and thinking about it made him look oppressed. "Yes," he said, eventually. "Like every other Rathen in the past thousand ages, I have always entertained the heartfelt belief that I know the best way to everything. Being King indulges that fantasy – for all it teaches me my limits. I'm familiar with the issues, but I wasn't overmuch trained for rule, never expected to have the weight of that responsibility. And I suffer from not knowing everything that's changed, two hundred years from the Darest I understood. Most of the decisions have been Aristide's, though he makes a nice game of leading me to feed him back what he wants to do." Strake's mouth compressed. "Where is he?"

"His breakfast room."

"And the Fae?"

"Casting. Communication, I think. He's holding someone's sigil."

"Is he?" Hostility radiated through the lean body half wrapped around Soren. Then it broke, or was put away, and he sighed and pulled her closer. "They can wait an hour. Tell me about something else, something which has nothing to do with any of this. Your family, your home. I saw Carn Keep just after it was built. Talk to me about – oh, Sun, anything but that creature on the beach."

Half the morning had been lost by the time Soren returned to her bedroom. She could hear voices from her receiving room, knew perfectly well it was Halcean and Aspen. Aspen had planted himself there, no doubt hot to tease her about the morning's gossip, and

Halcean had been unsuccessfully shooing him for rather too long judging from the tone of her voice.

Soren watched them joust while she washed and dressed and thought that despite Halcean's irritable manner she was in truth enjoying the game. Then she had to laugh at herself. Soren didn't know if what she and Strake had could become love – it was such a damaged thing – but it had felt so good to be able to touch him, to talk about innocuous things, to part with a caress. If that painted everyone else with a rosy glow, then so be it.

It also made it easier to walk into her receiving room and face the first of the many who would see her now as King's lover.

"I'm devastated, Champion," Aspen said as she emerged, starting in style. "Simply shattered. I don't know how you could do this to me." He smirked at her even as he complained.

"It was oddly simple," Soren said, "since I don't recall thinking of you at all this past day."

Aspen made a show of taking a wound to the heart, then rolled his shoulders to set teasing aside and said: "Well, I'm all over envy, but I always suspected myself out of the running. Outclassed in the competition? I will, as ever, declare myself entirely eager should you want something with more variety than a simple pairing."

"You're too kind, Aspen." Soren sat down, adjusting Kittredge's sword. Still too big and tiresomely awkward, but after last night she was far more inclined to wear it. "I'll be breakfasting with the King, Halcean," she added. "No Court business till this afternoon."

Halcean made the appropriate obedient murmurs and left. She'd spent a part of the morning writing a letter to her mother, relaying the news of Soren's pregnancy, but had otherwise shown no sign of sharing that most delicious piece of gossip. And she had not at all liked it when Soren had returned from yesterday's walk pale and unwilling to talk. Feeling slighted, with Soren's secrets standing between them.

"Kindness has nothing to do with it," Aspen was saying. "I've been marked positively seer-like for having had the good sense to cultivate you before you were important. You're a boon to my reputation, Champion."

Soren shook her head, wondering how to extract him without risking another friendship. Though Aspen was hard to bruise. "Dangling about my apartment, you're not doing a great deal for mine," she replied.

"If only I could convince them of that." He grinned outright, then turned serious, glancing to the door Halcean had closed behind her. "But it's not your reputation I wanted to talk about. Do you know what's been whispered this morning?"

"Other than the obvious?"

Aspen nodded. "I know rumours, Soren. I've started them often enough, embroidered them, countered them. They have a life of their own, a way of behaving that you grow to recognise. That fribble Fisk set yours off this morning, and it's gone the usual rounds. Champion in King's bed. Wedding in Spring, baby in Summer, all the rest. They'll have you naming your grandchildren before you can blink."

"This is all very interesting, Aspen–"

But he held up his hand with enough authority to silence her. "Last night, after that very creditable explosion, I heard a whisper which was new. The meaning of the black rose has been going around these past few days, and naturally people are tying that to Princess Sethane's death near Teraman, and whatever it is stalking Dariens. Predictable and unavoidable talk because it's very probably true. I'm not so sure about last night – of a sudden there was a new twist, talk of an offence against The Deeping, or the Moon herself. That these past two hundred years Darest has failed because our delectable Aluster had not paid debt with life. And that our troubles won't be over until he has."

Soren couldn't answer that. "You said a rumour this morning."

"Quite so. Evidently, trysting with you has led our King to a falling out with the Diamond. A noted chill, when half the Court was of the firm opinion that this Spring festival they're planning will see the Diamond given a truly royal reward."

"Oh yes?" Soren merely raised her brows and looked to where Aristide sat beside a sunny window, drawing intricate patterns in one of his books. He did not do this often, but displayed considerable talent, and was quite absorbed. No sign of brooding pique.

"Oh yes." Aspen shook his head at her. "There's all sorts of talk of due justice, an insult to the Diamond. But it's not the content of the rumour, my lovely, though that has its interesting factors. It's the distribution. After last night, I made sure to pay particular attention, and sure enough, soon after Fisk had let the cat out of the bag this little item turned up. From nowhere to everywhere. It's not unnatural for people to speculate about the Diamond's love life and ambitions. Sun knows, I've contributed to that body of work. But everyone doesn't come up with the same idea within moments. It was fed to them, Soren, just as I'd wager that piece about blood price was. There's a few busy little mouths out there."

"Lord Aristide does have enemies."

"Many. And, well, the throne was as good as his. The question of whether he'd try and take it back is something even I mulled over. But though I may be the laziest creature that e'er was birthed, I do have precocious talent. I know the implications of that pretty knot of lines our Diamond has in the palm of his hand and I can feel the power of it even before he walks into a room. But that won't do him much good if King Aluster is killed, because a *saecstra's* bound to the one who takes the oath, and the Diamond wouldn't be able to prove it was genuine, after the fact."

"It's not something we haven't anticipated, Aspen. We're keeping an eye on that quarter."

He snorted. "You refer, no doubt, to the twisted schemes of Lady Arista? Please. If our less-than-beloved Lady Regent had the least intention of seeing her son as gallows-bait, it would have happened long ago. That's not her point at all."

"What is then?" Soren asked impatiently.

"To make him *fail*, of course. To put his utmost into something, just as she did, and watch it slowly sour." He gave her a pitying expression which was a too-emphatic reproduction of Aristide's sweetest smile. "Sun and Sky, Soren! The last thing Lady Arista would do is kill our delectable King, even if that left the Diamond locked away for the crime. The situation's too perfect the way it is. Aristide never able to take the throne and permanently in service to a Rathen King? I don't say that she was entirely ready to step down, but she is getting old and these past few years she's been looking about almost obviously for ways to keep the Diamond from power. If I might be so crude, I'd bet our White Lady creamed herself when she heard about that rose."

Gloating pleasure had indeed been the impression Soren had taken during her interview with the Regent. "I have a feeling I should start paying you, Aspen."

"A detailed description would go some way to settling accounts."

Soren shook her head, exasperated. "But why not just disinherit Aristide? Appoint someone else her heir? It can be done. It's not as if the Regency was dictated by the Rose."

"My darling innocent. You don't understand the game at all, do you? Why not chop off his head and spike it on a pole by the palace gate? The point isn't to be expedient."

"Do you think Aristide knows this?"

He looked at her. "I'm not even going to dignify that."

It was, in fact, almost exactly what Soren recalled Aristide telling them, with merely the emphasis shifted. He'd never claimed that his mother would try to kill Strake, had simply stated that if it came to that, blame would fall to him. He'd said her goal would be to ruin their plans.

Because it had been Jansette who had warned them about the knife, Soren had been assuming Lady Arista was plotting assassination. There were others she watched, true, but she'd kept Lady Arista at the back of her mind, pictured her pulling strings from behind the scenes. Maybe she was, but Aspen made good sense. Someone else was orchestrating an end for her Rathen.

"Who? Who's behind it?"

"Now if I knew that, I would have at least dropped a hint already. I'm calling in my favours."

"Thank you."

"Ah." He waved a hand negligently. "Fors tells me that now he's no longer Court Mage he can't 'prentice me. Told me to refer myself to the Councillor of Mages. Which is a simply delightful thought, but I didn't get very far before. Unless I improve myself in the Diamond's estimation I'll have to face some less than inspiring choices." He grimaced. "Though I can just imagine the amount of work I'd be buying into. The Diamond's such a perfectionist. Oh, and one last thing..."

"Yes?" Soren turned her attention away from Strake, who was already at his breakfast table and looking more worried than impatient. *Imagining her dead in the next room?*

"The Diamond's heard these rumours too. This morning's and last night's. Usually he'd have them countered, or at least probed. Keeping track of this sort of thing is part and parcel. But my source says he hasn't. Listened, yes. Caught at least some of the implications, almost certainly. Done nothing. Lingers over breakfast. Puts off a practice session with the Captain of the Guard."

Goes into a sunny room and draws patterns in a book. His face was perfectly composed, the expression very like that he wore when staring at the ceiling each morning. And as ever, Soren had no idea what was going on behind it.

Twenty-Three

The book was neatly face down, pen and inkwell beside it. Aristide had not risen, but gestured toward the seat opposite him before speaking. "What can I do for you, Champion?"

"The King is planning to speak to the Tzel Aviar shortly, and would appreciate you joining him," Soren said, formally passing on a message. She decided then that with Aristide it was best to be direct. "And I wanted to ask you about trump knives. You said you could not steal one. Do you know who could?"

He studied her, as ever seeming faintly amused by her questions "It would have been more correct of me to say I don't know a way to accomplish it," he said. "Or did not. I have considered the matter, and suspect that if a person knew me very well, or I had some strong link to them, there might be a way. Not easy, especially in not alerting me, but as with any kind of magic little is impossible if only you know the method. I am not entirely certain I could bring it off, which should give you some guide to the calibre of the thief. Or their luck."

"Who in Darest could?"

"There are some possibilities in the latest batch of spies, few of whom are without some casting ability." Aristide's lips curled, derisive. "Darest has not previously warranted such talent. The ambassadors, too – Celaury is well-known, and Kindraffen. Among Dariens, I would not rate more than a handful so high. Frid Calder is the strongest I've seen outside The Deeping, but directs all her focus into Shaping and has barely met me besides. Choraide, Baron Mirallon, Lessitar – all have the base ability, but I would doubt the learning and the skill. Saman Kitreggar I imagine would be possible, if only barely. But the only method I can see requires not just skill and strength, but a tangible connection to or exacting knowledge of the subject. There is of course my mother."

Mockery gleamed as he refrained from pointing out blood tie and long enmity. Soren just nodded. "Do you have any idea how long the knife's been gone?"

"I reset the casting some two months ago, and would need to do so again in another month."

"And could stealing it be accomplished from a distance?"

"Now that I doubt. You are, I collect, wondering whether they may have been visible to you?" He paused, then reached for his book and turned to an early page before handing it to her. "This is the knife. Convenient, I must admit, if you should happen to see it lying about."

Soren turned her attention to the picture, a carefully inked rendering of a thin blade covered by subtle whorling patterns. But the handle was plain, not at all unusual; hardly a weapon which would draw the eye.

Head bent over the book, Soren was very aware of Aristide's face, for she suspected it was precious to him. But the brilliant blue eyes had turned to the window, almost as if he'd lost interest. Distracted.

She had raised Aspen's concern about Aristide over breakfast, but Strake would not be drawn into trying to analyse his Councillor. The most he would say was that no matter the cause, the warped spell which had ruined their hunt would probably weigh on any mage. And shrugged acknowledgment that this was precisely the opposite of the attitude he'd taken when Aristide had claimed responsibility. Soren suspected Strake simply couldn't judge the depths of Aristide's loyalties. The Regent's son might be plotting something so complex it would side-step the *saecstra*. Or he could be ill, heart-weary, anything. It would never show on the surface.

Whatever else, she was sure news of Champion and King would hardly overset him. No surprise when he had been first to know of the Rathen heir Soren carried.

"And what do they look like? Calder and Kitreggar and the rest?"

With an air of being obliging, Aristide summoned an illusion of a tall, hearty woman with curling brown hair, and then a wispy blond man, another woman, a man she vaguely recognised, then one of the

Barons, other people who sparked vague memories, naming each. Soren filed away their images. "And–" How to ask this? "I understand your father is an accomplished mage. And not Darien." A wildly intrusive question, and she was pleased when her voice came out steady. It was about all she knew of the man, for Lady Arista had followed a practice common to mages and contracted a sire for power's sake.

Without hesitation another image appeared, a tall man with the distinctive fair skin and coppery-red hair common in Cya. There was only the faintest resemblance to Aristide, most strongly in the star sapphire eyes. Again it was no-one she recalled seeing, but he had said someone with a tangible connection, and blood was the most obvious thing to pursue.

Still, the question did not seem to have bothered Aristide. She understood why when he said, in a very patient tone: "A not unreasonable deduction, Champion, and he even had links with the Cyan Crown to hang all manner of suspicion upon. I am sure, however, that someone would have told me if he'd risen from his grave."

"I–" She could not keep back the flush.

"Some twenty years ago." Another image appeared, this time a man with darker blue eyes and a deeper red shimmer to his hair. He was tall, broad-shouldered, did not look like Aristide but was oddly familiar in the way a blood relative of someone you knew could be. Closer inspection showed the same shape around the eyes.

"My half-brother, also Cyan, and very active on that land's behalf. I've had his current location checked, but be sure to let me know if you see him lurking about the palace. And I do believe the children of my mother's aunt aspire to word-magery, if you wish to make a catalogue of every relative I can claim who owns some thread of magic."

"If you consider them a possibility," Soren replied, recovering just enough to not look mortified. It was part of her role to ask these things, and she would do it.

"Not in the least." He remained very dry. "I have not forgotten the matter, Champion. Wherever the knife is kept, it seems to be shielded, for I cannot trace it. Using it to strike against the King would see blame nicely muddied, but there is still the difficulty of the actual attack. I will admit to being obliged to the talented Lady Denmore. Knowing a particular weapon allows me to fashion some measure of counter. Not ideal or infallible protection, but a shield on the wall. There is another issue more imminent I think."

That would depend on when the thief chose to strike, but Soren merely nodded acquiescence when Aristide rose. Strake's meeting with the Tzel Aviar would be difficult enough without delays to try his temper. She would consult with her Rathen before pushing further.

Aristide had cut up at her less than she'd expected, had been quite forbearing in fact. Only a light serving of mockery and no taste of venom. What this meant she could only speculate, but she did not feel it was a good sign, an acceptance of changing circumstances. She felt instead that an edge had been taken from a knife, that he had compacted in on himself somehow. Simple preoccupation?

There was so much, when she spared the time to think about it. What had gone right for Aristide, this last month? A Rathen heir taking the throne. The humbling decision to serve rather than battle. Yesterday rattled by two shocks to a mage's esteem – first the stolen trump blade and then the warped spell. And it was obvious Lady Arista was the prime candidate for thief. How could that be anything but a blow? For, despite everything, the former Regent was Aristide's mother. She had no more attempted to kill him than he her during their years of battle. Was he uncertain whether that had changed?

Sometimes Soren wondered whether Aristide lay in bed each morning steeling himself to face the world.

Surprised by a sudden rush of sympathy, Soren decided to set her doubts aside. She had accepted Aristide as an ally, but not given him her trust, or offered him her friendship. She'd demanded far better treatment for herself, when faced with Strake's pain. Could she be so cowardly as to not hold a hand out to someone because she found them more than a little overawing?

"Lord Aristide?"

"Champion?" Halfway to the door, he looked back at her.

She stumbled over good intentions, because she could not imagine a feat of subtlety capable of opening up so opaque a diamond. Any question she asked would be rebuffed. Why would he admit to weakness, after all? She'd do better to keep quiet.

But that was just her cowardice again. If she had decided Aristide wasn't her enemy, she was damn well going to act like it, and accept the consequences. It would be a novelty for him, at least, to be treated like a person. So she asked, with blunt simplicity: "Are you all right?"

That brought the smile back at least. It bloomed to highly entertained width, his light brows lifting to add an extra leaven of incredulity. Concern became clumsy intrusion, an ignorant donkey prying into the secrets of a unicorn.

"Passing well, Champion." The words were sugar-dusted highly pointed derision. "And yourself?"

Fighting the tide of heat, Soren refused point-blank to be cowed. "Spare me courtier's arts," she said, with an edge of her own. "You haven't seemed yourself. I just wanted to – are you all right?"

He had no intention of being disarmed, offering her a wonderfully judged courtesy in return, a little illustration of grace. "Your concern charms me, Champion. What have I done to warrant it? If you must think me troubled, consider this: our whirlwind King came very close to dying last night, and the action which so exposed him, which left him blind and stumbling at exactly the wrong moment – that was mine." He touched the palm of his hand, the swirling pattern of the *saecstra*.

"I don't–"

"Don't what, Champion?" The tone had become weary, and his mouth flattened. She had finally stepped too far, and succeeded in annoying Aristide Couerveur. "Did I frown over my breakfast? Fail to keep to routine? Delighted as I am at your interest, your solicitude is misplaced."

It was a momentary flash, in hand even before the last word. He lifted his brows again, the curl of the lips this time suggesting amusement at his own loss of control. "But we must not keep our King waiting, Champion," he said, and inclined his head with every appearance of respect before turning to the door.

Ruefully, Soren followed. She had achieved what she intended, she supposed: shown that she cared about the isolation she was only beginning to see. As reward she was now perfectly clear on how very much he disliked the idea of the Champion's palace-sight. Aristide was a fortress in the centre of the Court's whirlpool, with defences so subtle-fine no-one could pierce them. He did not want nor need her clumsy good intentions.

Her Rathen was waiting in his private audience chamber, and since Soren and Aristide met the Tzel Aviar at the door there was no chance to confer about their approach. Soren hoped Strake was not going to be as icy as he looked.

But it was Aristide who took the floor, serenely himself as he bowed to his King and nodded to Tzel Damaris. "I have been considering the implications of a natural defence which warps magic," he said. "It may provide some explanation for your sudden appearance so many years out of the proper order. In the last moments of your first encounter with the Deeping killer, you said you cast. What was it?"

Strake had become intently focused while Aristide spoke. Now he shifted, putting a hand flat on the back of a chair by the room's central table. "It was scarcely formed. Pure power, shoved in one direction. I knew it was behind me, didn't think I could turn before it struck. Panicked." There was condemnation in the word, and Soren knew Strake would never forgive himself for blindly thrusting Vahse's body away.

"And this was followed by darkness, disorientation. And stories of sightings of a ghostly prince near Teraman. Your casting, barely formed as you say, must have struck the killer. And warped. And pushed you both...away."

"Produced a kind of Walk between years." Strake was staring into the past.

"It fits."

"And brought that thing with me."

Aristide answered with a small movement of one hand. "I doubt that he is immune to the castings he warps, that he is completely unaffected by magic. You spoke for instance of blood at the site of an explosion, when magical traps were set. In that, I think we also discover a reason why he has not attempted the palace."

"Which reeks of the Rose's power, the protections wound throughout. Anyone with the slightest talent can sense it." Strake was thinking rapidly. "I don't think the Rose is capable of making exclusions in its observation. If the killer entered the palace, the entire enchantment of the Rose would be warped."

Unpredictably and probably catastrophically. The examples of warping so far had mainly consisted of the spell unravelling, the caster's sudden death, or a large explosion. The appalled look Strake turned on Soren brought that thread of thought to the worst conclusion possible for a man who'd just bedded the focus of the Rose's enchantment. It was the same reason why they couldn't destroy the Rose themselves. All the Deeping killer need do – an effortless feat for an invisible man – was step inside the palace, simply touch its outer wall, and Soren would die. Small wonder the Rose had hysterics whenever the killer came near.

"But casting does work on him," she blurted, in a hasty attempt at denial. Everyone was at risk, according to this interpretation. "The Rose tracks him when he's anywhere near Strake or me. Your theory has to be wrong, or he must be able to control it somehow, or that could not happen."

"It can." Tzel Damaris, speaking at last. Not a hint of regret or apology shaded the words, no sense that he was aware how furious he'd made Darest's ruler. "The power of that enchantment is focused on Champion and those of Rathen blood. It does not act upon anybody else – a sensible precaution to prevent its detection. From the rune transcription we know that it works by making audible a particular kind of sound, with filters in place to add meaning. And it appears the killer's protective warping does not extend to his breath."

"Does that mean–" Strake broke off, frowning, his hand tightly wrapped around the top of the chair's back. "If we transmuted the air around the killer to a gas which was not in itself magical, he could not counter it?"

"Very likely."

That was news Strake had been hoping to hear. He let go of the chair at last and turned with a kind of instinctive affirmation toward Aristide, who nodded once. Something they could do. But 'very likely' wasn't a guarantee, and the beginnings of a plan of action would founder unrealised when there were so many other answers needed. Boy killers and Fae assassins. The look Strake turned on the Tzel Aviar was a full return to icy resolve. And was forestalled.

"I have been instructed to request your presence at the Court of the Fair," Tzel Damaris said.

Strake's brows came together. Soren felt her mouth sag and saw that even Aristide could not quite hide surprise. Even when The Deeping had not been drawing away from contact with humans, the Court of the Fair had been closed to outsiders. It was said that Domina Rathen had been so honoured, but it had been an extraordinarily long time since humans had been invited to the Queen's Court at the heart of The Deeping.

Strake managed not to gobble at the travel involved, and didn't waste time questioning the purpose of the meeting, simply boiling his response down to: "When?"

"Midday." The Tzel Aviar's eyes never wavered. "Vostal Hill would be an ideal venue, if it is permitted."

"Very well." Strake had shut surprise away, and inclined his head rather than question how such a thing would be possible. The entire Court of the Fair, coming to Darest in a matter of hours? Fae truly did live among the kind of magic others only encountered in legend.

Without another word, the Tzel Aviar left. Soren flicked her attention after him, out into a palace still buzzing with the morning's gossip, and stirring at new interests. She felt her face go stiff.

"I don't think I'll even speculate," Strake said. "Tell me whether you think it possible for us to track the killer as the Rose does."

But Aristide didn't answer, was studying Soren's face. "Are you all right, Champion?" he asked, but mockery was blunted by his frown.

Soren knew her expression had gone awry and corrected it, all the while wishing that these things would not come at once. And said: "I didn't know Lady Arista had returned to Tor Darest."

 Twenty-Four

Aristide hadn't known. Or, at least, his star sapphire eyes were briefly veiled, then the corners of his mouth drew up in that smile of pointed appreciation.

"I am remiss in paying my respects," he said. "If Your Majesty will excuse me?"

Strake's expression revealed faint exasperation as he watched his Councillor go. "Like a compulsion," he said. "Can't help but run to sting and dart."

Surprised, Soren turned her attention away from Lady Arista's entourage. "She has been his major opponent for – well, for his whole life. And might well be ours."

"Might be. Has been. She's not the one who set that boy on me, whatever else. And I don't see what reason you have to act like an army was at the gate, just because one of my Barons comes to the palace."

Her Rathen was feeling very uneasy, was annoyed out of concern. Soren touched his shoulder, enjoying the freedom to do so, and he gripped her hand briefly.

She told him of her conversation about possible thieves. "Would it really be as hard as he says? To take the knife?"

"Oh, yes. I've been puzzling it over and it seems to me that what you'd have to do is get into the structure of the spell's trigger and modify it so that it obeys you and not him. You could have the knife delivered into your own hand. To do that without alerting the owner is challenge enough, but to access the trigger you'd need to convince the casting that you were the one who set it up in the first place."

"You'd need to pretend to be Aristide?"

Strake's suddenly sharpened attention told Soren she hadn't kept her voice under control. "What is it?"

"I—" She pulled a face at herself. "Nothing. The rate I'm going I'll suspect the whole world. Aristide already said he wasn't capable of the casting." The look Strake gave her told Soren she couldn't leave it at that, so she went on reluctantly. "Aspen Choraide. I know he's a true-mage, and a strong one, but he's not worked at it. Aristide discounted him as a suspect."

"For all he apes the man in dress and manner, and probably knows him as well as — as anyone is able to. And you'd rather not consider him a suspect."

"It's just not the sort of thing he'd do. He's no reason for it. Besides, Aspen's more interested in you both alive, not dead."

"You know him so well?" Strake managed derision and jealousy in the same five words.

"He's a friend," Soren said, helplessly. "And—" She thought of Aspen, glorying in the games of Court, chasing pleasure, gossiping and teasing her. What did she know of him, beyond his deliberate cultivation of the Rathen Champion, and the fact that he had a finger in every pie in Tor Darest? "Aristide discounted him," she repeated, falling back on her belief in the Diamond for want of better argument.

"If you say so." Strake was hardly mollified. "It's knowledge of Aristide which is the critical factor. It's no real challenge for a mage to look like someone else — but what you'd need to do is taste like someone else. You'd need to know how a person acts, thinks, is. And—" He leaned back. "And better still if you've blood to work through. Choraide might be a possibility — if he'd hold of a piece of Aristide — but Lady Arista is the prime and probably only person I think could pull off such a theft."

And Lady Arista was now back in the palace.

"Could the Rose detect when someone's casting? If the knife was taken since your return, would it have known?"

Strake shrugged. "There's a limit to the amount of divinations Domina Rathen could practicably establish. It might be capable of knowing something magical was being cast within the palace, but it simply doesn't have the facility to pinpoint who was casting or what was being cast. I'd have a better chance, especially when you — when the Rose's focus is not a mage. If it were sigil casting, blood magic, something the Rose could visually identify–"

"How did Rathens protect against magical attack, then?"

"Rathens are mages." He said it quietly, looking toward her stomach. Tiny creases pulled at the corners of his mouth, and he went on with deliberate focus. "The palace's enchantments do make it hard to detect casting, though. Something like this theft – the modification of that trigger – I'm less than likely to have caught that. The challenge would be keeping it from Aristide, since the pocket where the knife was kept would follow him around. It would help to be close, it would help if he was asleep. If you have enough time, and enough strength, you can do a lot to hide any trace of casting." He paused. "What's Lady Arista doing?"

"The Chamberlain mustn't have known she was coming," Soren remarked. "He's hastily evicted someone and given her apartments in the residences. Aristide's just reached her and they're being polite to each other."

"Very useful."

The exchange proved a short one. "They're heading toward the Hall of the Crown now."

Strake grunted. "You'd better tell Fisk to cancel what's left of my morning. And the afternoon as well, given our midday excursion. I'll see her in here."

There was just enough time before the two Couerveurs arrived to dismay Fisk, and for it to occur to Soren to wonder whether they would be expected to host the Court of the Fair for more than a meeting on Vostal Hill. The palace was already close to capacity.

Aristide came in ahead, that faint appreciative smile playing about his lips as he said: "I believe my mother wishes to present an opposing view."

"About?" Strake said, but didn't wait for an answer, gesturing impatiently for Aristide to bring her in.

It was odd to see them standing side by side, both so pale and shining, one all in white, the other splashed sapphire and emerald. Their relationship was visible in colouring, build, the shape of their faces, the small, exquisitely shaped mouths. They shared most of all that extreme self-composure; in Lady Arista's case it became an imperiousness which was a tangible echo of thrones and power. Decades of rule.

"Please be seated," Strake said neutrally, when she stopped at the far end of the table to subject him to a highly critical survey. Aristide moved to a chair opposite, but Lady Arista remained standing, pale eyes coldly shifting to Soren then returning to Strake.

"You are being taken for a fool," she said.

"Very likely." Directness didn't trouble Strake. "I hope you have something more useful to say to me than that, Baroness."

Lady Arista inclined her head, looking perfectly equal to facing down the Sun, let alone a Rathen king. "You have invited the Tzel Aviar into Darest." She made no attempt to keep condemnation from her pale blue eyes. "The situation with The Deeping has always been caught on lack of proof. The Tongue appears an obvious encroachment, but no-one has been able to discover any form of enchantment. There has been for centuries talk of a curse, but if it exists, it is so amorphous it cannot be divined. Opinion varies wildly over whether the Rathen line was directly attacked."

"Are you leading somewhere?"

Strake's tone had chilled, but Lady Arista did not so much as flicker. Reaching into the folds of her robe, she withdrew a thick sheathe of paper and placed it on the table in front of her. "The Fae would take back Darest. Don't aid them in that."

She turned and left. It was quite five breaths after the door had shut before any of them moved. The roll of paper was more eloquent than any argument.

Face exceedingly blank, Aristide stood and collected the folded sheets. He passed them on to Strake, "No sign of enchantment," his only comment. His eyes seemed darker than usual, but he sat back down and managed to look entirely unconcerned. Strake turned the first few pages, paused, then divided the bundle into three and handed Soren and Aristide each a share. It was impossible to interpret the expression this provoked in his Councillor, but Soren thought it possibly the most diplomatic thing her Rathen had ever done.

Looking down at the top of her pile, she saw that it had been written over sixty years ago. A report to Lord Everett, Lady Arista's father, little more than an outline of suspicion gone nowhere. The failure of Shaping experiments with perfume trees was, according to the writer, related more to the delicacy of the species than any interference from outside Darest.

The next document was only ten years old, and just as unhelpful. Weather patterns had been disrupted all over Sumica. Darest had suffered most of all because it had comparatively few mages to shift the situation in its favour. There was no indication of any other factor.

It was all like that. Reports of deaths and accidents, failure and misfortune. Even the plague had been investigated, more than two centuries ago when Rathens still ruled. And there was nothing at all; just suspicion and frustration. After her initial surprise, Soren felt cheated. That shifted to a bruised kind of anger, though she wasn't sure whether at the Fair or Lady Arista.

Having exhausted his papers, Strake shuffled them neatly into a pile, face neutral. "A clever woman, your mother."

It was acknowledgement of the force of the presentation. Basing an argument on such an extensive lack of proof would have been fatal. But in the same way Aspen had powerfully brought home Lady Arista's relationship with her son, simply handing over this history of investigation had given weight to suspicion even as it repeatedly went nowhere. There was just so much.

"Has she convinced you, then?" Aristide sounded merely curious, turning over another sheet.

Strake's mouth twisted. "What need? I was already well served with doubts about the Fair. She's given me nothing I can fling in their faces."

Pragmatic restraint was perhaps not what Aristide expected from his whirlwind king. He wore a very thoughtful expression as he handed back the papers.

"And what of you?" Strake asked. "Has all this nothing shifted your views?"

"No." Fine lips curved into a curiously peaceful smile. "I have never been a great believer in coincidence."

It took a moment to register what he meant. The papers had not convinced him because he too was already converted to their argument. They both stared at him. But Strake didn't fire up, just blinked, then looked supremely sour. "So glad to have earned your trust."

Aristide inclined his head, every bit as imperious as his mother, no glimmer of irony in the gesture. He believed the Fair in some way responsible for Darest's decline, and had judged his King due that dangerous honesty.

"But why court them?" Soren asked, and was immediately made to feel the outsider as Aristide turned mocking eyes on her. He would not soon forgive her probing.

"We are in no condition to fight any kind of war, Champion," he replied, ever so courteous. "Outnumbered, outclassed on every side, dying by inches. Our neighbours are all very anxious we don't reforge alliances with the Fair, because they are in truth Darest's greatest strength, the reason none of the West has quite dared invade. With Fae help we may be able to recover, become the power we once were, while moving into direct conflict with The Deeping would only hasten Darest's end. As all this paper suggests, we have been caught in a trap, suffering from something we cannot prove. Ten thousand intangibilities. In theory Darest is protected by the former Fae Queen's edict that Dariens be left alone, but her successor has made a practice of not questioning events which seem to us so suspicious. 'Courting' the Fair, as you say, may give us the opportunity of obliging her to do so."

He looked at Strake. "Perhaps more quickly than anyone could have anticipated. The Tzel Aviar was perfectly placed to witness what can hardly be termed anything but Fae interference in Darest. The result is an unprecedented audience with their Queen. It is –" He paused. "– far more than I hoped."

It seemed Strake was not the first bitter pill Aristide had forced himself to swallow. Believing his home under attack by The Deeping, the man had not followed his mother and grandfather's route of hostility. He had sought their teaching, made overtures, then lined up his Rathen king as a demonstration. Played to win.

"Do you have an approach in mind?" There was displeasure in Strake's tone, but no boil-over of anger. Today he was, she realised, more like the person he had been before the Rose's assault. Still irritable, but far more in command.

Aristide's steady gaze acknowledged the shift, though he did not give any appearance of being relieved his king had accepted being made unwitting part of a complex stratagem. "Listen to them," he said. "This is not an opportunity we can force."

Vostal Hill at midday was bronzed by the sun and tossed by a wind carrying wood-smoke and brine but mainly chill. Autumn was shifting.

They had ascended to its flat peak in dignified silence, the Tze Aviar leading the way, Aristide, Strake and Soren following in a row, and Captain Vereck bringing up a lonely and determined rear guard.

How, Soren wondered, would the Fair come? Through a Walk, just as she and Strake had travelled? Or by one of their air-ships, a fabled piece of magnificence so long unseen no-one outside The Deeping was certain they had ever existed. She stared up into the sky, pale with a tracery of white, then down over grass curving in every direction.

The killer had been here – could it be only yesterday? Stalked her Rathen, then made an unexpected plea and paid the price of exposing himself. He might be dying even now, a problem spawning new questions even as it was solved. And he'd left her feeling hopelessly exposed, vulnerable to any Fair assassin who chose to materialise into existence. The small squad of guards waiting at the foot of the hill were ready with their crossbows, but short of decking him out in full armour, Soren could not think of a way of adequately protecting her Rathen.

Along with the guards, they had a further audience decorating several balconies of both the old and new palaces. There even seemed to be an unusual number of figures lingering along the low sandstone wall which rose above the opposite bank of the river's mouth. No-one close enough to hear or even properly see what was going on, though the arrival of the Court of the Fair would hardly be unobtrusive. She wondered if Lady Arista was one, and how many would be longing to see this encounter fail. Meeting the Fae Court was going to be the most unpopular thing Strake had done so far.

Tzel Damaris seemed to be studying the grass, which had been only lightly grazed, ankle-high in some places. The hill was, it had to be admitted, a more suitable location for a picnic or kite-flying. Would they offer the Queen of The Deeping a seat in a tussock? And a mug of something hot to off-set the wind?

"If you would wait at this spot, Your Majesty?"

Without pausing for an answer, Tzel Damaris paced slowly around them, then stopped some three feet behind, in the direction of the palace. Kneeling, he ceremoniously set down the only object he'd brought with him: a flat case of sueded leather. As meticulously as if he were performing the Service to the Sun in the grandest of temples he opened the case and folded back a velvety cloth to reveal a dozen felt-backed partitions, the largest of which held what for a moment Soren thought was Aristide's trump blade.

It was the decorations; whorling, swirling knots faintly etched. But a moment's attention showed the thing not to be a knife at all. Instead, it was a round spike of metal set like a blade. Balancing it lightly between his palms, Tzel Damaris lifted it to the height of his face, then plunged it into the ground.

Bemused, Soren shifted so her arm brushed her Rathen's and felt him stir in response, but his eyes did not waver from the Fae. From the case Tzel Damaris now selected a thumbnail-sized object, glossy brown, which he dropped into the hole he had made. A seed. The remaining partitions all contained seeds. Did the Fae plan to grow a portal?

Without a glance in their direction, he closed the case, stood and walked past them. Pacing with even stride to a point nearly thirty feet south, he knelt once again.

Imagining how this must look to those who watched from the palace, Soren checked Aristide's expression and found only absorption. Strake wore the beginnings of a wary frown, half inclined to demand explanations or order a stop.

"Well, you said you wanted a garden," Soren whispered, and succeeded in startling a smile from him. He switched his attention briefly, grazing her hand with his, enough to make her glow. Then it was back to watching the Tzel Aviar, who planted six seeds in all. After the two north and south, he moved further out and set one each north-west, north-east and so forth, to form a rectangle about the initial pair. Then he closed and sealed his case and moved into the centre of the area he had defined.

After inclining his head in recognition of Strake's patience, Tzel Damaris unhurriedly raised his eyes to the sun and said: "The Court of the Fair is called."

It was a proclamation, echoing despite his quiet tone. Strangest of all was that Soren understood it, for the words had not been spoken in Darien. There was no immediate result, but both Aristide and Strake reacted as if to a sudden, distant noise. Then the seeds grew.

The four outermost were lorams, slender trunks of black stretching up clean and clear for over thirty feet before curving inward, reaching out branches to twine into an amber-gold roof. The two planted facing each other seemed to be some kind of maple, their smooth brown bark twisting into wide, high-backed forms, garlanded with triple-lobed leaves shading from vivid red to dried rust. Living chairs. Thrones of fire and blood.

It took no more than a count of ten for Vostal Hill to assume its crown, and in that time the Court of the Fair came to Darest. Not aloft in a winged ship or stepping through a portal blazing with magic, but simply there. They dwarfed the Dariens as even the trees did not, sheer height becoming secondary to the weight of their numbers. There were surely more than could be held within the area Tzel Damaris had circumscribed. Some seemed to be occupying exactly the same spot, yet there was not the tangled intersection of form which should result.

Every one of them, Soren realised as she struggled with awe, was standing in their own pavilion of loram. Not in Darest at all, but somewhere balanced between a dozen different hills and meadows and forest glades. She could see those places, fragments of elsewhere past people who weren't really on Vostal Hill. Straight ahead she could see a city of lakes and bridges, arches and vaults of white stone dripping with foliage in every Autumn hue. Celoras, the Heart of The Deeping, fabled and forbidden. And yet, she could still see the Bay of Diamonds, the images laid on top of each other and lent an air of complete unreality by some property of the light, which had a sharp, blue-washed quality.

A tiny bell chimed, just once. Small as it was, the sound rang clarion-clear and parted the crowd like reeds in the wind, a corridor opening down the centre of the pavilion. And as the note died it brought with it awareness that it was the only sound, that the rush of Autumn breeze and distant surf and any incidental clatter from a living city had been sealed outside the loram frame as solidly as if behind stone. In this hush stood Desteret, Queen of the Fair, one hand raised to touch the wrought maple arm-rest of the other throne.

Soren had expected the Deeping Queen to be haughty, but instead she stood looking over the small group of humans with calm interest: unsmiling, but not cold. That intelligent regard was the first thing Soren took in, even before the typical Fae height, the smooth beauty of her oval face, and the long black hair, elaborately dressed. Her gown was in the eastern style, fine linen of elegant cut, the pale cream cloth embroidered with white thread in scarcely visible patterns.

The bells were in her hair, great strings of them, each no larger than the nail of Soren's smallest finger. Suspended on combs, silver ropes of them framed her face. Others were wound about the thin braids which weighted the mass of hair allowed to flow down her back, and there was a single chain about the wrist of the hand which rested on the throne.

As she folded into her best courtesy, Soren watched Strake from the corner of her eye and saw him incline his head, the greeting of one monarch to another. The Fae Queen had such a singular presence that Soren could scarcely believe it when she returned the gesture. It was like a mountain had noticed the capering of ants. Desteret Saw them.

The silver ropes, so perfectly still a moment ago, swayed but did not give tongue. Then she moved, seated herself, still without sound. It was grace underlined. Soren felt the very ground should tremble.

Strake was stiff in contrast, the suspicions stressed by Lady Arista perhaps playing in his mind, but he took the seat provided.

Rearranging themselves so that Aristide stood on one side of their throne and Soren and Vereck the other gave Soren the chance to look away from Desteret. She needed that somehow – to look away, to rest her eyes, as if she had been gazing at the sun.

Groups emerged to her eye, each clustered around some central figure just as the Dariens bracketed Strake on his blazing throne. Each of these would be a Deeping lord, owing fealty to their Queen as Strake's barons did him. Except these 'barons' held dominion over lands as large as Darest itself.

There were perhaps a dozen groups, and in some she found the chill she'd been expecting, in most a kind of tolerant attention which left Soren feeling like a stripling urged upon a stage. The Queen had half a dozen about her, including two of the small *eisel* or 'lesser folk' more common in the eastern reaches of The Deeping. Only the Tzel Aviar stood alone, and it was to him that the Fae Queen turned now, those strings of bells again swaying but not sounding.

"You have called Council, Damaris of the Wryve." Desteret's words were in the Fae language, yet again somehow comprehensible. And the air trembled with the effort of carrying them: they resonated in Soren's bones, as if that soft, measured voice carried with it the weight of the very earth. "Open the matter."

Tzel Damaris had placed the case of seeds at his feet and stood upright and alone in the very centre of the pavilion. Among his own kind he looked diminutive, but that composure was unassailable, his voice without ripple as he lifted it and said:

"A child of the People has been Shaped."

Twenty-Five

No race was more closely linked to Shaping than the Fair. Their jealously guarded fields and vast forests were populated by plants and animals found nowhere else in the world, to their immeasurable profit. On occasion they undertook specific commissions for lesser realms, and produced a crop suited to adverse conditions or an animal to combat a seemingly incurable local trouble. The best grains, whose high yields allowed all Sumica to keep famine at bay, were said to have been an ancient gift of The Deeping.

With their long lives and comely features, it was widely assumed that the Fair had practiced their skills on their own kind, with notable success. But the reaction to Tzel Damaris' statement made it clear that if this had ever been the case, it was no longer. It was as if every member of the Court of the Fair stopped mid-breath. Their eyes widened in disbelief and anger, and beneath that there was a dismay which trembled on the verge of something more.

Soren's own first moment of reaction had been an ambiguous irritation, thinking that Aristide's machinations would go nowhere if the Fair were more interested in the condition of the killer than his purpose in Darest. To see them so palpably shaken left her reliving her own scrawling horror, particularly that lonely ordeal in the Tongue. Was this boy something so dreadful even the Fair could not deal with him?

During the initial shock, the Queen had shown as much reaction as the Sun. And when the Court turned to her in a body, instinctive need not put to words but made abundantly clear, that mountain's regard had a quality which brought nothing so much to Soren's mind as an impending avalanche. When the Queen of the Fair said: "Base your claim," Soren found herself sure that if the Tzel Aviar did not, he would fall far. This was an accusation with consequences.

Tzel Damaris lifted one hand. There was no other warning before the pavilion was gone and Soren, her eyes dazzled and blurred, was seeing a beach at night. There were guards running toward her and, as the vision flickered, a brief image of Strake close by, sword in hand. Her sight flickered again – Damaris blinking, she realised – and then she was looking past the guards, beyond the figure of Aristide to a dark-haired woman in a black surcoat worked with silver and gold. She was holding a sword out at nothing and despite the distance her face was clear, an illustration of paralysed fright, the effort of taking a breath. The sword shook.

Then he was there, a figure in black blocking that of the woman. Damaris had started to move, not running but rapid strides which had him perhaps forty feet away when the woman turned her head sharply and looked up the nearby hill. The figure in black followed her gaze, and Damaris had focused on the profile of a boy, young and startled. Then a quick glance up the hill, but rocks blocked more than a glimpse of the archer. Damaris had looked back in time to catch the boy vanishing too late. Sand kicked up, and then it was the pavilion once again, that flat blue light, the many-layered view.

"There was no discernible use of reserve or trigger, no time at all for structuring force," Damaris continued, ever unwavering. "I judge his abilities to be [innate-constructed-not external]."

Soren, angrily trying to push aside the resurrection of disabling terror, had to blink at the final word, which her ear heard as *coralith*, but which compounded itself on her mind as three different things at once. The enchantment translating for them could not provide a single expression in Darien which would fully encompass its meaning.

Whatever it meant to be *coralith*, the Tzel Aviar was obviously not alone in considering it a conclusive argument. The dismay in the pavilion was tangible. Having heard all her life tales which extolled the power of the Fair, it was unnerving to realise that they were truly afraid.

Beneath her throne's crown of Autumn leaves, Desteret turned the weight of her attention to her Court. "Who has knowledge of this?"

With a transgression of such obvious magnitude, simply asking seemed as likely to win a positive response as Soren's attempt to be nice to Aristide. And yet, one group stirred.

There was a waterfall behind this cluster of people, a thin streamer bathing dark, moss-laden rocks with mist as it fell to a fern-shrouded pool. Two men and a woman were reluctantly stepping aside, as if they wanted to shield their fourth, a pale, dark-haired woman dressed in colours to echo the moss, with a single heavy silver wristlet weighting her arm. Although her face was no more lined, she was the oldest-seeming Fae Soren had ever seen. The grace of her carriage owed more to care than ease and her slender body, though very upright, spoke its frailty.

"Seldareth would speak," she said, moving to the centre of the pavilion. Her voice had a tenuous quality, woven through with threads of fatigue.

Beside Soren, Strake leaned forward. Seldareth was the name of the Deeping land directly north of Darest. The 'North' which, like 'East', had once disputed possession of Darest. And the place where Vahse had died. On the throne opposite, Desteret moved just enough to set those silver ropes silently swinging once again, granting permission.

Damaris, unselfconsciously collecting his case, moved aside and the woman, who could only be Seldareth's lord, took the central position.

"The boy is Moon-cast," she said, fragile voice apparently finding this a statement almost beyond its ability to deliver. "His purpose is laid upon him beyond the blood, but his structure has not been altered."

A thrill of disbelief ran through Soren. 'Moon-cast' meant nothing to her, but she could scarcely credit that this woman had admitted before the full Court of the Fair that she knew the identity and purpose of the killer who had attacked Princess Sethane's hunting party. It was far more than she had expected from this Council, something entirely solid and real to make firm centuries of unprovable suspicion. The Fair had known. And if they had done this, what else could be marked down to them?

Worried, she glanced at her Rathen. Hands resting on his throne's arm-rests – because they gave him something to grip – Strake seemed to be biting the inside of his cheek, his eyes boring through the woman's thin back. But he did not speak, leap up and demand answers, or even blink. As Aristide had counselled, he was listening. The Court, though still less than sanguine, had seemed to find the news mild relief. Moon-cast was apparently not so bad a thing as Shaping.

"Laramae of Seldareth's skill in drawing the Moon was unparalleled." Desteret showed no sign of shock or anger, but each word she spoke next fell with momentous clarity. "Lay clear this matter."

The woman, Seldareth, gave a tiny nod of acquiescence, then paused as if to muster her thoughts. It was impossible to see her expression while she faced Desteret, but she retained a frail dignity, her stance upright and determined. Was this their enemy?

"It is not excuse but explanation to say that in the years before her death I believe Laramae of Seldareth – she who was my mother – suffered from [fault-distortion-backlash]."

Another fractional pause. The word had been *azrhul*, and lingered unpleasantly. Her companions had lowered their eyes at it, a gesture Soren thought might be grief, or resignation.

"Her purpose in creating the boy lay in a discovery made by Acander of Seldareth little more than a century after Daseretal's Gift." Seldareth's voice firmed as she continued, as if beginning this tale had been the hardest thing. "When Daseretal laid upon the People that none should act against the human possession of Telsandar, there was great resentment. But none broke the interdiction. Acander watched closely as Telsandar became Darest. He hoped, I believe, to discover–" Minute hesitation. "– some failing in the Gift which would warrant Daseretal breaking the Covenant and expelling the humans. This he did not find. Instead, over several decades he isolated something new. The ill-will held by many of the People toward those who had been given Telsandar was a powerful thing. There was more than one who said they would rather see the Morning Reaches stand forever empty than have them trampled by the blind and unknowing. Over time, this resentment gained substance, drew power from those who would not relinquish it. What Acander found was a malison, no structured enchantment or distinguishable curse. Merely dissatisfaction taken on life."

Biting back her own increasing anger, Soren had watched Strake throughout this speech, but her Rathen remained tightly intent. It was Aristide who reacted. The smile had long been absent and now his lips parted, just a fraction. He had gone beyond pale.

"The effect of the malison," Seldareth continued evenly, "could not be considered an act against Darest. There was no choice in it, no single will driving it. It simply was. Well-pleased, Acander waited for the Darien endeavour to fail, for defeat to spread, for all but the luckiest and most stubborn to be driven out. He knew very well how this would be interpreted among the People.

"And it did not happen. Darest waxed in power, grew populous and flourished. The malison remained, but it was impotent against them. It was Laramae of Seldareth who found the reason why."

Seldareth stopped speaking again, and stood very still, then turned part of the way around, looking first at Strake and then directly at Soren. Her eyes were moss green, and for some reason struck Soren as too dark, an incongruous note she clung to against the dragging weight of Seldareth's grief. She didn't want to feel sorry for this Fae lord, who, even if she spoke like a spectator to events, had known and not told. Who had kept this secret while Darest withered like an orchid in winter.

Who looked like she'd never known a moment free of regret.

"The Covenant of the Gift was sealed by enchantment," Seldareth said, holding Soren's gaze a moment more before turning to again face her Queen. "And that enchantment maintained by every heir of the kingdom. It turned the malison aside as if it did not exist. Thus the boy."

She lifted one hand, a command to one of her companions, who turned with great reluctance and departed the pavilion. For a moment sound broke in from outside, a hush of falling water, the murmur of distant voices. Bird song. The Court simply waited, while Soren uneasily wished this was over, heard Captain Vereck shift from foot to foot, saw Strake's hands relax their hold. Aristide's colour had returned to its usual alabaster clarity.

Was this woman saying that the boy had been created to kill Rathens? That their deaths had been secondary, that it was the Rose which had been the target, all along? That it was the Rose which protected Darest from this malison.

And yet, if the boy disrupted magic as the Tzel Aviar claimed, why not simply send him straight to Tor Darest and remove the enchantment at the source? And why hadn't he attacked her?

That brief intrusion of sound came once again, and the man walked forward, carrying with him a leather-bound book, old and well-used. He paused for direction, then handed it to Tzel Damaris. Although the two men were in different pavilions, in different countries, the transfer was accomplished without any sign of difficulty.

"It was a lie, of course," Seldareth said, as if she had never paused. "Self-deception and semantics. Killing the line of Domina Rathen to weaken Darest's protections is an act against the Darien possession. Against Law. The boy was an attempt to muddy matters further, to place the act at one remove, to give it the same status as the malison. Laramae wished to create a creature whose very being was fused with death, whose purpose was put on him beyond the blood, so that no-one need command him to seek out Rathens and slay them, any more than a moth is ordered to fly to a flame. She wished for a perfect killer, caged force rather than a servant, untraceable, untouchable and impossible to hold to account.

"The enchantment took hold beyond the boy's blood: power and purpose were endowed as she had wished and showed every sign of increasing as he passed out of infancy. But he was still a child of the People, possessing will and frailties, far too easy to detect, capable of resisting the casting. And the need to kill extended far beyond the Rathen line. For Laramae's purposes, flawed in almost every way. She studied him, searching out her errors in hope of correcting them. But the Moon would not answer a second attempt, and I was born unaltered."

Bottomless silence. Of course the killer had to have parents. Being Fae made that an inescapable progression of logic. From there it was only a single step more to conclude that the most readily available child to a Fae enchantress would be her own. The boy, and this woman. Soren refused to allow her hand to creep toward her stomach.

Seldareth forged on, like a runner bound by a need which surpassed exhaustion. "He can resist the kill," she said. "As the Moon wanes he becomes more in command of himself, and if he avoids...everything, he can pass without shedding blood. Laramae – our mother had him provided with a steady stream of small animals, and – he would adopt them, go through agonies of care and live in horror of the waxing of the Moon. It is one of my earliest memories. Watching my brother weep, clutching to his chest the corpse of the latest pet he had slaughtered."

The line of her back shifted minutely, and there was another of those pauses Soren was beginning to dread. Each time, it seemed only to herald some worse revelation. This was their enemy? A boy made monster by his own mother? Another child no more than a failed experiment? How old would Seldareth have been when this happened? Twelve? Ten? Even younger? Decisions had been made for her, and she had borne the weight of them ever after. But, she too had kept this secret. It had to be remembered.

"He grew in strength far more quickly than Laramae anticipated. Barely fifteen and he was gone and my mother and his keepers lay torn beyond recognition. The bodies were not discovered for days, and before that there were other deaths. Seradonthial – he who was my Regent – called in the Tzel Aviar never realising the identity of the killer. It was only after the death of the Darien Princess Sethane that the record of Laramae's endeavour was uncovered. My brother had vanished as suddenly as he had escaped, was thought dead. Out of cowardice or shame, Seldareth kept its silence. Then came the plague. No doing of ours, but it accomplished precisely what my mother had wished. Many Rathen heirs died, the protective enchantments spent themselves trying to sustain them. The malison began to gain ascendancy, though it has yet to attain complete victory."

And Seldareth ground to a stop, standing mutely in the centre of the pavilion. There was a collective sense of a breath taken, the Court's focus shifting back to the figure of the Queen. The ropes of silver looked as if they had not moved since the Sky spat out the world.

"Who gave the order for his death?"

"I did." Seldareth lifted one hand an inch from her side, then let it fall. "It seemed best."

For a moment something touched Desteret's eyes, clouds crossing the face of the Sun. But her face remained clear and still, and her voice unhesitant as she pronounced judgment:

"Asterall of Seldareth, the People turn their face from you. You have no lands. You have no title. You have no name. Walk into the Heart and seek an end."

Soren, who had been more than eager for retribution a moment before, immediately wanted to protest. This Asterall's role had been so peripheral, more a victim herself. What of this Serandor thial, and the others who must have known? There was no balance here. But the Court's only reaction was to bow their heads in grieving acceptance. Glad, perhaps, that a suitable scapegoat had presented herself?

Without a word Asterall unfastened her wristlet, placed it on the grass at her feet and walked, head high, from the pavilion. Soren could mark the faint resemblance to the boy now, this woman's older brother. For some reason, as she walked out through the mist of the waterfall, her step was lighter than before. She looked almost happy.

Then the Queen's gaze was on Strake, and Soren could feel him turn into knots beside her. This wasn't even close to over.

"Seldareth will make compensation for the act of Laramae against your possession, and this malison will be investigated. Blood price is yours to name." The Queen was austere, but Soren imagined she heard the echo of distant thunder, felt that mountain-weight poised above them. "Aluster of Darest, the Aseratal would beg mercy for the child," she continued, each word distinct and exact. The silver bells swung, though there was no movement to disturb them. "The imperative placed on him is a [weight-aegis-must] we bear."

Every muscle in Strake's face spoke his reaction, the painful need for revenge and the affront he felt at her request. She wanted them to let the boy go, to never hold him personally accountable for Vahse's death, for any of the deaths. On Strake's far side, Soren saw

Aristide look down, pale lashes shading brilliant sapphire eyes. But that was all he did. This was Strake's moment of vengeance.

"I have a question."

The bells swayed.

Strake's voice was hoarse, as if it was an effort to speak beneath that gaze, but very much under control. "During your rule, this boy began killing. No explanation was made of the deaths. Then my family began to fail, rapidly. Then Darest followed suit. I understand the Couerveur regents requested aid during various incidents, then registered protests, made accusations. These were denied, or not answered. I would hear why."

There was a new stillness when Strake stopped speaking. Soren pictured herself at the foot of a cliff, looking up, heart thumping, because a single pebble had fallen. The Queen of the Fair was not one lightly held to account.

But she gave them their answer.

It was the Tzel Aviar who spoke, the faint movement of those silver ropes translating to direct command.

"Telsandar, now become Darest, was one of the oldest parts of the land of the People. A sacred place, which suffered a disaster which is [taboo-impolite-repugnant] to speak of. Those who dwelled there perished, and the region was held to be tainted. Seldareth and Calondae's increasing enmity was considered evidence that the taint endured. But the lands of the west – now Sax and Ceria – showed no such effect. Daseretal of the Fae formed the view that healing would only come by removing Telsandar from our influence, that only those not of the People could safely dwell there. So it was excised, given as Gift."

"A poisoned chalice," Strake said. His eyes had gone very dark.

"The experiment subsequently appeared only to have blunted the peril, and Darest declined as you have described. It was felt that if Telsandar's taint could adapt, then its current inhabitants would in time grow more and more susceptible to it. The petitions were not answered because a decision had been made to allow Darest to die."

This was beyond candour. The previous Queen had made it against Law to act against the Darien possession. This one had done precisely that, purely by doing nothing. Like standing on a beach, watching a man drown.

Strake's eyes glittered black and dangerous, but still he maintained control. "Is this...malison an expression of the older problem?"

One of the bells sounded, a flat, discordant note which somehow set a flutter loose in Soren's chest. Wrongness. Then the Queen spoke again, seven words:

"I do not know, Aluster of Darest."

Their eyes were locked: Strake fulminating, Desteret with ultimate calm. In a roundabout Fae way she had admitted error. The Fair had mistaken the effect of the malison as a symptom of something worse. And instead of warning Darest, attempting to hold back the threat, or even making a clean blow of it and breaking the Covenant, they had said nothing and waited. Allowed generations of Dariens to struggle and fail. And now they asked for a favour.

A pulse beat visibly at Strake's temple, and his hands had again found that stranglehold on the throne. Soren bit her tongue to keep from speaking, to leave him to face this himself. In truth, she didn't know what she wanted to say. Her first impulse toward sympathy had been countered by anger at Desteret's unapologetic admission. And, lingering at the back of her thoughts, the fact that a powerful Fae who was inexorably driven to kill Rathens was not the sort of person with whom they could afford to be lenient.

"I will accept blood price in his stead." The words were forced out, and Strake sat back in the throne as if immediately wanting to repudiate the concession. Soren bit her lip, sure she was happier her Rathen wasn't so expedient as to have the boy killed for the sake of prudence, certain she would rather not have to face the threat he posed. Telling herself that was so. She felt bruised, crushed between mercy and fear, and the Queen's response only made her feel angrier.

Desteret simply inclined her head. She did not look grateful, say thank you, or even appear pleased, just turned to the Tzel Aviar, his arms full of book. Done with them.

"It is laid on you, Damaris of the Wryve, to deliver the Moon-cast child."

Imperturbable as ever, Damaris bowed, and the Court shifted, as if an end had been signalled. All without a word of apology or regret. Laramae of Seldareth had schemed to kill Rathens, and her successor had kept it secret. Desteret had decided Darest was a failure and shut a door in the face of the Couerveurs seeking a solution. Her predecessor hadn't even warned Domina Rathen about this oh-so-mysterious taint lurking beneath the surface of her gift.

Strake, glancing up at Aristide, looked more than ready to be shut of the Fair. He had shown himself a King capable of placing his land above his feelings, and Soren thought he had done right, and wished it didn't feel wrong. Then came a final note from Desteret's bells.

"Who has knowledge of the forest known as the Tongue?"

This was patently unexpected, and Soren had a strong impression that among the groups one stood silently appalled. She searched and found, well before anyone stepped forward, three men and a woman who had turned to each other in wordless question. Then, his face setting to stone, one of the men walked to the centre, stopping just short of the silver wristlet left by Seldareth.

"Calondae would speak," he said, any sign of reluctance wiped from his voice. This, then, was East. He was a blond man, golden and beautiful in tunic, hose and cloak shading through azure to aquamarine. A simple circlet of silver rested on his head.

"Calondae not infrequently uses the loram trees as conductors when encouraging the growth of our orchards," the man said, voice and stance suggesting perfect ease. "Calondae has not been unaware that the effect might carry over the border into lost Telsandar."

Breath hissed through Soren's teeth, and she clenched her fists, finding in this sudden turn a hoped-for villain. 'Not unaware' indeed! When she thought of all the damage the Tongue had done–! And his tone! This man deserved the title 'The Indifference' far more than the Tzel Aviar.

The Queen's response was not even sufficient to set the ropes of bells swaying. The tiniest alteration in the contour of her lips, a fractional drop of smoky lashes. Nothing more, while Calondae remained standing with fitting formality before her. But with every moment a ponderous balance seemed to tilt, a looming potentiality which crushed upon the proud blond head. Soren could see the effort it took him to hold his position, and wondered if the only thing preventing him from dropping his gaze was the presence of that silver wristlet at his feet. Then:

"Calondae acknowledges calculated malice." His tone was exactly the same, the admission emerging as forthright statement. "Recompense is offered."

Desteret's relentless gaze shifted to the throne opposite. To Soren's shock, Strake simply nodded, his mouth twisted with sour disgust.

"Go then, Calondae," the Queen said. "Know that your voice has diminished in this Council."

Calondae bowed, and returned to his small group, which then left the pavilion into a grove of Autumn trees. He never once so much as glanced at Strake.

Soren found herself aching to throw things, to jump up and down and shriek and completely shatter this measured progression of question and decision. Why was this man, who had been far more actively working against Darest, let off so lightly? Asterall of Seldareth's crime had been one of silence, while Calondae had been deliberately destroying the lives of Dariens, had broken their spirits and driven them from their homes. Calculated malice. How could payment and some slight loss of status possibly balance that? She wanted at the very least to see him crawl.

It was all too inadequate, revelation becoming an anti-climax where the Fair dictated the terms and retribution was lost in a morass of formality. But her Rathen showed no sign of firing up at the vagaries of Fae justice, and the cool voice of reason was already throwing water on Soren's temper. They had what they had wanted – admissions and solutions, two centuries of failure explained. The compensation would surely be of immeasurable value to Darest, and there was no point going to war over a lingering sense of injury, even if it were possible to win. Shouting about the perceived shortcomings of the Fae Council would achieve nothing at all.

This, Soren reflected, must be something like how Aristide had felt, when he had given Strake his oath.

The Queen was studying each of their faces in turn, and Soren found her knees suddenly inadequate, her breath short, and was greatly relieved when the Fae's gaze moved on. Strake was pale, but Aristide looked as if he had just recalled some particularly fine joke, and he did not quaver.

Desteret lifted one hand. "This Council has ended."

Twenty-Six

Wind punched over them with force enough to make the lorams roar, sending golden leaves tumbling toward the ocean. The shielding blue light had gone and taken the Fair with it, leaving a day grown grey with the threat of rain.

Soren turned sharply about, the Rose bringing her the breath of too many observers at once, but no-one was close. A clot of several dozen at the foot of the hill and throngs at every balcony and window of the palace. More lined the foreshore across the mouth of the river, but they were apparently too far to be detected by the enchantment. All of them staring up at the pavilion of trees, its two thrones, and the five who remained within.

The Tzel Aviar moved first, walking forward to collect the wristlet Seldareth had set on the grass, which had failed to vanish. He stowed it in an inner pocket before turning his composed gaze on Strake.

"With your permission, Majesty, I will study Laramae's notes and report my findings to you."

Strake's response, a nod as minimal as the Queen's, made clear how out of charity he remained with any Fae. Tzel Damaris simply inclined his head in return, then bowed more formally and walked away, heading unhurriedly toward the palace.

"Issue an order that if anyone stumbles across the boy, they should keep their distance," Strake said to Captain Vereck, his curt tone not inviting argument. "We'll leave it to the Fair to 'deliver' their own."

Reluctantly accepting the clear invitation to make herself scarce, Vereck also bowed and followed the Tzel Aviar down the hill.

"How did the enchantment on the Tongue work?" Soren asked, as they watched Vereck go. "Why wasn't it detectable?"

"Transmission," Strake replied. "He couldn't have meant anything else."

They both looked to Aristide for confirmation, and he nodded agreement. "Only a formidable casting could have produced something as extensive the Tongue," he said. "A blanket enchantment – something periodically sweeping the entire area or even permanently established – would have been blazingly apparent to anyone in the region. Most investigation focused on discovering the kind of things which radiate power in a defined area – rune stones and so forth. Anything present in the forest which could be proven to be emitting an encouragement to growth. Even squads of Fae mages. But nothing was ever turned up, so less obvious solutions were tested. Transmission was one of them – that is, using something which is not enchanted in itself but is capable of channelling magic, much like pipes direct water. The flow can be sent great distances without overmuch effort, and is a mouse to the blanket enchantment's bull. The casting could be periodic, and thus unlikely to be detected unless a suitably sensitive mage was on site at the right moment. But there are few substances capable of acting as transmitters. Rare crystal, the bone of a certain creature – scarce enough that it did not seem a likely solution, especially when none could be found in the area. If the loram can be used for such a purpose, it is a secret the Fair have kept well."

Strake stared up at the arch of black and gold above them. "Would Desteret have asked about the Tongue if I had not spared the boy?"

"Very likely not."

Another gust stripped leaves from the thrones and brought a spatter of premature raindrops. Strake switched his gaze to the choppy waves and fell silent, mouth a flat, harsh line. Soren wanted to ask precisely what 'Moon-cast' was, but kept it for later. This was a moment for celebration, really, if only they could bring themselves to enjoy it. If her Rathen could accept his own decision to place Darest above avenging Vahse.

Usually smooth hair bedevilled and disordered, Aristide stood with an air of infinite patience contemplating the pavilion. No hint of strain lingered, whatever his opinion of the revelations of the Council. Would apologies matter to Aristide, or did he consider this an unqualified success? Compensation and an identifiable target in the malison, even a favour to weigh the scale in future dealings with

The Deeping. If he too felt sourly cheated, he was not going to show it.

After the pavilion had exhausted his interest, he switched his gaze to Strake and said: "If Your Majesty is planning to brood up here all afternoon, I'll take leave to go deal with the business of the Court."

The tone had been one of perfect courtesy, the words provoked brows-together surprise from his King. Then an outright scowl. "I loathe being managed."

"That was a little obvious," Aristide conceded, unperturbed. "Perhaps if I'd solicitously asked your Champion if she wished a heavier cloak fetched?"

Strake shot a searching glance at Soren, who contrived to appear perfectly warm in her layers of uniform and cloak. He let out a little tuh of breath, then looked annoyed again because Aristide had succeeding in distracting him. Eyeing the wonderfully bland expression his Councillor had assumed, he shook his head. "Provoking me will only take you so far." But the frown had lifted.

"I'll keep that in mind, Your Majesty," Aristide murmured. "Shall we go down?"

"My friends call me Strake." Strake said, not moving.

The faint smile did not falter, and if Aristide's eyes narrowed, the fine blond hair being whipped about his face could be blamed. "The rib of a ship?" he asked, after the shortest of pauses.

Strake just lifted a shoulder, waiting for a response. Friendship was not something he offered lightly. Nor, Soren thought, was it a thing Aristide was in the habit of accepting. She found herself far less dismayed than she would have been a week ago, to see Strake taking a step closer to his Councillor. Was she so sure of her Rathen? Or was it that she had changed toward the Diamond Couerveur?

Eyes blue-grey beneath the clouds, he stood considering his King, just one corner of his mouth faintly curving. Still a dangerous, far too self-possessed man who wanted control of the throne. But he was – had become – more than a threat. For both their sakes she didn't want this gesture refused.

"What are you going to ask for?"

It was a side-step: though the question was bare of formal address, the words still held that finely measured distance he'd always kept between himself and his King. Hardly eager acceptance of the proffered friendship, but Strake only looked amused as he gazed up at his Councillor's fine profile.

Then he flipped a hand over, choosing not to push. "Labour," he replied, with a measure of anticipation. "They can winnow out the Tongue, restore the road and orchards. And Aramond. That's something which will outweigh any amount of coin. The thing we need most, and worth – worth forbearance." He paused, and looked tired. "Would you have done differently?"

"No." Aristide's gaze shifted to Soren, then returned to Strake. The grey cast the clouds gave his eyes didn't suit him, made him look bleak and wintry. "There are times I would raze The Deeping to the ground, given the chance," he added. "But in this, I am – pleased." The words were very clear and exact, and prompted Strake to lift a hand as if to reach out. Then he caught himself and let it fall back. Aristide didn't miss the motion, but his response was confined to a slight drop of his lashes. The way he had said it reminded Soren somehow of the Fae Queen. Aristide might never have worn a crown, but in his heart he was as much King of Darest as Strake.

"Yes, it's a bitter thing to have no-one to practice retribution on," he continued. "But I need only think of what comes next, how greatly recompense will tip the scales. We should estimate how much we can demand from the Fair, alter the Spring festival to take advantage of today's events. And this malison – naming it, knowing more of its origins, I can try and isolate it, study it, see if it can be unmade. And I want to get out of this wind."

This last was unexpected enough to make Strake laugh, a brief spurt which banished the aftertaste of compromise. And Soren discovered that when Aristide was genuinely amused, his eyes smiled while his mouth did not.

"Out of the wind first, then," Strake said, standing up. He glanced toward the palace at the still-transfixed crowd, but only suffered a mild flicker of exasperation. Touching a hand to Soren's back long enough to show her not forgotten, he started down.

"It makes cleaning up the docks an almost viable proposition," Aristide said as he fell in step. "Or would you prefer the garden first?"

"The garden," Strake said, and looked back up the hill. The pavilion was a grand if lonely spectacle, and he paused to enjoy it, then visibly started plotting out a suitable frame for the lorams. A moment later he shook his head and turned. "But it will be the docks. The garden is a very long-term project, and one I don't mean to hurry. I'll have it done in stages over the next few years, and quite possibly sensibly budgeted. It couldn't be more than a design until Spring anyway."

They started down again, plunging into detail about priorities and resources, circling the issue of who was currently Baron of the Oaks and the Baron of Fyse, the two demesnes overwhelmed by the Tongue. And almost as quickly they detoured into the Spring festival, which continued to consume much of their energy. With a subtle shift of manner Aristide now displayed a certain pleasure in sharing his plans, but he was never going to forget whose decisions were final in Darest.

Nothing about the boy, Soren thought as another speck of rain scored her chin. Today was a turning point, and now they're full of the future, as if the big problems have been overcome and all that's left is tidying up. With Aristide's trump blade still in the hands of someone who can't mean any good, and 'the Moon-cast boy' in Tor Darest, wounded and alone and bound inexorably to seek out Rathens and kill them. They're looking further ahead than they should, because those two things are the ones they don't want to deal with.

But Soren was Champion, and could not afford such indulgence. When they reached the palace, the first thing she did was look with palace-sight into the Garden of the Rose. And saw with sinking heart but no measure of surprise the velvety black symbol of a doom which had not been altered.

They made a proclamation. Strake didn't want it, but felt it necessary. Bare words in a hastily convened Court: Calondae had admitted to the Tongue. Reparation would be made. Soren watched the faces hidden by the crowd. Arista completely blank, the ambassadors concealing dismay, Aspen disbelieving and delighted. Overall there was bewilderment combined with anger, a little joy, and a strong undercurrent of relieved anticipation. Darest had taken Strake's return as a sign of changing fortune, and a weighty blood price was an unexpectedly early fulfilment of that promise. But Strake was not alone in wishing for vengeance above compensation, and there was an ugly undercurrent in the overcrowded room as they left.

With Strake and Aristide anxious to bury themselves in their planning, Soren returned to her apartment, her attention on the continuing ripples of the proclamation. She watched Lady Arista particularly, especially when Baron Mogath accompanied her for a short time. There was a brief, tight-lipped conversation which Soren studied with every scrap of her attention. But if these two were allies, they were not easy ones, parting without any visible appearance of accord.

The ambassadors all returned to their rooms and made reports. It was a fascinating illustration of how to spot a caster. Various sigils were produced. Some chanted, some stared with fixed concentration into the distance, some waited while one of their entourage performed the casting for them. In a couple of cases she could see a little image of the person they were talking to. None of them looked particularly happy.

"This is the most danger we've been in since the King returned."

Halcean, in the process of handing her a mug of cider, looked suitably startled. "Why so?"

"We've done just what everyone seems to have particularly not wanted. True, we've not precisely put ourselves on good terms with The Deeping, but they are – so far as I can tell a support which had been withdrawn is now returned. And the compensation will change everything for Darest."

"It's that significant an amount?"

"Nothing's been fixed – I suppose they'll negotiate exact terms through the Tzel Aviar. But they spoke of having Calondae actually restore the lost orchards." She shook her head, rather awed by the image. The baronies of the north-east had once been the richest, a far cry from the abandoned, isolated communities which survived. "Even the excess trees alone, the labour involved in cutting them, preparing the wood. Aristide will know just how far we can push. Between Calondae and Seldareth–"

"Seldareth? The North?"

"Is, in a distant kind of way, behind the killings. That's still to be resolved, but at least we've some hint of what to look for now. And Seldareth will more than owe us a favour after, even if no formal debt's been declared. I should think that between two Fae kingdoms we should get enough to not only arrest Darest's slide, but to firmly turn us around. Aristide will probably even be able to start this ship-building venture he's so enamoured with."

"Ships?" Halcean stared at her.

"He'll have the wood for it, if not the expertise. And probably enough free coin to attract a few shipwrights away from Cya or the East."

Halcean, looking shaken, said: "I see what you mean now. Lord Aristide and King Aluster are – too formidable. Too much to hope that someone won't decide they have to be stopped before they manage to drag the region back to the way things were before."

When Darest's wealth and stability had let it dominate the West. "Not likely to happen in our lifetime," Soren said. But it was possible. Strake was not going to be popular with his neighbours. Or with all Dariens.

"Do you think – Court gossip gives me a different story every time – but I don't know what to believe of Lady Arista. Do you think she hates the Fair enough try and stop this no matter the benefit to Darest?"

"Who knows?" Halcean was turning her own mug between her hands, pensive. "The Couerveurs have made a tradition of devotion to Darest. You'd think that'd be all to the good, but it's too absolute to be healthy. And, well, I'm not going to pretend I don't think Lady Arista twisted. It's not so much the Fair which will bother her here – the Fair are admitting fault after all, and what could be better than that? It's her precious son – she might try and stop it because of that." A complex mix of emotion underlay Halcean's words, and she took a breath, composing herself.

"Aristide's–"

"Covered himself in glory. With your King's help or not, he's done just what she's been trying to do for years. Do you think she'll be able to stand that?"

Lady Arista was now meeting with Baron Peveric and the Marshall of the Army. They spoke with the air of discussing an unlooked-for problem. The Lady Arista still had her loyal allies, it seemed, and was the prime and possibly only suspect for the theft of Aristide's so-distinctive knife.

Bar one. Soren hated herself for thinking it, but she couldn't help but return to Aspen, currently talking excitedly to a small clutch of his closest confidants. He was mage, knew every scrap of gossip about Aristide, openly imitated him. And unless Darest's plethora of foreign spies had managed to infiltrate the Diamond's extremely secure household, Aspen was one of the precious few who'd had the opportunity as well. The knife was best stolen while Aristide slept, by someone who was not too great a distance away, who had some way of 'tasting' like him. Who could it be but Aspen?

Except Aristide discounted him on score of ability, and he had no discernible motive. And he was her friend. A friend who had cultivated her even when she'd been unimportant to the Court.

"Halcean–" Soren hesitated, not wanting to embarrass Aspen by passing on suspicion even to her aide. "You know Aspen's decided he wants to 'prentice himself to Lord Aristide? What do you think his chances are?"

"Slim to nothing," Halcean said promptly. But she frowned, evidently making connections.

"He's not that bad, surely?"

"Just not devoted enough to it. Too busy chasing scandal, or making it. More to the point, Lord Aristide's never taken an apprentice."

"There doesn't seem to be that many true-mages in Darest to 'prentice."

"I doubt that's the reason. He has the talent," she added carefully. "Instinct, strength, all the rest. But really, I don't think such a perfectionist as the Diamond would be interested." Watching Soren's reactions carefully, she added: "Unless Choraice's been putting on an act about not studying."

"Where would he find the time?" Soren said, shrugging it off. Halcean, it seemed, had already held suspicions.

Tired of watching and worrying, Soren did not at all want to pursue the idea of Aspen as two-faced assassin. Instead she would try and unravel a different thread from this endless tangle of suspicion. "Do something for me, Halcean?"

"Of course." Her aide was immediately on her feet.

"Ask Baroness Couerveur if she can spare me a short interview."

Lady Arista had given nothing away when told the Champion wanted to see her, and had settled in the cup of a heavy, high-backed chair while she waited. It was, Soren reflected, an arrangement designed to conjure memories of the Regent's Court.

"Do you bring messages, Champion?" Lady Arista asked, as soon as the door had closed behind Soren. She was intent, no doubt eager for details about the bargains made with the Fair. How much did she hate not being the centre of Darest's world? How much did she hate her son?

"Questions, Lady Arista," Soren replied, with all her self-composure. This was the kind of thing she needed to be able to do.

"Then ask."

Easily as unnerving as Aristide, her pale blue eyes beyond incisive. It was necessary for Soren to remind herself how much the balance of power had shifted, that she had become a person of considerable consequence while the Regent had been reduced to one of sixteen barons. Then she could manage to say: "Who was Jansette Denmore working for?"

There was not so much as a shadow of surprise. Soren's guess had been right – no-one as intelligent or frankly suspicious as Lady

Arista was reputed to be would have neglected to investigate those she took to her bed. Even Jansette's transparent beauty had not been sufficient to turn this woman's head. But would she answer?

"I am told Lady Denmore has been notably absent from Court, these past two days," Lady Arista commented.

"Recalled," Soren said, offering honesty in hopes of provoking it.

"Having lost access to the inner Court." Lady Arista's reaction was pure Aristide: she looked thoroughly appreciative, nodding to herself. To this woman, knowing her lover was a spy may have only increased the attraction. "Why is this important, Champion?" she asked then, gaze sharpening until Soren wanted to move out of its way. "All the West has spies in Tor Darest. They change them on so regular a basis it's scarcely worth tracking the rotation."

Soren hesitated, aware that Lady Arista marked her indecision. But she couldn't admit to the theft of the trump blade – any mention of Aristide would surely bring the conversation to an inglorious conclusion, even if Lady Arista wasn't directly involved. She had an awful sense of having taken hold of the tail of a tiger.

"I want to test some information Lady Denmore provided," Soren said, stamping on her nerves. "To do that, I need a better idea of her loyalties."

"Jansette Denmore provided you with information?" The tone was intrigued, not threatened. The only answer Soren gave was an uncommunicative nod and the former Regent's gaze became all the brighter, her interest very evidently roused. Then, with the faintest edge of malice, she launched into a tangent. "Tell me, Champion: is the Tzel Aviar to remain long in Darest?"

"I don't believe a definite period has been set," Soren replied, after only a small pause. Wanting to know more about Jansette, she had put herself in a position where Lady Arista could press for answers of her own. She decided to pre-empt matters a little, adding: "He is to capture the Fae killer who has been stalking the King."

"An individual the Darien guard has been ordered not to harm."

"To not approach." Soren looked down, thinking about conspiracies and the nature of her duties, then went on to give Lady

Arista a detailed and unadorned account of the events on Vostal Hill. The former Regent was not a woman to be underestimated, and certainly not to be treated as a fool. A clear understanding of the day's sour victory might stave off any plan of Lady Arista's to move against Strake.

When Soren's recital reached the point of Desteret's departure, she stopped, unsure how effective her strategy had been. Lady Arista simply sat back with a contemplative air, and said: "Thank you, Champion. You may go."

Before Soren had done more than take breath in disappointment, she added a single word:

"Sax."

It hadn't brought her any forrader. Watching closely, Soren had seen no sign that Lady Arista was at all perturbed by the thought of Jansette passing on information, as she surely would have been if the Regent had displayed Aristide's knife to her lover. That did not rule out Jansette having seen more than Lady Arista had realised, but was not nearly enough to verify the former Regent's place at the head of their list of suspects.

Could she at least put Sax at the bottom? The kingdom took up much of Darest's western border, and when the mines were at their peak had positively longed to change that boundary. But those mines were known to be failing and Sax's King was a cautiously greedy sort of man, the kind who advanced by increments rather than a sudden coup. Since it was unlikely Jansette would have revealed a plot of her own country, Soren could be at least moderately certain Sax was not behind the disappearance of the trump blade.

Cya was the foremost enemy of Sax, trade rivalry occasionally escalating to diplomatic falling-out, with open war in living memory. If a Saxan spy had a choice of secrets to spill, they would most definitely be Cyan. But how would a Saxan have known a Cyan had stolen Aristide's knife?

Jansette's proclivity for flitting from window to bedroom would have provided plenty of opportunity to discover all manner of things, but that only widened the field of suspects. It could be anyone. Lady Arista, a Cyan spy who had slipped through Aristide's nets, a mage hired by Everett Rothwell before his downfall, or someone she didn't even know to worry about. There were simply too many people to watch.

Dispirited, Soren made her way back to her apartments. Lady Arista stayed enthroned, head resting on one fist. Mogath was writing innocuous-seeming letters, and Peveric, various other barons, were all doing things she couldn't call suspicious. The Tzel Aviar was reading Laramae of Seldareth's notebook, as he had been all afternoon. Aspen had found an adventurous girl to chase about his cramped room, and the ambassadors were making Soren dizzy with their comings and goings.

Strake and Aristide had abandoned lists and diagrams to talk to each other with frowning absorption. It seemed to Soren she would be best served taking a bath.

To her faint surprise, soon after she'd returned to her apartment her Rathen bid Aristide good night and left to join his Champion in soapy caresses, urgent and intense, with not a word between them until they were tangled damply in his bed.

"Feeling better?"

"Immeasurably." But he looked tired, and again more regretful than pleased. Her Rathen had given in to wanting her, but he didn't like himself for it.

She told him what little she'd learned, and he listened with brooding attention. "The blood-price will be paid to Darest, with or without me. They'd be best advised to get rid of both of us."

"And who rules then?"

He lifted himself onto an elbow, looked down at her face.

"Lady Arista?" Soren asked, not flinching.

"I'll have to suggest that to Aristide." Amusement flickered, then was lost. "She may well be a good choice, if he were gone. She'd at least not be promoting her heir in our child's stead." He touched a hand to her stomach, eyes darkening. "Sun. Go to sleep, Soren. I can't talk about this just now."

She didn't protest, but sleep was not easily won for either of them. The palace marched through Soren's mind until, an hour or more before dawn, her dreaming sight showed her the Tzel Aviar moving through the shadows of Fleeting Hall. His hands were empty and his face grave as he walked into the Garden of the Rose and looked at the black bloom which represented Strake's life. Then toward the concealed cluster of leaves which heralded a Rathen child.

Twenty-Seven

T he steady gaze of Damaris of the Wryve turned toward the focus of Soren's palace-sight and fixed there. Tangled up in Strake, Soren struggled into full consciousness, and found that it definitely wasn't a dream. The Tzel Aviar stood in the Garden of the Rose. Waiting for her?

Confused and curious, she worked her way carefully out of the bed, managing to not disturb her Rathen. After a brief stop in her apartment to dress, she slipped out into Fleeting Hall, where it was cold enough to steam breath and goose-pimple skin. Glancing toward the guarded entrance to the Hall of the Crown she briefly considered an escort, rejected the idea, and then was filled absurdly with guilt, as if she went to some clandestine assignation. It would help if she could begin to guess what the Fae wanted.

Palace-sight showed Tzel Damaris turn his head as she walked into the garden. Her own eyes could only make out shadows: the upright of walls and curve of arch, the dark mass of vines dripping in the wake of the rainstorm. The smudge beneath all this which might be a man. The storm had left not so much as a breath of wind to stir the leaves, and Soren discovered an odd reluctance to speak, to break the black silence. The place was cold and close and crushingly still.

Vision apparently unhindered, Tzel Damaris was studying her face, gauging something she was not certain she wanted to know. In the dark he was a more concentrated kind of man, as if something had risen out of that bottomless well and was looking at her over the rim. She felt like she'd never met him before, and wished she hadn't now. Even in this place, where she had so much power, he had somehow become a thing which made the hair on the back of her neck stand up.

"I have completed my perusal of Laramae's journal," Damaris said then. Decorous, formal, pure Warden of the Borders. It almost made things normal again.

Soren took a breath, dismissing fear and trying not to show her discomfort. Business. Like Aristide, he was always and ever focused on business. Standing expectantly about the Garden of the Rose had been a clear message, but why did he suddenly want to speak to her? He should be reporting his findings to Strake. What was she supposed to do?

What should the Rathen Champion want to do?

To ease the increasingly awkward silence, she said: "I wished to ask what Moon-cast meant."

His gaze shifted to the waning moon above. "Moon-sourced," he explained. "The power supplied outside the caster, thus making possible very strong and, more usually, long-lasting enchantments. While the Moon endures, so will the spell."

"Oh." Soren knew enchantments had to either be maintained or renewed to prevent them simply wearing off. That was one of the many reasons Shaping was considered so superior.

"To successfully draw power from the Moon is by no means easy, so Moon-casting remains a rarity. But the link once forged is extremely durable. That is what I wished to speak of to you."

"The link?" She sounded like a cowed fool, and wished that she could rid herself of this ridiculous sense of threat. It helped to look at him only through palace-sight, and focus on the measured calm of his words. He had no reason to want to hurt her, was just a man who would live for centuries, who looked human but was not. Like the boy.

"Enchantments can be lifted, Champion. While the Moon is waning, the link will be weaker. It should be possible to break the casting, removing both the boy's need to kill and the abilities which make him so difficult to capture. Along with the drive to hunt Rathens."

This was better than good news. Soren looked up at Strake's rose, hoping for the first time to see it some other colour. But—

"I'm no mage, Tzel Damaris. What would you have me do?"

The question was full of unease. Above their heads the Rose uncoiled, sending icy drops of water to patter down around them. But there was no ripple of response from the Tzel Aviar, even when a tendril descended to pass just behind him. He had returned that unflinching gaze to Soren, did not seem even to have noticed the movement.

"Laramae conducted many experiments to discover the limits of the child she had created," he told her. "Although not truly Shaped, placing the enchantment beyond the blood gives the effect of making the boy a child of the Moon herself. The death-urge is one part of that. But the Moon is Death and Life."

He stopped, and above them the Rose coiled again as Soren realised what it was he meant, why she could help where Aristide could not. "The baby."

"The boy has approached you twice. That which impels him should have been overwhelmingly urging him to strike you down for the Rathen you bear. That same child is what affords you protection."

"How would he know?" Soren, after all, had not. She could scarcely have been pregnant, the first time. That had been less than half an hour after Strake had run from her.

Thoughts tumbling over timing, Soren took a slow breath. How much did the Rose know? Had it known pregnancy would protect her? Had that been another factor in whatever reasoning had led it to force her and Strake together? And—

It didn't matter, not right now. The Tzel Aviar was standing here, his steady gaze saying as clearly as any words that if he knew she was pregnant the boy certainly did. Child of the Moon, death and life welded into one. Killer of a previous Tzel Aviar, a Crown princess, Strake's Vahse, too many others. Did Damaris really expect Soren to risk her own child to aid someone whose purpose was to cut down her Rathen? Someone who had stood before her, silver eyes wide, and asked her to stop him?

"What is his name? The boy – did the book say?"

"A name is power, Champion. A foothold for resistance against imposed will. He was not given one."

The northern lord had treated her children like tools, Soren thought. Her insides were knotted with sick confusion, anger leaking into fear and all bound up in uncertainty and an intense desire to be anywhere but here. "Why did she use people?" she asked, the question a protest. "Why not an animal?"

Damaris had turned his face slightly away from her, although palace-sight showed her that his expression had not changed. "Laramae of Seldareth did not record her reasons," he said. "Only her results. Perhaps because the Moon is more responsive to the People, or because a mind is the greatest weapon a hunter can own." He looked now towards Strake's rose, black with impending death. "There are other ways I can approach this problem, Champion, but this places the fewest possible in danger. Your enchantments allow you to detect his presence. And it was to you the Moon-cast child made his appeal."

And you the Queen gave the task. But Soren was torn by the memory of silver eyes, a feeling of being on a precipice about to take a step over the edge. "What – what is it exactly you want me to do?" she asked.

"Hold him." That assessing gaze had returned. "I believe I can strike at the enchantment where it lies on him, beyond the blood and outside the defence which warps casting. But it will not be a quick thing, and I will need to be touching him, drawing the Moon. You he cannot harm, and you are also powerfully bound to this land by the enchantment of the Rose, which will offer some measure of protection against any side-effects of my attack."

He was making no attempt to hide that there was danger. How could Soren possibly do as he asked? Strake had only just accepted his desire for her, he was – after all the loss he had suffered, this would be the last thing he would be able to bear. Quite aside from the threat to herself, she was carrying his child. Heir to Darest. Involving herself directly in trying to rescue the nameless Fae killer was simply out of the question.

Except that anyone else would be more at risk, and if they did not move quickly the boy's need to kill would grow with the Moon. He had slaughtered the Rathen hunting party effortlessly, and was quite capable of turning Tor Darest into a charnel house. He would remain a threat to all Rathens, unless this was done. He had looked at her out of those unnatural silver eyes and said 'please'.

And Soren was Champion.

"I need to ask." Ask her Rathen to risk his Champion, his lover and his child. She couldn't even say it.

Tzel Damaris simply nodded. "It must be done before the Moon is black."

She wondered how he expected to find the boy, have him conveniently to hand for the attempt. They couldn't just go continually walking on Vostal Hill in the hope that he would turn up. But those were details, and nothing beside the hurdle she had to take first. Strake. An argument, unavoidable and potentially terrible. Why had Damaris had to ask for her help and put her in this position?

Staring at the shadow beneath the dripping Rose, Soren found herself full of angry distrust. His priority was the boy, not Rathens. The Fair had been willing to let Darest founder over a secret. How could they be trusted?

"What happened to the Fair who once lived in Darest, Tzel Damaris?" The words were forced through stiff lips. "What is the taint which lies beneath all this?"

"That is not spoken of outside the People."

The words were as quietly unperturbed as anything else he had said to her. And yet foreboding crawled beneath Soren's skin, took her by the spine and pulled her back. It should not be possible to feel this isolated, here where she was strongest. But she did and it was only despite knees which threatened to knock together and a throat inconveniently frozen that she managed to ask a question which had been at the back of her mind since the Council on the hill.

"Were they Shaped?"

Damaris of the Wryve simply turned and walked away.

"A midnight stroll?"

Soren's stomach dropped. Caught up in sick anger transmuting to queasy relief, she hadn't been paying attention to Strake's breathing. He lay in his bed, still curled around the space where she had slept, watching her walk toward him from the door.

"The Tzel Aviar wanted to see me."

Blunt, because he was not going to like anything to do with the Fae, no matter how she couched it.

"He asked me to help him," she went on, as Strake sat up. "Laramae's notes say that because he's tied to the Moon, the boy can't attack someone who's pregnant. The Tzel Aviar wants me to hold the boy while he tries to break the casting." She sat down on the edge of the bed, meeting Strake's eyes. Her stomach sank further at what she found there, but she managed to take a deep breath and add: "I think I should do it."

"Do you?" Incredulous, scathing.

"It's what I'm here for," Soren explained, determined not to cringe. She felt odd inside. Her title had been awarded for reasons she thoroughly disliked; only by her actions could she earn the right to bear it. "Rathen Champion: protector of King and country. If I don't help him, how many might die before he captures the boy?"

"He can find some other woman." There was no room for compromise in her Rathen now, and Soren bowed her head under the beating force of his anger. She was making him hate her again and it felt even worse than before because he'd only just started to see her as something other than a trap. Wasn't it also her duty to support him, to be there for him? And didn't it make far more sense to find someone whose child wasn't heir to the kingdom, who wasn't Soren's own child, to make the attempt first?

"I can't do that." The words were wrung out of her. "How can I send some random pregnant woman into danger when I have all the protections of the Rose?"

"The Rose places you at greater risk!" The mattress jerked beneath Strake from the recoil of his body. "That Moor-forsaken monster disrupts enchantments. You're the last person to send out after him!"

She could argue at least on points of accuracy, even as the half-contained explosion blasted away at her resolution. "He disrupts spells cast on him," she said, holding her head high. "I'm not about to do that. And we don't know if the Rose was a factor stopping him from striking at me before. We do know that he's stood as close as you are to me now, and not raised a hand to me." Her voice wobbled, but she swallowed, determined at last to be Champion in more than name. She made herself still inside and stood firm, refusing to crumble. "I couldn't live with myself, Strake. If it's the Rose which protects me, and someone gets killed because they were sent in my place – I just couldn't."

Strake flung out of the far side of the bed and stood there, naked and seething and apparently too furious for words. He should look ridiculous, but all Soren could think of was that she really was in love with him and that she was driving back the wedge it had taken so much to remove. The price of this stupid need of hers to be something other than a woman who looked good in a uniform.

"So you want me to sit here – locked up and ignorant – while you lay your life on the line?" His voice was shaking, and those dark blue eyes were entirely black.

"I–" Soren stopped, pierced by a sudden, thankful realisation. Strake was as angry as she'd ever seen him, but the hate which had so battered her before wasn't there. Her choice would cost her, but not nearly so much as she'd feared. "I was thinking that they're the same," she said obliquely, finding this an odd moment to be so happy.

"What?" His voice had risen in pitch.

"The Rose and the boy – the..." She stumbled and looked up at him, and something in her face at least made him hold his tongue. "They were both constructed to perform certain tasks – they were truly made to be something. The Rose to protect Rathens, the boy to kill them. They're horrible things and we hate – want to kill them both. And can't, either of them. And – they're just doing what they've been made for. Puppets. The boy at least fights against it."

"Do you expect me to be sorry for Vahse's killer?"

"Aren't you?"

He tossed his head, turned to one side. It wasn't something he was going to admit, any more than the obvious parallel between his own temper and the murder laid on the boy.

"You called me a composite, once," Soren faltered. "Something made to get a child off you. Let me be more than that."

"Is that what you think? Damn it, Soren—" He came toward her, anger washed out by dismay. Snaring her fingers he found his black frown once again. "Your hands are like ice."

"That's the weather." She tried not to think about the boy, injured and somewhere out in the night. "You could watch from the residences."

This did not impress. "I'm not going to simply stand by while you—" He shook his head, squeezed her hands. "I'll talk to the Fae. This can't be the best solution. Even if it was, there's no way I'd let you go out there unless I was with you—"

"So that we can spend all our time trying to make sure you didn't get killed?"

"Soren—"

"I'm Champion, Strake. I'm – I need to do this."

"No."

There was just enough uncertainty in the word to bring a frantic look to his eyes, and he covered it with sudden, urgent passion. It did nothing to solve the impasse, but served to set it briefly at a distance and return them to tangled warmth in the bed.

Dawn was creeping up on them by the time he had exhausted everything but slow caresses. The Tzel Aviar was asleep and Aristide had woken early, was blinking in the dark. The doubled patrols of the palace looked bored and restless, and the kitchens were starting to stir.

"I...vowed never to marry you," Strake said abruptly. "Stupid, hot-headed thing to do, guaranteed to turn around just as it has. But the kind of vow I made – it's not easily broken."

Soren didn't answer for the moment, sorting out the idea of having Strake and marrying him. "Does it make a difference?"

"Of course it does." He sounded annoyed, then sighed. "Quite aside from having to deal with the Court's expectations for my bedding arrangements, I want – I want that. I want our child to have that."

A declaration of intent, not love. Like Aristide, Strake had faced his impossibilities, that mass of anger and desire, and found a compromise. Despite all that the Rose had done to them, he was going to try to make the best of it.

She should feel happy, should catch hold of this fragile thread of hope, and look for a future with a partner not an adversary. But there was another issue, something the risk to her made suddenly important to establish.

"What about Aristide?"

"What? What about him?"

"If you're talking Court's expectations, that's one which hasn't wavered. They're all expecting you to marry him."

Strake snorted. "He's not."

"No. But he—" Soren broke off, thinking of future possibilities, watching Aristide staring at his ceiling. "It feels unbalanced. When he swore that oath to you, I think he was gambling on your death. Now – he serves you more than well and will continue to do so. Forced to, no matter how he feels about it. I don't know why it bothers me so much."

Her Rathen, unusually, did not fire up or grow irritable, but looked at her with long dark eyes which saw far more than she'd expected. "Perhaps because you're forced to serve me, no matter how you feel about it," he said.

"Strake—"

"Without the Rose you would be in Carn Keep, and I would not be King." Strake's tone was meditative. "I would have returned to a land where Queen Arista had withdrawn from rule, where Prince Aristide was the focus of a fascinated Court. Feared quite possibly, and thoroughly disliked by those whose ambitions run counter to his. But – ah, I was not an hour back before I realised the rest of them hang on his every word. They were eager to have him rule, but instead they have me. And Darest has one King too many."

"Because of the Rose."

"Oh yes. Far too much in this land is 'because of the Rose', good and bad all tangled together and no way to undo it. The Couerveurs were kept as regents rather than kings, which is certainly good for me, for the Rathen line. It was terrible for Darest. You and I – how different would it have been, if the Rose had not made you Champion, but had left you in Carn Keep for me to one day see and want without feeling you were being forced down my throat? Let alone–" His voice quivered, and she felt his entire body tense. "Let alone the rest of it."

"The boy did not kill me because–" She couldn't quite say it, hurrying on. "We're safe in the palace because of the Rose, but it – I hate being in the palace for the same reason. And it keeps the malison from completely destroying us."

"From warping us. The malison's effects you can see most in Lady Arista. Not dead or broken, but turned in on herself. In Darest the one who sits the throne, the ruling line, is never something as simple as the one at the top of the pile."

She went still. "But that would mean–"

"That I'd be impacted by the malison without the Rose." His voice was bitter. "Or even with the Rose, given the lack of Rathens to power it. But it will give some measure of protection. Another Sun-blasted chain about my throat."

Soren touched his cheek, his temple, feeling heat, the throb of pulse beneath skin. "And you'd throw it off in a moment, if it wasn't for the risk to me." She knew perfectly well it was true, didn't need to see him nod his head, eyes squeezing shut in his pain. "Do you think it could be the malison which has formed this instinct in the Rose?"

"Who knows? It doesn't matter – take away the malison and the Rose would still be what it is now, just as Arista Couerveur would continue to war against her son. There's no escaping the thing."

He was working himself up to anger again, but stopped and touched her face, shivering. "Good with bad. Bad with good. And you're right to be worried about Aristide. His greatest strength is this singular devotion to Darest. It kept him from killing me, because he saw more harm than good would come out of it. Now, the *saecstra* will hold him, whether he wants it or not, but – as I said, he's near as much King of Darest as I am. The malison has to be effecting him, or will eventually, and I can't guess where that will take us. I do know marrying him won't fix things."

"Because he still wouldn't be King?"

"Exactly. I've no doubt he'd hate the prospect, no matter how much or little he felt for me. It would lessen him, in a way."

Never simple. Soren shifted, tracing the curve of his ribs. "Do you want him?"

Strake didn't answer immediately, the tension creeping back into his body. The question bothered him. "I can barely reconcile lying here with you, without Vahse," he said, eventually. "Aristide would be too much."

That was not quite an answer. Soren touched his cheek and after a moment he reluctantly went on: "There's a lot about him I admire. I suppose in other circumstances I'd be tempted. But I don't want or need another lover. And he doesn't want anything of the sort. I'd like – I'll admit at least to wanting to make him stop 'your majesty-ing' me."

Would that be enough? If something happened to her, Strake would need someone, and Aristide was by far the most logical person. They were suited in so many ways, and surely Aristide couldn't be completely indifferent? Soren didn't like the prospect of leaving her Rathen alone.

"A tribond would probably circumvent my vow," Strake said then, completely shattering her equilibrium.

"What?"

"You'd have to want it," Strake said, eyes glittering. "Want him. Could you?"

Impossible question.

"I don't think Aristide...is himself with me," she said, without a great deal of enthusiasm. "I'm not sure he's himself with anyone, really. You, perhaps, on occasion. I won't deny he's attractive, but he–" She shook her head, trying to push away the images that were filling it, unable not to look at the man as he stood before a mirror, dressing with slow precision. Unreadable as ever. "He's not what I thought he was. How can I tell whether I want him if he doesn't let anyone know him? Court him? I'm not even sure I've *met* him."

Strake's smile was one of a man who has demonstrated a point. Lining up Aristide as her replacement would founder on the rock of Aristide's self-imposed isolation. And could never balance the risk she wanted to take. But the air of triumph was short-lived, and he slid his hand across her hip to rest it flat on the bed on her far side.

"I don't know what I'm doing," he whispered. "Here with you, without Vahse. He was the one who wanted children, was far more determined to find a third than I. And I already knew that anyone he liked enough to want to have children with, he'd want as part of a tribond. Pragmatic contracts weren't the sort of thing he could do." His hand and his eyes both closed, and his voice dropped even further, tense with misery. "He talked a lot about how we would make sure we didn't know who fathered which child, but he wanted one so much that I was going to make certain at least the first was his. The perfect man to be a father – he always gave his love so unconditionally. He would have adored you, made me jealous. Made a game out of what could have been the most horrible rivalry. Exhausted himself making sure you loved me as much as him, and then been quietly hurt, despite all good intentions, if we spent too much time together. Then laughed at himself. Keeping the world in proportion was so easy for him."

For a moment there were three in the bed, a mage-conjured image of a Rathen man with a wry smile and dancing eyes lying beside them. Then it was just Soren and Strake, and her Rathen's face was all planes. "I can't let you go out there."

It took a long time to find the answer. "One of the worst things I can think of–" she began, and found that her throat had stuck and she had to swallow to make it work again. "One of the worst things would be if the boy managed to run from Tor Darest. If the capture went wrong or if he overcomes this Moon-shaping and flees from what's been set on him. How long before he came back? I don't want to be terrified of letting our child outside the palace walls, Strake. I don't want to have this sick dread every time you so much as set foot outside the door. I'll be damned if I have that."

His hand had found her stomach, undistorted by a child still months in the future. "No," he repeated, and this time the word was full of fear.

Twenty-Eight

Every question Strake asked the Tzel Aviar only made it clearer that the risk to Soren was considerably less than that posed by any other approach. It was the Rose's senses Strake couldn't argue away: the fact that it would let her know where the boy was, and be actively doing everything it dared to keep her alive. Finally, whether because of Soren's determination or the undeniable risk posed to Darest, he gave in.

Tzel Damaris' solution to getting the boy within arm's reach was to construct a massive knot of illusory writing on Vostal Hill — a sentence in Fae script which Aristide translated as: "Come an hour after sunset". And an hour after sunset she and the Tzel Aviar once again walked out on Vostal Hill.

Feeling that it was better than nothing, Strake was watching from a balcony. Soren regretted suggesting it, picturing the boy maddened by his distant presence, trying to leap up the side of the palace. From the hillside she could only see the shape of two men, side by side on the unlit balcony, but the boy would still know exactly where his target was. That was why Aristide was at Strake's side, and four guards lurked beyond the doors into the palace proper.

Soren tucked chilled fingers into her armpits as they neared the top of the hill. She'd managed to leave her gloves behind, despite a stone-faced Halcean trying to kit her out in everything including a mail shirt. Her aide had worn an air of impending doom, eyes dark and troubled but her mouth closed firmly on her fears. Just like her Rathen.

Having promised to remain in sight, Soren slowed as they approached the pavilion, listening to the leaves rattle, and scenting salt and lavender on the evening breeze. The sky was clean and clear above, with the sliver of the Moon just beginning to rise. On her back the sword felt reassuringly solid, but the Rose was completely silent and there was no hint of a killer's breath.

She hoped that the boy could read.

"Tzel Damaris—" she began, then decided the Fae simply would not have overlooked that point. When he turned enquiring eyes on her she hesitated, then said: "Seldareth – Asterall – is the 'end' she's supposed to seek death?"

"It may be." He stopped just before the shadow of the pavilion and gazed across at the mouth of the river at the lights of Tor Darest. "That one will walk alone to Celoras, and into the Lake of Essence. Many who do this do not emerge. Should she survive, the name of Asterall will still be recorded among the dead, and she will seek a new one by...complicated means. She cannot return to the person she once was."

This seemed to Soren an unimaginable thing. To have everything you were taken away, and to have to search out a new purpose, a new self. "It seems harsh," she said, inadequately. "She did so little."

"Asterall faces death for ordering the murder of Seldareth's heir."

Seldareth's heir. Of course. The boy was the elder.

"The land will remain under regency until he is able to assume the title," Damaris continued. Without palace-sight she couldn't see the subtleties of his expression, but that perfectly even voice held some fragment of acknowledgment for the difficulties of installing someone with so much blood on his hands as North's lord. Strake would hate it.

Unable to muster any meaningful comment, Soren fell silent. Why did every problem partway dealt with birth a litter of consequences? Being Champion of Darest was like fighting a hydra with a thousand heads, and none of them nice, solid, visible ones you could just lop off and forget. Even if you were competent enough to swing a sword. Everything she did still felt wrong.

He came from the south, walking with steady ease, pausing occasionally as if to survey what lay ahead. When his breath first sighed into audibility the Rose fluttered in response, a memory of unease at the back of Soren's chest. But there was none of the panic of previous encounters. Soren made herself take heart from this, for it suggested the Rose agreed with Tzel Damaris' plan. It at least had made no attempt to stop her leaving the palace – there'd been none of the weak-legged confusion which had delayed her effort to reach Strake in the Tongue.

If only she could be so sanguine. One thing to decide she had to live up to the title of Champion, to argue for the right to risk herself. Quite another matter to actually play hero. She still couldn't believe she was out here. But there was no backing out of this now, and she sounded almost calm as she warned Tzel Damaris.

"I will explain to him what I intend to do," Damaris replied. "It is unlikely he will run, but if he does I will attempt to block him. Take hold of his arms, for his hands are his weapons, and keep him as still as you are able. I have laid protections upon myself to shield against a strike, but I am not certain they will be effective."

The Fae's instructions produced a marvellously tangible sense of discomfort. What harm in a little reassurance? Or at least a show of fellow feeling, some awareness that it was not easy to stand out here beneath a swimming sliver of moon, listening to a child made monster approach? Tzel Damaris simply gazed in the direction she'd indicated, his stance suggesting concentration, certainly not fear.

Soren had enough of that for both of them. Fear of death and her own inadequacy, concern for her barely-real child and for her Rathen watching so impotently. She'd always thought herself better able to face danger than cope with Court subtlety, but perhaps she simply hadn't hunted enough killers. Sick helplessness had taken her by the throat and she thought it entirely possible she might just stand there and watch while Tzel Damaris was torn apart.

On the far side of the pavilion, the boy stopped again. It was a poised, anticipatory kind of hesitation, speaking palpably of suspicion and the memory of an arrow striking home. Then he crossed from one throne to the other and out into the open. Only ten feet away when he stopped, while Soren's spine tied knots and the Rose became tangibly intent. But she stood her ground.

The Tzel Aviar began to speak, evidently tracking the boy's progress by the crackle of trodden grass. This time there was no convenient enchantment of translation, just the quiet flow of incomprehensible words. Nor did the Fae's tone suggest threat or plea; his face was as imperturbable as ever.

Finally, Damaris fell silent, waiting. Soren couldn't guess the boy's reaction, for there had been no clue in the even pace of his breathing. What if he fled? Rejected whatever Damaris had said and ran? The offer, after all, would take as much as it gave. Freedom from the purpose written on his blood in return for the strictures of the Fae Court and the loss of the powers which made him so dangerous. He was only a few steps away – shouldn't she leap forward, grab him, so that the Tzel Aviar could work his magic?

But it seemed important to give the boy the chance to choose. And terribly unlikely that a sudden leap would be at all successful. And even as Soren took an unsteady breath, and closed her hands to wait, a killer appeared before her.

A scavenged jacket hung loosely over rough bandaging. The arrow must have hit deep in the meat of his shoulder – not an impossible wound to dress without help, but difficult. The fine features carried an edge of weariness, but his clear silver gaze was far from the desperately ill and pitiful image conjured by Soren's conscience. He caught her gaze and held it, then stepped forward and offered his hands to her, wrists together.

That Fae confidence was lost with the gesture, eyes becoming wide and young despite their inhuman light. The hands, slim but hard-used, shook. And Soren shook too. A final blow against the image of the monstrous hunter.

She reached out and touched the back of one hand; warm skin soft beneath her fingers. Even as she quailed internally, a need to face the practicalities reasserted itself. According to the Tzel Aviar his hands were his weapons, and he was fully Soren's height, though his young male strength was probably weakened by injury and deprivation. Her role here was to protect Tzel Damaris, but also to expose herself as little as possible.

Awkwardly she took hold of the back of one wrist, glancing up into eyes which now matched her own uncertainty. Then she stepped behind him, reaching with her other hand for his free wrist. Uncomfortable as it made her, she pressed against his back, positioning herself for maximum leverage should he attempt to fight or flee. He offered no resistance, adjusting to her bracketing hold with a wary respect for his injured shoulder. And waited.

As a mage, Soren had measured Tzel Damaris against Aristide: probably stronger, certainly more experienced, able to tell when she watched him with palace-sight. In truth, until he began to draw the Moon, she had had no comprehension of what he was capable of doing.

It began quietly enough. He cupped his hands together as if to hold water and lifted his eyes toward the tranquil sliver of Lady Moon. Those who watched from the palace would not be able to hear the low sibilance of chant which threaded itself through the night, and she could not guess if they sensed what it summoned.

Lady Moon, whose cycle holds birth and death. Honoured certainty of all who lived, known before the first breath is taken and finally met after the last slips away. But this was not the Lady's quiet regard, familiar from temple visits. This was a dreadful immediacy. This was the sudden realisation that with each heartbeat there was no reason but the Lady's will that there be a next.

Soren was stitched into crushed immobility, a mouse before a parliament of owls, bound small and trembling with fear. She had never truly felt the authority which sparked and snuffed life. Sunlight was more forceful, that balming, burning touch a constant reminder of what fuelled daily existence. But here, in a reflection of moonlight glimmering against the curve of an impassive Fae mage's fingers, was something beyond angry heat. In Lady Moon was the essence. Tzel Damaris stood there, his chant fading to the wind's night-soft whisper, holding souls in his hands.

And Soren was supposed to keep *him* safe.

A small movement forward with those cupped hands, and the boy mewled, a naked little animal sound which gave her bare warning of a young man's back becoming a bow drawn taut, his shoulders against her neck, arms raised toward his own throat, sinews wire-strung beneath her straining grasp. She thought she could smell death in his hair, old and dried with fear. But he was not struggling, was caught in the grip of some agony, ecstasy, as the Tzel Aviar brought his hands up to the bandaged chest and began to call from the child made monster the power bound beyond his blood. Like to like.

Her challenge was to hold him upright, vibrating beneath the touch of the Tzel Aviar. He was phasing in and out of visibility and the next time he was visible his hands were encased in sharp-edged light, shifting glimmers of edges and points which formed gauntlets rather than claws. The light left little trails, as if the air itself took wound from its passage. Flesh would not heal so readily. This was what killed Vahse.

Sheer good fortune that the boy's response continued to be directionless agony, for Soren could barely hold him as it was. The Rose's unease began to increase, a murmur turning to a constant hum, tangling with Tzel Damaris' steady winding chant and the raggedly tearing gasps of the boy they were trying to save. Soren's head rang from the breath of giants, from the struggle to which she was spectator rather than participant, and wished for strength of resolve and purpose rather than this blank desperation which was the only thing which kept her grip in place.

For it was becoming terribly apparent that Tzel Damaris was losing the battle. The boy's periods of invisibility were becoming more and more frequent and each time he vanished Soren was treated to the sight of a Tzel Aviar being crushed by effort. Slowly a line etched itself onto the clear brow, the colour leached from fine skin. He continued his chant as if each word was a basket of rocks he must lift above his head, and at every syllable another stone was added. And into his eyes, those steady Fae eyes which had surveyed them all with such detachment, crept the waver of a man who finds himself in a trap and sees no way out. Even the Fair could lose their course.

Then he looked up at her through the space where a killer strained to remain in existence, and broke his chant, slid into it two words which could well have been boulders for their cost.

"Name him."

Panic-fuelled memory immediately proffered the explanation the Tzel Aviar had given her beneath the dripping Rose. "A name is power, Champion. A foothold for resistance against imposed will. He was not given one."

A name, an identity away from the purpose the boy was constructed for, might make all the difference, for it was obvious Tzel Damaris did not have strength enough to break the Moon-cast enchantment. But Soren jerked back in instinctive rejection, a host of consequences unreeling through her mind. Even if she had the slightest idea what an appropriate name for a Fae lordling was, it would be a link, a permanent tie, in its way an act of shaping which she was hardly fit to make, Rathen Champion or not. Define the life of this boy-monster-prince?

But she couldn't not do it, any more than it had been possible to send a substitute out here in her place. With her mind full of Daseretals, Asteralls and Desterets, Soren leaned forward and said the only name she could manage: "Shaol. You're Shaol. Shaol of Seldareth."

And that was it. With a sound like wire violently snapped, a bond was broken. The Tzel Aviar grunted, an earthily human sound, and the boy – Shaol – sagged back into Soren's hold, nearly tipping them both over. He twisted, shuddering, then turned to look at her and his eyes were as green as his sister's, but full of tears.

"My thanks, Champion," Tzel Damaris began, rediscovering his composure, but Soren wasn't listening. All her attention, her whole focus, had been swallowed by the panic of the Rose. And Aristide and Strake, still together, both gasping as if they could barely spare a moment to draw breath.

"Can you get me into the palace? Right now?" Her voice was high with panic.

The Tzel Aviar glanced toward the balcony where Strake and Aristide were supposed to be watching in safety, but didn't trouble her with questions or argument. Two steps and he had a firm hold of Soren's waist, stooping to lift up the boy and murmur something to him.

The words must have been 'hold on' because a moment later they launched into the air. Hopelessly precarious, as his grip immediately slid from waist to armpit and Soren had to cling to prevent herself from plunging to the suddenly distant ground. The thin light of the moon spared her a good view of the effort this sudden flight cost him, but it was a close thing, for they did not so much land on the balcony as drop on to it.

The palace exploded through Soren's mind, and she stumbled but remained upright while the Tzel Aviar went to his knees and stayed down. The scene before her sprang into precise focus. Strake doubled backwards over the corner of the balcony, a slender knife flaring into white existence at his throat, and black lines streaking Aristide's pale hands as he held it there. But his hands were more on the blade than the hilt and the blood was Aristide's own. He was holding the knife back, struggling against nothing Soren could see.

Strake hadn't called out. The guardsmen still loitered on the far side of the doors, oblivious to the drama out in the night. Summoned, they would surely leap to cut down the person holding the knife, not knowing he was keeping their King alive. And be left with a perfect scene of traitor and the man he had murdered.

The Rose was flinging scenes of the palace through her mind, person after person, standing, sitting, sleeping. Trying to find who or what was controlling the trump blade. But Strake had said it wasn't able to sense magic of itself, that it would have to rely on visual signals. And no-one, none of them, was conveniently sitting in a circle, chanting and scribing ominous symbols.

Soren looked straight at Lady Arista. The woman was standing just inside the door of her apartments, eyes intent on nothing, head tilted in concentration. It was so marvellously easy to reach out through the Rose, to summon glass-glimmer thorn ghosts and—

"Don't kill her."

Aristide, his gaze fixed on the region of Strake's collar-bone, face completely expressionless. Asking her to spare the life of the mother he hated. Soren blinked at him, then turned her attention back to that distant room where, the beginnings of a frown creasing her brow, Lady Arista reached out with her hand as if plucking some unseen string. Light flared around the hilt of the dagger, and abruptly Strake and Aristide between them were able to move it a fingers-width back. Aristide began muttering some attempt at counterspell while Strake inhaled sharply, as if he had been holding his breath.

"Mimic casting," he said, in a tight but remarkably unflustered voice, even as the knife began edging toward his throat again. "Spell tastes of Aristide, as if he activated it. But it's not. We won't be able to hold it much longer."

Soren stared back at Lady Arista, who was now gazing with considerable affront at the thorny vines surrounding her. But not casting. She'd just *interfered* with the attack – that had been obvious enough. Which meant it was someone else, one of the palace *hundreds* was doing this. The Rose's panic, fury, competed with her own. This was her greatest test, where she had to truly be the Champion, use the tool of palace-sight, save her Rathen.

And she couldn't! She was staring at them all, all she knew to be mages, all she suspected, anyone at all. At Aspen, staring at the door of his room. Barons, ambassadors stilled in the middle of evening activity, reacting to a second sudden excess of power nearby. Any of them could be the caster.

Frantically, Soren tried to expand her focus, to see them all at once, every person in the palace, all of them, searching for the one who shammed or betrayed effort, malice, anything. Lady Arista reached out again, doing something which made the knife flare, slip back.

And there, at the palace's heart, someone reacted. A slight jerk, a frown, then leaning forward as if to push harder.

"Halcean?!"

Off in the Champion's apartment's, Soren's aide reacted to her name, her eyes widening, focus shifting. She had heard.

"Halcean. Stop." Soren could scarcely believe what she saw, but she could still deal with it. All around Halcean, seated so innocuously in her room, the palace's defences uncoiled. Milk-white threat. Soren couldn't keep the hurt from her voice, but her tone still made clear the consequences of refusal: "Stop now."

And, face white, Halcean obeyed. Surrounded by thorns as long as her forearm, she made a simple chopping gesture. The light surrounding the trump blade went away and both Strake and Aristide let out their breath. Metal rang as it fell to the balcony.

"Why?" Soren asked then, struggling against roiling anger larger than her own. The Rose was fully roused, still curling and twisting at the back of her mind even though the crisis was past.

She watched dismay war with fear on the woman's face and she spoke, but lip-reading was still beyond Soren. Only sorrow was evident, and regret.

Strake touched her arm then. "Your aide?" he asked, shortly. He was staring at the Tzel Aviar, still kneeling, and the boy who stood behind him. Huge moss-green eyes in a smudged face, blood on his clothes, and hands which could not cut. Soren tried to think with a head which thrummed with second-hand fury, anxious to divert her Rathen from any confrontation.

But Strake simply and very deliberately turned his back on Vahse's killer. Aristide reached with bleeding hands for the fallen trump blade. Lady Arista emerged from her apartment in search of the source of the casting and the guards on the far side of the balcony door seemed finally to realise something was wrong. And the vines about Halcean stirred.

Inside her but separate from her Soren felt anger turn to malice, to vengeance. Eyes widening, she pulled the vines back, willed them away. They swayed, lifted, then coiled down.

"No." The words were a whisper through frozen lips. Just loud enough to bring Strake's attention back to her, to see the strain on her face as she pushed again, harder, with all her will.

"What?" Strake had hold of her arm.

"It wants to *kill* her." Numb words, forced out. She was shaking now, sweating with the effort it cost her to hold the vines back. Halcean, eyes huge, sat mouse-still in her chair, watching a vicious tip turn inches from her face. But Soren wasn't going to let it happen. Halcean had betrayed them, yes, tried to kill Strake, and she would pay for it. But not like this. Soren would not allow it.

Then, on the heels of this absolute resolution, the Rose pushed her almost negligently to the back of her mind, reached out, and cut Halcean to pieces.

Twenty-Nine

"I am Darien, boy. You would do well to remember that."

Arista Couerveur had not taken kindly to being suspected of attempting regicide, nor to the amount of time she'd been kept waiting before she'd been permitted to see the King. Soren, sitting in the audience chamber opening off the throne room, listened to Strake reacting to being called 'boy', and his brusquely polite termination of the meeting. She watched her Rathen pass a hand across his face as the former Regent stalked away, and Aristide's face as he passed his mother. Briefly Soren glanced at the Tzel Aviar, putting a freshly scrubbed killer to bed, then returned to gazing at the guards in the process of removing pieces of person from the Champion's apartments.

After the thing behind her eyes had fallen back satisfied into nothingness, Soren had been overwhelmed with a new kind of anger. It swelled in her chest, burning, choking, urging her to scream and rant and tear at her face. But instead she'd very carefully said: "She's dead," then closed her mouth on all the other words which wanted to pour out.

The ominous silence she'd maintained since was no doubt the inspiration for the expression on Strake's face as he and Aristide came into the audience chamber and sat down. Frank worry. Aristide looked at her intently, but then succeeded in acting as if nothing at all out of the ordinary had been happening. He'd taken off his blood-stained demi-robe, but the white undershirt was also spotted with patches of red, and his hands were swathed with bandages.

"A third child of my father's," he began, his voice thoughtful, detached. "No doubt originally intended to be a spy rather than an assassin, but circumstances in Darest have altered of late."

Purpose-built to get every advantage out of Tor Darest. Halcean had told Soren that, quite directly. She'd called Court a game, apparently been happy to play the part she'd been set. Deliberately cultivated Soren, cast suspicion on Aspen, pretended loyalty. But she hadn't been happy to be made assassin. Another tool. Another puppet.

Strake snorted. "Does this Veth family even exist?"

"Vereck checks all residents of the palace. A Runath family, settled in Darest out of the east some twenty years ago – my sister would have been an infant, and I doubt the Veth woman was her blood mother. They purchased the semblance of a title and land close to the Saxan border and have been rigorously ordinary since. The local garrison has been contacted, but there is little chance of finding them there."

"And what redress do we have?"

The smile which touched Aristide's mouth now was faint, and very cold. "Her paternity is clear. I will have her body delivered to my brother. Beyond that? Accusation, counter-assassin, harsh words? We can certainly go to war with Cya if you wish it."

For a moment Strake looked tempted, then he made a disgusted motion with his hands. "*You* don't."

It was open acknowledgement that it was as much Aristide's choice as Strake's, but neither of them marked the gesture with so much as an eye-flicker. "I want a successful Spring festival," Aristide said, very mild. "And to build ships, which I suspect is what made our lives too costly for Cya. This is a distraction. Our energies are better spent."

Strake shook his head, not angry but frustrated. He knew perfectly well they'd lose a war against Cya or any other land, and was twisting on a need for vengeance gone unfulfilled. The night's drama had left him with a small cut on one hand, a great deal of nervous energy, and a rigorous determination to avoid all mention of Vahse's killer.

Head buzzing, Soren shifted her attention to the Fair. Damaris was holding someone's sigil, no doubt reporting success. The boy sat in the middle of a vast bed: clean, clothed, bandaged and miserable. There would be a price to pay for naming him, Fae princeling, murderer, monster. Shaol.

He looked up, mossy green eyes fixing on the point where she watched him through the Rose.

"Do your injuries limit your ability to cast, Lord Aristide?"

The words were quiet, marvellously calm. For the first time in her life, Soren had found an absolute certainty. It left doubt quite behind, and brought that worried foreboding back to Strake's face. He mightn't fully understand why she had struggled against Halcean's death, but he could hardly fail to recognise the blasted fury locked beneath her rigid composure.

Aristide's expression barely changed. "I am not a follower of the Tybol School. Few castings would be unmanageable."

"And do you think yourself equal to sewing with lightning?"

This was quite incomprehensible to Aristide, but Strake knew what she meant, the only possible course of action left to her.

"Soren, it can't be done—" he began.

"It *has* to be!" She shouted it, loud enough for distant guards to lift their heads. She found herself bent forward, her hands flat on the table. "Has to be, Strake. Right now it's the weakest it's ever going to be. The longer you're here, the more Rathens you produce, the bigger the power backlash will be. Am I right?"

"Quite true." It was Aristide who answered, unblinking. "But weak is a relative term, and you are not equipped to survive so much raw power. I could try and shield you from it, but your chances are slim."

"I know that." She was still staring directly at Strake, at her Rathen. "Your rose isn't black any more." It was, in fact, a very bloody red. "Hypocritical of it to kill Halcean for attacking, when it was quite ready to let you die a week ago. That's what it is, Strake. Something prepared to do whatever it needs to survive, something full of anger and malice. Inside me."

"This isn't the way, Soren," Strake said, shaking his head. "The price is too high."

Soren turned away from him, looked at star sapphire eyes which did not mock. "You said it slept. That it was something which had grown inside the Rose, not particularly developed. What happens if it does? Isn't it inevitable? What do we do when it's awake all the time, when it's more than a sleeping bear? What if the next person it kills is someone we do mind being dead?"

"Yours isn't a life I can throw away!" Strake shouted it, was on his feet. But this time she remained steadfast.

"What happens if, next time it rouses, it makes it impossible for us to stop it, puts a blank space in our minds for that? Or simply decides to replace me with a more complaisant Champion, as soon as this child is born? Or sooner. You know, after all, that it's willing to sacrifice individual Rathens. And it can always get another child off you."

He went white, veins standing out at throat and temple, hands clenching. But he couldn't deny it, knew very well she was speaking bare truth. "You're asking me to kill you."

She took a deep, sobbing breath, full of hate and fear. "Strake. If you don't destroy it, I'll go take a sledgehammer to it myself."

And he bowed his head.

"I'll never forgive you for this."

"No." He probably wouldn't.

"But I'll miss you."

For the first time her determination wavered, and Soren quickly put a hand on his arm. "Please don't make this harder." She couldn't keep the quaver from her voice.

"There isn't any way to make it easier."

Aristide, politely not noticing their embraces, studied the reflected moonlight patterning the walls beneath the great bell. After a suitable interval he said: "I cannot cross this."

"No." Strake's arms tightened convulsively around Soren one final time, then let go. "Only King and Champion. You'll both have to stay here."

"Very well." Aristide glanced at Soren. "Has it shown any awareness?"

"Nothing." That had been Soren's great fear, the reason this had to be done now, tonight. It could so easily stop them, once it read this resolution in her mind. The next time the worm at the Rose's heart roused, it would know.

Her Rathen walked away from her, very tall and upright, with a face from the frozen north, but paused at the entrance of the room beneath the bell.

"Aristide–" He glanced at his Councillor's face. "I doubt I'll forgive you, either."

For not sewing with lightning. Aristide's eyelids dropped, but no smile touched those exquisite lips. This could put King and Councillor at each other's throats, and only their awareness of the potential for disaster, their forbearance, would save them.

"I imagine not," was all Aristide said.

Strake nodded, and walked down the stair into a black, unlit room of runes, outside the limits of her palace-sight. He didn't look back.

Quite perfectly expressionless, Aristide turned and looked at her. Soren could only guess at his thoughts, at how he felt to participate in the destruction of the enchantment which had kept him from the throne. Did he curse her for oversetting all plans, or did his mind race with possibility, of the turning tide of fortune? After this, only Strake's life to keep him from the crown. Would his oath hold him over a lifetime of servitude?

The faintest curve of lips suggested he read her face a little too well, but all he said was: "Ground the sword."

Obediently she drew the overlong shaft of metal, that pleasurable tingle running through her arm. She touched its tip to the treasury floor, and Aristide nodded.

"It will help, a little," he explained. "It, at least, was created to channel power." He came to stand beside her, lifted one bandaged hand and rested it lightly on the back of her neck, placing the other on the wrist of the hand holding the sword. And turned his head as the sibilant murmur of casting came from down the moonlit stair.

Soren's stomach twisted, and a shudder ran through her. She was really doing this rather than compromise, rather than accept bad with worse. "Will the – could the *saecstra* strike at you because of this?" she asked, needing distraction more than an answer. Her voice shook, betraying her terror.

She couldn't read the look Aristide gave her then, but he answered with perfect composure. "Be assured, I will be making every effort to preserve you. That should fulfil the terms of the oath."

"I'm glad." She didn't need any more lives on her conscience.

Because that was the worst of it, what none of them had said but all had known. Her baby, unwanted, forced on her. Her child she was willing to risk too, to take with her into not quite certain suicide to save it from becoming a puppet of a festering enchantment.

"Selune forgive me," she groaned, hating herself, refusing to turn back from this. It had to be done.

Something stirred behind her eyes.

"It knows!" She felt it uncoiling, twisting up to jar her thoughts awry. The panic of unlooked for attack, of threat, of fear and fury.

"Too late." Aristide's brilliant eyes were unwavering, fixed on her face as the soft chant in the darkness fell silent and there was a moment of nothing, then a tiny little ticking sound.

It burned!

Her back arched, spine curving, throat distended, every muscle in her body locking as her head snapped back. Unseen fire ran the very length of her, up through her feet, scorching the course of her bones, twisting joints to their limits. Her eyes bulged and her jaw cracked as that burning force rammed itself past throat and tongue and blasted with a rising scream out and up and away. Agony, all-consuming and complete, beyond compass.

Fragmentary things touched her. Rage, the worm in the Rose, boiling with fear, fury and no way to save itself. Aristide's hands tightening on her arm, the back of her neck. Palace-sight, the images carving into her mind. She knew every true-mage in the palace by the way they leapt in shock. Guards, battering the treasury door. The Tzel Aviar dropping a silver sigil. Shaol with tears in his eyes.

The sword was drawing some of the power, channelling it in a focused and purposeful manner. That, in some way, was also the

Rose. But too little. Her heart was going to burst, a knot crushing her chest, pushing out her ribs.

Then a crack, like a frozen lake in winter melt: sharp, echoing, absolute. Soren's scream cut off.

She sagged and Aristide went down with her, borne over by her greater height. A scrape of boot on grit heralded Strake's arrival, and she heard him moan as he flung himself to his knees, snatched her into his arms. She coughed, all she could do with the pain it caused. Her hand wouldn't work, the fingers fused around the hilt of the sword, melted together. It hurt. So much.

"Soren. Oh, Sun, Soren." Strake was weeping. She could hear it. There was a lot of banging, which she belatedly connected to the guards trying to break down the door. Her head rang with every blow.

Aristide moved beside her, there was a cool touch on the back of her wrist and the pain went away.

"It worked." She heard the delight in a creak of voice scarcely recognisable as her own. "It's gone. It's all gone. I'm not dead." She found Strake with her undamaged hand, touched his face. Smiled. "Not dead. It worked."

He made a choked noise and clutched her all the more.

"The baby?" she asked then, and waited a very long moment before his sigh, pure relief, gave her an answer. She cried then: release, guilt.

"The Rose was shielding it," he said, to her surprise. "Not this instinct, but the Rose itself, still carrying out its basic function. Shielding it and you, preserving the Rathen heir and Champion."

"Ah." She tried to feel some gratitude, but there was only relief. Then she turned her head toward him, started to lift a hand to her own face, and stopped. It seemed an insignificant thing, compared to the life of her child. She thought about it, then added, almost apologetically: "I don't seem to be able to see."

Enthroned in the King's bed, all bandages and exhaustion. Healing was a tricky thing, even for the best of mages, and the burns on Soren's hand would require many days of work. She wouldn't lose use of her fingers. Her eyes were beyond repair.

It had taken Strake a long time to accept it. When his own and Aristide's divinations had failed to give hope, he'd even gone so far as to summon the Tzel Aviar. But although magic was good at hurrying healing, and doing straightforward things like binding bones and warding against infection, living bodies resisted enchantment which replaced or made as new. She was blind.

Strake and Aristide had stayed a long time away after escorting the Tzel Aviar out. Soren drifted on the edge of dozing, feeling she should stay awake, feeling it was all unreal and that she'd died after all and was only dreaming she still lived. Any moment now, surely, the Moon would welcome her back.

A step at the door told her it wasn't true. Strake, though the Rose was no longer there to underline the guess with perfect awareness. She felt the bed shift with his weight as he sat beside her, and then the echo of another step as someone else crossed from the door.

"Champion–" Aristide began.

"Not Champion any more." She said it with open pleasure, and heard Strake swallow.

Aristide responded with that light, polite, almost chiding tone which had once made her writhe: "There was a Champion before there was a Rose. And is one after."

"Blind Champion?" She thought that funny, made a little hiccupping noise.

"Yes." All hint of mockery had gone. "Without the Rose, Darest is now exposed to the full force of the malison. Strake will bear the brunt of that, and you will be a vital shield against its effects. There are many ways to serve: don't underestimate this one."

She supposed he meant she'd take the edge off Strake's temper, keep him human, or sane. Save him from Lady Arista's fate, from becoming a grieving, brooding king, a whirlwind eating out its own heart. A most important factor for Aristide, bound to serve. But something else was more interesting.

"You called him Strake." She said it in an awed, dizzy kind of way, and had the signal pleasure of hearing Aristide Couerveur laugh.

"So I did. Remiss of me."

Soren wondered if it was possible to shield Aristide as well. Two kings in Darest, and the uncrowned just as important, but before she could say anything he went on.

"We cannot repair your eyes, Champion. But we have been to view the structure of spell which allowed the Rose to see, and I believe we can adapt it to our purposes."

"Palace-sight?" She sounded appalled, and shook her head to underline that. To suffer that overwhelming press again – she'd rather the alternative.

"It wouldn't have the same range," Strake said quickly. "The bounds of a room, no more. And you'd be able to go out of the palace. You'd not be able to see into the distance, though, and we'll have to keep renewing the thing, but – Soren –" He gripped her uninjured hand painfully.

"We will attempt a casting tomorrow morning," Aristide said, with an amused edge to his voice. "Until then, Champion. Majesty."

He went out. Soren wondered if he was smiling, and knew that she'd be glad to see again. She especially wanted to see the look in her Rathen's eyes, right this moment.

"This isn't your fault, Strake," she said softly.

"Does that make it any better?" He leaned over her, pressed his cheek against hers and inhaled as if he, too, couldn't quite believe the Moon hadn't taken her, and had to have some proof beyond – sight. "You screamed, Soren. I've never heard anything worse."

"Well it hurt." That seemed so obvious. "But I'd do it again."

"You should never have had to do it in the first place."

"Maybe not. Who can know what Darest would have been if Domina Rathen had never created the Rose? Perhaps the Kingdom would have died young, or would have been taken back by The

Deeping these past couple of centuries. Or perhaps Aristide would be King, and doing very well indeed. I do know I couldn't go on as a puppet, and I'm so happy to have my mind my own I can barely stop myself screaming. And that there's one thing that hasn't changed, even without the Rose."

"What?"

"You're still my Rathen."

He was silent, and Soren found her inability to see his expression suddenly overwhelming. Could she somehow be wrong? Had they not come far enough?

Then a touch on her uninjured hand, and his fingers curled through hers.

"I'm Strake," he said, and that was all the reassurance she needed. Not her Rathen, but her friend. Without the shadow of the Rose, it was a way forward both of them could accept.